Forget Me Not
The Journey Continues

Forget Me Not
The Journey Continues

Previous works by Valmai R. Harris **Forget Me Not**

The Journey Continues is the second part of a trilogy involving the characters created for Forget Me Not. They have moved beyond the end of World War 1 and into 1919, where the Spanish Flu impacts heavily on Australian lives.

This is a work of fiction, and any similarity between my characters and persons living in that period, is purely coincidental.
Certain names and place names have also been changed.

Valmai Harris

Copyright © 2019 Valmai Harris
2nd edition copyright © 2021
ISBN -13:9780645072709

valmairuthharris@gmail.com

Cover design created by Joanne Livingstone
joliving@westnet.com.au

Author photography
imaginepictures.com.au

All rights reserved. No part of this book may be reproduced or transmitted, in any form or by any means, electronic or mechanical, including photocopying, recording or by any information storage and retrieval system, without prior permission in writing from the author.

Produced and Printed in Australia by IngramSpark

Introduction

January 6th 1919

The fighting in Europe has ended, and battle-weary troops are making their way home to Australia, to loved-ones who have not seen them for two, maybe three years. This is not so for every family.

For our heroine, Jess, the homecoming was not to be. Her beloved Jack lies buried far away in England, and she will never know the excitement of welcoming him back into the family fold.

The future looks bleak for Jess, and she has succumbed to grief, isolating herself from those around her, and unable to rise above it.

Christmas has come and gone.

She sits on the front verandah, staring forlornly at a handful of crushed forget-me-nots, and remembering the day Jack left for the training barracks at Williamstown. That was September 28th, 1916.

Today I picked forget-me-nots,
And pressed them in a book for you.
A keepsake to remind you
That my love is always true.
Think of me when I'm far away
On a distant, war-torn shore,
And remember, just like the forget-me-not,
That it's you I'll be fighting for.

Now it is her turn to fight the feelings of self-pity and melancholy, and she must, for the sake of her three children.

Sometimes it is just too hard, and she escapes to the solace of her empty bedroom, to think of Jack and all that she has lost.

She hears a dog bark, and looks up from her musing. Beau, the one constant in her life, is standing on the steps below her, a smile on his scarred face. He has been her anchor in all the turbulence of the past few weeks, and tomorrow he goes back to Sydney, to his work with returning soldiers who are unable to adjust to civilian life.

Her two boys stand beside him now, and they are all looking in her direction. At Beau's feet lies the terrier, Mack.

"We're going to the park, Jess, and wondered if you'd like to join us."

The park? Jess doesn't want to go there. That was where they had spent the last day before Jack went away.

"No," she says abruptly.

"Come on, ma!" There is eagerness in Edward's voice. "Mack's coming too, and we're going to play ball."

"Please, ma!"

Jess sighs, and places the crushed forget-me-nots in Jack's worn copy of 'Gulliver's travels'.

"Very well, I'll get my hat."

She has to do this.

Part One

Coming to Terms with Loss

Farewell

A hot breeze ruffled the red geraniums that grew beside the brick wall of the Bendigo railway station, and sent dry leaves swirling around the feet of passengers waiting for the morning train from Swan Hill. Conversations were at a minimum; a quiet murmur broke the silence.

Jess and Beau stood side by side, each looking straight ahead.

"I hate this place," said Jess softly, almost to herself.

Beau turned grey eyes in her direction. "Why is that, Jess?"

"It's where everybody says good-bye." A tear slid down her pale cheek.

Beau squeezed her arm gently, forcing her to turn her head.

"This is not good-bye, Jess. I have to go back to Sydney. That's where my work is, but I promise I'll be back as soon as I can."

"You promise?" It was just a sigh.

"Yes." His brow furrowed. "Izzy will be coming down from Swan Hill in a few days, and you have Jean and Margaret." He brushed the tear from her cheek. "You'll be alright, Jess."

"I know." Jess forced a smile, as the sound of a train whistle broke the silence. "Thank-you, Beau, for bringing me back from…" Her voice faltered, and she left the words unsaid.

The train screeched to a halt beside them, issuing forth hot steam. Beau picked up his case, and smiled at Jess.

"Farewell for now, Jess." He leaned forward and brushed a kiss across her cheek.

Jess was unable to answer, so she merely nodded, and watched as Beau made his way on to the train. He opened a window, and stood watching her as passengers pushed their way to vacant carriages.

"Goodbye, Beau," she managed to mouth, as the train jerked forward, and slowly departed the station.

She was alone. People hurried for the exits, anxious to get home out of the heat. Jess made her way slowly up the steps of the pedestrian bridge that spanned the rails. An overwhelming feeling of dread surged through her body, and she bit on her lip to stop from screaming out loud. Jack was never coming home. Her life must go on without him, and she had no idea how she was going to do that.

Everybody had been so kind and sympathetic, but Jess knew that this would come to an end, and she would have to face the future alone.

She shuddered in spite of the heat, and forced her legs up the hill that would take her home.

The Grey Goose hotel was shimmering and silent in the sunshine. Jess walked slowly in the shadow of the south wall, and on towards the corner of the street. Crossing the road she headed along Oleander Street to her own front gate.

Taking a deep breath, she opened the gate. It creaked, as it had always done. Jess stood on the verandah for a moment, before opening the door.

A cool rush of air greeted her as she entered the passage, and she heard childish laughter coming from the kitchen. She headed towards the sound.

The kitchen door opened to her touch, and she stepped into the room where her three children and their grandmother, Margaret, were seated at the table, a game of snakes and ladders opened before them.

Margaret looked up as Jess entered. "So he's gone then?"

Jess nodded. "Yes." She swallowed hard. "He said he'd be back."

Margaret smiled. "Don't doubt that, Jess. Beau is a man of his word."

"I know." Jess removed her straw hat and hung it behind the kitchen door. She tied an apron around her waist. "Time to think about lunch."

"Ma?" Edward looked up from his game.

"What is it, Edward?"

"It's just us now, isn't it?"

Jess felt her eyes well up. "Yes, it is, Edward. It's just us."

The words sounded hollow to Jess's ears, and she moved to the sink to hide the tears from her children.

Margaret read the signals. "Time to pack up the game now, children," she said quickly. "Then Ben and Edward, you can go and gather the eggs. We'll make omelettes for lunch."

The boys packed up the board and put it away in a drawer of the kitchen dresser.

Grace slid from her chair and padded across to the corner where her dolls lay. She was a 'big girl now', so her playpen had been relegated to the sleep-out.

The screen door slammed as the boys made their way outside. Margaret moved across to Jess, and placed an arm over her shoulders.

"You are strong, Jessie; you can do this. Remember what Jack said in his letter? You must be brave and try not to be too sad." She took a deep breath. "Remember what you had, and it WAS good. You know it was good." Her voice shook.

Jess fumbled for a handkerchief in her apron pocket, and wiped her eyes. She stared out through the kitchen window. The boys were at the chook pen, shooing the hens away from the eggs.

"You know the hardest thing about this, Margaret?"

"What is it?"

"It's having nowhere to go and talk to Jack; nowhere to lay flowers and no plaque to say that this is where he lies. I'll never get to see where he lies."

Margaret was silent for a moment.

"Talk to Billy Maitland. He's home now, and he saw where Jack was buried."

"What of Martin Weatherall? Did he come home?"

"Yes. According to Izzy, he's home in Swan Hill at present, but he plans on returning to France, to help with the rebuilding. It must be awful for those poor people, having to now rebuild their homes and towns."

"This war has brought nothing but suffering!" Jess's voice was sharp.

Margaret squeezed her shoulder. "I know."

They both watched the boys coming across the grass, a bucket of eggs swinging precariously between them.

"Come on," said Margaret, "Charles will be here shortly for his lunch, and you know how he hates waiting." She chuckled briefly.

*

True to form, Charles walked through the kitchen door at two minutes to midday.

"Nearly ready, Charles." Margaret slid an omelette on to a plate.

Charles reached for a slice of bread. As he cut it in half, he looked up at Jess. "So the good doctor has gone, eh?"

Jess nodded. "He has patients to attend to in Sydney; he couldn't stay any longer."

"Hm." Charles waited while Margaret served the rest of the omelettes.

When she was seated, Charles said grace. The clatter of cutlery broke the silence.

As she ate, Jess looked covertly at Charles. He had said very little since the news of Jack's death. It was almost as though he had shut it away from his consciousness. Jack had been away for two years, so nothing was any different.

Margaret had confided in Jess that Charles didn't speak of his son. Was it because it was too painful or was he unable to accept the fact that Jack would not be coming home? Tears sprang to her own eyes as she thought of this.

Charles caught her watching him. He frowned, and Jess looked away.

"Are you coming home today, Margaret?" Charles wiped his mouth on a serviette.

Margaret looked swiftly in Jess's direction before answering.

"Well," she began, "if Jess thinks she'll be alright on her own."

"Yes, yes, of course, Margaret. You go home. I have to do this sooner or later."

"Are you sure?"

"Of course. I know where you are if I need you."

Margaret nodded and smiled at Charles. "I'll be home this afternoon, Charles."

"Good, now how about a cup of tea before I return to work."

The two women glanced at one another, and Margaret raised her eyebrows ever so slightly. Jess turned away, hiding the smile that tugged at her mouth.

Charles would never change, and Margaret would always look after him.

Beau

Beau stood looking out the window of his second floor office, across the Sydney harbour, with its white caps shimmering and dancing in the sunlight. Sailing boats rolled at anchor around the quay, and the ferry was preparing to leave on its afternoon trip across to Manly. Everything seemed normal; nothing out of place.

Beau heard the door open, and a sharp female voice cut through his reverie.

"Oh! So you're home, Beau?"

Without turning, Beau said quietly, "I am."

"Where were you, may I ask?"

"I had to go to Bendigo."

"Bendigo! I thought you'd seen the last of that place!"

Beau turned. Celia stood in the doorway, hands on her slim hips, and a frown on her otherwise smooth brow. She was a beautiful woman, and even at forty, Beau had to concede that she carried herself with all the elegance of her youth. Her sleek dark hair was pulled back into a bun on the nape of her neck, and her dark eyes were even now, challenging him. She had always challenged him.

"I had to see Jess," he said simply, meeting her gaze.

"Why?"

Beau turned back to the window. "She needed me." *Something you'd know nothing about, Celia.*

Celia snorted. "What?"

"Her husband didn't come home from the war."

"He was killed, you mean?"

"No, he died of that viral epidemic that's been sweeping the world."

"Oh. I'm sorry." Celia paused just long enough to appear sensitive. "Matthew wants to see you. He needs your advice on a patient out at Serendipity Lodge."

Beau felt a shiver go through him at the mention of Serendipity Lodge. It was where he had spent the first three months of his recovery therapy, after he had tried to take his own life. He couldn't go back there.

"Serendipity Lodge." He said it slowly.

"Yes, Beau!" Her voice had an edge. "Could you go and see Matthew, now, please?"

Beau watched the ferry bobbing on the waves, as it moved towards the Heads.

"Beau! Are you even listening to me?"

Beau turned, picked up his jacket, which he had flung across the back of a chair, and walked towards the door. Celia moved aside, shaking her head as he passed her. She closed the door after them, and followed Beau along the passage that led to Matthew's office. Her heels clicked on the linoleum as she walked.

Beau knocked on the door with the gold plaque, which read: Dr. Matthew Morley.

He shrugged himself into his jacket, and opened the door as he heard a voice from within. Celia followed.

"Ah Beau, you're back. Good." Matthew's aquiline features showed a ghost of a smile. "Did Celia tell you that I want your help with a lad at Serendipity Lodge?"

"Yes, she did."

Matthew looked from Beau to Celia, and back again. Where these two were concerned, he had always been aware of friction. Now, with Beau still living on the edge of his wartime experiences, that friction was even more palpable. It was no wonder their marriage had failed. His eyebrows arched as he looked at Beau.

"Right! I'd like to go out there this afternoon."

Beau shrugged. "Yes, alright, Matthew."

"You don't sound very enthusiastic. This lad needs your firsthand knowledge, and I would appreciate your co-operation."

"You will have it, Matthew," said Beau smoothly, "but as you know, Serendipity Lodge does not hold good memories for me."

"I can appreciate that, Beau, but it did set you back on to the path of normality."

"You have a job to do here," said Celia sharply, "so please, Beau, keep your mind on it. Bendigo is in the past. Leave it there!"

Beau thumped his fist on Matthew's polished oak desk.

"You know nothing about my friends and what they are enduring, Celia. If I want to go back there, I will, with or without your consent!"

"Calm down, Beau." Matthew raised his hands, as the two in front of him, glared at one another. "Celia, you are not helping." He lowered his hands. "Now, if we can get back to the business at hand, I would like to be ready to go out to Serendipity at two this afternoon. Beau?"

"I'll be ready, Matthew." Beau turned on his heel and headed for the door. It swung shut behind him.

Celia leaned on Matthew's desk.

"He must not go back to Bendigo, Matthew. It does him no good."

Matthew shrugged. "We can't stop him, Celia."

"We may have to use the power of persuasion." Celia straightened her slim-fitting black skirt, as she drew herself up to her full height. "He has to listen to sense. He has the idea that he owes his life to this woman. That is nonsense of course."

Matthew frowned as he looked up at his wife.

"Not entirely, Celia. By the way, the woman's name is Jess, and without her, he may not have survived."

"Well, anyway, we need his full attention here."

"We do, I agree, but we mustn't push him, Celia. He is still very fragile."

Celia shrugged her elegant shoulders. "I suppose you know best, Matthew."

"I do, so leave me to deal with Beau in my own way."

Celia smiled knowingly. "You were always the forceful one, Matthew." She blew him a seductive kiss, turned, and exited the room.

Matthew ran his hands through his thick greying hair, and sighed heavily.

*

Beau stood on the gravel path, looking up at the two-storey sandstone building with its green painted window frames, and massive oak door. Wide concrete steps led up to a covered verandah, where two large ceramic dogs stood guard beside the door. Matthew took Beau's arm.

"Come on, Beau, it's not going to gobble you up, you know."

Beau looked at his companion, smiling broadly from beneath the brim of a straw hat.

"I know, Matthew, but the sight of this place gives me the horrors."

Matthew propelled Beau up the concrete steps and on to the verandah. The massive door swung open to his touch, and they stepped into the cool entry hall. Black and white linoleum covered the floor, and squeaked beneath their feet as they crossed to a service window. Matthew pressed a bell, which stood on the wide window ledge, and a fresh-faced young woman, with her brown hair cropped short, appeared, opened the window and smiled at Matthew.

"Good afternoon, Doctor Morley." Her gaze shifted to Beau and her eyes widened with recognition. "Doctor DuBois, how nice to see you again."

"Hello, Shirley." Beau smiled at the young woman. "It's nice to see you, too."

There was an awkward silence for a moment.

"We're here to see the Evans lad, Shirley," said Matthew.

"He's upstairs, Doctor, in room eight."

"Good. Thank-you, Shirley."

Matthew led the way towards the staircase, and Beau followed. His legs were heavy as he climbed the stairs, and the sounds of men in torment, reached his ears. He stopped, unable to continue.

"I can't do this, Matthew," he said through gritted teeth.

"This boy needs you." Matthew looked down beseechingly at his companion.

Beau drew a shaky breath, and reached the top of the stairs. He followed Matthew along the corridor that reeked of disinfectant, until he stopped outside a door marked: Isolation. Matthew peered through a window, and then turned to Beau.

"This is Charlie Evans, Beau. He's eighteen, and managed to slip into the trenches at the age of seventeen. He remains in a foetal position most of the time, rocking backwards and forwards. His mother brought him to us a week ago, and he hasn't spoken a word in all that time."

Matthew put a key in the lock, turned it and opened the door. Beau looked beyond Matthew to a figure crouched in the far corner, rocking and whimpering softly. The room was bare, save for a single cot, covered with a grey blanket, a chair, and a bucket for the patient to relieve himself, if he remembered what it was for. The odour suggested otherwise.

It was a bleak room, with no window to the outside. Beau stood for a moment, as his mind took him back to his time here.

"Does he have to be in this semi-darkness, Matthew?" said Beau slowly. "He doesn't even have a window."

"I know. The outside world is not what he needs right now."

Beau stepped forward, picked up the chair, and sat beside the pyjama-clad figure.

"Hello, Charlie, my name's Beau. I've come to see how you are getting on, and whether there's anything I can do for you."

The young man continued rocking, as he turned fear-filled eyes in Beau's direction. Beau immediately felt a bond with his torment. He leaned forward.

"I want to help you, Charlie," he whispered. "I know something of what you are experiencing, and I also know that we can make you well, if that's what you want."

The brown eyes darted around the room, and rested on Beau's face. He reached out a hand and touched his scar.

"I got that in the war, Charlie. I try not to think about it now."

The boy tucked his head back under his arms and his shoulders shook.

"Charlie, how would you like to go with me to see the garden?"

"I don't think that's a good idea, Beau," came Matthew's sharp retort.

Beau looked up at his companion. "We need to gain his trust, Matthew. You of all people should know that."

"I do, but at this stage we don't know what's going on inside his head, and until we do…"

"He's not going to open up while he's cooped up in here. Trust me on this, Matthew. I have been in a similar place."

Matthew sighed. "Very well, but I'll make sure that a couple of staff members are close by, in case he does a runner."

Beau knew exactly what he meant by 'staff members'; men with the appearance of wrestlers, and dressed in white coats.

"If you must, Matthew, but tell them to keep out of sight."

Matthew turned on his heel and hurried along the corridor. Beau stood up and reached out his hand to Charlie.

"Come with me, Charlie. Let's go and have a look at the garden."

Charlie eyed him suspiciously, and then slowly stretched out his hand. Beau took it, and helped him to his feet.

Standing upright, he was taller than Beau, his frame gaunt beneath the striped pyjamas. His brown hair was long and unkempt, and fine stubble covered his chin. He stared down at Beau, and his brown eyes were fearful.

"Come," said Beau quietly. "There's no need to be afraid. Hang on to me."

Together they took slow steps towards the door. Charlie stopped as they reached the corridor, and leaned forward to look in both directions.

"There's nobody there, Charlie. Nobody's going to hurt you, I promise."

Together they moved slowly along the corridor, and down the polished staircase.

All the while, Beau talked in a soft tone, which immediately brought thoughts of Jess, and the way she had used her voice to calm him on more than one occasion.

Charlie shuffled along in slippers that were too large for him. Beau reminded himself that he must do something about that.

When they reached the large oak front door, Charlie stiffened and began to whimper. Beau opened the door, and sunshine streamed into the entry hall.

"There's nothing out there to hurt you, Charlie. Trust me. We don't have to go far. We'll sit on that seat you can see from here, near the roses."

Beau gently propelled Charlie across the threshold, down the steps and on to the gravel path. Charlie blinked in the unaccustomed sunlight, but he let Beau lead him to a seat some yards away from the house, in an arbour of well-tended roses.

Beau looked around for the duty nurses. He didn't see any, but a movement at one of the first floor windows, suggested that someone was watching.

"Do you like roses, Charlie? Just nod your head if you do."

Beau turned to look at his companion, sitting like a coiled spring beside him. He saw his head jerk in a nodding motion. This was a surprise. He hadn't expected a reaction so soon. "I'm glad you do, Charlie. I think they are beautiful." He paused. "Would you like to walk a bit further and see what other flowers we can find?"

Charlie's head nodded once more.

Beau stood, and took the younger man by the hand. Charlie shuffled beside him, as together they made their way along the gravel path. Summer blooms were growing alongside the walkway, and Beau pointed out geraniums, pansies, hydrangeas in the shade of tall gumtrees, and colourful perennials turning their faces to the sun.

"I spent time in a place like this, Charlie," said Beau quietly, "just like you. The doctors didn't give up on me, until I was well enough to face this world that we find ourselves in. If you can trust me, I know we can do the same for you. Do you understand me, Charlie?" His head nodded. "Good. That's all I need to know. Now I think we have walked far enough for one day. I'll come back…"

Beau felt Charlie wrench his hand away, and the next moment, the boy was running in his ill-fitting slippers.

Beau caught a glimpse of white coats, and heard heavy footsteps along the gravel. He could only watch helplessly as two male nurses grabbed the stumbling figure, and began hauling him back along the path. Seeing Matthew hurrying in his direction, Beau whirled to face him.

"What do you think you're doing, Matthew? Everything was under control!"

Matthew wiped his perspiring face.

"You were out of our sight, Beau. Anything could have happened."

"He was responding. Didn't you trust me?"

"I didn't trust Charlie, Beau."

Beau drew an angry breath. "Well, he's not going to trust me again. It's back to the beginning, Matthew, and it could have been the start of his recovery."

"I'm sorry, Beau." Matthew hurried to catch up with Beau as he stalked in the direction of the Lodge.

As they approached the front steps, a woman, possibly in her early forties, ran from the building, her hands pressed against her chest.

"Doctor Morley!" she cried angrily. "What's happening with my Charlie? What have you done to him?"

Matthew and Beau stopped as the woman clattered down the steps. She was attractive in a care-worn sort of way, and her brown hair hung loose.

Matthew stepped in front of her, and laid a hand on her shoulder.

"I'm sorry you had to witness that, Mrs. Evans." He turned towards Beau. "Doctor DuBois had Charlie out for a walk in the grounds, and I sent staff members to bring him back."

Brown eyes stared accusingly at Beau. "You took him for a walk?"

Beau shrugged. "I was getting somewhere with him. He responded to me."

"Well!" The brown eyes blazed. "He's not responding now." She turned back to Matthew. "I thought you'd do the right thing by my boy. I was wrong. I'll take him away from here, and find someone else who can help him."

The woman turned to go back up the steps, but Beau stepped forward.

"Please don't be hasty, Mrs. Evans."

She swung around to face him, her expression hostile.

"He's my boy, and I'm taking him away from here." As a parting shot, she added, " I thought the Germans were bad enough!"

Izzy's Arrival

Jess looked up as she heard the whistle. Her sister, Izzy, was arriving on the morning train from Swan Hill, and for the first time, Jess was not at the station to greet her. It was a place of much heartache for her. Izzy had understood, when asked if she could make her own way to the house.

Jess was seated on the wooden stool on the front verandah, where she had spent many hours lately, reflecting on the direction her life had taken. It would never be the same as it was, and even with Jack being absent for two years, there had always been the anticipation of a homecoming. Now there was only emptiness. She brushed impatiently at a tear that escaped, and rising from the stool, opened the front wire door.

"Gracie! Auntie Izzy is on her way!"

Running footsteps could be heard along the passage, and Gracie appeared. She was now an active three year old, with bouncing golden curls and an impish grin.

"Auntie Izzy!" she exclaimed, as she headed across the verandah. "Let's go, ma!"

Jess shook her head as she followed her daughter down the front steps. Gracie pulled open the front gate, which squeaked loudly, and jumped down the step to the footpath.

Together they headed right, towards the Grey Goose Hotel, and soon they saw a familiar figure walking slowly towards them, a large carpetbag in one hand.

"Auntie Izzy!" squealed Gracie as she ran towards the approaching figure.

Jess stood and watched the reunion, as Izzy put down her bag, and gathered the small child in her arms. She swung her around, before looking in Jess's direction. The two sisters smiled at one another.

Izzy put Grace down, picked up her bag, and took the child by the hand. Jess noticed, with some amusement, that Izzy's flowing blue dress was shorter than usual, and her blonde hair barely reached her shoulders. She always did love fashion, thought Jess wryly, as she stood in the cotton forget-me-not dress that represented her love for Jack. It had always been his favourite, and she knew that Izzy would wrinkle her nose, but she didn't care, not now.

Jess waited until they were directly in front of her, and then she lifted her arms to embrace her sister. They clung together, while Jess's tears fell, unrestrained.

Izzy let her cry. "I still can't believe it, Jess. How are you coping, little sister?"

Jess groped in her pocket for a handkerchief to wipe her streaming eyes.

"It's been awful, Izzy, but I know I have to keep going, for the children's sake."

"That's my girl." Izzy cast a cursory glance over her sister, but said nothing. She picked up her bag, which had been dropped on the footpath. "Time for a cup of tea. I'm parched, and the wretched train didn't have a buffet carriage." She linked arms with Jess, and they headed towards the house.

"It's very quiet, I must say," remarked Izzy, as they stepped into the cool passage. "Where are the boys?"

"They're back at school after the Christmas holiday."

"Of course. I don't have to think about that yet for a while. Freya is only two."

When they reached the kitchen, Jess moved to the stove where the kettle was singing quietly. She lifted down the tea caddy from the mantel, and scooped tea into the brown earthenware teapot. Gracie went to the corner where her dolls were silently reclining.

"Have you left Harry in charge of Freya?" Jess moved to the pine kitchen dresser.

Izzy pulled a chair out from the big table, and sat heavily. "Yes and no."

"What do you mean by that?" Jess took two cups from the dresser.

"Harry has to look after her at night, and I'm afraid I've enlisted the services of Nancy Weatherall to mind her during the day, while Harry is busy in the shop."

"That's a wonderful idea." Jess put the cups on the table. "Is Martin home yet?"

Izzy noticed the tremor in her voice, and looked up sharply.

"Yes, he is." Izzy paused. "Jack would be very proud of the way he has turned out. He's a very nice young man, and he plans on going back to France soon. It seems he has a French lass waiting for him."

Jess busied herself with the tea. "He was very close to Jack, right from the start." Her voice faltered. "I'm pleased he's found some meaning in his life." She looked up at her sister. "How is Nancy?"

"She's very well, I must say. Freya loves her. She's become quite a regular visitor, so Harry is thinking about giving her a job in the shop. We are doing much better now that the war is over."

The ensuing silence was broken only by the sound of Gracie murmuring to her dolls. Jess poured the tea.

"And mother? How is she?"

Izzy shrugged. "I've had to move her in with us. Actually, Nancy is very good with her, and takes her for walks occasionally. We can't really let her out of our sight now. She tends to wander."

Jess pushed a cup across to Izzy.

"Why don't you move into the family home? It shouldn't be standing empty."

Izzy brushed her fingers through her thick blonde hair.

"We are thinking about it, but Harry would have to drive to the shop each day."

"It's not that far, Izzy. Actually a walk would probably do him good."

Izzy's eyebrows arched. "You're probably right, Jess."

The two women sipped their tea in silence.

"How is Beau?" asked Izzy, putting down her cup.

Jess looked straight into her sister's frank blue eyes.

"He's well." She stopped, before continuing. "He brought me back, Izzy. I didn't want to live, and he made me see that although Jack was gone, his children needed me, and that I owed it to them to keep going." She stopped to wipe her eyes. "He's gone back to Sydney, but he said he'll be back."

"I'm sure he will, Jess. You and Beau…" She stopped.

"What?"

"Never mind. He's been a very good friend, and that's what you need, little sister."

Izzy smiled at Jess's bemused expression. "And how is everyone else? Margaret and Charles? Jean? The boys?"

"They're all well. Margaret has been a tower of strength, and stayed with us until Charles felt she should go home."

"Charles felt she should go home! Jess, that man doesn't realize how selfish he is!"

Jess put her finger to her lips, to quieten Izzy's outburst.

"Well he is! Damn it, Jess, the man only thinks of himself!"

"Hush, Izzy! He's not as bad as he used to be." Jess nodded in Gracie's direction. "Gracie loves him, and it's actually reciprocated."

"Humph! Well that's something then, I suppose." Izzy smiled at Jess.

Charlie

Beau sat at his large polished desk, and toyed with a pencil. His last patient had gone, and all he had to do now was tidy up some paperwork, before heading to his lodgings and another lonely evening.

His thoughts turned to Charlie Evans, and he wondered about his future. His mother had been justifiably angry after seeing her son handled so roughly by hospital staff at Serendipity Lodge. Beau was angry. It should not have happened. What was Matthew thinking? Was he losing his grip, with all the new patients lining up for help?

Beau sighed and placed the pencil in his drawer. He closed the file before him, and rose from the leather seat. Opening a filing cabinet that stood beside the large window, he slipped the file into its appropriate slot. Closing the cabinet, he stood for a moment looking out on to the harbour. It never ceased to thrill him with its constant motion; its restlessness.

He turned as he heard a knock at his door. "Come in."

Matthew appeared in the doorway. "I'm glad you're still here, Beau. Can we talk?"

Beau looked beyond Matthew to see if Celia was following. She wasn't.

"Yes, Matthew."

Matthew closed the door quietly behind him, and sat opposite Beau.

"What is it, Matthew?"

"It's about Charlie Evans."

Beau looked up sharply. "Charlie? Funny you should mention him, Matthew. I was just thinking about him, and wondering what had happened to him. His mother took him, presumably?"

A frown creased Matthew's high forehead. "Yes, and I'm afraid she's not finished with us yet." He pulled a folded piece of paper from his pocket, and handed it across the table to Beau. "She wrote me this. See what you make of it."

Beau unfolded the paper. On it was scrawled the following:

Doctor Morley, I am very upset by your treatment of my Charlie, and I want you to know that I'm considering going to the newspaper, to let everyone know what goes on out at Serendipity.
The war has done terrible things to Charlie and many other young men, and they don't need rough handling to rid them of their demons. What they need is love and a lot of patience. They can't help the way they are now. Shame on you and your staff!

Edwina Evans

Beau laid the note carefully on the table, and looked up at Matthew.

"Has Celia seen this?" he asked.

Matthew shook his head. "I don't want her to see it. What do we do, Beau?"

"I'd like to go and see Edwina Evans, and try to explain our position."

Matthew sat back against the leather chair. "You'd be the best one to deal with her, I would say. Explaining your experiences might help." He groaned loudly. "We don't need this, Beau. It could damage our good reputation."

"I'll go and speak with her. What's their address?"

Matthew rose from the chair. "I'll get it for you. Thank-you, Beau." He gave a mock salute, and left the room.

Beau opened the bottom drawer of his desk, and reached for his tobacco pouch. It was times like this he needed to draw on extra reserves of confidence.

*

The street was narrow, and lined with shabby double-storey tenement buildings, crammed together to conserve space. Children played on the tarred roadway, or sat on the concrete footpaths. Beau stepped carefully between piles of overflowing rubbish, as stray cats darted out of his way. He had read in the newspaper that there was to be a garbage strike by the unionists. A rise in wages, was it? The smell was certainly ripe.

Beau stopped in front of building No. 18.

Two women sat on the top step, in front of the shabby wooden door. They stopped their chatter, and looked down at the man standing below them.

"What do you want?" one of them asked, as she spat close to his feet.

Beau stepped back. "I'm looking for Mrs. Evans."

They both laughed, a raucous sound. "Calls 'erself missus, does she?"

Beau ignored the rant. "I believe she lives here, at No. 18."

"Yeah, she does. Upstairs. Her an' that crazy boy."

The women refused to move, as Beau made his way carefully between them. After opening the heavy door, he stepped inside. His nostrils were assailed with a combination of urine and damp. Paint peeled from the walls, and the signs of neglect were everywhere. He made his cautious way up the creaking stairs to the second floor, holding his breath as he did so. Did people really live like this?

Beau knocked on a door with the number 7 painted roughly in yellow paint.

He waited.

Finally it opened, and the woman he had seen at Serendipity, stood on the other side. She looked at him, and then attempted to shut the door, but Beau was too quick for her. He pushed his hand against it.

"Mrs. Evans, I need to speak with you, please."

"Why? Haven't you done enough damage? I don't want to speak to you!"

"Please? Just hear me out."

The woman hesitated, and then with a sigh, opened the door.

"Thank-you," said Beau, as he stepped inside the small living room, which, although sparsely furnished, was clean and tidy.

The woman motioned him towards a faded velveteen chair, while she sat stiffly on another. Pressing her hands on to her lap, she looked up at Beau, her brown eyes questioning.

"Well, what do you have to say to me?"

"Firstly, I want to apologize for what happened the other day, and I'll try to explain my involvement."

A bang coming from behind a door opposite Beau, made him look up quickly.

"It's Charlie," said the woman evenly. "I have to keep him locked in his room when he starts to behave strangely. I'm afraid he'll try to run off if I don't."

Beau nodded slowly. The scenario was all too familiar. He licked his lips.

"I have first-hand knowledge of what Charlie is suffering, Mrs. Evans. I've been there myself."

The woman looked at the scar on his face. "The Germans did that?"

"Their shrapnel did." He paused. "Tell me about Charlie."

She shrugged. "What do you want to know?"

Beau noticed that she spoke well, in spite of her poor circumstances.

"Why did he enlist? He must have been very young."

"He was seventeen. His father had died… so he took it upon himself to follow some of his friends. They all put their ages up, and there was nothing we, as parents, could do about it."

"He finished up in France?"

"Well, yes, but one of the doctors there had him sent back to England, because he worked out that Charlie was under age."

"And his mates?"

"I don't think he saw them again. Somehow he managed to find his way back to France." She smiled, and her thin features softened. "He always was a determined little sod." She looked down at her hands.

"What happened then?"

"I'm not sure, but he became a dispatch rider, probably because he was a good horseman, and he was never afraid of danger." She looked up at Beau. "We didn't always live like this. We had property down south, and my husband was keen on the horses. He…" She stopped, and shrugged helplessly.

Beau noticed tears on her lashes.

"Dispatch riders were crucial along the trenches," he said quickly. "They were responsible for keeping lines of communication open, where there was a risk of interception from the enemy. They needed men who weren't afraid of danger."

"Something really terrible must have happened to Charlie. He refuses to talk about it." She brushed the tears from her eyes. "He keeps whatever it was locked up inside himself, and goes into these strange trances at the least little thing. I thought Serendipity would help him. It seems I was wrong."

"I can help him, Mrs Evans, if you'll trust me." He met her gaze. "Give me another chance, and I'm sure I can reach Charlie. He was responding to me, when Doctor Morley unwittingly interrupted. It won't happen again, I assure you. Doctor Morley was doing what he thought was right at the time." He held out his hand. "Will you let me help Charlie?"

She didn't take his proffered hand. "I'll think about it."

Beau stood up. "I'll come back in a few days."

"I won't write that letter," he heard her say as he moved towards the door.

"Thank-you, Mrs. Evans. I appreciate that."

Jess's Reunion with Martin

"Jess!" Izzy's voice could be heard from the kitchen. "You have a visitor!"

Jess pulled her apron off, brushed back the stray curls from her damp brow, and hurried along the passage to the front door.

Izzy stood aside as Jess appeared, and smiling at her sister, opened the door. Jess stopped in her tracks, and her eyes widened as she looked at the tall, handsome young man standing on her front verandah. He pulled the cap from his head, and brushed a hand through his blonde hair.

"Martin!" It came out as a croak, and Jess felt herself bubbling up inside.

"Hello, Jess."

She found herself immediately engulfed in a bear hug. Her feet left the floor, and she had a sudden recollection of three Christmases ago, when Jack had surprised her on a twenty-four hour leave pass. She caught her breath on a sob, as Martin released her. They stared at one another for a long moment.

"Are you two coming inside before the flies do?" came Izzy's voice.

"Yes, yes. Come in, Martin. It's wonderful to see you. Are you staying long?"

"No. I'm on my way to Melbourne to organize my trip back to France." Martin followed Izzy and Jess along the passage to the kitchen. "So I knew I had to pop in and say hello to you and then I'll go and see Billy."

"Yes." Jess's tone sounded forlorn, so Izzy rescued the moment.

"You will have a cup of tea, of course?"

"Yes, thank-you."

Izzy made the tea, while Jess and Martin sat opposite one another at the big table.

"So you're going back to France then?" Jess looked into the pale blue eyes.

"I am, Jess. We owe it to those people to try and repair some of the damage." He paused. "Besides, I met a girl. Her name's Fleur, and I promised her I'd be back."

"That's very commendable, Martin." Jess reached across the table and covered his hands with hers. "Did Jack meet Fleur?"

Martin's jaw trembled. "Jack was there the day we pulled her mother from the rubble of their home. Yes, he met Fleur." He cleared his throat. "He said she was a very pretty girl."

Jess nodded. "Good," she murmured.

They were silent for a few moments while Izzy slid cups of tea in front of them.

"I saw him buried, Jess." There were tears on Martin's fair lashes. "Jack was buried with honours, alongside others who died of that….influenza."

"It was deadly, then?"

"Took some out in twenty-four hours, it was that deadly."

"I'm glad you and Billy stayed to say good-bye to Jack, Martin."

"He was our mate, Jess." Martin wiped a sleeve across his eyes. "He was my best mate, and I was angry when the Sergeant said he had gone. It was so unfair!"

"I met the Sergeant, Martin, and his wife, Mary."

Martin's expression softened. "Oh, Jess, you should've heard nurse Mary sing; like an angel she was." He gave a short laugh. "I was smitten on her at one stage, and Jack told me that there were plenty of other fish in the sea. Mary was definitely not for me." His eyes met Jess's. "Jack was like a dad to me, Jess. I listened to his advice mostly." He smiled softly. "He did get on my goat occasionally, because he knew everything. Jack knew *everything*, Jess."

"I'm sure he didn't, Martin. It just seemed to you as though he did."

"No, Jess. He was a regular encyclopaedia."

This made Izzy snort. "Are you calling Jack a know-all, Martin?"

"No." Martin shook his head. "He wasn't like that. He just….well, he just took an interest in everything around him."

Jess wiped her eyes. "How does your mother feel about you going back so soon?"

"She's alright with it. She said if it's what I want to do, then I'd better do it."

"So you've left the Army?"

"Oh, no. I plan on gettin' some stripes this year. As a matter of fact, I'll be going back to France with a work party. I won't be on my own."

"Your mother should be very proud of you, Martin."

"She is, Jess, and she reckons I've turned out like this because of Jack's influence."

Are you staying for some lunch, Martin?" interrupted Izzy.

"No. I'd better get along and see Billy before I catch the afternoon train."

Jess took a deep breath. "I'm so glad you popped in to see me, Martin. Jack did think the world of you, even though you're nearly half his age."

Martin stood up. "He was a great bloke, Jess, and I'm sorry he's gone."

Jess nodded, unable to speak.

"Well, thanks for the cuppa." Martin stood awkwardly for a moment. "Look after yourself, Jess, and those kids of yours."

"I will, Martin." Jess swallowed hard. "I'll go and see your mother some time, when I've settled down a bit."

"She'd love that." He twisted his cap in his hands. "Good-bye, Jess." He nodded at Izzy. "'Bye, Mrs. Dalton."

"Call me Izzy, Martin." She smiled at him. "Come on, I'll see you out, before you both decide to flood this place."

*

Jean O'Malley wiped a handkerchief across her perspiring brow, and looked around the bar. It was getting close to lunchtime, and the usual crowd was in, enjoying a cold beer before she brought out the sandwiches.

Her son, Rodney, was still with her after six months, and didn't look like moving back to Sydney. It meant that she didn't have to look for another barman. The ending of the war had created an influx in the number of men looking for work, but Jean felt too tired to be bothered training a newcomer.

She stretched her gaze out through the far window, and could see flurries of leaves moving randomly along the street. There was a north wind out there, and the temperature gauge behind the bar was nudging 70 degrees, which meant that on the street, it was likely to be close to 100.

Jean turned to make her way out to the kitchen, when she saw two young men enter. They were laughing and jostling one another as they headed for the bar.

"Hello, Mrs. O'Malley," rasped Billy Maitland cheerfully, seating himself on one of the high stools. "Two beers, please." He cast a glance around the crowded bar.

Jean nodded towards Martin. "One of your army buddies?"

Billy slapped Martin on the back. "This is Martin Weatherall, Mrs. O'Malley."

The smile on Jean's lips faded. "Oh! You're Jack's mate then?"

Martin nodded. "Yes, I am."

There was an awkward silence for a moment.

"You here to stay, Martin?" asked Jean.

'No." Martin cleared his throat. "I came down from Swan Hill to see Jess and Billy, then I'm off to Melbourne to organize my return to France."

"You're going back?" Jean voiced surprise as she slid a beer glass across the bar towards Billy.

"Yes, I am. There's a lot to be done to make the country liveable again."

"I see." Jean slid a glass in Martin's direction.

"Besides," said Billy, picking up his glass, "Martin found a real nice French girl, didn't ya Martin?"

Martin's fair skin flushed slightly.

Jean smiled. "Did he, indeed?" Seeing Martin's discomfort she added, "How is Jess?"

"She's doin' alright, considering." Martin wiped the froth from his lips. "It was a real shock to all of us, Jack dyin' like that." He shook his head. "So unfair."

"Yes, it was. I must pop along and see Jess, once this weather cools down." Jean mopped her perspiring brow. "Now that Beau has gone back to Sydney, she might be needing some company." Jean smiled at the two faces in front of her.

"Beau?" Martin had a puzzled look on his face. "I thought he died."

Jean shrugged. "It's a very long story, Martin, but no, he didn't die. He's working in Sydney, looking after returned servicemen who are suffering the same as he did."

"That's good then." Martin nodded his head sagely. "Nice bloke, Beau."

"Yes, he is." Jean paused. "Are you two staying for some sandwiches? I was just about to get them when you arrived."

"Yeah," rasped Billy. "We'll stay, won't we, Martin?"

Martin was still pondering the unexpected return of Beau.

"Why not. The train doesn't leave 'til 2.15."

"You've got plenty of time, mate!" Billy slapped Martin on the back.

Charlie Evans

Beau knocked on the door with the yellow number 7, and waited. He heard a noise within, and then the door opened slowly. Edwina Evans peered out at him, before opening the door wide enough for him to enter.

"You came then," she said softly.

"I said I would," answered Beau as he stepped into the darkened room.

The atmosphere was stifling and he sensed immediately that all was not well. He looked closely at the woman in front of him. Her face was in shadow, but he saw the bruise on her cheek.

"Did Charlie hit you?"

She put a hand up to her face and nodded briefly. "It was my own fault," she whispered. "I tried to take something from him, and he lashed out. It's not like him. He's never done that before."

"Where is he now?"

"In his room. I locked the door and I'm waiting for him to calm down."

Beau frowned. Violence was not an indicator that he was looking for in Charlie. The lad was deeply troubled, but he needed to discover what it was that had led him to violence against his mother.

"Can I have the key, please?" He held out his hand.

Edwina reluctantly handed Beau the key. He walked across the room and stood in front of a door. Muffled sounds could be heard coming from within the room.

"He's banging his head against the wall," whispered the distraught mother.

"Charlie," said Beau loudly. "Can you hear me, Charlie? It's Beau." He paused. "Do you remember me?" The banging stopped. "I want to come in, Charlie. Is that alright with you? Bang once on the wall if it is."

There was silence for a long moment, and then a single bang was heard. Edwina stifled a sob. Beau smiled encouragingly at her, and slid the key into the lock.

"It might be an idea to let some light into this room," he said as he slowly opened the door.

Charlie was standing against the far wall, his hands pressed against his chest. He looked very dishevelled. His brown hair hung limply around his face, and all his shirt buttons had been ripped off. He clutched something in one hand, and Beau wondered whether this was what his mother had tried to take from him. He couldn't see what it was, but it was small and dull grey in colour.

There was a look of desperation in his brown eyes, and Beau had an immediate recollection of Jess holding him tight when he was paralysed with fear. His forehead beaded with perspiration in the airless room.

Beau took a step forward. Charlie backed into the corner, and began to whimper. His eyes darted past Beau to where his mother stood motionless.

"There's nobody else here, Charlie," murmured Beau. "I promise you there's only myself and your mother. You are quite safe."

Charlie made a clucking sound as he slid into a crouching position, and hid his face in his arms. Beau could now see the object he held in his hand. It was a button, from his shirt perhaps? No, it was the wrong colour.

It dropped to the floor. Charlie made a grab for it, but not before Beau saw it, and a shock ran through his body. It was from a German Infantry uniform. He recognised the crown, although speckled with rust. Where had it come from?

"Charlie," said Beau softly, "come and sit in the living-room. Here, take my hand." He held out his hand. "Don't be frightened. I'm not going to hurt you, I promise."

The brown eyes drooped and Charlie reached out hesitantly towards Beau. He took the trembling hand and led the boy from the room that had become his prison.

Edwina had opened the curtains, allowing light to stream into the cramped living quarters. She stood back as Beau led her son to one of the faded pink chairs.

"Very good, Charlie." Beau looked across at Edwina. "Perhaps you could get Charlie a glass of water? It's very hot in here."

She hesitated, before turning to the sink that occupied one wall, and along with a black-leaded wood stove, served as the kitchen.

Beau pulled up another chair, and sat beside Charlie, who was fidgeting nervously. His mother handed him a glass of water. He looked at it, and then at the two who were watching him.

Suddenly he lifted his arm, and was about to hurl the glass, but Beau was too quick for him and grabbed his wrist. Edwina gasped and stepped back.

"No, Charlie!" panted Beau. "It's water for you to drink."

"Not water! Not water!" The rasping sound startled both his mother and Beau.

"That's the first words he's uttered since he's been home!" Edwina gasped.

Beau was beginning to formulate a picture of what had happened to this boy during his time in the trenches. He turned to Edwina.

"We need to get him back to Serendipity. I'll take full responsibility for his welfare, but you must trust me." He turned back to Charlie. "I want to help you, Charlie. I know something of what you have suffered, but I must take you back to the hospital, where you were before. Do you understand me, Charlie? Nod your head if you do."

Charlie's head drooped. "Yes," he croaked.

Beau looked across at Edwina, who was sobbing quietly.

"I'll do my best for him, I promise," he whispered fervently.

*

Beau stood at one side of the desk, while Matthew sat on the other side, leaning back in his big comfortable leather chair.

"I hope you know what you are doing, Beau," said Matthew carefully. "The mother could still cause us problems."

Beau leaned on the desk. "Not if you leave Charlie to me, Matthew, without any interference."

"Interference? From whom?" Celia had entered the room, and crossed to the window behind Matthew.

The two men looked at one another.

"Beau wants to be solely in charge of young Charlie Evans."

"Oh?"

"I think I've discovered what he was subjected to while in France, and if I can get him to open up to me, we should have a chance of pulling him through this." Beau looked directly at Celia. "There'll be no white coats, no dark rooms and no shock treatment. If I want help I'll ask for it."

Celia raised a delicate eyebrow. "You are not the psychiatrist, Beau. Please remember that." She placed her hands on her husband's shoulders. "Matthew has the final say, don't you, darling?"

Matthew swivelled around to look up into the chiselled features of his wife.

"I'm going to trust Beau on this one, my dear. I shall observe."

"Thank-you, Matthew." Beau let his gaze rest briefly on Celia.

Realization

Jess stood looking out the kitchen window, feeling the intense loneliness of her surroundings. The summer heat was still baking the landscape, and her garden wilted under the sun's fierce blaze. She knew that she would have to do something about it, or there would be no vegetables left to pick. Fruit lay rotting at the base of the gnarled old apricot tree, and the tomato vines hung shrivelled on their wire frame. She sighed loudly.

Izzy had returned to Swan Hill, the boys were at school, and Gracie was with Margaret, so she had no excuse not to be out there tending her plants.

Turning from the window, Jess crossed the kitchen and headed along the passage to her bedroom. She opened the wardrobe, and flicked through the clothes hanging there, until she found her grey gardening pinafore.

Bending to retrieve her boots from the bottom of the wardrobe, her eyes rested on a pair of Jack's boots. Her resolve crumbled, and she dissolved into tears. It was nearly two months since she had learned of Jack's death, and the bitterness of that moment, had not left her. She stood and closed the wardrobe door.

Taking a handkerchief from her pocket, Jess wiped her eyes before donning her pinafore and boots and walking from the room. There was work to be done and she must do it. Gritting her teeth, she marched resolutely towards the neglected garden, pulling on a straw hat as she went.

She would start with the apricots. They needed raking into piles and covering with dirt. There would be no apricot jam this year, she thought wryly, as she wrestled the garden rake from its tight position among the tools in the shed.

The sun was hot as she laboured underneath the tree, and wiping the perspiration from her brow she heard Jack's voice.

"Jess! Have you taken leave of your senses?"

She smiled as she pictured him taking the rake from her hands, and leaning over to plant a kiss on her perspiring forehead. *"Go inside and let me do this."*

"Jess! Did you hear me?"

"Jack!" His name quivered on her breath.

Jess turned, hardly believing her ears. A figure strode towards her. The sun was in her eyes, so she shielded them with one hand, while she rested the shovel against the tree trunk. Her heart was beating a tattoo in her breast.

Jess felt hands on her arms, and she cried out, "Jack!"

"No, Jess, I'm not Jack!"

Until this moment, Jess had never seen any resemblance between Jack and his father, but as she stared at Charles standing before her, she wondered how she could possibly have missed it. She rested her head against his chest and sobbed.

"I thought Jack had come back to us."

"He's not coming back." Charles's voice was thick as he held his distraught daughter-in-law. "He's not coming back." There was a sigh of resignation.

Jess lifted her head. Charles, who was never demonstrative, dropped his arms to his side and stepped away.

"I'm sorry, Charles," Jess wiped her streaming eyes. "I thought you were Jack."

Charles took a deep breath.

"I've been in denial myself, Jess. I just couldn't let go. The whole idea of Jack being gone was preposterous." He drew an envelope from his shirt pocket. "I received this today; that's why I'm here."

"What is it?" Jess took the envelope in trembling fingers, pulled out a sheet of paper, and opened it.

"It's an answer to my letter to the Department regarding Jack's personal effects." He paused. "There's also a copy of his death certificate. That makes it final."

The words danced before Jess's eyes, as she read the following:

> *Dear Sir,*
>
> *I acknowledge receipt of your letter of the 4th ultimo, written on behalf of Mrs. J. C. Stanley, regarding the personal effects of the late No. **** Private J.C. Stanley, 21st Battalion, and state that these packages are packed by A.I.F Headquarters, London, and forwarded to this office for transmission to the person entitled to receive them. Therefore upon receipt of a reply, Mrs. J.C. Stanley will be communicated with.*

There was a signature scrawled at the bottom of the page.

Jess looked at the small slip of paper which was headed: REPORT OF DEATH, and there written beneath was Jack's name, Regimental No., his age, (34) cause of death, (Influenza pneumonia) time and place of death, (14/11/18, Military Hospital, Sutton Veny) and the date at which interment would take place (18/11/18).

She looked up at Charles, and was startled to see tears glistening on his eyelashes. For the first time in their association, she felt a pang of pity for the man. She smiled softly, as she handed back the envelope.

"That's it then." She wiped her hands down her pinafore. "Come inside and I'll make us both a cup of tea." Charles followed as she walked towards the verandah. "It really is too hot out here."

As they sat sipping tea some minutes later, Jess thought it ironic that she and Charles should have this empathy for one another. It had never happened before. They had never sat sipping tea together.

"If you need the garden tended to, Jess," Charles was saying, "you only have to ask. I have a couple of lads I could send around. Work in the plumbing business is slowing down. People are hanging on to their money at present, as they see which way the economy is going to go, now that the war is over."

Jess nodded. "Thank-you, Charles." She placed her cup on the table. "I might have to get a job myself, to supplement my income. The ironing I do for Jean O'Malley isn't enough, with three growing children."

Charles raised his bushy eyebrows, and Jess waited for the retort that would surely come after such a revelation, but there was none.

"Margaret and I are here for you, Jess. You don't have to do this on your own."

"I know that, Charles, and I suppose I am luckier than most war widows, but I want to be as independent as I can be."

The word 'widow' suddenly struck Jess like a blow to the head. It was real. It was official. She was a widow, and at the age of thirty, had a long lonely road ahead of her.

Charlie's Treatment

"So, you've moved the lad back to Serendipity, have you, Beau?" Matthew sat back in his comfortable leather chair, his fingers drumming on the polished desk.

"Yes, I have." Beau stood facing Matthew.

"Is that a wise move?"

"Matthew, his home environment is sadly lacking in amenities."

Matthew shrugged. "How will you monitor him? You can't be there twenty-four hours a day."

"No." Beau paused. "I'm moving his mother to a room nearby, so that she can be on the spot when I'm not there."

Matthew's fingers stopped drumming, and a scowl creased his high brow.

"What? Beau, this is not a home away from home! It is an institution, which relies on professional care. This woman is not trained to deal with these people."

"She is a mother, Matthew, who has seen what the war has done to her son. She is, in my opinion, qualified to deal with him." Beau stopped and took a deep breath. "Charlie's recovery depends solely on her. My role will be to support her, and gain an insight into what actually happened to the boy. I do have my suspicions."

Matthew scratched his head. "This is unprecedented, Beau, and I don't know that I can allow it. We have staff trained to deal with these people."

"'These people' as you call them, Matthew, have suffered enough for their country, and deserve to be treated with respect." Beau's voice rose as his anger increased. "A little human kindness will go a long way, in my humble opinion."

"Very well." Matthew sat upright. "We shall see how it goes, but I assure you, Beau, I will be observing closely."

The two men stared at each other for a long moment.

"You wanted me to take a personal interest in this lad, Matthew, so that's exactly what I am doing." Beau turned stiffly and headed for the door.

Matthew watched him leave the room, and then sat back, rubbing his hands through his hair. Beau was becoming very high-handed, and he hoped that wasn't going to be a problem.

*

"Why are you doing this? Is it because you're afraid I'll go to the newspaper?"

"No." Beau looked into Edwina's serious brown eyes. "I know you want to see your son get better, more than anything else. Bad publicity is not what Charlie needs, and I think you know that."

The woman turned away, and looked around the room in which they were both standing. It was small, but clean and freshly painted, with a bed settee at one end, a round table with two straight-backed chairs, and by the window which looked out on to the tree-lined street, was a bench with a sink. On the bench stood a single gas ring, with a kettle, and above, in an overhead cupboard, there were cups, saucers and plates.

Edwina moved to a door adjacent to the entrance, and opened it. She saw a small washbasin, and a toilet. There were no bathing facilities. Her eyes rested on a cup in which stood a toothbrush, and moved to a towel hung carelessly over a rail. She looked enquiringly at Beau.

"It's a shared bathroom, I'm afraid," he said apologetically.

Edwina shrugged. "Oh! Well, I'm used to that. I just hope my neighbour is friendly." She walked back into the living room. "What happens now, Dr. DuBois?"

"We go and see Charlie. Serendipity Lodge is only a couple of blocks from here."

"What happens with my room over on East Street? I can't afford both."

"You keep paying your rent there, and I'll take care of this room."

Edwina's eyebrows arched. "I can't let you do that. I'll pay for this room, and collect my belongings from East Street. God only knows, I haven't got much."

Beau turned to face her, and was met with an intense stare from those brown eyes. In spite of her situation, Edwina Evans was a proud woman.

"Very well," he said slowly. "If I say the hospital will pay for your room here, will that make a difference?"

She stared at him for a long moment, and Beau guessed that she had seen through his little deception.

"Alright, Doctor DuBois, we'll do it your way."

"Good." Beau smiled. "That's settled. Now let's go and see Charlie."

*

"What can you tell me about the German button that Charlie has?"

Their footsteps crunched on the gravel as they walked the path to the Lodge.

Edwina shrugged. "I know nothing about it, except that he refuses to let it go."

"I didn't notice it the last time he was here." Beau's brow furrowed as he tried to remember his earlier encounter with Charlie.

"No. Charlie is very cunning, and he probably had it hidden somewhere."

They climbed the wide concrete steps, and Beau opened the door for Edwina to enter the cool interior. As he crossed to the service window, Shirley looked up from her work.

"Hello, Doctor DuBois!" she breezed.

"We're here to see Charlie Evans, Shirley." He turned to Edwina, standing quietly beside him. "This is Charlie's mother, Mrs. Evans, and she'll be assisting me with Charlie's care."

"Oh? Does Doctor Morley…" She stopped, as she read the expression in Beau's eyes. "That's fine then." She looked at Edwina. "You won't need to come to the service desk each time, Mrs. Evans. You can just go up. Charlie is in room ten."

Beau took Edwina's arm and steered her towards the staircase.

"Doctor Morley will be extremely interested in what happens with Charlie," he said quietly, "but I've asked him not to interfere. I know he'll respect my wishes, but if he questions you at any time, just refer him to me."

Edwina nodded. "Certainly."

Reaching the top of the staircase, they headed along the corridor to room 10, which was just opposite the nurse's station.

As they approached, a nurse smiled at Beau from beneath her white veil.

"Hello Doctor DuBois."

"Hello Susan. This is Charlie Evans' mother, and she'll be a regular visitor here."

The young woman greeted Edwina with a broad smile.

"Nice to meet you, Mrs. Evans."

Edwina nodded in response.

"Any noises coming from Charlie's room, Susan?"

"No, Doctor. He's been real quiet."

"Good." Beau opened the door of No. 10. "He has a window now, and the garden to look out on," he added as they entered the small room.

Charlie was seated on the wide window ledge, his knees under his chin and his face pressed against the glass.

"Hello Charlie." The boy turned.

He looked beyond Beau towards his mother, and his hostile expression softened. Edwina crossed the room, and took her son by the hand.

"Hello, Charlie," she whispered, pressing his hand against her breast.

As Beau waited for the right moment to interrupt their reunion, he glanced around the room. It was light and airy, and contained a single cot, a chair and small table, a washbasin with soap and towel, and the usual bucket for emergency use by the patient. There was a strong smell of disinfectant lingering in the air.

He was pleased to note that there were no restraints visible, and the cot did not have extended sides. What he did notice, however, was that Charlie still wore the slippers that he had promised himself he would replace.

He stepped towards the window, and Charlie immediately stiffened.

"It's alright, Charlie," said Edwina quietly. "Doctor DuBois is here to help you. You remember him, don't you?"

Charlie frowned, and then nodded.

"You can see the rose garden from here, Charlie," said Beau lightly. "You'll be able to see the gardeners taking care of it. Maybe one day soon, you can help them. Look! There's one now, cutting off the dead blooms."

Charlie pointed a finger at the window, and a grunt escaped his lips. Edwina looked enquiringly at Beau, who was watching Charlie intently. The lad didn't have the German button in either hand, so where was it? Was it in his pocket?

"Do you think he'll be able to talk again, Doctor?" whispered Edwina.

"Oh, yes," said Beau quietly. "Trauma has paralysed his vocal chords. Once we get to the bottom of his fear, I have no doubt he'll talk freely again."

Edwina leaned against her son, and attempted to cradle him in her arms, but he stiffened, and sucked in his breath in great gasps. She stepped back, afraid that he might lash out at her as he had done once before.

An anguished cry tore itself from his lips, and Beau noticed that he suddenly clutched at his pyjama coat, right over the left pocket. The button had to be there.

It was significant, and Beau knew that it was the key to freeing Charlie from the memories that haunted him.

"Charlie!" Beau spoke firmly. "Your mother wants to help you. I want to help you. There's nothing here that will hurt you, I promise."

Charlie looked around desperately, before hiding his head in his arms and rocking backwards and forwards, from his precarious position on the window ledge.

Beau took Edwina's arm.

"I don't think we're going to get any more out of Charlie at present. Why don't we go and get you settled into your room, and then perhaps you can come and see him later on." They walked quietly from the room. "He obviously doesn't want too much human contact, so let him initiate the next move."

As they headed along the corridor, Edwina stopped suddenly.

"Aren't you going to lock his door?"

"No. He won't try to escape. He has a fear of open spaces."

"Are you sure?"

"As sure as I can be." Beau smiled suddenly. "Besides, he wouldn't get far in those slippers. I thought I'd buy him some new ones."

They had reached the top of the staircase, and Edwina turned to face him.

"You're going to do what?" Her tone was sharp, stopping Beau in his tracks.

"I'll buy him some new slippers."

"You'll do no such thing! They were his father's and…" She hiccoughed loudly.

"I'm sorry," said Beau. "I meant no offence. They're too big for him, and I just thought it was the least I could do."

"I think you're doing enough, Doctor. I don't want charity!"

"It's not charity, I assure you."

"Well, whatever your motives, I can't accept this. If he needs slippers, I'll get them." Edwina began to descend the stairs, and by the set of her straight back, Beau knew that he would have to tread very carefully in future.

Jess Makes a Decision

Jess smoothed the last tablecloth in to the big cane basket, and thought about her future. As she had told Charles, she needed to get a job if she was to keep her family together. She wouldn't rely on her in-laws, although she knew they were willing to step in. It was her responsibility, and hers alone.

On Monday she would go to the Trades hall and see what was available for a woman with three children, one not yet at school. She was clutching at straws, even thinking that there might be a job out there for her, but she had to try.

She sighed loudly. It might even be worth speaking with Jean, when she delivered her ironing, to see if she needed a kitchen hand. At least she would be able to take Gracie with her.

"Ma! Ma! Come quick!"

Jess stopped in her tracks as Ben's voice rose to a crescendo in the back yard. Something was wrong. She headed for the back door, slamming it behind her as she raced across the verandah and down the steps.

"What is it, Ben? What's happened?"

Ben's voice became a sob. "One of my chooks is dead, ma!"

Jess ran to the chook pen, where Ben was pressed against the wire fence. As she flung open the wooden gate, she saw what Ben was staring at; the mangled remains of one of his prize chooks. She grabbed his hand and pulled him towards the gate. The rest of the chooks scratched nervously in the dirt.

"It must have been a fox," said Jess breathlessly, as her eyes scanned the bottom of the wire enclosure. Sure enough, there was a hole dug beneath the fence, allowing access for a wily fox.

Ben was sobbing beside her, as she manoeuvred him out of the pen.

"That was Speckles," he said tearfully. "She was my favourite."

Jess closed the gate, and put her arms around her distraught son.

"I'm so sorry, Ben." She wiped the tears from his cheeks. "We'll have to fix the fence so it doesn't happen again." She took his hand. "Come on inside and I'll see what I've got to mend a broken heart." They walked towards the house.

"I'll have to bury her, ma," said Ben, wiping a sleeve across his face, and then in all innocence, added, "and then I can go and talk to her whenever I like."

Jess felt the blow to her heart, as though she had been physically struck.

"Yes, Ben, you can," she murmured, as the tears prickled her eyelashes.

Life, with all its ups and downs, was going to continue, and she had to prepare herself to be the one to deal with all of it.

Edward met them at the back door, as they entered the house. He stared at his brother's tear-streaked face. "What's wrong with you, Ben?"

"A fox has killed one of Ben's chooks," said Jess quickly.

"Which one, Ben?" Edward followed them eagerly into the kitchen.

"Speckles." A fresh wave of tears coursed down Ben's cheeks.

"Ooh! Can I have a look?"

"No, Edward! You cannot!" Jess retorted sharply.

Edward had his hand on the wire door. "Why not?"

"Because I have said so! Don't you disobey me, Edward?"

Edward's shoulder hunched, but he turned from the door, and with a scowl in his mother's direction, headed slowly for his room.

Jess turned to Ben. "Let's see if we can find a box big enough to bury your little friend, Ben."

*

Later that day, after the remains of Speckles had been buried, and Edward's morbid curiosity was finally satisfied, Jess and the boys walked to the Grey Goose with Jean's basket of ironing, and half a dozen eggs.

They entered through the side door, and into the ladies Lounge. The loud hum of male voices filtered through from the bar, and Jess told her boys to wait while she went to get Jean.

Standing at the door of the bar, she could see Jean and her son Rodney, busy serving beer to the packed bar. It was Saturday afternoon, and the weather was still pushing up the barometer to the one hundred degree mark.

Jean saw Jess hovering in the doorway, turned to say something to Rodney, and headed in Jess's direction. Her florid face was beaded with perspiration, and she wiped it with her handkerchief as she reached Jess.

"Hello Jess, dear," she said as together they headed for the Ladies Lounge. "Brought my ironing, have you?"

"Yes, I have." Jess was feeling concerned for her friend. "You need to rest more, while this heat continues, Jean."

Jean sat her ample frame on a chair, and fanned her face with her handkerchief.

"I know, Jess, but who will do it if I don't?"

Jess almost said, *Rodney could do more for you,* but stopped herself just in time.

"Is there anything I can do, Jean? In the kitchen perhaps?"

Jean stopped fanning her face and squinted up at Jess.

"Are you looking for a job, Jess?"

Jess nodded. "I have to do something, Jean. My pension is not really enough, with three children to raise."

"What about your in-laws? Surely they can help you."

"I'm responsible for my children, Jean, not Margaret and Charles."

Jean looked at the two boys standing watching them. They were certainly growing fast, and keeping them in clothing was probably Jess's main concern. She looked up at Jess.

"I'd like to help you more, Jess, I really would, but I'm struggling as it is, and Rodney, well, he does like to spend money, not always wisely, I might add."

"That's alright, Jean." Jess smiled at her friend. "No harm in asking." She nodded towards Ben. "We have some eggs for you; only half a dozen today, because a fox got into the chook pen, and killed Ben's best layer."

Jean stretched out a hand to Ben. "I'm sorry to hear that, Ben. You love those chooks, don't you, lad?"

Ben nodded as he handed Jean the box of eggs. Jess noticed that his eyes were moist and he blinked rapidly.

"Tore it to bits, Mrs. O'Malley," said Edward, eager to pass on the gory details.

Ben took a swipe at his brother, hitting him in the stomach. Edward doubled over.

"That's enough, you two!" Jess grasped each boy by the arm, as she looked apologetically at Jean.

Jean lifted her heavy body from the chair, and shuffled towards the door.

"I'll get you some money, Jess. Wait here."

She returned several minutes later, and pressed some coins into Jess's hand.

"I really would like to help you, Jessie love, but the way things are at present, with all the returning soldiers looking for work, I'm more or less obliged to employ a man." She shrugged. "Not that I'm going to, of course."

"I understand, Jean." Jess patted the older woman's hand. "I'll find something."

"Why don't you go to the Repatriation Office, just near the fountain in Charing Cross? They might know what jobs are available."

"Yes. Maybe I'll do that." Jess smiled. "Now, we'd better get home, boys. Grandma will be bringing Gracie home soon, and we have a fence to mend before it gets dark." She turned to Jean. "You get some rest if you can, Jean."

The older woman nodded and shuffled back towards the bar.

*

First thing Monday morning, when the boys had gone to school, Jess and Gracie headed for the town. Jess had dressed herself neatly, in a plain grey skirt, white blouse with a high neckline and long sleeves, and a straw hat covering her unruly curls. Gracie was dressed in a blue pinafore with lace across the bodice. On her head she wore a straw hat, tied at the chin with blue ribbons. She looked up at her mother as they walked.

"Where are we going, ma?"

"Ma has to go and see if she can find work, Gracie."

"Oh! Why?"

"Because you children are growing so fast, I can't keep up with you." Jess took hold of her daughter's chubby hand. "Now come on, let's cross the road before we get trampled on by horses or run over by a motorcar!"

Gracie giggled, as together they negotiated the busy Charing Cross, with its impressive Alexandra Fountain. They reached the footpath, and Jess stopped. Ahead of them stretched a queue of mostly men, and with a sinking heart, Jess realised that they were waiting their turn to step into the Repatriation Office.

"I don't think this is a very good idea, Gracie," murmured Jess, as they took their place in the queue. "However, we are here now, so I suppose we wait."

Men in front of her, turned to look at the attractive redhead with the small child, and Jess could hear their whispered comments, as she stood uncomfortably behind them. She was about to make a hasty retreat, and forget the whole idea, when she heard a raspy voice at her elbow.

"What are you doin' here, Mrs. Stanley?" It was Billy Maitland.

Relief flooded over her.

"I'm so glad to see somebody I know, Billy. I'm here for the same reason as everyone else, I imagine. What about you? Haven't you got a job?"

"Oh, yeah, I do," he rasped. "I'm here to see what can be done about me brother, Frank, and what me mum's entitlement should be."

"Oh, yes, of course."

Billy glared at the two men immediately in front of them, who were staring openly at Jess, grins on their whiskered faces.

"What are you starin' at?" he muttered gruffly.

"Good-lookin' filly y've got there, mate," said one of them, a dishevelled young man with yellow teeth and long greasy hair.

"You shut ya mouth!" warned Billy. "I didn't fight the Hun for nothin'!" His fists balled, and his thin cheeks flushed.

"We all fought the Hun, mate," said the other man, also young, in spite of his unkempt appearance.

Jess put a hand on Billy's arm. "We're not here to fight," she said quietly.

"You heard the lady," muttered Billy. "Now turn around and don't let me see ya ugly mugs again!" He winked at Jess as the two men turned their backs on them. "Cheeky buggers!"

Jess smiled and looked down at Gracie, whose eyes were as big as saucers.

They stood in the heat for nearly an hour before it was Jess's turn to walk through the doors. She approached the big desk, and stood silently until the clean-shaven young man with droopy eyes and a condescending air, looked directly at her.

"Name?" he said imperiously.

"Jess Stanley."

"Age?"

Jess swallowed hard. "Thirty."

"Marital status?"

Jess took a deep breath. "I'm a widow. My husband died in England."

His droopy eyes surveyed her, and then looked down at Gracie standing solemnly beside her. He pursed his lips.

"And what can I do for you, Mrs. Stanley?"

"I would like to find employment."

The young man looked her over disdainfully.

"You saw the line-up of men out there? They're all looking for employment. You have a widow's pension, I presume, if your husband was a serviceman?"

"Yes, I have a small pension. I also have three growing children, who now have no father. I need to have a job."

"I'd like to be able to help you, Mrs. Stanley, but you must realise that these men must hold priority over you." He paused. "What skills do you have?"

"I've worked in haberdashery, I can cook, I can sew and I'm not afraid of hard manual work."

He raised his eyebrows. "I'll make a note of these things." He scribbled on a piece of paper. "I can't promise you anything. Please send in the next in line. Good day to you, Mrs. Stanley."

Jess grabbed Gracie by the hand, and hurried outside into the heat. Billy Maitland was the next in the queue.

"How'd ya go, Mrs. Stanley?" he rasped.

Jess shook her head. "I hope you have more luck with your mum's entitlement." She smiled wanly. "You're next."

"Righto."

Jess watched Billy stroll jauntily into the 'lion's den', before turning and heading along Mitchell Street. *That was a waste of time*, she pondered heavily.

*

That night, when the children were all in bed, Jess sat at the kitchen table and wrote a long letter to Beau. She missed him terribly, and the next best thing to being able to talk to him, was to pour out her concerns on paper.

Beau would understand; he had always understood.

Jess's Letter

Celia closed the front door of the Norlane Street office block, and leaned against it for a few moments. The air outside was sticky, and she had really noticed it as she walked the short distance from the terrace house that she shared with Matthew.

The large elm trees lining the street did very little to combat the heat on this particular day.

Celia looked down to where a pile of letters lay scattered at her feet. There would be more cries for help; more people unable to cope with the everyday task of living a normal existence. She sighed and bent to pick up the envelopes. Flicking idly through them, she came to one addressed to Beau. Celia turned it over and frowned as she saw the name *Jess Stanley* written on the back.

Celia felt a twinge of annoyance, mixed with a feeling that she had always had where Beau was concerned. He no longer belonged to her, but somewhere inside, she still retained a degree of possessive jealousy. She pursed her lips, and slipped the letter into her jacket pocket. Beau could do without this right now. He had work to do here. Feeling completely justified in her action, Celia headed up the narrow stairs. After all, she was only protecting Beau from himself. He had always let his heart rule his head.

Her heels clicked on the polished linoleum, as she walked along the corridor. Reaching Beau's room, she slipped the key into the lock, and let herself in. The room was in semi-darkness, with the curtains pulled across the window. Celia dropped a pile of mail on to the desk, and walked over to the window. She pulled the heavy blue drapes open, to let in the sunlight. Beau liked to stand at this window; she had seen him on numerous occasions.

Celia looked out across the harbour, and marvelled at the water reflecting the rays of the sun. It was peaceful, serene even; in sharp contrast to the turmoil that existed on the streets below her. That was where the flotsam and jetsam of society were trying desperately to piece together the remnants of their lives, in a world that had been turned upside down.

Celia heard the door open and turned as Beau entered the room.

"Good morning, Beau," she breezed, giving him her warmest smile.

"Good morning, Celia." Beau slipped off his jacket, and threw it over the back of his leather chair. "I have three patients this morning, Celia, and then I'll be off to Serendipity." He flicked through his mail. "Is this all?"

"Yes, why? Are you expecting something?" Celia's tone was sharp.

"No, I'm not expecting anything."

"Good. I'll leave you to it, then." Celia left the room, creating a breeze as she shut the door behind her.

Beau sat behind his desk, and began opening the letters before him. There were no surprises. People were desperate to find answers to the problems that their loved ones had brought home from the war with them. The military hospitals were filled to over-flowing, as were the psychiatric institutions, and help seemed so far out of reach. He would like to be able to help every one of them, but he knew that was impossible. It was difficult enough, reading the pleas, and having to decide which ones were in the most need.

As he sat there, his thoughts inevitably strayed to Jess and the family. He wondered how she was getting on, now that a new year had begun. It was time he wrote to her to find out. He had put it off, because he didn't want her to think that he was being over-bearing. He smiled to himself as he recalled the time when she had told him exactly what she thought of the attention he had been giving her. What was it she had said? *I don't need looking after; I'm perfectly capable of looking after myself!*

She was right, of course, but sometimes a man needed to prove his worth.

The door opened and Celia's head appeared.

"Are you ready for your first patient, doctor?"

"Yes. Send him in."

"It's 'her', actually." Celia placed a folder on his desk.

"Very well, send her in."

"Doctor DuBois will see you now, Miss Harper."

Beau looked up as a young woman entered the room. Beau guessed her to be in her early twenties, with blonde hair swept back from her face. Her blue eyes were wide and luminous above hollow cheekbones. She stood uncertainly for a moment, before Beau beckoned her forward.

"Miss Harper?" She was staring at the scar on his face. "That's my legacy from the war," he said as lightly as he could.

She sat before him. "I'm sorry, I didn't mean to stare."

"That's alright. You're not the only one who does." Beau opened the file in front of him. "You were a nurse on the front line?"

"Yes." Her voice quavered.

"Do you want to talk about it?" Beau relaxed back in his chair.

The young woman pressed her fingers into her eyes. "No. I just want something to make me sleep; something to make me forget." She looked up at Beau. "If you were there, you must know what I mean."

"Yes, I was there." He leaned forward. "Do you have anyone you can talk to?"

"No-one who'd understand. My mother thinks I need to just 'get over it', as she puts it. You must know that it's not as simple as that."

"No, it's not. Are you currently employed?"

"Yes." She plucked nervously at her light cotton blouse. "I'm at the repatriation hospital at Randwick." Her eyes were blinking rapidly.

"Still exposed to trauma?"

She nodded bleakly.

"Do you have friends?"

"Nobody in particular. My close friends from the front, have all gone their separate ways, so I haven't seen them since we arrived back in Australia." She leaned forward anxiously. "Please, I only want a sleeping draught."

Beau studied the girl carefully. She showed all the signs of drug dependence, and as he glanced down at her notes, he saw that she had not been previously to the clinic. "What made you come here?" he asked.

The girl jumped to her feet. "I didn't come here to answer questions!" she burst out. "Are you going to prescribe me a sedative, or not?" She stood glaring at Beau.

"No," he answered bluntly. "Not until I know your medical history." He met her wide-eyed gaze.

"Fine! I'll find someone who will!" The door slammed behind her.

Beau sat for a moment, with his fingers pressed to his eyes.

"What did you say to her?" Celia's sharp voice came from the doorway. "She certainly left in a hurry, and without paying her dues."

Beau sighed. "I wouldn't prescribe sleeping pills for her."

"Why not?" Celia stepped into the room, and faced Beau, hands on hips.

"Because, Celia, the girl is obviously dependent on medication."

"And depriving her is going to fix her problem?"

"No, but I have no doubt she'll find someone who'll give her what she wants."

Celia rolled her eyes. "Honestly, Beau, you're not here to play judge and jury over the patients."

"Without knowing her medical history," he pointed to the paper on his desk, "I couldn't, in all conscience, prescribe barbiturates."

"So you sent her out to find the nearest quack! Honestly, Beau, sometimes I despair of you." Celia flounced out, slamming the door shut.

Beau closed his eyes. He had been prepared to help the girl, but not on her terms, so now he was left to wonder what would become of her. Maybe Celia was right; maybe he was playing judge and jury.

*

Celia stormed out of Beau's office, marched the length of the corridor, and clattered down the narrow staircase to the street below. Opening the front door, she stepped out on to the footpath and looked in both directions. She saw no sign of the young woman among the faces of the passing population. She had gone.

Celia entered the building. Climbing the stairs at a slower pace than she had descended, she put her hand in her pocket and immediately felt the letter between her fingers. Pulling it out, she looked at the front, turned it over, and then glanced up the stairwell. All was silent, so she tore open the envelope and pulled out a sheet of paper. The handwriting was neat, and her practised eye scanned the contents. It began:

> *Dear Beau,*
> *I hope this finds you well...*

Celia snorted. *Why were people so formal when addressing each other on paper?*

> *I know you will be working hard, and I think of you often.*
> *The children and I are managing reasonably well. I plucked up the courage to go to the repatriation office today to see if I can find employment. The boys are growing so fast; I fear I won't be able to keep up with their needs shortly.*
> *I am not hopeful of a job, as the man at the repatriation office politely informed me that men must have priority, and with all the servicemen returning from the war, there are more men than jobs.*
> *Still, I do have a small pension, so I must count myself lucky.*
> *Izzy came to spend a few days with us, and she hasn't changed, Beau; she still calls a spade a spade. While she was here, I had a visit from Martin Weatherall. It was lovely to see him. He's going back to France to help in the rebuilding. That's very commendable.*
> *Poor Ben is upset at present. A fox got into the chook pen, and made a meal of one of his hens. We've mended the fence, but I can't guarantee that it won't happen again.*
> *Charles and I have a newfound respect for each other. He was in denial*

about Jack's death, until he received confirmation that Jack's possessions will soon be sent home. We also received a copy of his death certificate. That made it final.

I am worried about Jean. She doesn't look well, and I think her son, Rodney, is causing her a lot of anxiety. I will keep my eye on her.

We look forward to receiving a visit from you, when you have the time.

Fondest regards, Jess
(and the children, of course)

Celia folded the letter, slipped it into her pocket, and continued up the stairs.

Charlie Opens Up

Beau stood at the door of Charlie's room, and looked across at the hunched figure on the window ledge. Charlie had his face pressed against the glass, so he didn't see Beau enter.

"Hello Charlie," said Beau quietly, so as not to alarm the boy.

However, Charlie swung around, overbalanced, and landed on the floor. Beau covered the distance and sat beside him, his back against the wall.

"I didn't mean to frighten you, Charlie." He smiled into Charlie's startled eyes. "Have you seen your mother today?" Charlie nodded and pointed to his slippers.

"She's gone to get you some new slippers?"

Charlie nodded. Apart from his fall from the window ledge, Beau noted that the boy was relatively calm, so he decided to bite the bullet and see what happened.

"I'd like to ask you some questions, Charlie, and some of them may be difficult. If you'd like to write the answers for me, then I'll get you some paper. Would you prefer to do that?"

Charlie studied him for a moment before nodding.

Beau smiled reassuringly. "Good. I'll get you some paper." He rose to his feet.

Beau crossed the corridor to the nurse's station, and shook the bell that stood on the desk. A young nurse appeared from somewhere along the corridor.

What can I do for you, Doctor?" she asked breathlessly.

"Some paper and a pencil, nurse, please?"

"Certainly." She bent to open a drawer, and produced two sheets of paper and a pencil, which she handed to Beau. "Are they for Charlie?"

"Yes, they are." Beau smiled. "Thank-you, nurse."

Back in Charlie's room, Beau handed him the paper and pencil.

"What is it you're afraid of, Charlie?" began Beau. "You see if I am to help you, I need to know what it is." Charlie was looking out into the distance. "Before you answer, Charlie, can I tell you what happened to me?" The brown eyes swivelled around to meet Beau's, before he frowned, licked his lips and nodded sharply.

"Very well," continued Beau, his tone never altering, "I was sent out with a platoon, to set traps for the enemy on no-man's-land. We were all afraid, and our nerves were on edge. The enemy discovered us, and fired into our midst. One of our boys panicked; a young man named Tommy. He tried to run, and became entangled in barbed wire. We were given the order to retreat, but I couldn't leave Tommy there, so I went after him. I tried to free him from the wire, and in the process we both got shot. Somehow I managed to get him back over our front line, but I became like you, Charlie, and refused to talk about it. I was sent home, and I finished up in an institution, not nearly as good as this one, and I lived in my own little world for a long time." He stopped. "It wasn't until I met someone who actually cared, that I took an interest in life again." He turned to face Charlie.

"I'd like to be that person for you, Charlie, if you'll let me."

Tears were streaming down Charlie's face, and he opened his hand to reveal the German military button.

"Tell me about it, Charlie," whispered Beau. "Where did you get it?" Beau took the button from Charlie's hand. "If you can't tell me, write it down, or draw me a picture. I need to know, Charlie."

Charlie wiped a sleeve across his tear-streaked face, and with a trembling hand, picked up the pencil and paper. Beau watched as he drew a very crude sketch of what looked like a hut, surrounded by rolls of what Beau guessed to be wire.

"You were a prisoner, Charlie? In a German camp?" Charlie nodded twice. "How?"

Charlie's fingers were drawing rapidly now, and Beau deciphered a person on horseback. "Was that you, Charlie?" He nodded. "You were a dispatch rider, am I right?" Another nod. "You were caught by the Germans and imprisoned?"

Beau looked down at the button. "So who did this belong to, Charlie?"

Charlie's energy was spent, and he curled up into a ball, shaking his head. Beau knew that he wasn't going to get any more information out of the boy, but they had made great strides. He knew more now than he had done a few minutes ago.

"It's alright, Charlie," Beau said soothingly. "You have done very well. I won't ask you anymore today, but I'll leave the paper and pencil, and if you want to, you can draw me some more pictures. They have been very helpful." Beau held out the button. "Do you want this back?"

Charlie lifted his head, and with trembling fingers, took the button from Beau's hand. It was crucial to the story, Beau felt sure. Now that Charlie had started opening up, there would be a way forward.

Beau rose to his feet, as Edwina made her entrance. Her smile faded as she looked from her son, in his hunched position, to Beau.

"What's happening?" she asked sharply.

"Everything's fine," answered Beau smoothly. "Charlie has done very well today."

"Have you, Charlie?" Edwina knelt in front of her son. "Look, Charlie, I have new slippers for you." She held out a pair of tartan slippers.

Charlie lifted his head, and reached for the slippers. Edwina frowned when she noticed his tear-streaked face. She looked up at Beau.

"I hope it wasn't an interrogation, Doctor," she said icily.

"Not at all," answered Beau. "Can you step outside for a moment, please, Mrs. Evans? I need to talk to you."

Edwina stood up, and followed Beau from the room. He moved a little way along the corridor, and then turned to face her.

"Charlie has made remarkable progress today, Mrs. Evans. I now know that he was taken prisoner by the Germans."

Edwina drew in a shaky breath. "Oh, God!" she murmured.

"He showed me the button. It's from a German soldier's uniform, what rank I'm not certain, but most likely the equivalent to our Private."

"How did he come by it?"

"I don't know that yet. I've asked him to draw for me what he remembers, so I'll see what happens tomorrow." He smiled at Edwina's troubled face. "We will get to the bottom of this, Mrs. Evans," he said quietly. "I promise. Now go back in there and make a fuss about his new slippers." She walked away. "Men rarely talk about their experiences at the Front, Mrs. Evans, whether it be from fear or guilt or sometimes shame."

"But my Charlie is just a boy," she whispered, her eyes filled with tears.

"All the more reason for us to find out what's troubling him."

*

An hour later, Beau sat in Matthew's office, facing him across the large polished desk. Celia stood at the window behind, looking out on to the harbour.

"So you've made headway with Charlie, have you, Beau?" Matthew was saying.

"I have, Matthew, and I'm confident that he will give me the rest of the story in his own time."

"He trusts you now, does he, Beau?" Celia spoke without turning.

"I think he does, yes."

"What did you learn?"

"I know that he was taken prisoner by the Germans. He also carries a button from a German soldier's uniform, and I want to know why, because I suspect that it holds the key to his condition."

"What methods are you using to extract this information from a boy who refuses to talk?" Celia turned to face Beau, her chiselled features stony.

"Methods?" Beau shifted in his chair. Celia was trying to unnerve him, he felt sure. "I asked him to draw what he remembers. His pictures led me to the conclusion."

"Drawings?" Celia snorted. "They're not conclusive. What do you think, Matthew?"

"Maybe not, Celia, but it's a start," said Matthew diplomatically. He smiled thinly at Beau. "What's your theory on the button, Beau?"

"I'm not sure yet, Matthew, but he refuses to let it go. It holds some importance, and I intend to find out."

Matthew nodded as Beau rose from his chair.

"You have patients here, Beau, who need your attention," said Celia sharply, as Beau headed for the door.

"I'm aware of that, Celia," said Beau patiently. "I'm going to my surgery now."

"What about the young nurse from this morning?" Her voice followed him as he stepped into the corridor.

"What about her?" Beau turned slightly.

"Are you going to follow her up, seeing as she left in such a hurry?"

"What are you two talking about?" Matthew interrupted. "What nurse?"

Celia gave Matthew a dazzling smile. "Nothing for you to worry about, Matthew."

"Don't patronize me, Celia! What nurse? Beau?"

Beau stepped back into the room, and shut the door.

"A young nurse came to me this morning, wanting barbiturates, and I wouldn't prescribe her any."

Matthew shook his head. "You know what she'll do now, don't you, Beau?" Beau nodded. "Then you'd better find her."

Beau opened the door, but not before he saw the smirk on Celia's face. Anger rose like bile inside him. *Why is she doing this? She has what she's always wanted.*

Jean

"There's a thunderstorm coming, for sure." Jean mopped her perspiring brow, as she sat on Jess's front verandah.

Jess, sitting beside her on the old wooden bench, looked up at the sky. There were certainly storm clouds gathering, and the air was hot and still.

"You're right, Jean. We need a good soaking to clear the air. It's been a very hot summer."

Jean turned to her friend, and her eyes were anxious.

"You're probably wondering why I came to see you, Jess."

"Friends can go and see each other, Jean. They shouldn't need a reason."

Jean nodded. "I know, but I need to tell you something."

Jess's heart sank. "What is it, Jean?"

Jean brushed her fingers through her untidy grey hair, and adjusted the combs.

"I've been to see the doctor, Jess."

"Doctor Simmons?"

"Yes. I've been feeling a little unwell for some time, but I just thought I needed a tonic." She paused.

"And?" urged Jess.

"He told me I have a heart murmur and I have to take it easy."

"I'm not surprised to hear that, Jean." Jess patted her friend's hand. "What is he going to do for you?"

"Medication, but I need to rest." She looked into Jess's green eyes. "It's not that simple, with Rodney there at the pub."

"He should be helping you, Jean."

Jean shrugged her plump shoulders. "I know, but unfortunately Rodney's like his late father; bone lazy."

"Well, he'll have to step up to the mark, Jean. Have you told him you're not well?"

Jean looked down at her work-worn fingers. "I have, but he just laughs and says that's nonsense. I'm as fit as a fiddle."

"You'll have to convince him otherwise."

"There's something else, Jess."

"What is it?"

"Rodney likes the horses too much, and he's got himself into debt."

"His debt, not yours!" Jess turned to face her friend. "Don't tell me you're paying his debts! Jean? You mustn't be so foolish!"

Jean crumpled, and her shoulders shook. Jess had never seen her friend like this before. Jean was always so strong. She placed an arm across the heaving shoulders and felt suddenly helpless.

"How much have you paid out for him, Jean?" Jess knew nothing about horse racing, but she did know that some men were seriously addicted to it, at the expense of everything else, including their families.

"Twenty pounds," sobbed Jean.

Jess was aghast. "Twenty pounds is a lot of money."

"I know." Jean wiped a hand across her eyes. "I could get my roof fixed for that."

"What are you going to do, Jean?"

"I can't tell him to go. Then where would I be? Without a barman." She blew her nose. "Oh, I wish Beau was still here. He was the best barman I've had."

Jess smiled wistfully. "I think we all wish that Beau was still here," she murmured.

Jean stared at her before taking a deep breath, and rising from the stool.

"We can't turn the clock back, Jess, no matter how hard we try."

"No, we can't." Jess paused as she thought of the men who had gone from her life: her father, Jack and now Beau. She looked up at Jean. "Let me help you, Jean. I need something to take my mind off my own troubles. I could come and work for you, whatever needs doing, except perhaps the bar."

Jean turned. "I can't afford to employ you, Jess. I can't afford to employ anyone at the moment."

"No, no! You won't need to pay me. I'll do it as a friend. You've helped me through a lot of difficult situations, so I'd be returning the favour."

"I can't let you do that, Jess. You told me recently that you need employment. I can't let you work for nothing."

"I have to be realistic, Jean. I'm not going to get a job, not now, with all the men out there looking for work."

Jean turned, looking in the direction of her beloved Grey Goose Hotel. She would hate to have to relinquish it. She wouldn't relinquish it!

"Alright, Jess," she sighed. "We'll give it a try, but only until you get paid work." Jean smiled at her closest friend. "Come in tomorrow morning, and we'll see what we can arrange." She walked heavily down the front steps. "Oh, and bring Gracie with you, unless of course, Margaret has her."

"I'll bring her with me, Jean." Jess stepped down from the verandah as Jean reached the footpath. "You try to get some rest. Put your feet up for a while." *Let Rodney do some work, for a change.*

"Chance would be a fine thing," called Jean as she shuffled along the street.

Jess's step was lighter as she went back inside. She now had a purpose, and that was to help her friend who had always been there for her and the children.

A loud crack of thunder rent the air. The storm was coming.

*

That night, Jess and her children sat on the big bed, listening to the rain falling on the tin roof, and talking about their day. Thunder rattled the windows from time to time, and three bodies ducked under the covers, pretending to be afraid.

"Come on, out of there," laughed Jess. "The bed has suffered quite enough for one night." Three tousled heads appeared.

Jess patted the quilt. "Come and sit quietly now. I want to tell you something."

They scrambled to sit close to their mother, and looked up at her in anticipation.

"Are we going somewhere, ma?" Edward asked eagerly.

"Are you getting me another chook?"

"Is auntie Izzy coming back?"

"Hush! No, no, no! None of those things."

"What then?" Edward was obviously disappointed.

"I'm going to work for Mrs. O'Malley." Jess waited as three young brains processed this information.

Ben was the first to speak. "Are you going to be a barmaid?" His expression registered concern, and Jess immediately saw Jack looking at her.

"No, Ben." Jess touched his tousled brown hair. "I won't be a barmaid."

"What then?"

Jess shrugged. "Everything else that needs doing in a hotel, I expect, like washing and making beds, and preparing lunches."

"But you do that here," said Edward matter-of-factly.

"I know, but I'll be helping Mrs. O'Malley."

"She's got Rodney to help her." Ben was puzzled and a little disappointed that he wasn't going to get another chook like Speckles.

Jess smiled at their dilemma. "Rodney tends to the bar and the customers."

The three children lost interest at that point. Their mother's plans no longer concerned them. Jess saw their disinterest and concluded that children had enough resilience to be able to accept change and not be greatly affected by it.

She slid out of bed, and clapped her hands. "Time to go to your own beds!"

They scrambled off the bed just as a loud clap of thunder rattled the windows. As one they shrieked and scurried along the passage to their bedrooms. Jess followed, reaching the boys' room in time to tuck them under the sheets.

As she kissed Ben goodnight, he flung his arms around her neck.

"I love you, ma," he whispered, "and I really wouldn't care if you were a barmaid."

"Thank-you, Ben." Jess stroked the brown hair, so like Jack's, and blinked away the tears. She had lost Jack, but part of him would always be with her.

*

The following morning, when the boys had gone to school, and the house was tidy, Jess set off with Grace for the Grey Goose. She had dressed in a light floral cotton dress, and her hair was tied up in a green silk scarf. Gracie, dressed in a blue cotton pinafore, skipped alongside her.

"Can I play with Mack, ma?"

At the mention of Mack, Jess was immediately reminded of Beau, and she wondered whether he had received her letter.

"Ma?" Gracie's voice brought her back to the present. "Can I play with Mack?"

"Yes, darling, you can play with Mack. I'm sure he'll enjoy that."

They entered the side door of the hotel, and immediately felt the coolness of the old brick building. As they entered the Ladies Lounge, Jean appeared from further along the passage, and Jess frowned as she noticed that the combs in her grey hair were askew, and her apron was grubby.

"Ah, Jessie, you're here." Jean smiled down at Gracie.

"Is everything alright, Jean?" Jess asked hesitantly.

"Yes. Why?" Jean kept her eyes on Gracie, who tugged on her apron.

"Can I play with Mack, please?"

"Yes, dear. He's out in the back courtyard. You know your way, don't you?"

Gracie nodded, and with a look in her mother's direction, left the Ladies Lounge and disappeared along the passage.

Jean now turned to Jess, and her plump shoulders slumped.

"No, everything is not alright, Jess," she whispered. "I told Rodney that you had offered to help me out here, and…"

"I've changed the barrels downstairs," came Rodney's loud voice behind them, "and I'm going out for a while."

Jean turned to face her son, who stood in the doorway of the bar. "Well, you'd better be back before opening time, Rodney."

Rodney shrugged his thick shoulders. "I should be." He glanced at Jess. "Good morning, Mrs. Stanley. Come to do some work, have you?"

"Yes," said Jess stiffly. "I've come to help your mother."

"Good." The smile didn't quite reach his eyes. "Then I'll leave you both to it." He headed back into the bar. The two women heard the main door slam behind him.

Jean turned to look at Jess. "What am I going to do, Jess? He's probably going to see his bookmaker. He's become a liability to me."

"I don't know what to suggest," said Jess helplessly, "except that I wouldn't be lending him any more money."

"Lending him money!" Jean laughed harshly. "Rodney doesn't see it as a loan." Her eyes darted wildly about the room. "He thinks I've got plenty, and have a right to share it with him." She looked back at Jess. "I don't have unlimited funds, Jess. I have a hotel, and a good name, and that's about it."

Jess patted her friend's arm. "Then we'll have to make sure it stays that way." She smiled suddenly. "Rodney might not like it when he has two women to deal with."

Health Warning

Beau stood gazing down at the scene below his window. The street was a moving mass of people, each with their own problems; their own private concerns. Somewhere down there, a young nurse was probably doing the rounds of the medical practitioners, in the hope of receiving the drugs she needed. Maybe she already had them. In spite of Celia's remonstrations, he still felt he had done the right thing. If the girl hadn't walked out, he would have proposed another course of action for her. Now there was no chance that he could find her.

Charlie was another problem. He had refused to divulge any more information at subsequent visits, and Beau knew that he would have to be patient. The boy had closed down, and had even refused to see his mother. Edwina had not been happy about that, but she, too, would have to wait for Charlie to open up again.

Beau shifted his gaze to the sparkling waters of the harbour, and his dark mood lightened temporarily. He loved his work here, but there was a cost, and that was his own personal freedom. After his brief taste of life on the open road, there were times now when he felt trapped. Never had he felt more alone.

At times he longed for the peace of a small country town, where people knew who you were, and cared about you. Here nobody really cared. Oh, they said they did, but Beau knew from experience that feelings were shallow, particularly in the circles in which he had to move.

His thoughts turned to Jess and her family, and he would have given anything to be able to sit and have a cup of tea with her, and discuss the day's events. How was she getting on, he wondered?

His reverie was broken by a voice at the door.

"Good morning, Beau." It was Celia. "I have the newspaper here. There's an article that you and Matthew need to read. It's about a possible epidemic that you had better be prepared for." She threw the Sydney Morning Herald on the desk.

Beau glanced down at the headline:

Pneumonic Influenza has appeared in Sydney.

"Be prepared to have people coming in their droves to be vaccinated," said Celia, as Beau read the finer print.

There was definitely cause for concern, as the virus known as the *Spanish Flu*, had already hit Melbourne. It was thought that the returning servicemen had brought the virus with them. All public places would be closed down, and effectively turned into temporary hospitals for the victims, and people would be advised to wear masks to protect them from the germs.

Beau sucked in his breath. This was the influenza that had killed thousands of soldiers at the end of the war. Beau knew that it was deadly.

He looked up at Celia.

"This is serious, Celia," he said hoarsely. "This is what killed Jess's husband three days after the Armistice."

"Then we must be prepared." Celia moved towards the door. "I'll make sure that we have enough of the vaccine for our patients. Other than that, there's little else we can do."

Celia closed the door swiftly behind her. Beau stood for a moment, taking in the severity of the situation. His head was spinning. He needed to contact Jess to make sure that she had herself and the children vaccinated. He would telephone Margaret and ask her to give Jess a message. The virus had already reached Melbourne, so if she knew about it, she might have already taken the necessary steps to protect her family.

Beau would have to use the telephone in Celia's office, as it was the only one available to the Clinic. Leaving his surgery, he headed along the corridor to Celia's office and patient waiting room. He knocked on the door. There was no answer. He walked in and crossed the room to where the telephone sat on the back wall. What was Margaret's number? He would have to ask the exchange. Stepping back to Celia's desk, he reached for a pencil. As he did, his eyes rested on an envelope lying on the desk. Beau frowned. It had his name on it. He picked it up. It was a letter addressed to him, and it had been opened. Turning it over, he read Jess's name and address on the back. He felt a surge of anger. Celia had opened his mail. By mistake, he wondered?

The door opened and Celia appeared. She looked from Beau to the letter he held in his hand, and shut the door quickly.

"You opened my personal mail, Celia," said Beau, trying to be calm. "Was it by mistake, and were you going to give it to me?" His tone was stiff.

"No, it wasn't by mistake, Beau, and no, I wasn't going to give it to you." Celia met his hostile stare.

"Why would you do that?"

Celia let the seconds tick by before she answered. "You don't need any of this right now, Beau. I was looking after your interests."

"You had no right to open my mail, Celia!" Beau's voice rose dangerously. "My personal life has nothing to do with you anymore!"

Celia tossed her well-groomed head. "It has everything to do with me, Beau, because you work for Matthew, and I will not have this Clinic put at risk."

"At risk of what?"

"At risk of you walking out of here."

"What's going on?" Matthew's head appeared at the door.

Celia swung around to face him, with a smile.

"Nothing for you to worry about, Matthew," she said lightly. "Beau and I were just having a difference of opinion. Now, please leave my office, I have things to do."

"Have you seen this morning's paper?" Matthew laid the Sydney Morning Herald on Celia's desk.

"Yes, we have, Matthew," answered Celia quickly, "and I need to procure supplies of vaccine, before they run out." She waved her hands at the two men. "Now, will you both go and let me get on with it. Patients will be arriving soon."

Matthew picked up the paper, frowned, and turned to leave.

Beau pushed the letter into his pocket, and with a look in Celia's direction, followed Matthew. At the door he paused, and turned to Celia, who had her hand on the door handle. "This is not finished, Celia," he said quietly.

Celia smiled benignly. "I think it is, Beau."

In the corridor, Matthew turned to Beau with a puzzled expression.

"What difference of opinion, Beau?" he asked.

"As Celia said, Matthew, it's nothing for you to worry about." He added quickly, "Our opinions always differ, Matthew. You should know that by now."

"Hm." Matthew stopped outside the door of his surgery. "This epidemic is going to cause some problems for us. We'd better be prepared for the worst."

Beau nodded. "I agree, Matthew. A lot of soldiers died during the last months of the war, and it is extremely contagious, and I doubt whether the vaccine we have will be enough to suppress it." He looked at his watch. "Now if you'll excuse me, there's something I must do before I begin surgery this morning."

"Anything I need to know about, Beau?" There was a tinge of annoyance in Matthew's tone as he called after Beau's retreating figure.

"No." Beau shook his head.

He needed to find a telephone. The closest one was probably at the Post Office, two streets away. Beau headed down the stairs and out on to Norlane Street where he joined the jostling crowd, all going about their own business. He would read Jess's letter once he found a quiet spot.

As he reached the Post Office, his steps slowed. Would Jess think he was being overly concerned about her welfare? Well, this was a serious issue, and he needed to know that they were all protected. Returning soldiers would be unaware that they posed such a risk to the community, but according to the newspaper, the virus was spreading rapidly. Beau hurried up the brick steps and through the heavy wooden doors. This was no time to procrastinate.

*

Matthew sat behind his desk, contemplating the friction that existed between Celia and Beau. Surely they should have settled their differences by now. He would sit down with both of them, and insist that they tell him what it was all about, instead of humouring him all the time. It wasn't good for their working relationship, if his wife and his colleague were continually baiting each other.

Celia breezed into the surgery at that moment, a list of patients in her hand. She placed it on Matthew's desk, and leaned over towards him.

"Today's schedule, my dear," she breathed, smiling sweetly.

Matthew looked straight into her dark eyes, always so beguiling.

"The matter between you and Beau must be resolved, Celia. I can't work under these circumstances. I'm completely in the dark, and I don't like it!"

"I've told you, Matthew, that it's..."

"I know! It's nothing for me to worry about, but unless we are all open with each other, then this working relationship is not going to last."

"You worry too much, Matthew."

"Then stop giving me cause to worry."

Jess's Concerns

"Where are you, Jess?"

"In the kitchen, Margaret. Come through."

Margaret appeared at the kitchen door, and the smile on Jess's face vanished as she looked at her mother-in-law. Margaret's face was chalk white, her brown eyes large and fearful.

"Whatever's wrong, Margaret?" Jess stopped kneading the bread dough, and wiped her hands on her apron.

"I've had a telephone call from Beau." Margaret was breathing hard.

"From Beau? What about?" Jess immediately felt concern.

Margaret pulled out a chair, and sat opposite Jess.

"He wanted you to know that the virus that killed our Jack, has now reached Australia, and we should all go immediately to the doctor and be vaccinated. He sounded very concerned, Jess. Soldiers are still returning from overseas, and they are bringing it with them. It's already reached Melbourne, and now Sydney."

Jess took a deep breath.

"Then we'd better do as he says." She looked across at Margaret. "How is Beau?"

"He's very busy, and now with this news, they're preparing for an epidemic."

"Did he happen to say he'd got my letter?"

Margaret thought for a moment. "Yes, I think he did say he had just received a letter from you, but hadn't had a chance to read it. At least I think that's what he said." She smiled vaguely.

Jess sent her mother-in-law a troubled look, as she placed the kneaded dough into a tin and set it on the hob beside the stove.

"How have you been getting on, Margaret?"

Margaret looked up at Jess, and her eyes were brimming.

"I think it's all just sinking in now, Jess," she said slowly. "At the beginning, there were things that had to be done, so I didn't really have time to think about the reality of it, but now…" She shrugged. "If it wasn't for the children, I think I would go mad."

Jess nodded. "And Charles? He seems to have accepted it at last."

"Yes, he has, fortunately." Margaret gave a sigh. "We don't want him having any more heart attacks because of all this."

This gave Jess the perfect segue into the matter of Jean.

"I'm very worried about Jean, Margaret. She's going to have a heart attack if she's not careful."

Margaret looked up quickly. "What makes you say that?"

"Doctor Simmons told her she has a heart murmur."

"Goodness! Isn't her son still helping her with the hotel?"

Jess gave a short laugh. "Rodney has become more of a hindrance than a help."

"So what's she going to do?"

Jess hesitated before answering. "I'm helping her."

"Helping her? How?"

"I work in the kitchen, and help with the rooms."

"Is she paying you?" quizzed Margaret.

"No, Margaret. I'm helping her as a friend, that's all."

"She should be paying you."

"We'll see how things go." She added, "I did go to the repatriation office recently, to put my name down for a job, but I'm not likely to get one. There are too many returning soldiers out there looking for work."

"You went looking for work?" Margaret's tone expressed horror. "Jess, there's no need for you to do that. If you need financial help, Charles will see to it."

"I want to be independent, Margaret."

"Fiddlesticks! Don't let me hear you talk like that again!"

Jess suppressed a smile, as she heard Charles speaking. The kettle began to sing.

*

Jess was coming down the stairs from the bedrooms at the Grey Goose, a load of sheets in her arms. As she reached the lower floor, and turned to go to the washhouse, she heard Rodney's voice, raised in anger. Her steps slowed. For a moment she thought he was yelling at Jean, but then realised he was on the telephone in the hallway. Jess stopped, before she was seen.

"I'll get it to you, alright! Just give me a couple of days." Silence.

"I know. She's got a friend working here now, so I have to be careful." Silence.

"Tomorrow? That's impossible! Two days."

There was another long silence, before the receiver was slammed into the cradle. "Bloody mongrel!" Jess heard Rodney mutter.

His heavy footsteps moved towards the bar, and the door slammed.

Jess took a deep breath, tiptoed along the hallway, and through to the back of the building. Entering the detached washhouse, she took another deep breath.

What was that all about? He obviously owed more money to someone. Jess bit her lip in consternation, as she lifted the sheets into the copper. Was Jean about to be fleeced again by her son? Jess couldn't tell her what she had overheard.

As she pushed the sheets into the steaming water with the sturdy wooden washing stick, Jess heard a childish voice at her elbow.

"Ma! Where's Mrs. O'Malley?"

Jess turned. "I don't know, Gracie. Perhaps she's in her special room." Jess wiped an arm across her perspiring brow. "Knock on the door and see."

Gracie ran off, followed by the Jack Russell, Mack. Jess resumed her plunging, until she was satisfied that the sheets were done. One by one she pushed them through the wringer and into the concrete trough of cold water. There they were dunked until the water was clear, and pushed through the wringer once more.

Soon the sheets were flying high in the hot breeze. Jess went back inside the hotel. The passage was silent, and she headed towards Jean's sitting room. She knocked.

There was no sound from within.

"Are you there, Jean?" she called, and received no answer.

Jess opened the door quietly. The room was empty. She frowned. There was no sign of Jean or of Gracie. Jess headed towards the bar. She pushed the door open. It was just a few minutes to opening time.

Rodney was at the till. He looked up as Jess opened the door, and slammed the drawer closed. Scowling, he shoved something into his pocket.

"What do you want, Mrs. Stanley?"

Jess hesitated. "I was looking for Jean."

"She's not here."

"I'll check the kitchen."

Jess closed the door and leaned against it for a moment. Had Rodney taken money from the till? Her legs trembled as she headed towards the kitchen.

"Mrs. Stanley?" Rodney's voice stopped her in her tracks.

Jess turned. "What is it, Rodney?" Her mouth was dry.

"I don't know what you thought you saw in there, but I would appreciate it if you said nothing." He demonstrated by running his fingers across his mouth.

"Were you stealing from your mother, Rodney?" Jess's heart was pounding.

"Call it a loan." Rodney's eyes narrowed. "Not one word, do you hear?"

"Are you threatening me, Rodney?"

"No, just offering you some advice." Rodney turned to go back to the bar. "I have to open up now. Not a word, understand?"

The door closed behind him. Jess felt physically sick, and took a moment to settle her trembling, before entering the kitchen. Jean and Gracie were both there, and Jean looked up from making sandwiches, as Jess walked in. Gracie was standing on a chair, handing Jean pieces of ham.

Jess smiled brightly. "Washing's all done, Jean, and with this weather, it will be dry in no time. Gracie, love, we have to go. We have an appointment with Doctor Simmons."

Gracie climbed down from the chair. "Now, ma?"

"Yes, now." Jess smiled apologetically at Jean. "I'll come back later and bring in the washing, Jean."

"No need, Jess. Rodney can do that for me. Your visit to the doctor, it's nothing serious, is it?"

"We're all having a jab against the influenza virus."

"Oh?" Jean screwed up her face. "I did read where it's becoming a problem here."

"It's more than a problem, Jean, it's an epidemic. Beau telephoned Margaret from Sydney, to tell us to have the vaccine. It's now reached Sydney, and the doctors are preparing for the worst."

"Is that the virus that took your Jack?"

Jess nodded. "It's the same one, and the returning soldiers are spreading it here in Australia. It might be wise, Jean, for you to get a jab. You're in contact with returning soldiers, and with your heart condition, well..."

"I see what you mean, Jess. I'll certainly take your advice."

Jess took Gracie by the hand. "I'll be in tomorrow if you need me."

"'Bye, love. 'Bye, Gracie. See you tomorrow."

Jess hurried out, anxious to avoid seeing Rodney. Leaving by the side entrance, she walked quickly past the bar door, and across the road. She had a dilemma, and she wasn't sure how she should handle it. Jean was her best friend, and she couldn't sit by while Rodney stole from her, she just couldn't!

"Ma!" wailed Gracie, "You're walking too fast!"

Jess slowed her pace. "I'm sorry, sweetheart. Ma has her mind on other things."

Jack would have known what to do, and so would Beau. Izzy, too, would not be slow in confronting the man, but they weren't here. She wouldn't seek advice from Margaret or Charles, although she knew that Charles would have plenty to say. There was nobody else she could confide in; she was on her own with this problem. If she talked to Jean, Rodney would soon know, and she was reluctant to go down that path.

Jean would surely know if the till was short at the end of the day. Another thought suddenly occurred to Jess, and a cold feeling swept through her. She could be blamed for the theft. No, Jean would never believe that! However, it was a possibility, and if Rodney was desperate enough, then he could lay the blame on her. Jess shivered in the heat of the day. She would have to watch and wait.

*

The surgery waiting room was crowded, when Jess walked in with her three children. She squeezed on to a seat, beside an old man with a hacking cough, and tried not to face him. The three children sat on the floor at her feet.

They sat for some time, in the room filled with crying children and coughing adults. Jess was becoming increasingly uneasy about the delay, and the prospect of being infected with germs that were surely present in the waiting room.

Finally the nurse called her name, and Jess hurried her children into Doctor Simmons' surgery. He looked up from his desk as the family entered.

"Ah, Mrs. Stanley, how are you?" His keen eyes swept over the children. "You have the whole family with you, I see." He stood up and extended a hand across the desk. Jess took it. "My condolences to you for the sudden loss of your husband." His eyes looked sympathetic. "Charles told me what had happened. I expected I'd see you before this."

Jess sat and the children stood around her. "Thank-you, Doctor Simmons." She hesitated. "I was taken good care of at the time, by Doctor DuBois."

The heavy eyebrows lifted. "Doctor DuBois?"

"Yes."

"So you managed to make contact with him again after…"

"After his attempted suicide? Yes, he made contact with me, as it happens."

Doctor Simmons pursed his lips, and his eyes travelled around the family group.

"I see. What brings you all in here today?"

Jess breathed hard. "The influenza virus that killed my husband is spreading out here, as you probably know, and I have been advised to have the vaccination."

The thick brows knitted, and Doctor Simmons stared at Jess.

"I don't believe it's necessary here. In the cities maybe, but not here in the bush."

Jess met his gaze. "Soldiers are returning to the country towns as well as the cities, doctor, and I would like to have myself and my children vaccinated, please."

"Is this under the advice of Doctor DuBois?" There was an edge to his tone.

"It is, but I don't see what difference that makes." Jess's back stiffened.

"Very well," he said slowly, "I'll make arrangements for you to visit the hospital."

"Thank-you, Doctor. This virus killed my husband and many others, in a matter of days. It is not to be under-estimated."

Doctor Simmons opened the file that lay on the desk in front of him.

"Hm," he muttered. "Seeing as you're here, I'll give you all a check-up."

"Thank-you, Doctor Simmons."

Rodney

The following morning, Jess decided to leave Gracie with Margaret, while she went to the Grey Goose. If there was to be a confrontation with Rodney, she didn't want her daughter to be subjected to it.

Margaret was both surprised and pleased, and fortunately didn't want to know the reason for Jess's change of plans. She had plans of her own as soon as Gracie set foot inside the house.

"We'll go to the park!" she exclaimed excitedly, as she took Gracie by the hand. "There's a band playing there this morning, and I know granddad wants to go and listen." She turned to Jess. "We also have to go to the hospital to have our vaccination. Have you organised yours, Jess?"

"I've been to see Doctor Simmons, and he's arranging for us all to go to the hospital. Mind you, I don't think he wanted to. He seems to think there's not much risk in the country areas. I disagree."

"Charles had a word with him." Margaret smiled. "He may think differently now."

"I see." Jess could picture Charles convincing the doctor that it was best to err on the side of caution.

"If you like," Margaret was saying, "we could take Gracie with us, and then you'll only have the boys to deal with."

"Good idea, Margaret." Jess bent to kiss the top of Gracie's head. "Now I must go. I don't know what Jean has in store for me today."

"Don't you work too hard," Margaret called after her, as she headed down the steps to the front gate.

Jess waved a hand at her, and wondered what would be in store for her.

As she reached the Grey Goose, her footsteps slowed, and her heart did a little skip. She opened the side door, and let herself in. It was too early for opening time, and Jean had entrusted her with a key.

The passage was cool and quiet. Jess took an apron from its hook on the wall, and tied it around her.

"Jean!" she called tentatively.

The door to Jean's sanctuary opened, and the lady appeared. Jess stared at her in dismay. Tears ran from her puffy eyes, and she held a handkerchief to her nose.

"Whatever's the matter, Jean?"

"Come in, love," sobbed Jean. "It's been a terrible morning."

Jess followed Jean into the small sitting room, but declined a chair.

Jean sank into her favourite lounge chair, and wiped her eyes, while Jess waited for what seemed like an interminable length of time.

"We've been robbed!" stuttered Jean finally, a fresh wave of tears falling.

"What?" Jess felt dazed.

"Last night somebody broke in and took all the takings from the till, plus bottles of top shelf liquor." Jean blew her nose. "We're waiting for the police to arrive. This is something that's never happened before. I can't believe it!"

Neither can I, thought Jess, as she sought the safety of a lounge chair. *Is this just a horrible coincidence, or would Rodney stoop that low?*

At that moment, the door opened, and Rodney appeared. His usually ruddy complexion was pallid, and his eyes were stricken.

"The police have arrived, ma, and they want to talk to you."

Jean rose from her chair, and pushing back her hair, headed for the door.

When she had gone, Rodney and Jess were left facing each other.

"I know how this must look," he began, "but I swear this is not my doing."

Jess looked at his pale features, now beaded with sweat. "If that's true, Rodney, I can't help thinking that possibly you know who did it." He stared blankly at her. "I overheard you on the telephone yesterday."

Rodney covered his face with his hands, and his shoulders shook. There was no menace in the man now, and Jess actually felt sorry for him.

"What am I going to do?" he groaned.

"You have to tell the police everything, Rodney."

Rodney wiped a sleeve across his eyes. "I suppose my mother told you what's going on. I'm such a bloody fool."

"Then you have to make it right, and hope your mother will forgive you."

"Do you think she will?" He looked helplessly at Jess.

"If you do the right thing."

"Will you?"

Jess shrugged. "Possibly."

"I'm a proper bastard, aren't I?"

Jess blinked. "I wouldn't put it quite like that, Rodney, but you can turn things around. Your mother needs you right now."

A cheerful face crowned with bright red hair, appeared at the door.

"Mr. O'Malley, could you come to the bar, please?"

Rodney looked at Jess, and she smiled encouragingly at him.

The young constable turned to Jess. "Do you work here, too, ma'am?"

"I suppose I do, yes."

"Then you'd better come too." He opened the door, and Jess followed Rodney along the passage to the bar. Jean was seated on a stool as they entered, and she looked up at her son, her eyes filled with tears.

"Who could have done this?" she said wearily, as she gestured towards the open till. "Just the night I was too tired to count the takings."

Rodney stepped towards his mother, and placed an arm across her shoulders.

There's something I need to tell you, ma." He looked at the two constables standing beside them. "There's something I need to tell all of you."

"You know who did this?" asked the redheaded constable.

Rodney nodded. "I believe so."

So the story of Rodney's gambling debts came out in a rush, while four people stood silently and listened. He had availed himself of the doubtful services of a moneylender, by the name of Seamus Oliver, who had put pressure on him, forcing him to seek money from his mother. It had not stopped there, and Rodney had found himself being pressured even more, resulting in his own theft of the till. This was what Jess had witnessed, and she had to acknowledge the fact that Rodney had warned her about telling Jean.

"You did what?" Jean stared at her son in disbelief. "Rodney! How could you?"

"I have apologized, ma, and I feel really stupid."

The two policemen were watching Rodney closely, and looked at one another when he had finished speaking.

"Well, Mr. O'Malley," said the redhead, "we will be following up on Seamus Oliver. He is known to the police, and has the reputation of being a thug and a bully. You will need to come to the police station and make a statement." He looked at his watch. "Now, I believe its opening time. We'll be in touch, and in the meantime, may I suggest you make sure the till's empty at the end of the day."

When they had gone, the three looked at one another in silence, until Jean spoke.

"I can't believe my son would stoop so low as to rob his own mother." She shook her head sadly. "However, you have seen fit to come clean, so I can probably forgive you for that, but to threaten Jess, my best friend, I don't know whether I can forgive you for that, Rodney." Her eyes glittered.

Jess stepped forward, and took Jean by the hand.

"We have to wipe the whole slate clean," she said simply.

"So you forgive him?"

Jess looked at Rodney. "I think so."

Jean rolled her eyes. "It might take me a while." She rose stiffly from the stool. "In the meantime, we have a pub to run, so get to it, Rodney! I'll be in my sitting room, letting all this sink in." She turned to Jess. "You can have a rest today, too, Jess. Rodney will have to manage." She shuffled off, without a backward glance.

"Serves me right," said Rodney, as the door closed behind his mother.

"She'll come round." Jess smiled at his dejected countenance.

"This won't be the end of it, you know."

"Maybe not, but at least you're no longer facing it alone."

Rodney nodded slowly.

Later that afternoon, when Jess had relayed the story to Margaret and Charles, their eyes were wide with horror.

"What kind of man steals from his own mother?" bellowed Charles.

"He's a very contrite one right now," said Jess, "and one who's learnt his lesson."

"Humph! I doubt that, Jess. He's a gambler, and they don't change."

"We'll see," smiled Jess. "Now, what's been happening here in my absence?"

"We went to the park, ma, and then we had a needle. See?" Gracie pulled up her sleeve to reveal a red mark on her arm. "It hurt, ma."

"So granddad bought us all an ice-cream, didn't he, sweetheart?" Margaret's eyes were shining as she looked from Gracie to Charles.

Jess smiled. Well, it seemed that some people could change, and for the better.

Panic on the Streets

The door to Beau's surgery burst open, and Matthew strode in, his face set in hard lines. He leaned heavily on the desk.

"We have been asked to release rooms at Serendipity to the Coast Hospital," he muttered, "so they can set up quarantine wards. This virus is spreading quicker than anticipated."

"How many spare rooms do we have?"

"No more than four." Matthew's brow creased. "We'll have to give them the four rooms at the back of the building. I don't want to risk our patients being infected."

"They'll all have to have the vaccination."

"That's not a guarantee against this virus."

"Agreed, but it's all we've got."

Matthew ran his fingers through his thick, greying hair, and began to pace the room. "This is not going to go away, is it, Beau? The word on the street is that many have died already, and people are beginning to panic. They think the medical profession is bullet-proof, but we're not, and this is all new to us." He turned worried eyes in Beau's direction. "Face masks are being distributed as a precaution, and those in the sex industry are being warned about spreading this dreadful influenza virus. They're calling it the Spanish Flu, God knows why."

"Matthew, I know all about it," interrupted Beau. "Jess's husband died from it. He didn't even make it home."

"Yes, I'm sorry." Matthew stopped pacing. "We need to get over to Serendipity this afternoon, after surgery, and see what can be done." He turned and headed for the door, stopping before he went out. "By the way, how are you going with the young lad, Charlie? I haven't seen any report about him recently."

Beau shrugged. "Charlie has shut down for the time being. He refuses to tell me any more. His mother is becoming rather frustrated, naturally, as am I, but we can't push him. He'll come around in his own time. In the meantime, at least he is settled. He spends most of his time watching the gardeners from his window."

"I suppose that's something." Matthew turned the door handle. "Shall we say two this afternoon?" Beau nodded. "Good!" Then he was gone.

*

At precisely two that afternoon, Matthew's head appeared at Beau's door.

"Ready?"

"Yes." Beau shrugged himself into his jacket, locked his desk drawer and placed the key in his shirt pocket.

In the drawer was a half-written letter to Jess, and he didn't want Celia finding it. Matthew and Beau headed down the stairs and on to the street, where evidence that there was a viral epidemic, was very prevalent. People walked with their heads down, most of them with their faces covered by handkerchiefs or masks.

Matthew made his way to his shiny black Ford Motorcar, which was parked further along the street, and in no time, they were weaving their way between trams and horse-drawn carriages.

"It won't be long before everyone will have a motorcar!" shouted Matthew, as he honked his horn at a slow-moving pony and trap.

The pony shied, and the driver mouthed something obscene at Matthew, but the sound was lost in the noise of the traffic.

After leaving the busy central district behind, they drove out through leafy streets until Matthew turned into the long driveway that led up to Serendipity Lodge. He parked on the gravel near the massive front door, and both men alighted and headed up the steps.

The foyer was cool and smelt strongly of phenyl. Matthew and Beau climbed the stairs to the second floor, and made their way along the passage, past the wards that were occupied, and along another passage that led to four unoccupied rooms at the rear of the building.

"They should be far enough away from our patients to not cause too many problems," said Matthew, as they opened each door in turn.

The rooms had not been used during Matthew's time at Serendipity, but they each had a bed and a washstand.

"Shouldn't take much to get these into running order," said Matthew, as he stood at the window of one of the rooms.

He looked out over the back of the building, across a green landscape of grass and tall gum trees. Beyond the boundary lay the rest of suburbia: crowded, congested and noisy. Matthew turned to Beau.

"I think life in our professions is about to get a lot more complicated, Beau."

"It's complicated enough as it is, Matthew, but I do agree with you."

"Psychiatry and medicine need to become more inter-active, because the mind and the body cannot be separated." Matthew smiled thinly at Beau. "Welcome to the twentieth century, old chap."

"We've been in it for eighteen years, Matthew."

"Yes, I know, but it's only just making its presence felt, thanks to the war." Matthew clapped his hands together. "Right! We need to get these rooms disinfected and fresh linen on the beds." He turned to Beau. "I wonder if Mrs. Evans would like a job while she's here. Milly would welcome her, I feel sure."

Beau nodded. "We could ask her. She sits and watches Charlie most of the time."

"I'll leave her to you, Beau, and I'll go and rattle Milly's cage. I'd better let kitchen know as well."

"Who will be staffing these quarantine wards?"

"Certainly not our nurses. The Coast Hospital Board will have to see to that."

"Don't be too sure about that, Matthew."

Matthew was gone.

Beau shook his head, and followed. Walking back to the occupied rooms, he opened the door of No. 10. Edwina Evans was seated on Charlie's bed, a book in her hand, and Charlie was in his usual spot, on the window ledge. Edwina looked up as Beau entered.

"Hello Doctor." She closed her book.

Beau looked from Charlie to Edwina. "How is Charlie today?"

She shrugged. "No different. All he wants to do is look out the window."

Beau walked across the room to Charlie, who turned then to look at him.

"Anyone working in the garden today, Charlie?" Charlie turned back to the window and pointed to where a man was turning over the soil with a shovel. "What's he doing, Charlie?"

Charlie gave a grunt. "Digging," he said slowly.

Edwina crossed the room to stand beside Beau. Her eyes were glassy.

"What did you say, Charlie?" she whispered.

Charlie turned to look at his mother. "Digging." He said the word slowly.

"Yes, Charlie, he's digging." Edwina looked at Beau, and smiled tremulously.

"Very good, Charlie," said Beau quietly, "and what is he using?"

Charlie swallowed hard, and his brow puckered.

"A shovel," he whispered eventually.

Edwina was crying, and reached out to touch her son, but Beau gently pulled her arm away. "Not yet, Mrs. Evans; one step at a time."

He saw her frustration, as she clasped her hands in front of her.

Beau turned back to Charlie. "What is he planting, Charlie?"

Charlie looked out the window. "Roses?"

Edwina gave a small hiccough, and covered her face with her hands.

"Yes, Charlie, they are roses," said Beau, as he took Edwina by the arm and led her back to the bed. "This is what we've been waiting for," he whispered, "and we mustn't get ahead of ourselves. Charlie will dictate the moves." He smiled. "We have to take small steps."

Edwina nodded and wiped a hand across her eyes.

"I came in today to see you on another matter."

"And what's that?"

"We've been asked to open any spare rooms as quarantine wards for people suffering from the influenza virus that's taken hold across the city."

"Yes, I've been reading about that."

"We have four rooms here that can be used, but they need to be cleaned and made ready for any new arrivals."

"How can I help?"

"Would you like a job as cleaner while you're here?"

"It would certainly help pass the time."

"And you will be paid for your work."

Edwina looked across at Charlie, and then back at Beau. "Alright," she said slowly. "I'll do it. When do I start?"

"As soon as we can organise equipment for you. Thank-you, Mrs. Evans."

"Please call me Edwina."

Beau smiled. They had made great strides this day.

*

"I suppose this means we all have to wear masks," sighed Celia, as she, Matthew and Beau stood in Matthew's office later that day.

"Unless you want to catch this confounded virus, you will, Celia," muttered Matthew, as he sat behind his desk and pulled a sheet of paper from the drawer. "We need to lay down a few rules for Serendipity, if it's to be invaded by people with this infection." He reached for a pen, checked it for ink, and began to write. "Firstly, we don't want them using the front entrance. They can use the back stairs to gain access to the rooms that we've made available. We can't have their nursing staff mixing with ours."

"Hold on just a minute, Matthew," interrupted Beau. "We might find that it's our staff who will ultimately be responsible for these people, in which case, our nurses need to be briefed and warned of the dangers."

Matthew swivelled in his chair to look at Beau. "What are you saying, Beau?"

"I'm saying that we're not going to escape the consequences of opening up these rooms to a public hospital."

"Our nurses will have to wear face masks," said Celia. "What about our patients?"

Beau frowned. "That could be a problem, as most of them are suffering mental trauma. Wearing a face mask might unsettle them further."

"It certainly will," conceded Matthew. "We can't foist that on them. It would tip most of them over the edge."

"What do we do then?" Celia looked at both men.

"We have to keep the wards and the nurses separated." Matthew put down his pen. "The back rooms will be subjected to quarantine regulations, which means if anyone needs to access them, for whatever reason, strict rules of protection will apply." He sighed heavily. "Vaccination will be compulsory for everyone. We don't want this thing to spread any further. We need to have a Board meeting."

*

Later, in the privacy of his own room, Beau unlocked the drawer and took out the half-written letter to Jess. What could he say now? That they were all at risk of falling victim to Influenza Pneumonia?

An Unexpected Surprise

Jess stood at the letterbox, and opened the letter from Beau. It began:

> *Dear Jess and children,*
> *Finding time for the small pleasures of life, like writing a letter, is becoming increasingly difficult. Our workload at the Clinic is about to increase, as the Influenza Virus runs rife in our city. There is panic on the streets here, and masks have become an essential part of our attire.*
> *I do hope you have all had the vaccination. I know it is not a 100 percent guarantee, but it is all that's available at present, until science can come up with a new vaccine. You need to remain vigilant, however, and avoid places where many people gather. If any of you develop a persistent cough, don't waste any time in getting to see your doctor. Please take care.*
> *I did receive your letter, and it held a few surprises, I must confess. Firstly, it must have taken some courage to go and ask for work at the repatriation office. These places are not known for their sensitivity to people's needs. Please don't despair if you can't find work. You can always come and work for me. You have already proved your nursing skills. Do you remember?*

Beau, I will never forget the day you turned up in my sleep-out, your head bleeding, and your insistence that I stitch it up for you. It's etched in my brain.

Jess continued reading.

> *Tell Ben I'm very sorry about his chook, and I will send him some money to buy another one. Call it an early birthday present. I can imagine your reaction, Jess.*
> *I'm pleased that you and Charles are on better terms. It will make things a lot easier for both of you, and for Margaret as well.*
> *Tell Jean from me, not to overdo it, and to let her son do the hard work. She has earned a rest.*
> *Well, speaking of 'rest', there is no rest for the wicked, so I must close this letter and get on with some work.*
> *I would love to come and see you, but I don't dare leave the city at present. Easter is probably the earliest I can make it. I see that Good Friday is April 18th. I'll try to organise a visit then.*
> *Until then I remain*
>
> *Yours always, Beau*

Jess smiled as she folded the letter and put it back in the envelope. She would read it to the children after tea. In the meantime, after spending the morning at the hotel, she had work to catch up on at home.

Jean was slowly coming to terms with Rodney's confession, and the police had returned several days later to inform her that Seamus Oliver had been picked up, and was being questioned as to his part in the whole sorry saga. They assured Jean that he would cause her no more trouble.

"Maybe not," snorted Jean, "but it's my son who needs to mend his ways."

Rodney appeared to be doing just that, but time would tell.

Jess could report to Beau that they had all been vaccinated, and that she would remain vigilant. Each night she quizzed the boys about children with coughs at school, but they didn't really see what all the fuss was about.

"There's always someone coughing, ma," said Edward, in exasperation one night.

"Well, you make sure you keep away from them, do you understand?"

"Why?"

"Your father died as a result of a coughing virus, and although we've had a needle to prevent us catching it, we still have to be very careful. Make sure you wash your hands after playing football, or cricket, or using someone else's pencils."

"Ma!" Edward had rolled his eyes. "We'll be called sissies if we do that!"

Jess shook her head as she thought about her two boys. They were becoming harder to handle, without a father figure, and even their grandfather was letting them get away with things that at one time they would have been punished for. She would have to be firmer with them. After all, she had insisted that she wanted independence in raising her own children.

It was two in the afternoon, and Jess was preparing the evening meal, when she heard a knock at the front door. Taking off her apron, and smoothing her hair, she headed out of the kitchen.

Gracie ran out of her room and skipped to the door ahead of her mother.

"I'll get it, ma!" she cried gaily, as she pulled the heavy door open.

Jess stopped in her tracks, and sucked in her breath when she recognised the couple standing on the verandah. She hadn't seen them since that awful day at the docks, when they gave her the news about Jack. Her hands flew to her mouth.

"Hello, Jess." Mary Walker was smiling at her from beneath the brim of a large straw hat, and in her arms she carried a young child.

"I don't believe it!" gasped Jess, and recovering her composure, she opened the screen door. "Come in! Come in!"

She was too bemused to initially notice that the Sergeant was walking with the aid of a stick. He followed Mary as Jess led them to the kitchen.

"Please sit down!" Jess pulled chairs out for her guests, and then began to clear the table of her cooking utensils. "You'll have to excuse the mess."

"Don't let us stop you from what you're doing, Jess," said Mary, seating herself beside her husband, and removing her hat. "We thought it was time we came to see you, and to introduce you to our son, Lachlan Jack Walker."

Jess was suddenly still, and her eyes misted as she looked at the child in Mary's arms. He was bonny, with a fair complexion, blonde hair, and startling blue eyes.

"He's beautiful," whispered Jess. "What do you think, Gracie?"

Gracie was standing on tiptoe, peering at the baby in Mary's arms.

"He hasn't got much hair." She frowned up at her mother.

Mary laughed softly.

"His hair will grow, Gracie," said the Sergeant, smiling proudly.

Mary looked up at Jess, her brown eyes suddenly serious.

"We named him after your Jack."

Jess brushed a tear from her eye, and touched the tiny face. "Jack would be very pleased and honoured, Mary." She breathed deeply. "Now, you must tell me all of your news. I'm sorry I haven't tried to contact you since…"

"Don't be sorry, Jess," said Mary quickly. "We understand, don't we, George?"

The Sergeant nodded, and it was at this moment that Jess realised he hadn't come in on crutches.

"Your leg..." she began tentatively.

"I have an artificial leg, which makes it easier to move about." George smiled at Mary. "I was very much against it at first, but my dear wife insisted that I at least try one. I have to admit that she was right."

"I'm not often wrong, George." Mary returned his smile, and Jess, watching on, caught her breath. Here was a couple very much in love.

She turned her attention to more practical matters.

"You will stay for tea?"

"If it's not too much trouble, Jess," said Mary. "We must get back to Melbourne tonight, and the last train goes at six."

"Then we'll have early tea, and make sure you don't miss your train." Jess smiled.

Mary stood up and placed the baby in George's arms. "I'll help you, Jess."

Sergeant George Walker looked quite at ease with the small bundle in his arms, and Mary smile indulgently down at him.

"Two peas in a pod," she quoted. "Sometimes I wish all the long-suffering Privates could see him now." She laughed. "They wouldn't believe it."

"So you're back at the barracks, Sergeant?"

"I am, but I'm no longer a drill Sergeant. I'm confined to a desk now." George's blue eyes met Jess's. "By the way, call me George."

Jess smiled, and Mary took her arm. "Jess, I haven't asked how you are coping. It was all such a shock for you."

"I think I'm alright now. There are times when I wonder how I'm going to face the next day, but we have to, don't we? Nobody else can do it for us."

"I agree, Jess," said the Sergeant, and his eyes were moist as he looked at the two women. He had known the pain of losing his first wife.

There was silence as each one contemplated the losses in their lives.

Jess looked up at the clock above the mantel. It was three o'clock.

"I must get this stew in the oven," she said, "or we won't get tea. I hope you like stew and dumplings."

They both nodded.

*

At five-thirty, Jess, the children, and their unexpected visitors, walked slowly towards the station. The boys were fascinated by the Sergeant's artificial leg, and wanted to know how he could walk on it without tripping himself up.

Jess and Mary watched on in amusement as the Sergeant patiently explained to the boys that at the knee there was a pivot, so that he had some bend. The top of his leg was encased in a leather sleeve, and a strap went up over his shoulder.

"Like braces?" chirped Edward.

"Yes, like braces."

"What's it made of?" Ben asked politely.

"Wood and leather," said the Sergeant patiently, "and as you can see, it's made to fit my boot, so that I don't just wear out one."

"You've got a limp like Beau."

The Sergeant looked enquiringly at Jess.

"Oh," she said hastily, "Beau is a friend, who has a war injury which has left him with a limp."

By the time they reached the platform, the interrogation had stopped, and the boys were more concerned about seeing the train. The Sergeant looked visibly relieved.

As they waited, Mary pulled a mask from the bag she was carrying.

"Time for the masks, George."

"Here, let me do that for you," said Jess quickly. "You both have your hands full."

She tied the surgical masks on their faces.

"We take no chances when we're in public places," said Mary.

"Very wise," said Jess. "We've been advised to do the same. It's the same virus that took Jack." She paused. "Cover the little one, too."

"Oh. I will, Jess." Mary placed her free arm around Jess's shoulders and gave her a gentle squeeze. "Thank-you for today, and we will keep in touch."

The train rattled into the station in a cloud of steam.

The Sergeant gave Jess a quick kiss on the cheek, before turning to the children.

"Good-bye, children. Look after your mum. She's the only one you'll get."

He hurried awkwardly after Mary, and they boarded the train.

The whistle sounded and the great wheels moved. Soon they were out of sight.

Charlie's Secret Revealed

Beau turned Jess's letter over in his hands. It was still sealed, so he knew that Celia had not interfered with it. He opened it carefully, and drew out the sheet of paper. There was a faint hint of lavender. It reminded him of Jess.

His eyes scanned the page, and he frowned when he read about her encounter with Jean's son, Rodney, and the unexpected outcome.

Please be careful, Jess. He was remembering her encounter with the scoundrel, Sid O'Connor, after Jack's departure, and the possible consequences to that. She was too trusting, it seemed.

Jess went on to talk about the surprise visit from Sergeant Walker and his wife, Mary, and their tiny son, whom they had named after Jack. Beau had not met them, but Margaret had told him the story of their friendship with Jack, and their meeting with Jess that fateful day on the docks.

She finished the letter with the words:

> We look forward to seeing you at Easter, and you must stay for the procession on the Monday. I will see if Izzy and Harry can join us.
> Until then,
> Jess and the children

Beau folded the paper, slid it back in the envelope, and placed it in the drawer. While he was pondering its contents, the door opened and Matthew appeared.

"Well, old chap, it seems as though our spare wards at Serendipity have been filled, and we now have a new set of hygiene rules to abide by." He sat on the edge of Beau's desk. "Care to come out there this afternoon and check it out?"

"I had planned on going to see Charlie," said Beau absently, "to see if he is ready to talk to us yet."

"It's taking him a while, isn't it?" Matthew moved to the window. "His mother has settled in to her job. I'm thinking seriously of hiring her fulltime, if she wants it. She's very thorough, and nobody escapes her scrutiny." He laughed.

"Good."

"Are you alright, Beau?" Matthew turned from the window. "You seem very distracted lately and don't tell me it's nothing for me to worry about! I keep hearing that from Celia, and I get the feeling she's just fobbing me off."

Beau looked up at Matthew, and felt a slight twinge of pity for his friend. Matthew had known Celia as long as he had; they both knew she liked to be in control.

"I'm fine, Matthew."

"Hm. Well, in that case, I'll see you at about one, shall we say?" Matthew looked at his watch. "Celia wants me to take her to lunch at a new restaurant down by the quay. It's her birthday today, in case you hadn't remembered."

"No, I hadn't. Do you think it's wise to eat in a public place at this time?"

Matthew shrugged. "I don't think it will be a problem, Beau. Returning soldiers aren't likely to be dining at Mario's."

"Mario's? That's a bit flash, isn't it?"

"You know Celia, Beau; nothing but the best." Matthew opened the door. "Do you know what's wrong with you, Beau? You need a woman to jolly you out of your sour mood."

Beau laughed harshly. "Who's going to want to be seen with me socially, Matthew?"

"Come on, old chap. You don't look as bad as you think you do. Besides, it's what's on the inside that counts."

"Tell most women that, and check their reaction, Matthew."

"What's going on in here?" Celia appeared in the doorway.

"Nothing for you to worry about, my dear," said Matthew quickly, and received an impatient shove.

"Very funny, Matthew!" retorted Celia. "I've come to remind you both that your first patients have arrived, so masks on, please, and get ready to work."

*

At one o'clock, Beau stood outside the office building on Norlane Street, waiting for Matthew to arrive from lunch. As he leaned against the wall, he thought of what had been said earlier in the day, and he knew that Matthew was right. He also knew that while his thoughts were so preoccupied with Jess, he couldn't even consider keeping company with a woman, even if one could be found for him.

He thought about the heady, passionate whirlwind romance he'd had with Celia, so long ago, and the endless round of parties and good times that they had enjoyed.

Then had come the war on the other side of the world, and he, along with many others from the medical field, had joined the army, and moved to the barracks to train in combat, with the idea of heading across the seas if they were required.

Life at the barracks had not pleased Celia, and even then he had the feeling that she was after better things. Matthew had a motorcar, and an apartment in the centre of the city, so her social life had continued without him.

No, he had not been enough for Celia, and now, looking on at her relationship with Matthew, he wondered whether any man would be enough for her.

"Sorry I'm a bit late, old chap," he heard Matthew's voice, and looking up, saw him grinning from the driver's seat of his motorcar. "The meal was absolutely divine. You should have joined us."

"Three's a crowd," said Beau, as he climbed into the passenger seat.

"I dropped Celia off at the apartment." Matthew had to shout above the noise of the traffic. "She was feeling a little tired, and thought she'd have a rest."

Beau nodded, and the motorcar jerked forward.

"Damned gears!" muttered Matthew, as he steered his way out into the traffic.

*

"Doctor Morley, can I speak to you for a moment?" Shirley's voice stopped Beau and Matthew as they crossed the highly polished foyer at Serendipity Lodge.

"What is it, Shirley?"

"It's about that new cleaning lady, Doctor."

Matthew and Beau glanced at one another.

"Mrs. Evans? What about her, Shirley? Isn't she doing a good job?"

"Oh, she's doing a good job alright. Milly Saunders, our regular girl, is ready to quit if she doesn't stop ordering her about. Fanatical she is, according to Milly."

"I'm very pleased she is fanatical, Shirley. We don't want the 'flu virus spreading through the whole building." Matthew paused. "You tell Milly Saunders to come and see me if she is unhappy."

"Yes, Doctor Morley."

The two men crossed the foyer and made their way up the stairs. As they reached the second floor, the sound of raised voices could be heard along the passage.

"Doctor Morley will have something to say about this!"

"Doctor Morley put me in charge of hygiene, and I am only following his orders."

Matthew looked at Beau and groaned.

"We obviously have some very unhappy people here," he muttered, as he hurried forward to where a plump duty nurse stood with her hands on her ample hips, glaring at Edwina Evans.

"What seems to be the trouble, nurse?" Matthew smiled benignly at the angry girl, who jabbed a finger in Edwina's direction.

"She's trying to tell me my duty, Doctor! She's only the cleaning lady, and I don't take my instructions from her."

Matthew raised his hands. "No, you don't. You are all answerable to me. We are in the middle of a medical crisis, with this virus, and we all need to co-operate fully. I have revised the rules on hygiene to include things like the wearing of masks while dealing with patients, and diligent disinfecting of all public areas. Mrs. Evans is following my instructions to the letter, and I'm confident that this will stop the germ from spreading." He stopped, while the two women stared at him. "What is the issue you have with Mrs. Evans, nurse? Let's clear it up now."

"Well," the nurse turned her attention to Edwina, "she wants me to make sure I wipe down the telephone each time I use it. I haven't got time to do that."

Beau noticed that Matthew was trying very hard to keep the smile from his face. He cleared his throat.

"This is diligent disinfecting of all public areas, and Mrs. Evans is right."

Two red spots appeared on the nurse's cheeks. "What!" she exclaimed angrily. "Do you mean to say that I have to do what she says?"

"In a word, yes." Matthew turned to Edwina. "Perhaps, Mrs. Evans, we need to speak about this, and draw up a more comprehensive list for the nurses."

"Certainly, Doctor Morley. Even in an institution as clean as this, there are places for germs to spread."

The nurse gave a snort of indignation, and hurried off to answer a bell that was ringing behind her desk.

Matthew glanced at Beau, pulled a surgical mask from the pocket of his tweed jacket, and proceeded to tie it over his face.

"Come on, Doctor DuBois," he said lightly. "Time to head for the danger zone." He nodded at Edwina, before striding off along the passage.

Beau smiled at her, before following Matthew.

"I'll check on Charlie before I leave," he said over his shoulder.

Matthew had already disappeared around the corner.

The four wards set aside for the influenza victims, were full. In fact two of the rooms held two people. Matthew queried this, and was told by a young man in a white coat, that those patients were simply being monitored. They did not display full-blown symptoms.

The smell of phenyl penetrated the surgical masks, and Beau found himself coughing, which amused the young man.

"If the virus doesn't kill you, the disinfectant will."

One door was closed. Matthew moved to open it, but was immediately stopped by the young man.

"You can't go in there," he said quickly.

"Why not?" Matthew wanted to know.

"The young woman in there was picked up on the street last night, with drug-related issues as well as respiratory symptoms. Her outcome doesn't look good, but she is receiving the best of care."

"Who is the Doctor in charge of these patients?" asked Beau.

"Doctor Freeman, from the Coast Hospital at Randwick."

"And he's here often?"

The young man shrugged. "Once a day, I believe."

Beau frowned. "Is that enough?"

"The doctors are run off their feet at present. They're doing all they can."

Beau looked at Matthew. "I could free up some time to come and assist in here."

Matthew pursed his lips as he considered what Beau was saying.

"If you think that will help, Beau, by all means give it a try. I'll contact Doctor Freeman and suggest that you do mornings. I can take up your patients at the Clinic." He stopped. "By the way, do you know how to drive a motorcar?"

"I drove trucks during the war."

"Good. You can borrow mine."

*

Beau pulled the surgical mask from his face, and took a deep breath. He could still smell phenyl. Charlie's door was open, so he knocked and entered the room. The lad was sitting in his favourite place, on the window ledge, and he turned as Beau entered. The ghost of a smile flitted across his pale features.

"Hello Charlie." Beau seated himself beside the crouched figure.

Charlie nodded, and turned to gaze out the window.

"Picture," he said slowly, and Beau looked down to where a sheet of paper lay on the ledge beside him.

"You've drawn me a picture?" Beau picked it up. "Very good, Charlie."

He studied it closely. There were three simplistic figures: one standing, another crouching and a third lying flat. Beau pointed to the prostrate figure.

"Who is this, Charlie?" Charlie slowly opened his hand to reveal the button, and his eyes were glistening as he looked at Beau. "Is this the German soldier?"

Charlie nodded, so Beau pointed to the crouching figure.

"And this is… this is you, Charlie?"

Charlie nodded again, and wiped a sleeve across his eyes.

"And this one, Charlie, what is he doing?"

Charlie slowly raised his right arm, and demonstrated the firing of a gun.

"He shot this one?" Charlie gave a brief nod. "Who is he, Charlie?"

Charlie touched the button, and began to cry.

"It's alright, Charlie." Beau's head was spinning. He pointed to the upright figure.

"Is this a German soldier, too?" he whispered hoarsely.

Charlie lifted his tear-streaked face. "Yes."

"What happened, Charlie?"

Charlie pointed to the prostrate figure, and the words tumbled out. "He tried to help me, so he was shot."

"By one of his own men?"

"Yes."

"What happened then, Charlie?"

Shaking his head, Charlie resumed his crouching position, his hands clasped around his head as he rocked backwards and forwards.

Beau looked up to see Edwina standing in the doorway, her eyes streaming. She had heard. A German soldier had tried to help a young Australian soldier, and had been shot down by one of his own men. Where was the common human decency in all this?

Moving off the window ledge, Beau made way for Edwina to hold her son.

"Thank-you, Doctor," she whispered.

"Everything will move forward from here, Edwina." He smiled at her. "I'll leave you now, and I'll talk to you later." He patted Charlie on the shoulder. "Well done, Charlie. Your mother and I are both very proud of you."

Charlie nodded from the comfort of his mother's arms.

Beau headed down the stairs, and out into the sunshine. Crossing the gravel path, he made his way to where Matthew was seated in the motorcar.

"So, how did you go with young Charlie? Opened up yet, has he?"

"Yes, he has." Beau climbed in to the passenger seat.

"And was it as you had suspected?" The wheels crunched on the gravel as Matthew turned the vehicle towards the driveway.

"I don't know the full story yet, and it may be worse than I had feared."

"In what way?"

"He was taken prisoner, and saw a German soldier shoot one of his own men, who was trying to help Charlie."

Beau unfolded the picture that Charlie had drawn. Matthew glanced down at it. "And you got all this just by looking at what Charlie had drawn?"

"No, Matthew. The boy has finally spoken."

"Well done, Beau!" Matthew reached over and patted his colleague on the shoulder. "You are in the wrong part of the profession, old chap! You should have done psychiatry." Matthew laughed.

"No, it was more good luck than good management, Matthew. I suppose my war experience must have taught me something." Beau smiled grimly.

"Well, anyway, you can tick that one off."

"Not yet, Matthew. I believe Charlie will tell us the rest in his own time."

*

Beau rolled a cigarette, as he sat on his tiny balcony, two stories above the street. He heard the clanging of the trams as they made their slow way around the city.

The occasional honking of a horn, and the clatter of horses' hooves on the hard road surface, indicated the competition for space on the crowded streets.

Laughter drifted up from the restaurant below, and lights were beginning to wink, as darkness fell over the city.

Beau exhaled, and watched as the smoke curled into the night air. He thought of his progress with Charlie, and pondered on the rest of the story. The button that he had clung to so desperately all this time was obviously his reminder of a man who had died because of him. How this had come about, Charlie had yet to reveal, but Beau felt sure now that he would.

He shifted his gaze to where the stars were beginning to light up the night sky, and his thoughts strayed to Jess, so far away and yet with him constantly.

He must send Ben some money to buy himself a new hen. He had promised as much. Jess would be annoyed with him. Beau smiled as he crushed out his cigarette butt, and stood up.

Stepping into the small room that he called home, Beau shut the door and sought the cold comfort of his bed. Tomorrow would come around soon enough.

Jean

"A letter came for you today, Ben."

Jess picked up the letter from the table, as the two boys rushed through the back door. She knew it was from Beau, and she also knew what it contained.

"A letter for me?" Ben threw down his schoolbag. "Who from?"

"Open it and see," said Jess calmly, handing Ben the envelope.

Ben ripped it open with great haste, and out fell a pound note. His eyes popped open with surprise, while Jess sucked in her breath. A pound note!

"Is this for me?" squeaked Ben, fingering the precious note.

"I expect it is," answered Jess, her voice tight.

"You're lucky, Ben," said Edward. "Who's it from?"

Ben opened the paper that had been around the note.

Dear Ben,
Please buy yourself another hen, and I look forward to eating its eggs when I see you at Easter.
Tell your mother not to be too angry with me, and if there is any money left over, buy her something nice.
Your friend, Beau

Ben scowled. "Why would you be angry with Beau, ma?"

"I'm not angry, Ben. Beau likes to do these unexpected things for us. You must write back and thank him, immediately."

Ben nodded enthusiastically. "I will, ma!"

Ben grabbed his schoolbag, and headed off to his room.

"Why did Beau send Ben some money, and not me?" Edward asked petulantly.

Jess ruffled his blonde hair. "Because Beau knew that a fox had taken one of Ben's chooks, and he wanted to..." She didn't quite know what to say.

"He wanted to help him get over it?"

Jess smiled. "Yes, Edward, that's exactly what he wanted to do."

*

The next morning, Jess walked Gracie to her grandparents' house, and arrived at the Grey Goose at precisely nine o'clock. She unlocked the side door and let herself in. As she took an apron from the hook behind the door, she noticed that Jean's sitting room door was ajar, and she heard Doctor Simmons.

"Mrs. O'Malley, we need to get you to the hospital. You appear to have suffered a mild heart attack, and I need to run some tests on you."

"A heart attack!" It was Rodney.

Jess hurried to the door and entered quietly.

Jean was in her favourite chair, her usually florid face deathly pale, and beaded with perspiration.

"What's happening?" Jess whispered to Rodney.

"Ma's had a heart attack." Rodney also looked pale beneath his ruddy complexion.

Doctor Simmons stood up, and folding his stethoscope, turned to Rodney.

"We need to get your mother to the hospital." His eyes flicked over Jess, and he nodded curtly.

"I'll call the ambulance," said Rodney, and rushed from the room.

Doctor Simmons turned to Jess.

"Are you working here, Mrs. Stanley?" he asked politely, to which Jess nodded.

"Mrs. O'Malley should be alright, but I need to x-ray her chest, to make sure, and of course she will have to go on medication, and try not to do so much."

"A bit hard in this job," wheezed Jean, as she struggled to rise from the chair.

"Nevertheless, you must obey orders from now on. Let your staff do the work."

"Staff!" Jean looked at Jess. "You mean my son and my best friend?" Her eyes glistened with tears.

"We can do it, Jean." Jess clasped her friend by the hand. "You must do as the doctor says, and let us worry about the hotel."

"But can I really trust Rodney?" Jean stared intently at Jess.

"Of course you can, ma!" Rodney had entered the room. "I've learnt my lesson."

Doctor Simmons frowned, unaware of the background to Rodney's statement.

"Is the ambulance on its way?"

"It's on its way." Rodney smiled at his mother. "Don't worry, ma, everything's going to be alright."

*

When the ambulance had taken Jean, and Doctor Simmons had driven off in his black motorcar, Rodney turned to Jess.

"This is all my fault," he reproached himself. "If I hadn't been so bloody stupid, none of this would have happened."

"You don't know that, Rodney." Jess tried to be positive. "Jean has been unwell for some time, and we should have all read the signs, but we didn't."

"But what I did was unforgiveable, and probably brought on this last attack."

"Well, whatever the case, Rodney, we can't change what's happened, so we have to make the best of it, which means that you and I have to hold the fort while your mother is in the hospital." She smiled at his downcast countenance.

"How long will she be there?"

Jess tried to remember how long Charles was in the hospital after his heart scare the previous year. "Probably only a couple of days." She patted Rodney's arm. "Come on, we have a hotel to run, and it's almost opening time."

*

Jess threw herself into the task of helping Rodney behind the bar, but refrained from actually serving the drinks. She took money, gave change, and answered the many questions from curious customers who wanted to know where their popular publican was hiding.

"Maybe we need to write an explanation on a board, and hang it above the bar," Jess jokingly said to Rodney after one such quizzing.

"That's not such a bad idea."

At fifteen minutes to midday, Jess slipped into the kitchen and prepared a tray of sandwiches for the lunchtime customers. It was something Jean had always done, and everybody expected it.

The afternoon flew by, and when Jess looked at the clock above the bar, she discovered to her horror, that it was almost three o'clock.

"Rodney," she said hurriedly, "I have to go. The boys will be home from school shortly, and I must be there, or they'll wonder where I am."

Rodney nodded. "You go, Jess, and thank-you for your help." He grinned suddenly. "We might make a barmaid out of you yet."

"I don't think so," laughed Jess. "I'm happy to do everything else."

At the door she turned. "I'll be in tomorrow morning. If you need me before then, you know where I live."

As she hurried along the street, Jess felt more invigorated than she had felt for a long time. She might not be paid for her efforts, but she was doing something constructive. The people who frequented the hotel might not have been on her list of acquaintances, but they all had their stories to tell, and what's more, she had listened to them. She had laughed at their jokes, and had not been offended by the occasional expletive. Yes, she had to admit that she had enjoyed herself.

Jess unlocked her front door, and let herself into the house. The passage was cool and quiet. The boys weren't home yet. She headed for the kitchen, where she checked the stove. The fire had died down to glowing embers, so she carefully laid some sticks on top and closed the firebox.

While the house was quiet, Jess opened the dresser drawer, and took out the chocolate box that contained Jack's letters. Placing it carefully on the table, she opened it. This was where she always came when she wanted to talk to Jack. She breathed deeply and picked up the last note that she had; not written by Jack, but containing the message that he wasn't coming home.

It was crumpled, where she had crushed it in her hand that awful day on the docks.

Jess slowly straightened it out, and her eyes misted over as she read his words once more:

Think of what we had together, and don't love me any less for leaving you.

"Oh, Jack," she whispered, "I will always remember what we had, and I want to tell you that I think we are going to be alright. Life will never be the same as it was, and I miss you every day, but today I finally found some purpose to my life. It might not be what you would want for me, Jack. In fact you might even be horrified, but I need to help Jean as she struggles with a heart condition, and working in a hotel is not all that bad."

"Who are you talking to, ma?" Ben's voice brought Jess back to reality.

"I was talking to your father, Ben."

A frown creased Ben's brow, as he looked around the kitchen.

"But he's not here, ma."

"Maybe we can't see him, Ben, but he is here." Jess put a hand over his heart. "He'll always be in our hearts, Ben, and don't be ashamed to talk to him. I talk to him often; usually when you children have gone to bed."

"Does he answer?" Ben still looked puzzled.

Jess shook her head. "Not in actual words, Ben, but occasionally I have a thought that comes to me out of the blue, and I like to think that it's your father looking after us."

"I talk to Speckles sometimes, when I really miss her."

Jess nodded. "I'm sure you do, Ben. It helps us to deal with our sadness."

Ben changed the subject. "How's Mrs. O'Malley?"

"I think she'll be fine, Ben. It will be a little bit like when granddad had a heart attack last year. We'll have to look after Mrs. O'Malley, and make sure she doesn't do too much." Jess looked around for Edward. "Where's your brother, Ben?"

Ben shrugged. "He's gone to play with Phillip Harvey, down the street."

"That's good." Jess brushed a twig from the front of his shirt. "When are you going to find a special friend, Ben?"

"I don't need one, ma." Ben picked up his schoolbag and headed for his room.

You will one day, Benjamin Jack.

Jess placed the letter in the chocolate box, closed the lid and placed it back in the dresser drawer. How much of that discussion had Ben understood? Perhaps he hadn't understood at all, but she didn't believe that. Ben was too much like his father to let things slip away from him that easily.

You'll always be close, Jack, while I still have Ben.

Part Two

Challenges Ahead

Serendipity Lodge

Beau negotiated the black Ford along the gravel driveway that led to Serendipity Lodge. He had enjoyed the drive from Norlane Street, and found the vehicle to be extremely responsive to his touch. Shutting off the engine, he alighted and headed up the stone steps, to be met at the door by a very agitated receptionist.

"What's the matter, Shirley?"

"Oh, Doctor DuBois, I'm so glad you're here! There's mayhem up in the quarantined wards. You'd better go and sort it out. I can't deal with it."

"What's the problem, Shirley?"

"One of the patients has attacked a nurse!" Shirley was wringing her hands in consternation. "She's threatening to walk out!"

"Who? The nurse or the patient?"

"The nurse, Doctor."

Beau patted her shoulder, as together they stepped into the foyer.

"I'll go up straight away, and see what I can do. How many nurses are there?"

"Probably only one by the time you get there."

Beau took the stairs two at a time, in spite of his war injuries, and ran the length of the corridor. As he turned the corner to enter the quarantined area, he pulled a mask from his pocket, and tied it across his face. A dark-haired young man in a white coat and surgical mask met him at the door to one of the wards.

"What is happening here?" asked Beau sharply.

The young man jerked his head towards the door. "The patient in there has gone berserk, and has bitten my colleague on the hand." There was a thumping noise coming from the ward behind him. "She needs restraining, Doctor."

Beau pushed past the young man and tried the handle, but it was locked.

"Where's the key?" he asked sharply.

The young man handed Beau a large key, which he slipped into the lock.

"Watch how you go, Doctor. That one is a proper wildcat."

"What's her name?"

"I don't know," stammered the young man. "I'll go and get the chart." He hurried to a desk on the other side of the corridor, and picked up a chart.

"Hasn't got a name here, Doctor."

The noise behind the door had stopped, so Beau slowly opened it. On the cot, lying face down was a woman. Her shoulders were heaving, and she was gasping for breath. Beau was beside her in two strides. He grasped her shoulder and turned her over. Blonde hair fell across her face, but Beau recognised her; she was the nurse who had come to him for sleeping tablets.

"Oxygen!" he screamed at the young man standing at the door. "Quickly, man!"

The young man leapt into action and sprinted along the passage.

Beau brushed the hair from the young woman's face, and attempted to loosen the collar of her blouse. He saw fear in the blue eyes that stared up at him, as she struggled for breath.

The young man returned, wheeling an oxygen bottle, and carrying a mask.

Beau grabbed the mask and proceeded to place it over the young woman's face. She struggled weakly, trying to fight him off, but to little effect. Beau soon had the mask in place, and the oxygen turned on.

"Try to relax," he said calmly, "and breathe slowly." He stroked her wet forehead.

Her struggling eased, and her chest rose and fell evenly. Beau sat back on the cot and looked up at the young man beside him.

"What would you have done, if I hadn't arrived?" he asked.

"I don't know, Doctor. I don't really know why I was sent here. Over at the hospital I mainly deal with bed pans and changing sheets."

Beau shook his head slowly.

"I'm sorry I screamed at you, but time was critical."

"You mean she might have died?" The eyes above the mask, blinked rapidly.

"Most likely. By the way, her name is Meg Harper."

"How do you know that?"

"She came to see me a few days ago, and that was my mistake."

The dark brows knitted together. "How come?"

Beau rose from the cot, not anxious to admit error to this young novice.

"It doesn't matter. Now, where's the other nurse? I need to see how she's faring."

"I think she's gone," said the young man miserably.

Beau groaned. "So it's only you on duty now?"

"It looks like it."

"Well, you'd better tell me who we have here. By the way, I'm Doctor DuBois."

The young man nodded. "James Wilson," he muttered bleakly.

Together they checked on the rest of the patients: four under observation, and one displaying significant symptoms. Beau ascertained that little more could be done for him. His thoughts turned to Jack as he looked at the pallid features, and saw the drops of blood seeping from his mouth.

They stepped out of the ward.

"We'll be calling for the undertaker very soon," Beau whispered to James.

He turned wide eyes in Beau's direction. "He's going to die?"

"That's a certainty. You make sure you disinfect yourself before you leave here."

"Are we likely to catch it?"

"Very likely, if we don't follow the rules. Now we need to make sure there's another nurse on duty. When does your roster finish?"

They were walking along the passage towards Meg Harper's ward.

"I don't finish 'til six."

"I'll telephone the hospital and explain that we need a nurse here immediately. In the meantime, I want you to keep checking on the four who are under observation. Do you know how to take blood pressure and temperature?"

James nodded vigorously. "Yes, I can do that."

"Good. Check them every hour, and write the results on their charts."

They stepped into Meg Harper's ward. She was lying quietly, and she turned blue eyes on the two men who entered. There was recognition as she looked at Beau, and immediately she tried to pull off the oxygen mask.

Beau stepped forward. "I'll do that." He turned off the oxygen and took the mask from her grasp.

"You!" She gulped at the air. "This is your fault!"

"Please don't distress yourself, Miss Harper. You have more to be concerned about than whether or not I'm to blame for this."

Meg struggled into a sitting position, but the exertion was too much for her and she slipped back on to the pillow. She started to cough; a harsh, agonising sound, and Beau noticed the spots of blood at the corners of her mouth.

He grabbed James by the sleeve and pulled him outside the door.

"I need to inject morphine, James. Could you get it for me, please?"

James sprinted away, and Beau returned to the ward. He looked down at the young woman, who had been courageous enough to work overseas during the war, and like Jack, had succumbed to the same deadly virus.

Blue eyes stared up at him, and her breathing was ragged as she tried to speak.

"I watched two men die from this during the war. Ironic, isn't it?"

"I'll give you some morphine to dull the pain," said Beau quietly.

"Morphine?" A laugh gurgled in her throat. "That's what I needed from you, doctor, and *now* you're going to give it to me?"

"I'm sorry. I was wrong."

James returned with a syringe and a bottle. Beau measured ten milligrams, and injected it into the young woman's arm. As he did so, he noticed the marks where needles had been inserted, and he was filled with a bitter sorrow, not because he had refused her medication, but because she had been brought to this as a result of the war.

"That won't be enough," he heard her whisper.

"It will be if I inject you every hour," said Beau, as he handed the syringe to James.

Her eyes closed and she expelled a long breath.

"It won't take very long." She sighed.

Beau looked at James. His dark eyes were filled with tears.

"Go and find something else to do, James. I don't want you to stay in here." Beau propelled the young man out of the ward.

"She's too young to die!" There was a sob in his voice.

"We'll do what we can for her, and see what happens."

The two men left the ward, and Beau closed the door.

"She'll sleep now, and I'll be back in an hour. In the meantime, I'll telephone the hospital and hopefully get another nurse; one who can administer drugs."

"What do you want me to do?"

Beau grinned. "Well, there's always the bed pans, and it will soon be lunchtime. If that's not enough to keep you busy, then try disinfecting the floors. I'm sure the cleaner will be thankful."

James laughed. "You're not like the doctor from the hospital. He wouldn't pass the time of day with me."

Beau shrugged. "This is a serious business, James, and sometimes it's good to lighten it just a little." He patted the younger man on the back. "Now I must go, and I'll be back within the hour. Miss Harper should sleep until then." As he turned to go, he added, "James, make sure you put her name on the chart."

"Yes, I'll do that, Doctor DuBois."

Before leaving the quarantine area, Beau made sure he had scrubbed his hands, and removed his surgical mask. He knew that the risk of catching the virus was extremely high, even with precautions in place.

After telephoning the Coast Hospital and explaining the situation, he was assured that a nurse would be sent immediately. He was also informed that the nurse who had been bitten, was already undergoing treatment for the injury, and had received the vaccine prior to her employment.

As Beau headed towards Charlie's room, he decided to take a detour, and spend a few minutes in the garden, where he could put the stresses of the past hour behind him. He sought a shady tree, and sank on to the grass, where he lay and closed his eyes. The sun was warm through the branches of the tall eucalypt, and the grass was cool beneath him. His thoughts travelled, as they did so often, to Jess, and he wondered what she would be doing. He longed to see her, and Easter was so far away. Maybe the virus would still be causing panic and…

"Doctor DuBois?" A voice broke through his thoughts, and he looked up, squinting in the dappled light. It was Edwina Evans.

Beau hurriedly sat up. "You caught me napping, I'm afraid," he said guiltily.

Edwina sat beside him. "You're allowed to, you know," she said softly.

"I was on my way to see Charlie, when I needed five minutes for myself."

"He's in the rose garden, actually," said Edwina, turning to look at Beau. "He told me the rest of the story."

"Oh? Let me hear it?"

"I'll tell you the story, as he told me." She paused to take a deep breath. "He was captured by these two German soldiers as he rode through one of the villages with an important piece of information for an Allied troop camped not far from the edge of the village. He was taken to a deserted farmhouse, where he was interrogated and forced to drink something that he managed to spit out."

"It would have been a drug to loosen his tongue," said Beau grimly.

"When that didn't work, the one soldier forced him to…"

Beau could see that she was struggling.

"I'm ahead of you on that, Edwina. What then?"

"He had to comply, while the other soldier stood over them, watching, his gun pointed at Charlie." She shuddered. "Afterwards he was forced to drink more of the liquid, but this time, the soldier who had been watching on, shouted something at his comrade, and sent the glass flying. Charlie had no idea what they were saying, but suddenly the one soldier turned on the other and shot him. He landed near Charlie, and he heard him say, in English, 'run, boy!' He tried, but another shot was fired, and he thought he'd been hit. He pretended he was dead, as the German began to drag his now dead comrade away from the scene. Charlie lay there until he thought it was safe to move, and that's when he found the button that had been torn from the uniform of the dead soldier. The man had saved his life."

"Did he find the Allied soldiers?"

"Yes. They had heard three shots and had sent a platoon to investigate."

"Three shots?"

"They found two dead Germans."

"Two?"

Edwina wiped her eyes. "The second one must have shot himself because of what he had done to his comrade."

Beau exhaled. "That wasn't quite what I was expecting."

Edwina turned tear-filled eyes in his direction.

"What does it matter, now? At least I have my boy back, thanks to you."

Meg Harper

Beau pondered on Charlie's story as he walked back upstairs to the quarantine wards. It didn't sit easy with him; there were too many questions that needed answers. For his own sake, he had to get Charlie alone, and try to get the whole truth of the incident. Charlie might still be reluctant to give a full account of what had really happened. At least his mother was happy to have her boy back.

What would they do now, he wondered? Edwina would be an asset to the Lodge, and maybe the Board would consider giving Charlie work in the garden. He would speak to Matthew about this.

Beau rounded the corner to the quarantine wards, and found his way barred by a rope on which hung a sign:

Quarantine Area. No unauthorized persons beyond this point.

He stepped over the rope, and was immediately accosted by an efficient nurse.

"Excuse me, sir, this is a restricted area. Didn't you read the sign?"

Beau was somewhat taken aback. "I'm Doctor DuBois, and yes, I read the sign."

"Oh! Doctor DuBois!" She squinted at him from behind heavy spectacles. "I'm Nurse Flanagan, and I must ask you to follow me to what is now the scrub room, where you will need to put on a mask, and scrub your hands."

Beau raised his eyebrows, but followed her nevertheless. How long had he been gone? An hour? Nobody was going to slip past on Nurse Flanagan's watch.

Beau followed the procedure, under her careful scrutiny, and when he was ready, awaited her instruction. She carried a pile of notes in her hand, and she referred to them as they walked along the corridor.

They stepped into the first ward, in which lay the man with severe symptoms. His breathing was laboured, and there was a pungent odour about him.

"What do you want me to do for him, Doctor?" whispered the nurse.

"Keep him comfortable with morphine. He had ten milligrams a little over an hour ago, so give him another dose now."

The nurse scribbled on her notes.

"What is his name?" asked Beau. The man was quite young: no more than thirty.

"His name is Michael Watson."

"Does he have family?"

"Oh, yes, he has a wife, I believe, and two young children."

Beau shook his head. They would soon be without a father, and he was powerless to remedy the situation.

"You'll see that they are kept informed, nurse?"

"Certainly, Doctor."

As they moved out into the corridor, Beau noticed James trying to catch his eye.

"What is it, James?"

Nurse Flanagan scowled as James came towards them.

"It's Miss Harper, Doctor. She's getting restless again."

"I'll be there in a few minutes, James. Keep an eye on her, will you, please?"

"That young man has a lot to learn about procedure," whispered the nurse.

"Then let's hope he's a fast learner," said Beau as they stepped in to the ward where two middle-aged women sat on their beds. Their conversation stopped immediately.

"Are you two ladies feeling alright?" asked the nurse, to which they nodded. "Good, then I'll send Mr. Wilson in to take your temperature."

They looked at one another.

"How long 'ave we gotta be cooped up in 'ere?" asked the older of the two.

Nurse Flanagan regarded them over the top of her spectacles.

"You'll be cooped up in here until we are sure you are not infected. You've both had sons return from overseas with symptoms, I believe?"

"Yeah," said the younger of the two, "but they're alright now."

"Nevertheless, you will stay here until we say you can go."

Beau turned away to hide the smile that was playing at the corners of his mouth. Nurse Flanagan was certainly not a woman to be trifled with.

The story was much the same in the next room, where two men languished.

"How much longer, doc?" asked a sandy-haired young lad with a cheeky grin.

"Mind your manners!" retorted Nurse Flanagan, bristling with annoyance. "This is Doctor DuBois, and you will give him his full title."

"Sorry, er...Doctor DuBois." He gave a mock salute, which aggravated the nurse even further.

"You'll stay here until I say you can go, if you're not careful, young man!"

"How long have you been quarantined?" Beau asked quickly.

The two men looked at one another and shrugged.

"Dunno," said the sandy-haired lad. "Two weeks all up, wouldn't you say, Joe?"

The young man called Joe nodded vigorously. "At least, I would say, Bill."

Nurse Flanagan referred to her chart.

"Hm, well in that case you're nearly ready to be discharged," she said tightly, " and count yourselves among the lucky ones."

We'll take one more blood sample," said Beau, "and presuming that it's clear, then you will be free to go."

"Thanks, doc...tor DuBois." Bill grinned as he watched Nurse Flanagan pull herself up to her full height, which was no more than five feet.

"The cheek of those two!" she exclaimed loudly, following Beau from the ward.

"It's alright, nurse, I've been called worse."

"That's not the point, Doctor! They need to show more respect."

Beau didn't comment as he walked into Miss Harper's ward. James, who was sitting by her bedside, sprang to his feet as they entered, relief visible on his face.

"I've been trying to cool her forehead," he muttered. "I didn't know what else to do. It seemed to settle her a little."

"Very good, James. That was an excellent idea." Beau stood by the bedside and looked down on the pale features with the staring blue eyes.

Meg recognised Beau, and a shaky laugh escaped her swollen lips.

"What can you do for me now, Doctor?" she whispered.

Beau felt his heart constrict, and a feeling of guilt overwhelmed him.

"I will try to keep you as comfortable as possible."

Her head nodded. "That's what we say to dying patients, isn't it, Doctor? I was a nurse, remember, on the front line? I saw a lot of men die, and I said the same thing to them." She coughed. "The end result was always the same."

She coughed again, and Beau noticed the blood. He turned to James.

"A clean cloth, please James, quickly!"

The young man hurried from the ward.

"There is something you can do for me." It was just a whisper.

"If I can. What is it?" Beau leaned over the bed.

"Not too close, Doctor!" warned Nurse Flanagan sharply.

Beau ignored the warning. He needed to hear what Meg Harper wanted to say.

"I need you to find my closest friend, and let her know what's happened to me." She paused to fight for breath. "Her name's Mary Walker...and we nursed together on the Western Front." There was another pause and Meg's eyes glistened as she stared at Beau. "She got married in the Field Hospital...on Christmas Day. It was so romantic..." Her fingers clawed at Beau's arm. "Please find her, Doctor. Tell her...tell her I tried to find her...and I did the matron proud. Tell her...."

Her voice petered out, and her chest rattled for a moment before a sigh escaped her swollen lips and she was still. Beau put a finger on her pulse. There was nothing.

He looked up to see James standing quietly beside him, a clean cloth in his hand, and tears streaming from his eyes.

"She won't need that now, James," said Beau quietly.

"I wonder if she was religious?" Nurse Flanagan asked nobody in particular.

"We can pray for her, nurse. You'd better notify the Coroner and I believe she has a mother who will need to be notified."

"Certainly, Doctor." Nurse Flanagan left the ward.

Beau sat back as the shock of what she had said, began to penetrate his brain. Could she have been talking about the nurse who knew Jack? What was the name of the nurse Jess had written about? He felt sure that it was Mary Walker, and if so, then he could fulfil a promise to a dying woman. He leaned over her bed.

"This is something I can do for you, Meg Harper. I promise I will find your friend and tell her of your bravery. Sleep in peace, now."

He heard James stifle a sob, and he looked up.

"The war is not over yet, James," he said quietly. "We must get used to this."

*

Later, in his office, Beau found Jess's latest letter, and quickly scanned it. The names Mary and George Walker leapt out at him, and he sat back in his chair, expelling a long breath. She had to be the Mary of Meg Harper's final words, didn't she? Beau needed to write to Jess. No, better still, he would telephone her. He needed to hear her voice.

The Telephone Call

Jess was walking home from the Grey Goose. It was just after three o'clock, and Rodney had assured her that he could manage. Jean was still in the hospital, undergoing tests, and fuming because she couldn't go home.

"I don't know why they want to keep me here," she had complained to Jess when she had gone visiting. "I'm alright, and I need to see what Rodney's up to!"

Jess smiled as she recalled trying to calm her friend's agitation.

"Jean, Rodney is not 'up to' anything," she had said, "so there's no need to be concerned on his account. We're working well together."

Jean had grunted.

"You always did see the best in people, Jess. What I'm saying is, watch him like a hawk, and don't believe everything he says."

So Jess was watching Rodney *like a hawk,* and saw nothing to discredit him. He had made one big mistake, and had escaped the consequences almost unscathed.

Jess opened her front gate, and checked the letterbox. There was nothing there. She was still waiting for word from the Base Records Office, about the return of Jack's few possessions.

As she looked up, she saw Margaret sitting on the old seat on the front verandah.

"Hello, Margaret." She looked around for Grace. "Have you brought Gracie home?"

Margaret stood up. "No, she's quite happy with granddad. I had to come and see you, to tell you that I've had a telephone call from Beau."

"Oh? What did he have to say?" Jess stepped on to the verandah.

"He needs to talk to you, so he's going to call again at four o'clock. I said I would make sure you were at our place."

"Did he say what it's about?" Jess unlocked the front door, and together they stepped into the passage.

"No, he didn't, but he sounds very forlorn, Jess. I think this virus is really taking its toll, especially on the doctors."

Jess entered the kitchen, removed her apron and headscarf, and hung them behind the back door.

"The boys will be home soon. I'll get their afternoon tea, and then if you wouldn't mind waiting for them, I'll go and see what Beau wants?"

"Yes, of course."

Within half an hour, Jess was knocking on Charles's front door. She heard running footsteps, and Gracie appeared.

"Ma! Granddad, it's ma!"

Jess opened the door and Gracie flung herself into her arms. Behind Gracie, she saw Charles, coming slowly along the passage.

"Ah, Jess, you've come to wait for your telephone call?"

"Yes, Charles." She put Gracie on the floor. "Margaret is waiting for the boys to come home from school."

"I thought she would. Come on through to the lounge."

They sat in the comfortable lounge chairs and engaged in small talk until the telephone rang loudly in the hall. Jess went quickly to answer it. Her heart was pounding, and she lifted the receiver cautiously. There was a loud crackle and she heard a female voice.

"Trunk line from Sydney. Are you prepared to receive it?"

"Yes," said Jess warily.

There was another crackle and she heard Beau's voice.

"Jess? Are you there?"

"Yes, I'm here, Beau." Her voice trembled, and she was close to tears.

"It's so good to hear you. I have missed you."

"I've missed you, too. Are you well?"

"Yes, and I have some extraordinary news to tell you."

"What is it?"

"I'll have to tell you briefly, in case we're cut off. A patient, who has just passed away with the influenza virus, asked me to find a friend she'd worked with overseas, during the war. That friend's name is Mary Walker. The name sounded familiar, so I found your last letter and I knew it had to be your Mary Walker."

"My goodness! What was your patient's name?"

"Meg Harper. Jess, do you have any idea where Mary lives now?"

"Her husband, Sergeant Walker, is at the Williamstown Barracks. That's the only contact address I have."

"That will do. I promised Meg that I would find Mary and tell her what happened to her dear friend."

"She would have known Jack, too."

There was a pause before Beau answered.

"Yes, I expect she did."

"You *are* looking after yourself, Beau?"

"As best I can, Jess. This virus has increased our workload." He stopped. "Look, Jess, we'd better say good-bye in case we're cut off. Take care of yourself, and don't you work too hard in that pub. I know what it's like there. Good-bye, Jess. If all's well, I'll see you in a few weeks."

"Good-bye, Beau. I'm looking forward to that. Please stay well."

"Are you extending?" a female voice asked politely.

Jess heard Beau say, 'no' and the line went dead.

After putting the receiver back in the cradle, she stood for a moment, composing herself before returning to the lounge. Jess realised that she hadn't told Beau about Jean's heart attack. She would have to write and tell him.

Charles looked up from his newspaper. "Everything alright, Jess?"

"Yes, Charles, but you won't believe what he had to tell me." Jess proceeded to tell Charles the details of her conversation with Beau.

Charles put down his newspaper.

"It's becoming a very small world, Jess, a very small world indeed."

*

Beau put down the receiver, and stood for a moment, looking out the window at the bay. He was in Celia's office/waiting room, and the silence weighed heavily on him. For a few moments, Jess had seemed almost close enough for him to reach out and touch her. Now he was alone.

The door opened and Celia appeared.

"Still here, Beau? I thought you'd gone home an hour ago."

"No. I had to make a telephone call."

Celia came to stand beside him. "A telephone call to whom?"

Beau turned his head to look at her. "To Jess," he said simply.

Celia groaned. "Stop making yourself miserable, Beau. Jess is miles away, and the whole situation is impossible! Can't you see that?"

Beau gritted his teeth. "Celia, the telephone call was to find out where somebody lives."

"Oh? Who?" Her brown eyes burned into his.

Beau shook his head. "Nobody you know, Celia."

She shrugged her elegant shoulders. "Suit yourself, Beau." Celia moved closer to the window. "It looks very calm and serene out there, doesn't it?"

"Yes, now if you'll excuse me, I need to go back to my office for some papers."

Celia's voice followed him as he stepped into the corridor.

"How are you going with the Evans lad, Beau?"

Beau turned. "He's talking at last."
"Good. And what does he have to say?"
Beau smiled thinly. "I haven't discussed this with Matthew, Celia."
Celia matched his smile. "So you're not going to tell me?"
"No."
Beau closed the door firmly behind him.

Charlie's Shock Disclosure

Beau tried to open Charlie's door. It was locked. He crossed to the nurse's desk.
"Susan, where is Charlie Evans?"
The nurse looked up from her paperwork, and smiled.
"He's gone, Doctor DuBois," she said cheerfully.
"Gone? Gone where?"
"He's been discharged."
Beau was mystified and a little angry. "Discharged by whom?"
"By Doctor Morley." The nurse could see the anger in Beau's eyes. "I thought you would have known."
"No. I wasn't told." His brow furrowed. "Where is Doctor Morley?"
"He went upstairs to the quarantine wards. They're now empty, and have to be disinfected and made ready for possible future cases. The cleaner is with him."
"Mrs. Evans?"
"No, Milly Saunders. Mrs. Evans went home with her son."
Beau was becoming increasingly angry. Not only had he been forced to catch the tram, he now discovered that Matthew had discharged the boy without even conferring with him. It wasn't like Matthew to do something like that.
Susan was looking at him apologetically.
"It's not your fault, Susan. I'll go and find him and see what's going on." Beau gave her a brief smile, before walking along the corridor.
He heard Matthew's laugh as he reached the cordoned off area, and stepping over the rope, he headed for the sound. It was coming from the room that Meg Harper had occupied briefly.
Matthew turned as Beau entered the small space.
"Ah, Beau!" he said hurriedly. "Sorry I didn't wait for you, old chap! To tell the truth, I couldn't find you, and Celia thought you'd gone home."
"No. I was waiting to make a telephone call."
"You may go, Milly." Matthew turned to the cleaner, who was standing coyly to one side. "See that all these rooms are meticulously disinfected."
"Yes, Doctor Morley."
Milly sidled past the two men, casting a sidelong look in Matthew's direction.
Beau frowned. Milly was young, and attractive in a common sort of way, but he had the distinct impression that something had been going on between them, and he had interrupted. Perhaps it was a timely intrusion.

"Don't look at me like that, Beau!" Matthew slapped him on the back. "It's just a bit of harmless fun, that's all! Nothing serious!"

"Harmless fun!" Beau glared at his colleague. "Matthew, you're old enough to be her father!"

"Come on, Beau! Don't look so shocked. These things go on, you know, or have you completely cut yourself off from the world?"

"I'm not ignorant, Matthew, but you of all people; I thought better of you."

Matthew laughed. "If it's Celia you're worried about, then I'm telling you now, she knows about my little indiscretions. I adore her, as you know, but we both go our own way at times. I thought you knew that."

"This is a little different, Matthew. Milly is the cleaner, for goodness sake!"

"She knows her way around, Beau." Matthew chuckled.

"Does she? Anyway, this is not why I came looking for you. I want to know about Charlie Evans. Susan told me he's been discharged."

"Yes. His mother feels that she can deal with him at home now that he's talking."

"And you didn't think to tell me?"

"I was getting to that, Beau, but you have been somewhat distracted, yourself."

"I need to see him," said Beau curtly. "Are they back at their old address?"

"Yes, I presume so."

Beau looked at his watch. "It's too late to go there now. I'll leave it 'til the morning. You'll have to continue with my patients at the clinic." He headed for the door.

Matthew called after him. "Do you want a ride back into the city?"

"No thanks. I'll catch a tram."

"Do you want my car in the morning?"

Beau looked at Matthew, and it was suddenly like looking at a stranger.

"I'll catch a tram." He turned on his heel and strode along the corridor.

*

Beau stood on the tram, as it rattled its way towards the city. He had always known that Matthew had a roving eye, but this was ludicrous. He smiled to himself as he thought of Celia competing for Matthew's affections with a cleaner. No, Celia would never compete. She knew exactly how to bring her men to heel.

"Mama, what's wrong with that man's face?" A childish voice interrupted his thoughts, and he looked down to see a young boy of perhaps five, pointing a chubby finger at him.

"I don't know, darling," whispered the woman sitting beside the child. "Perhaps he was in a fight." She stared up at Beau. "Men do that, you know?"

Beau turned away, the hurt and bitterness rising within him. *How little people know*, he thought, as he shouldered his way through the crowded tram. He wanted to scream, *a German gun did this*, but what was the point? A lot of people had very short memories.

The tram stopped and he got off. He would walk the rest of the way. He needed to clear his head. Working with Matthew and Celia was turning out to be more difficult than he might have imagined.

*

Beau knocked on the door with the yellow 7 painted roughly on it. He waited and then knocked again. Footsteps could be heard within, and the door slowly opened. Charlie stood there, fully dressed, his hair combed and his chin shaved.

"Hello Charlie," said Beau pleasantly. "May I come in?" Charlie opened the door wide, and Beau stepped into the room. "Is your mother here?"

Charlie shook his head. "She's gone to work."

"Good. It's you I've come to see."

Beau sat on one of the faded pink chairs, and drew some papers from his jacket pocket. Charlie stood in front of him, eyeing the papers suspiciously.

"Sit down, Charlie. I have a few questions to ask you."

Charlie sat slowly on the chair opposite Beau. He could see that the papers in Beau's hands were his drawings. Their eyes met and held for a moment before Charlie looked away.

"What do you want to know?" he asked slowly.

Beau held out the first drawing that Charlie had done; the drawing of the hut with what looked like barbed wire around it.

"Where was this, Charlie?"

Beau noticed the scowl that had settled on Charlie's features.

"It was a shed on the farm, where we were all held."

"So it wasn't just you imprisoned there?"

Charlie shook his head.

Beau pointed to the scribble around the shed. "Is this barbed wire?" Charlie nodded. "And the rider is you, of course?" Beau looked up at Charlie, as he placed the other picture on top. Charlie showed signs of agitation.

"This picture concerns me, Charlie. I don't think we have the whole story, and I'd like to hear it, however bad it might be."

Charlie was sucking in his breath, and his hands clenched and unclenched rapidly.

"I told my mum what happened! She knows!"

"Tell me, Charlie."

Charlie began to pace the room, while Beau waited. Finally he sat, and with his hands pressed between his knees, he stared at Beau.

"Two guards took me from the shed to the farmhouse. That's where they used to interrogate prisoners. I was really scared, because one of the other prisoners had told me that I'd be made to drink this stuff to make me talk. That's what they did, and I spat it out." He pressed his hands over his ears. "All the time they were shouting at one another, and I didn't know what they were saying." His hands moved to his eyes, and he gulped at the air. "Then the one guard pins me to the floor and starts to..." He began to rock backwards and forwards.

"He sexually assaulted you, Charlie?"

Charlie nodded, and his eyes filled with tears.

"Then he tried to make me drink that stuff again, but the other guard knocked it out of his hand, and shouted something at him. Then... he was shot! Just like that!

He fell near me, and I heard him say in English, 'run, boy!' I couldn't, but I got hold of his gun, and I fired. I missed, so I fired again and he went down."

Beau sat back. "So it was you who shot the other guard?"

Charlie nodded, his face awash with tears. "Mum doesn't know that."

"I know, Charlie." Beau paused. "And the button, Charlie? Did it belong to the guard who'd tried to save your life?"

"Yes."

Beau took a deep breath. It had taken a long time to get to the actual truth, but it was finally out. The lad had shot a German soldier, most likely at close range, and had suffered agonising guilt, fear and possibly shame, ever since.

"Tell me, Charlie, what did you do then?"

Charlie wiped a sleeve across his eyes.

"I couldn't do anything. I just stayed there 'til I was found."

"And the message you were carrying?"

Charlie winced and shook his head. "My brain was like mush, and I couldn't remember it!" He looked beseechingly at Beau. "Don't tell mum."

Beau patted his arm.

"She doesn't need to know, if you don't want her to, Charlie. I certainly won't tell her. She's satisfied with the story, as you told it to her."

Charlie reached into his shirt pocket, and pulled out the German button. They both looked at it.

"Does this mean that I can put it away now?"

"It does, Charlie. The man saved your life, and you can be forever grateful for that, but there's no need for you to feel guilty any more."

Charlie was silent as he contemplated the button and all it stood for.

"Why did he do it, do you think?"

"I don't know, Charlie. War takes men from all walks of life, and makes them do terrible things. Perhaps this man saw in you a son or a brother, and wanted to spare you from further torment." Beau smiled. "Anyway, put it all behind you, Charlie, and think about the future."

"I'd really like to work in the gardens at Serendipity."

"I thought you might. I'll speak with Doctor Morley and if he agrees, I think it would be the perfect place to start."

"Do you mean that?" Charlie's eyes lit up.

"Yes, Charlie."

*

Beau knocked on Matthew's door, and received permission to enter.

"Ah, Beau! Just the man I wanted to see." Matthew smiled up at Beau from behind his desk. "Did you get to see the Evans lad?"

"I did." Beau sat opposite Matthew.

"And?" Matthew spread his hands. "Why do I always have to prise information out of you, Beau?"

Beau ignored the comment. "I have the full story, and I'm satisfied that what I heard was the truth."

"I already know the story, Beau." Matthew sounded exasperated. "His mother told me what had happened."

"Good! So there's no need for me to enlighten you further?"

Matthew frowned. "Not unless there's more to tell."

"No." Beau sat back in the chair. "Charlie has come through his ordeal, but he'll never be completely free of the memories that haunt him. From time to time he'll experience panic attacks, usually triggered by something as simple as a sound."

"You're speaking from experience, of course?"

"I am." Beau paused, his brow furrowed. "He needs to be where we can keep an eye on him, so I told him that I'd speak to you about him working in the garden at Serendipity." Beau looked up into Matthew's eyes.

"Excellent idea, old chap! We can accommodate another gardener. I'll start the ball rolling, if you like?"

"Thank-you, Matthew." Beau rose from the chair.

"Oh, about the other day, Beau." Matthew's fair skin flushed. "I – er- I'm sorry you had to witness my little – er-"

"Indiscretion?"

Matthew nodded. "Stupid of me!"

"What you do is your own business, Matthew, but you know my opinion."

Matthew scowled up at his colleague. "Yes, I do, Beau. The trouble with you is you're too honourable. Falling from grace is not in your psyche."

"How do you know that?"

"I know you, Beau, and you're a better man than I'll ever be."

Beau laughed. "I think the difference between us is that I keep my feelings on a tight rein and you don't."

Matthew pursed his lips. "We've known each other a long time, Beau, and not once have I seen anything to discredit you."

"Well, maybe you don't know me as well as you think you do, Matthew."

"Are you telling me you've fallen from grace?" Matthew laughed. "Well! Well!"

"What have I missed?" Celia appeared in the doorway. "Something funny?"

A faint whiff of perfume accompanied her as she entered the room. "Well?"

The two men looked at one another.

"No, there's nothing funny, Celia," said Beau quickly.

Celia shrugged theatrically. "And you wouldn't tell me if there was, would you?"

"No." They spoke in unison.

"Well, I'll change the subject." She sat elegantly on the edge of Matthew's desk, and smoothed her slim-fitting black skirt. "It seems that the influenza virus is slowing down. The hospitals have reported no new cases in the last week."

"We already know that, Celia," said Matthew calmly. "We have been asked to keep our rooms at the ready, in case it flares up again, but at the moment, everything seems to be under control and the hospitals are coping."

"So life can get back to normal? No more wearing those wretched masks?"

"I wouldn't go that far, Celia," said Beau hastily. "We still need to be careful."

Celia shrugged and rolled her eyes. "If you say so, Doctor DuBois!"

Beau ignored the sarcasm, and turned towards the door.

"By the way, I'm planning on going away for the Easter, if all is quiet here."

Celia, who had been studying her painted fingernails, looked up sharply.

"Where are you going?"

"I'm going to Bendigo."

There was a shocked silence for several moments. Celia opened her mouth to say something, but Matthew cut in.

"You enjoy your time away, Beau. You've earned it."

"Thank-you, Matthew."

As he closed the door he heard Celia say, "Aren't you going to stop him, Matthew?"

He didn't wait to hear the answer.

*

"No, I am not going to stop him!"

Celia was silent for a moment. Matthew watched the changing contours of her face. She was searching for a suitably stinging retort. She found one.

"Daddy is still Chairman of the Board of Directors, Matthew."

"Meaning?"

"I'll tell him what's going on with Beau."

"There is nothing *going on* with Beau, Celia. You are the one who is being irrational, and I have to tell you that all this friction is getting me down." Matthew moved to the window, and stood looking out across the bay, his arms folded.

"Well, I fear that if Beau has his way, he'll leave here and head down to Melbourne, where he'll be closer to this woman. She has need of him, I fear."

Matthew turned to look at his wife, a scowl creasing his brow.

"And how do you know that?"

A faint flush stained Celia's cheeks.

"I saw a letter that she had written to him!" she declared defiantly.

There was a stony silence.

"You read his mail?"

"I did."

Matthew shook his head. "Why did you do that?"

"Because I needed to know, Matthew."

"I'm speechless, Celia! Did Beau find out?"

"Yes, quite by accident, he did find out. I wasn't going to give it to him."

"Celia, he is my friend and colleague, and you had no right to pry into his private affairs! No right at all!" Matthew turned back to the window. "This situation cannot go on the way it is. I'll have to give it some serious thought."

"We can't let him leave here, Matthew."

"We have no hold over him, Celia. If he wants to go, he can."

"And me? Do you wish me to go, Matthew?"

Their eyes met.

"No, of course not," he said raggedly. Celia walked into his arms. "You're my wife, damn it!"

Celia smiled sweetly. "Don't you forget that, Matthew."

Jean and Rodney

Easter was fast approaching, and Jess was becoming increasingly anxious. She had not heard from Beau, and she still had to purchase a hen from the money he had sent to Ben.

Jean had returned to the Grey Goose, along with strict instructions to take things easy, and not exert herself; both of which she ignored. She threw herself back into the role of publican with increased vigour, and not even the pleadings of her son or Jess, could stop her.

"This is my hotel," she voiced loudly one day, "and I won't have either of you telling me what I should or should not do!"

"You need to be following the doctor's orders, Jean," implored Jess, "or you'll finish up back in hospital. Is that what you want?"

"I'm feeling fine, Jess. I know how much I can do before I get tired." Jean was wiping down tables. "I really appreciate what you and Rodney have done in my absence, but I need to keep busy."

"You've had a timely warning, Jean, and it should be a reminder to retire to your sitting-room *before* you get tired." Jess picked up a tray of glasses and carried them to the sink behind the bar.

"Alright," sighed Jean. "I'll do as you say." She paused. "By the way, Jess, did I hear you saying that you have to buy a hen for young Ben?"

"Yes." Jess was busy washing glasses. "Beau sent him some money to replace Speckles, and I've done nothing about it. We're expecting a visit from Beau at Easter, so I need to do something fast."

"Beau's coming for Easter?" Jean smiled. "That will be nice." She flicked her duster at a pesky fly. "Harry Brown has chooks. Why don't you ask him when he comes in for his pint?"

"I might just do that, Jean."

*

Harry Brown was more than happy to sell Jess *'one o'me best layers'* for three shillings, and would even deliver it to their door. Jess was delighted, and so was Ben. The hen turned out to be similar in colouring to speckles, with bronze feathers and a spotted breast, so Ben called her Speckles Two.

"We'll have to make sure that Mister Fox doesn't get her, ma," said Ben, as he stood with his mother at the gate of the chook pen, and watched the hens strutting curiously around the newcomer.

"Hm," said Jess. "We might have to separate her from Midnight. She doesn't seem to like the intrusion at all."

"That's because she's the bossy one. She doesn't like any of the others, really." Jess laughed, and put an arm around her son.

"Well, I suppose they'll sort it out between them."

"I hope Beau likes her," said Ben quietly.

"I hope she lays some eggs."

"What'll I do with the rest of the money, ma?" Ben looked up at his mother. "Do I have to give it back to Beau?"

"No, sweetheart. Beau won't want it back. It was a present to you."

Ben was silent for a moment. "He said I could buy you something special."

Jess squeezed his shoulder. "I don't need anything, Ben. Why don't I put it in the bank for you? Then you can spend it when there's something you really want."

"That's a good idea, ma." They stood in silence. "Is Auntie Izzy coming for Easter?"

"Thank-you for reminding me, Ben. I'll write to her tonight."

*

The following day, after Jess had done her chores at the Grey Goose, and then posted her letter to Izzy, she opened the letterbox and found a letter from Beau. Sitting on the verandah seat, she opened it carefully and read:

> *Dear Jess and children,*
> *I am pleased to be able to report that the virus has slowed its impact on hospitals here in Sydney, so I am free to come and visit you all, over the Easter period.*
> *I will catch the train to Melbourne on the Wednesday night, and then hopefully the morning train to Bendigo. There's no need to come and meet me. You'll no doubt be busy. I am looking forward to seeing you, and catching up with all your news. I hope you have been keeping well, and out of contact with the virus.*
> *Jess, I have written to Mary Walker, explaining the death of her dear friend. There have been so many casualties, and I'll tell you about another one I've been dealing with, when I see you.*
> *Ben, did you manage to buy a new hen? If so, I look forward to meeting her.*
> *I must finish and get this to the post.*
> *Hope to see you soon,*
> *Beau*

Jess took a deep breath, and folded the letter back into the envelope. She really was looking forward to seeing Beau again. He had become her safe place in the storms of her life. She felt the tears prickle behind her eyes, and she felt sure that Jack would understand.

*

The following morning, as Jess was taking her apron from behind the door at the Grey Goose, she heard raised voices. Her heart sank. It seemed as though the temporary peace was shattered.

"I want you to go, Rodney!" she heard Jean saying. "I thought it was too good to be true, that you had turned over a new leaf."

"Ma, I can explain!"

"No! I've had enough. Pack your bags and leave!"

There was silence.

"You'll never manage on your own. Be sensible, ma! You need me!"

"No, I don't need you! I'll find another barman, don't you worry about that!"

"Very well, but you'll be sorry. Don't say I didn't warn you!"

The bar door opened, and Rodney appeared, flushed and angry. He glared at Jess.

"She's making a big mistake! A bloody big mistake!" He stormed off.

Jess walked slowly into the bar. Jean was sitting at one of the tables, her head in her hands. She looked up as Jess approached.

"What's happened?" asked Jess tentatively."

"That weasel, Seamus Oliver, has been sniffing around again, Jess." Jean wiped her eyes. "I won't have the reputation of this establishment soiled by the likes of him!"

"What has he done?"

Jean looked up at Jess. "I'm not waiting for him to do anything. I'm getting in first."

"You won't have a barman, Jean, if Rodney goes."

"I'll manage," said Jean stoically. "I've done it before."

"That may be, Jean, but you have a heart condition now."

Jean hauled herself to her feet. "I have you, Jess. You help me now, and I can pay you." She looked her friend straight in the eye.

"But I don't do bar work, Jean." Jess shrugged helplessly.

"Maybe it's time for you to learn."

Jess was silent for a moment, weighing up what Jean had said. *Do I have what it takes to work behind a bar?* She had her children to think about. They needed her attention when they weren't at school or with their grandparents.

"Well?" Jean's voice broke into her thoughts.

"I'm happy to help you, Jean, you know that, but I must consider my children. I wouldn't be able to give all my time."

"I understand that, Jess, and any help you can give me will be appreciated." Jean smiled thinly. "In the meantime, I can ask around, and see if there's a barman out there, looking for work."

Jess nodded hesitantly.

Jean touched her arm. "Think about it, Jess."

The side door slammed.

"I will, Jean."

Visitors

"You're a natural, Jess!" exclaimed Jean excitedly, as she watched Jess pull a perfect beer. "I don't know what you were worried about!"

"I'm slow, Jean. This won't work when the crowds come in."

The old man on the other side of the bar, gave her a toothless grin as she set the glass before him.

"If they want their pint, girlie, they'll wait, I c'n tell ya," he said before raising the glass to his lips.

"Do you think so?"

"We're sure, aren't we, Johnny?" Jean patted Jess on the arm, and the old man nodded. "Besides, with a little practise, you'll get quicker. We still have a week before the Easter crowds start coming though those doors."

"A week? Is that all?" Jess looked diffident.

"That's all, Jess." Jean leaned on the bar and surveyed her friend. "Beau will be here by then. Maybe he'll want his old job back?"

Jess looked up quickly. "I don't think so, Jean. He's moved on since then."

"You never know, girl. Perhaps he's tired of sickness, and needs some quiet."

"We all need that, Jean."

"Yes, I suppose you're right." Jean sighed loudly.

Rodney had been gone a week; packed his bags and gone. Jean had no idea where he was, nor did she really care. She only knew that she felt a sense of relief. Jess was proving to be more than capable, and as they worked together, she felt that her precious hotel would not suffer. Yes, she had made the right decision.

Jess was slowly working her way through the changes in her life, and with Margaret's support, she was able to assist Jean and get a small payment in return.

Her confidence was boosted daily, as the compliments flowed from regulars happy with the service.

Jean did remind her, however, that "men will always be men, Jess, so you be careful. You could be a good catch for someone out there."

Jess had raised her eyebrows at that remark. She had no intention of being a 'good catch.' The idea repelled her, as she thought of some of the hotel regulars.

*

The week leading to Easter, arrived at last, and excitement rose in Jess's household. Izzy had written to say that they would be arriving from Swan Hill on the mid-day train on Thursday. Sarah would not be with them, as Nancy Weatherall had agreed to look after her while the family was away.

Jess didn't know what train Beau would be on. They could all possibly arrive at the same time. She was feeling nervous and excited. The last time she had seen Beau was when Margaret had begged him to come and bring her back from the black abyss she had crawled into after learning of Jack's death. That was four months ago.

Not one to dress in black, Jess had not taken to wearing a widow's garb, but had preferred to wear the dress which reminded her so much of Jack; the dress with the forget-me-nots. She wore it on the Thursday, as the weather was still reasonably warm. Jean had been kind enough to give her time to meet her visitors, on the understanding that they all get together at the Grey Goose, after the six o'clock closing.

The boys were at school, and Gracie was with Margaret, so Jess had the morning to re-arrange bedding for the family. Margaret had suggested quietly that Beau stay with her and Charles, as it wasn't really appropriate for him to sleep at Jess's. Izzy and Harry would have her bed, and she would sleep in the boys' room. Ben would be out in the sleep-out, and Gracie was now in a 'big girl's bed'.

By eleven-thirty, all the arranging had been completed, so Jess wrapped Izzy's fringed shawl around her shoulders and stepped outside the front door. Her fingers trembled nervously as she put the key in the lock, and she took a deep breath to calm herself before heading for the station.

As she walked across the pedestrian bridge, Jess heard the whistle of the Swan Hill train as it approached Bendigo. She hurried down the steps, and along the platform to the board on which was written arrival and departure times. The Melbourne train was due in at twelve-thirty, on platform two.

The Swan Hill train thundered into the station, in a burst of steam. Jess waited anxiously for it to dissipate. Passengers poured on to the platform, and she stood on tiptoe as she searched the faces that passed by.

"Jess!" she heard eventually, as Izzy appeared out of the haze and enveloped her in a scented hug. "We're finally here!"

"How are you, Izzy?"

Izzy held her sister at arms' length, and surveyed her from head to toe.

"I'm very well, sis, and I must say you're looking better than when I saw you last."

Jess nodded. "I'm feeling much better." She looked past Izzy to see Harry, carrying Freya, and struggling with a large bag.

"Hello, Harry."

"It's good to see you, Jess." Harry put Freya on the ground. "She's all yours, Isobel. I'll collect the rest of the luggage."

Izzy swooped on Freya, who was now a chubby, energetic two-year-old, with blonde curls, and a fascination for the edge of the platform.

"My goodness!" said Jess. "Hasn't she grown?"

"And she's very self-willed," panted Izzy.

"Just like her mother," laughed Jess.

"It's not a laughing matter, Jess. She wants her own way in everything!"

"Discipline, Izzy," said Jess quietly. "Perhaps she needs some time with Charles."

Izzy looked shocked. "I don't think so, Jess."

Jess looked up at the platform clock. It was twelve-fifteen.

"I think Beau will be arriving from Melbourne on the twelve-thirty, Izzy."

Izzy looked up at the clock. "That's only fifteen minutes away." She turned her gaze on Jess. "What if Harry and I head on up to the house, and leave you to welcome Beau?" She smiled. "I don't think I could stay here with Freya for another fifteen minutes. She needs to have some lunch, and then a sleep."

"What's going on, ladies?" Harry stood beside them, a suitcase in each hand, and the bag under his arm.

"We're going on to the house, Harry, and Jess will wait for Beau. He's arriving on the next train."

"At least I think he is," said Jess quickly.

"Righto." Harry put down the bag. "All yours, my dear."

"How long are you staying?" Jess eyed the luggage with mild trepidation.

"'Til Tuesday," sighed Harry. "Looks like we're staying for a month, doesn't it?"

"Don't be like that, Harry," clucked Izzy. "Give me the key, sister dear, and we'll carry this circus up the street to your place." She laughed gaily.

Jess handed her the key. "You will have my room."

"Are you sure?" Harry was frowning.

"Yes, and there will be no argument."

"Come on, Harry." Izzy picked up the bag with her free hand. "This child is getting heavy, and I can put her down once we're over the bridge."

"Give me the bag, Izzy," said Jess. "I have to go across to platform two."

They made their way slowly up the steps, across the bridge and down the other side, where Jess handed Izzy the bag, and watched as the family made their way out of the station. She sighed, and headed for one of the wrought-iron seats.

It wasn't long before she heard the sharp sound of a train whistle, and her nerves began to tingle uncontrollably. *Stop being stupid*, she chastised herself.

The train arrived, and passengers spilled out on to the platform in a cloud of steam. Once again Jess scanned the faces as they poured past her.

As soon as she saw Beau's familiar figure stepping off the train, she pushed her way through the surging crowd, until she stood in front of him.

They stared at one another for a long moment, before Beau placed his bag on the platform, and opened his arms.

"Do I get a hug?" He smiled at her.

Jess fell into his embrace, her body shaking with emotion. Beau held her tight.

"It's so good to see you, Jess," he whispered against her hair.

Jess was trying not to cry, but had to succumb, and could only nod.

Finally she lifted her head to look at him. His hair was more salt and pepper than she remembered, and the scar seemed less pronounced, but his eyes were still that fathomless grey.

"You look well, Beau," she stammered, suddenly aware that her face was moist.

"And I can honestly say that you look much better than when I saw you last." Beau held her at arms' length, and ran a critical eye over her.

"Not you, too!" laughed Jess shakily.

"What do you mean?"

"Izzy said the exact same thing to me only a few minutes ago."

Beau looked around. "Where is she?"

"They went on ahead."

"Come on, you can tell me all the news while we walk."

Easter Reunion

That evening they all congregated in the Ladies' Lounge at the Grey Goose, and swapped stories of what had been happening in their lives since they had last been together.

Jean talked about Rodney, and how she had been forced to ask him to leave. As she talked she looked in Jess's direction, and her eyes misted.

"Jess has been a godsend, and I don't know what I would do without her now."

At this, Jess had blushed and cast a glance in Beau's direction. He returned her look, and smiled softly. This was not lost on Izzy, who changed the subject.

"Tell us, Beau, what's been happening with this terrible virus that's hit our cities?"

Beau shifted his gaze to Izzy.

"There's a drop in new cases at present, and the hospitals are managing to contain it, but the casualties have been enormous. We have to remain vigilant, because we never know when or where it will flare up again."

"So even in isolated towns like Swan Hill, we need to be wary?"

"Certainly. There's talk of setting up quarantine camps along the border, so that will include Swan Hill. If anyone has a sign of a cold or fever, please go straight to your doctor. I can't stress this enough."

Izzy looked across at Jess, who was seated opposite her. She noticed that her sister was struggling to remain in control, and Beau, standing beside her, placed a protective hand on her shoulder.

"I'm sorry, Jess." She reached across the table and took her sister's hand. "This must be very hard for you, but we need to know where we stand." She looked up at Beau. "So the crisis isn't over yet?"

Beau shook his head. "It could take months. We don't really know."

The room was silent for some moments.

"Someone we haven't seen for quite some time is Sally Mitchell." Margaret broke the silence. "Does anyone know where she is now?"

Jean answered. "Her grandfather died just before Christmas. I've seen neither sight nor sign of her since then."

"She did come to see us after Jack died," said Margaret hesitantly, looking in Jess's direction, "but I don't think Jess remembers, do you, dear?"

Jess shook her head. "No."

Jean smiled at Jess. "She probably decided to stay in Melbourne. She had made a new life for herself."

"We need to find out," said Jess. "She was always part of our get-togethers."

Everyone agreed.

By nine o'clock the conversations began to wane, and Izzy was the first to declare that it was time to get the children to bed.

"If the rest of you want to stay, Harry and I can take the little ones home, and get them to bed."

"No." Jess rose from the chair. "I'm ready to go." She pulled her shawl around her. "Thank-you, Jean. It's been lovely."

The evening had come to a close, and everyone headed out on to the street. In the waxy glow of a single street light, they all said goodnight before going their separate ways. Jess felt Beau's fingers brush her hand.

"Goodnight, Jess," he said softly, before following Margaret and Charles.

"Goodnight, Beau."

Jess turned and walked after Izzy. Harry, like the pied piper, was leading the four tired children towards home.

Izzy linked arms with Jess, and they walked several yards in silence, their footsteps echoing on the asphalt.

"Beau looks well," said Izzy, casting a sidelong glance at her sister as they passed underneath another streetlight.

Jess nodded.

"The man adores you, Jess," whispered Izzy, "in case you hadn't noticed."

Jess turned sharply. "Stop that, Izzy! You are shameless!"

"I'm telling the truth, little sister. I'm not blind, even if you are pretending to be."

"Izzy! I'm warning you!"

Izzy sighed. "Most of us only get one chance at real love, in this lifetime, but you seem to have two, if I'm not mistaken."

"I can't be disloyal to Jack, Izzy." Jess gave a stifled sob.

"Jack is gone, Jess. He's gone, and Beau is here. You need each other, little sister."

"Beau's not like that, Izzy!"

"Like what? He's a man, isn't he? Besides, why would he come all the way down here from Sydney, if it wasn't to see you?" Jess shook her head. "You can't tell me, Jess, that you don't miss the warmth of a man in your bed."

Jess wrenched her arm free.

"Now you are being vulgar, Izzy, and I won't listen to any more of it!"

"I'm being honest, Jess, and you know it."

Jess quickened her pace. Her sister's brutal honesty was too much for her.

"Are you two coming, or what?" Harry's voice filtered through the night air.

"Yes, Harry, we're coming."

*

Later that night, lying in her narrow bed, Jess recalled Izzy's words, and wondered why she was so transparent. Izzy had always been able to see straight through her, as if she were glass.

She couldn't have a relationship with Beau. It was too soon. Her emotions were still too raw, and her memories of Jack, too real.

"Oh, Jack," she whispered into the darkness, *"what should I do? Izzy is right, and if I don't want Beau in my life, I shouldn't be encouraging him. He is my safe place in all of this, and I miss him, too, when he's not here. Please know that whatever happens, you will always be in my heart."*

Jess awoke the following morning, to the sound of Ben's voice in her ear.

"Ma! Ma! Wake up, ma! Auntie Izzy is toasting hot cross buns for our breakfast!"

Jess blinked at Ben, and struggled to sit up.

"What time is it?" she yawned.

"I don't know, but if you don't hurry, you'll miss out!"

Jess groped for her dressing gown as she swung her legs over the side of the bed. Pushing her feet into her slippers, she stood up and ran her fingers through her tousled hair. She tied the cord of her gown, and smiled down at her son.

"Lead the way, Ben."

"Beau's arrived for breakfast, too." Ben was at the door.

Jess stopped in her tracks. "Beau's here?"

"Yes. He's come to see Speckles Two, so Auntie Izzy said he could stay."

Jess pressed her hands to her eyes. What was the time? It must be late, if Izzy was up and about.

"You go, Ben. I'll be there in a minute."

Ben needed no second bidding. He disappeared out the door.

Jess stood for a moment, contemplating her next move. She had to sneak into the bathroom, and at least tidy her hair. This she did, with mixed results. As she surveyed herself in the small mirror above the washbasin, she heard Ben shouting from the kitchen door.

"Hurry up, ma!"

Jess groaned, and accepted the fact that she had to greet Beau in her night attire, and there wasn't anything she could do about it. She headed for the kitchen.

The sound of laughter greeted her as she stepped into the warm room, and the smell of toasting hot cross buns made her mouth water.

All eyes turned in her direction, and a flush suffused her face, as she glanced quickly at Beau. He looked amused by her discomfort.

"Who let me sleep in?" She tried to sound nonchalant as she looked up at the clock, which read eight-thirty. "My goodness! Is that the time?"

"We didn't want to wake you," said Izzy, as she handed Harry a plate of buns to butter. "You must have needed the sleep." She nodded at Jess. "Sit down, sister dear. Margaret and Charles are at Church, so they will be in a little later."

Jess groaned inwardly. It was Good Friday, wasn't it?

They were all seated around the table: Harry, Beau, Ben, Edward, Grace, and Freya in the highchair. Jess sat beside Grace, and avoided eye contact with Beau, who was directly opposite.

"Right!" said Izzy, as she seated herself beside Harry. "Enjoy breakfast, everyone!"

They did, and the kitchen reverberated to the sound of laughter. The fact that it was Good Friday, a solemn occasion, did not seem to matter.

*

Later in the morning, when she was suitably dressed, Jess wandered out to the chook pen, where Ben was engrossed in a meaningful conversation with Beau, as they watched the hens preening and stalking each other.

"So this is where you two are?" She stood beside them.

"Ma, Beau thinks that Speckles Two is the best looking hen in the chook pen."

"Does he now?" Jess looked sidelong at Beau. "That's probably because she is the most expensive." Their eyes met and held.

"She lays three eggs a day!" Ben was saying enthusiastically.

"And we're going to gather today's eggs to paint as Easter eggs." Izzy had joined them. "I have enough paint to keep the children occupied for the afternoon."

"Good," said Jess. "You're in charge of that activity, Izzy." She stopped, and her face clouded. "That was usually Sally's task; to keep the children amused."

Ben opened the gate. "Come on, Auntie Izzy, let's see how many eggs we can find."

Izzy picked her way delicately through the droppings, before turning to Jess.

"Why don't you two take this opportunity to catch up properly? We can look after things here." She smiled encouragingly.

Jess looked at Beau. "We can go for a walk to the park if you like?"

"Wonderful idea." Izzy shut the gate. "Off you go!"

"I'll get a shawl." Jess felt suddenly nervous, and her legs were heavy.

Within minutes they were walking towards the town, their footsteps keeping perfect time on the asphalt. They were both silent.

Finally Beau spoke.

"I've really missed you, Jess. I hate being so far away, but it's not possible for me to leave my work at the moment." He sighed.

"I understand, Beau." Jess stole a glance at his profile. "We're very grateful that you were able to come down at all, the way things are at present."

He turned to smile at her.

"I don't think we should get all depressed about it. We should enjoy the time we have, and thank your sister for her intuitiveness."

"Her what?"

"She's a mind-reader."

"Oh, you noticed?"

They laughed, and Beau took her hand as they crossed the street.

They wandered slowly through the park, where people were enjoying the last of the summer blooms. They sat on the grass, and ate ice creams. Beau told Jess about Charlie and the mess that he was in as he bore the guilt of what he had experienced.

"You know," said Jess, after listening to the whole sordid tale, "it's perfectly alright to shoot someone during battle, but it's not alright at any other time."

"This wasn't a battle, Jess. It was two men trying to get information out of a boy. Charlie did what he had to do. He would have been killed otherwise. It was the trauma associated with it that sent him over the edge."

Beau's eyes took on a faraway expression, and his mouth was set in grim lines.

Jess put her hand over his. "It brought back memories?"

He turned to look at her. "Yes." He stood up. "Come on, the weather's too nice to get all maudlin." He took her hand and lifted her to her feet.

Beau tucked her arm in his as they continued their walk around the park. They stopped to listen to a brass band playing in the rotunda, they watched jugglers with their precision timing, heard poets reciting their lines and even saw an artist who insisted on doing a portrait of Jess.

"Let me draw your beautiful wife," he said with a strong Mediterranean accent.

Jess noticed that Beau didn't contradict him.

"I'd love a picture, Jess," he said quickly, making her blush.

The artist turned his dark twinkling eyes on Beau.

"She is not your wife, I think?" He nodded knowingly.

"No, she's not my wife, but she is very dear to me."

"Ah, I see."

"Will you please stop talking about me as if I wasn't here? Beau!"

"I'm sorry Jess, but I would love a portrait."

"Sit down, please?" The artist gestured towards a chair.

Jess sat, and Beau watched as he skilfully worked with crayon until Jess's face appeared on the paper before him. He caught his breath. It was beautiful.

When he had finished, the artist handed it to Beau.

"She is very beautiful. She should be your wife, no?"

Beau didn't answer, but reached into his pocket for some money.

"Let me see it," said Jess, and gasped at the likeness. "My goodness!"

Beau thanked the man with the twinkling brown eyes, and took Jess's arm.

"Are you hungry?" he asked as they moved away.

Jess nodded. "A little."

"Good. Why don't you sit on the grass and I'll go and look for something to eat."

Jess found a shady spot, and sat down to wait for his return. She thought about the speed at which things were happening, and she felt a little afraid. Beau was being very attentive, and she was responding with an eagerness that seemed natural. Strolling arm in arm was what lovers did, and although they were not lovers, Jess sensed that this could be the next transition. Her heart gave a little leap as she thought about this. Could she really give herself to another man?

"How does fish and chips sound?" Jess was startled by the sound of Beau's voice. He sat beside her and unwrapped the white paper.

"It looks and smells wonderful, Beau." Jess rubbed her hands together.

They tucked into the battered fish and crispy chips, until Jess sat back with a contented sigh.

"I can't eat another thing." She wiped a hand across her greasy mouth.

Beau wrapped up the remains of the chips. "The boys might like these. If not, I'm sure the chooks will eat them."

He lay back on the grass, his hands behind his head, and looked up at Jess. Her face looked surreal in the dappled light reflecting off the branches above.

"You look like an angel, Jess," he said softly.

She smiled down at him. "I've really enjoyed today, Beau."

"It doesn't have to end here, Jess."

"I know." She looked away, suddenly feeling afraid.

"I sense a 'but' in there somewhere, Jess."

"Let's enjoy our time together, Beau, and see what happens."

A shadow crossed his face, but it was soon gone and he smiled as he propped himself on one elbow.

"You're right, of course. I'm sorry, Jess. The longer we're apart, the more I realise how much I miss you." He looked down at the crayon portrait. "I have this now, and I can look at it whenever I feel lonely."

Jess touched his hand. "I think perhaps it's time we were heading home. The family will wonder what's happened to us."

Beau got to his feet, picked up the portrait and bundle of chips, and reached out a hand to Jess.

"Come on then. Let's report for duty."

*

The house was quiet when they walked through the front door.

"Izzy must be keeping those children extremely busy," commented Jess, "or they've all gone out."

She opened the kitchen door. There was nobody there. On the table sat a row of eggs, all painted in vibrant colours.

"Well, they have been busy, but all the birds have flown." Jess turned to Beau. "I'm dying for a cup of tea. Would you like one, Beau?"

"Yes, of course." Beau walked across to the window and glanced out at the back yard. All was silent. "Nobody outside, either."

"They must have gone for a walk." Jess busied herself at the stove. "Perhaps they've gone to see Margaret and Charles." Her nerves tingled. She was alone in the house with Beau, and after their conversation, she didn't trust her emotions.

"Jess?" He was standing close behind her. "Marry me, Jess."

She half turned. "What? Beau, I..."

"Before you say anything, please hear me out." He took a deep breath. "I can never replace Jack; I know that, but I love you, and I want to take care of you, and the children." Only the ticking of the clock broke the silence. "I don't mean right now. I can wait. If you'll just say you'll have me, I'll be the happiest man alive." Silence. "Jess?"

Jess turned and looked into those deep grey eyes. Her own eyes were swimming, and it took a moment for her voice to work. She tried to smile.

"I have a feeling, Beau, that you're not going to take 'no' for an answer."

"What does that mean, Jess? That you'll have me?"

"What it means Beau, is that I shall give the matter my careful consideration."

Beau frowned. This was not the answer he had expected.

"I'm serious, Jess." He looked somewhat perplexed.

Jess cupped his face in her hands, and gave him a watery smile.

"I know you are, Beau. That was just my attempt at a little light-heartedness. Forgive me." She paused. "I need time for it to sink in."

"So you're not saying 'no'?"

"I'm saying that I will be honoured to be your wife, when the time is right."

"You're saying 'yes'?"

"Yes, Beau." Jess gave a shaky laugh.

"Oh, Jess, you have no idea what that one little word does for me." Beau drew her into his arms. "Whatever happens now, I'll know that I have you." His eyes searched her face. "May I kiss my future wife?"

Jess nodded, and lifted her face for their first kiss. It was soft and hesitant at first, but increased with pressure as their passion increased.

Finally Jess broke away, breathless and trembling. She wasn't ready for anything else yet.

"Don't make me wait too long, darling girl," whispered Beau, who was also shaken by the heat of their desire for one another.

"Can we have that cup of tea now, Beau? I think we both need it."

As she turned towards the stove, the kitchen door burst open, and Ben and Edward tumbled into the room. The rest of the family followed.

"How was your day?" quizzed Izzy, as she removed her jacket and hat.

Jess kept her face averted as she answered.

"Oh, we've had a lovely day, haven't we, Beau?"

"Yes, we have, actually. The park is quite busy, and there's lots to see and do."

"We'll have to take all the children there tomorrow," said Izzy, as she picked up the portrait that Beau had placed on the table. "What's this?"

"That looks like ma!" exclaimed Edward loudly.

"Yes, it does, Edward." Izzy raised an eyebrow as she looked at Beau. "Who was the artist? It's a very good likeness."

"He was an Italian, I think," said Beau.

Jess, who now felt composed, turned to her sister.

"It only took him a few minutes."

"It's very good, Jess," said Harry as he sank on to the nearest chair. "Now I could do with a cup of tea. Looking after four children is quite a feat of endurance."

"Where have you been?" Jess poured water into the teapot.

"We've been to see the poppet heads," groaned Harry. "It was Isobel's idea of having an adventure."

"Oh, stop moaning, Harry. Don't tell me you didn't enjoy yourself."

"I wouldn't dare!" Harry winked at Jess.

*

Later that evening, when the children were all in bed, and the men were sitting on the front verandah, enjoying a quiet smoke, Jess made her way to the lounge and collapsed into the couch. She kicked off her shoes, and stretched her toes. It wasn't yet cool enough to light the fire.

She thought about the events of the day, and it all seemed surreal. She was going to marry Beau, when she felt the time was right. How would the family feel about it, she wondered? Izzy would certainly approve. She smiled to herself as she recalled the afternoon, and Izzy's surreptitious glances in her direction.

As if in response to her thoughts, Izzy appeared beside her, and settled herself into the couch.

"Well, little sister," she cajoled. "Out with it! I know something happened today, and you are going to tell me!"

"If you know so much," teased Jess, as she turned her green eyes on her sister, "then you tell me."

Izzy frowned. "When we walked into the kitchen today, we definitely interrupted something." Her eyes narrowed. "Did he kiss you? I noticed your cheeks were scarlet, in spite of you trying to hide the fact. Now tell all!"

Jess was silent for a moment, and Izzy wriggled with impatience.

"Beau has asked me to marry him."

The statement hung in the air for several seconds before Izzy's hands flew to her mouth, suppressing the squeal that rose up in her throat.

"He did?"

Jess nodded.

"And you told him 'yes', of course?"

"I told him that I'd be honoured, when the time is right."

"When the time is right?" Izzy threw up her hands. "And when will that be? You can't keep him waiting, Jess. The man is besotted, and that would be cruel. Besides, what are you waiting for?"

"There are a lot of things to be considered, Izzy, and I think it would be improper to jump into marriage too soon."

"Fiddlesticks! The world has changed since the war, Jess, and people must follow their heart. Love is too precious to waste, just because society has dictated the rules." Izzy flopped back on the couch and groaned. "Don't wait for the world to approve, Jess." She looked into her sister's eyes. "I think it's very obvious that you love him. Don't make him wait, I beg you."

"Don't make who wait?" Harry had walked into the lounge, followed by Beau.

Izzy looked up at her husband and smiled indulgently.

"These two have some news, Harry; some wonderful news."

"What news?" Harry looked bemused.

"Oh, Harry, sometimes you can be so frustrating." Izzy turned to Jess. "Tell him, Jess! Tell Harry what you have just told me."

Jess rose from the couch, and crossed to where Beau stood quietly. She took his hand, and smiled at him.

"I think Beau should be the one to tell you, Harry."

Beau squeezed her hand. "I've asked Jess if she'll be my wife."

Harry gave a loud snort.

"Well, I'll be darned!" He grinned at Jess. "You did say 'yes', of course?"

Jess nodded.

"Then let me be the first to congratulate you." Harry bounded forward, and planted a kiss on Jess's cheek, before grabbing Beau's free hand and shaking it enthusiastically. "That is wonderful news!"

Izzy lifted herself out of the couch, and kissed her sister on the cheek. Then she turned to Beau, and planted a kiss on his cheek.

"Don't let her make you wait too long, Beau."

As Izzy pushed Harry none too subtly from the room, Beau said, loud enough for Izzy to hear, "I don't intend to."

The door closed quietly behind them. Left alone, Beau drew Jess into his arms. Before his mouth closed on hers, she heard him say again,

"I don't intend to."

As the long suppressed feelings of desire swept through her body, Jess knew that her resolve had already weakened. Their need for each other could not be denied indefinitely.

Beau's Departure

Jess awoke the following morning, and lay for a time, reflecting on the events of the previous day. It all seemed dreamlike, and she feared that now she was awake, everything would evaporate, and life would be back where it had been before Beau's arrival. Had he really asked her to be his wife, or had she been mistaken?

She threw back the covers and swung her legs over the side of the bed. The linoleum was cold beneath her bare feet, so she slipped them hurriedly into her slippers, as she reached for her dressing gown.

Jess padded along to the bathroom, washed her face and hands and drew a brush through her hair. Surely she wouldn't be caught in her night attire again? Once again, she wondered whether that had really happened, or merely been part of the dream.

As she opened the kitchen door, she was just in time to see Grace throw her spoon, filled with porridge, towards the floor. Izzy made a grab for it, but was too late. Porridge splashed on her pink velvet dressing gown and on the floor.

"Gracie!" Jess cried sharply. "What are you doing?"

The child started at the unexpected appearance of her mother, and waved her arms around in angry little circles.

"I don't want it!"

She banged her chubby fists on the top of the table, and Freya, who was in the highchair beside her, burst into tears. Izzy attempted to console her.

"Now see what you have done! You are a naughty girl!" Jess picked up the spoon, and throwing it in the sink, grabbed a cloth to wipe up the mess on the floor. "What brought this on?" She turned to Izzy.

"I don't know, Jess." Izzy shrugged. "Her cheeks are a bit flushed; maybe she's coming down with something?"

"I hope not." Jess squeezed the cloth under the tap, and handed it to Izzy.

"It might pay to have Beau check her over."

"Yes, possibly."

As if on cue, Beau appeared at the back door, and let himself into the kitchen. He was dressed in his suit, and carried his travel case.

Jess's heart sank.

"Beau? Where are you going?" Gracie's outburst was temporarily forgotten.

Beau put down his case, crossed the floor, and took her hands.

"Jess, I have to go back to Sydney." His eyes reflected the sorrow in his heart.

"What?" Jess's mouth was dry. "Why?"

"I've had a telephone call from Celia; Matthew is very ill. She thinks he may have the influenza. I'm so sorry."

Jess shook away the indignation that had crept into her heart at the mention of Celia's name. Beau's expression was bleak.

"Then you must go," she whispered, fighting back the tears that threatened to spill over. "What time is the train?"

"I'll have to catch the ten-fifteen to Melbourne, and wait for the Sydney train, which doesn't depart until four."

Jess looked up at the clock. It was eight-thirty. She was supposed to be at the Grey Goose at ten. Jean would understand if she was late. She had to be at the station with Beau. Her heart was crying out for this not to be happening, but the look on Beau's face told her that it was real.

"I want to spend this time with you, Jess," Beau was saying, "because I don't know when I'll be able to get back again."

Jess looked in desperation at her sister.

"You get dressed, Jessie. I'll manage here. Quickly now! Harry's gone for a walk with the boys, so your room is free."

With trembling fingers, Jess pulled on a grey wool skirt and white blouse. She buttoned on her boots and threw Izzy's shawl around her shoulders. As her ablutions had been curtailed by Gracie's outburst, she fled back through the kitchen and outside.

On her return, she washed her hands at the washhouse trough, dried them, and took a deep breath. She hadn't had breakfast, or even a cup of tea, but all she wanted to do was spend the time with Beau. She was terrified of the possibility of history repeating itself. It couldn't, could it?

In the kitchen, Izzy and Beau were deep in discussion, and they both looked in Jess's direction, as the screen door slammed behind her.

"I'm ready." She tried to smile. Beau took her hand and picked up his case.

"Izzy says she'll explain to the boys, when they all get back." He smiled at her. "We'll go and have some breakfast somewhere."

"There's always Myers Cafeteria," said Izzy brightly.

"It won't be open at this hour of the morning," said Jess.

"You never know," replied Izzy. "Bendigo is buzzing with visitors. The shops won't miss an opportunity."

"Perhaps." Jess looked at Beau. "We could try it."

"Goodbye, Izzy, and thank-you," said Beau as he ushered Jess out of the kitchen.

"Think nothing of it, Beau. That's what families are for." Izzy smiled after them, and turned her attention to the children.

Soon they were walking along the footpath, heading in the direction of the town. Beau kept Jess close to him, and held her hand tight. They didn't speak as they made their way towards the Pall Mall.

"There's a tearoom just along the street," whispered Jess. "They might be open."

It was, and they walked through the door, the first customers of the day.

"What can I get you?" A bright-faced young waitress smiled as they sat at a table near the window.

Beau looked enquiringly at Jess.

"What will you have, Jess?"

"Just tea and toast, if I may. I don't think I could eat anything else."

Beau smiled at the waitress.

"Tea and toast for two, please, and maybe some strawberry jam?"

"Certainly, sir." She bustled away, leaving them to stare forlornly at each other.

"I'm so sorry, Jess." Beau clasped her hands across the table. "I hate leaving you like this, and I would give anything to be able to stay, but it sounds as though Matthew is very ill."

"Please take care, Beau." Her eyes brimmed. "I don't want to have to go through this again." Jess gripped his fingers.

"You're my whole world, Jess, and I promise I'll be back just as soon as I can." He smiled. "Now, come on, smile my dearest. I don't want to leave you with tears in those beautiful eyes. We have a wedding to plan, remember? Besides, you have a sister who is just itching to be part of the planning, if I'm not mistaken."

Jess did smile at this remark, and could just imagine Izzy taking charge.

"Yes, I fear Izzy will want to be a very important cog in the wheel."

She was silent for a moment, as she thought of Jack, and their wedding day. Her gown was in the camphorwood chest, along with the artificial berries that she had carried as she walked down the aisle. Was she really going to do it all over again?

Jess looked up into Beau's concerned grey eyes.

"What are you thinking about?" He squeezed her fingers.

Jess shook her head. "I was thinking about how life has changed, and how we have no idea what's ahead of us."

"You're not sorry?"

"I remember Izzy saying to me that there's always been something between us."

"Izzy said that?"

"She's very perceptive, my sister, in case you hadn't noticed."

Beau gave a short laugh. "Oh, I had noticed."

The waitress appeared beside them, a tea tray in her hands.

"Here you are then. Enjoy your breakfast."

"We shall," said Beau, as he reached for a linen serviette.

*

At ten o'clock, Jess and Beau were sitting close together on a station platform seat, their hands tightly clasped. It was happening all over again, the goodbyes and the promises to return.

"I hope Matthew will be alright, Beau."

"Yes, well Celia was extremely agitated."

"It all happened very quickly."

Beau turned to look at Jess. "What do you mean, Jess?"

Jess shook her head, and looked down. She was ashamed of the thoughts that had crept into her mind, but Celia had proved to be devious in the past.

"I just thought that maybe she over-reacted, that's all."

"Jess, what are you suggesting?"

"Nothing, Beau. I'm sorry. Forget what I said, please?"

He stared at her for a long moment.

"Jess, let's not spoil these last few minutes. I know Celia has done some outrageous things, but I think where it comes to Matthew, she's genuinely afraid."

Jess sighed. "Forgive me, Beau. I was so looking forward to these few days, and now that they've been cut short, I'm looking for someone to blame."

A whistle sounded further down the track. Beau stood up, lifting Jess to her feet.

"Be strong, darling girl." He wrapped his arms around her. "We will get through this, and there will be a future on the other side."

"I hope so, Beau; I do hope so."

The train thundered into the station, as Beau kissed her, and for a short time they were oblivious to everything and everyone around them.

Passengers spilled out on to the platform, anxious to begin their exploration of Bendigo and its Easter traditions.

"All aboard!" the voice over the loud hailer shouted.

Beau reluctantly released Jess.

"I'll telephone Margaret when I know what's happening, my love." He smiled. "Take care and know that I love you dearly."

Jess nodded. "Please be careful, Beau."

Beau picked up his case.

"Au revoir, ma Cherie. Je t'adore." He traced a finger down her cheek, and then he was gone.

"I love you, too, Beau," Jess whispered, but he didn't hear.

Telling the Children

Jess made her slow way back towards the Grey Goose, her thoughts decidedly bleak. How many times had she been through this scenario? Three times with Jack, and now this was the third good-bye she'd had to face with Beau.

How could she plan a wedding with so many walls tumbling around her? Maybe she needed to step back and not be so hasty in her decision to marry Beau? What if he caught the dreaded influenza? She gave a little sob. Could it really happen to her twice? She needed to talk with Izzy, and then perhaps her failing spirit would rise. Izzy had that knack of seeing the best of every situation.

As she passed the Grey Goose, Jess suddenly remembered that Jean would be waiting for her. She pushed open the side door, and walked along the passage to the bar door. It opened to her touch, and she entered. To her surprise, she saw Harry behind the bar with Jean. Both were laughing as they served the morning customers. Jean turned as Jess entered.

"Jess, love, you are not required this morning." Jean shuffled towards her. "Harry has agreed to help out while he's here." She smiled broadly at Jess. "I think he's relieved to get away from all the children."

Jess suddenly remembered that Harry had been a publican before taking over the general store in Swan Hill. She visibly relaxed.

"What a good idea, Jean. He's certainly in his element." She smiled at Jean. "Well, I'd better get home and take some of the pressure off Izzy."

"Before you go, Jess," Jean grasped her arm, "Harry's been telling me what happened. I am so sorry, my dear."

Jess shrugged. "History keeps repeating itself, Jean."

Jean's eyes twinkled suddenly.

"Harry also told me, and I hope you don't mind, that Beau has asked you to marry him. That's wonderful news, Jess dear, and I must say I'm not as surprised as I should be."

"You're not?"

"No. Heavens above, I've known that the man was besotted, long before he should have been." Jean chuckled. "I'm very pleased for both of you, and don't forget, if you're looking for somewhere to have a small gathering, then you'd better look no further than the Grey Goose."

"Thank-you, Jean. We're a long way from planning weddings at this stage. We have to get through this influenza crisis."

"Yes I know, love, but I'm just getting in first."

"I'm sure there won't be any other contenders, Jean, so I thank you for the offer."

"My pleasure, Jess. Now I'd better get back to the bar." Jean looked behind her. "Harry certainly has a way with the customers."

"Yes, he does." Jess smiled and made her way out of the noisy, smoke-filled bar.

*

When Jess arrived home, she found Izzy sitting out on the back verandah, and the children were all playing happily in the yard. Jess flopped into a chair beside her sister, and turned to look at her.

"Thank-you, Izzy, for sending Harry to the pub to take over from me. I really didn't want to face it this morning."

"It wasn't me, sister dear." Izzy affected surprise. "No, Harry was the one who suggested it when I told him what was happening." She sighed loudly. "He's probably enjoying himself immensely."

"Oh, he is."

They were silent for a few moments.

"Jessie, I feel so awful about what's happened. It's not fair!"

"I'm disappointed, naturally, but he did the right thing."

"Beau always does the right thing, Jess." Izzy took hold of her sister's hand. "He will do the right thing by you, Jess. He loves you deeply."

Jess felt her eyes fill. "But am I doing the right thing by him, Izzy?"

"It's only natural to have doubts, Jess, and you might feel that it's too soon, but you know my opinion, and I don't believe that waiting for a right time, is the answer. You must follow your heart." She leaned towards Jess. "Seize the day, little sister. You'll never forget your first love, and I feel sure that if Jack is looking down on you, he'll be saying, 'you couldn't have picked a better bloke, Jessie.'"

Jess sniffed, and wiped her eyes. "Yes, I know he would."

"Now, know that you are loved, and stop doubting yourself. Besides," Izzy stood up, "I want to be part of the planning committee for this wedding."

Jess laughed shakily. "Beau said as much."

"Did he now?" Izzy looked down on her sister. "Well, come on, Jess, we'd better get these children fed, and then decide what to do this afternoon. It looks like Harry is set for the day, so we can't count on him."

*

The family enjoyed a pleasurable day wandering around the town, trying out their skills at the sideshow alley and lining up for the more sedate of the fairground rides. They arrived home tired, and laden with stuffed toys.

After tea the boys vied for Harry's attention, as they displayed their trophies, and talked enthusiastically about their experiences. Harry smiled indulgently, and made all the appropriate noises. Izzy and Jess sat back and smiled.

"Help me out here, you two!" he whispered at one stage, looking beseechingly in their direction.

"You're doing fine, Harry." Izzy was unperturbed. "Jess and I have had them all day, so I think that a few minutes of your time is only fair, don't you, Jess?"

"Oh yes, certainly." Jess hid the smile.

Harry groaned. "I thought I could count on you, Jess."

"They'll be going to bed soon, Harry."

"Jess! Don't let him off the hook so easily!" Izzy was glaring at her.

"It's nearly eight o'clock, and I want to speak with them before they go to sleep." Izzy looked up at the clock, and immediately knew what Jess was saying.

"Of course, Jess." She turned to Harry. "It seems you're off the hook, Harry."

"Good." Harry pushed his chair back from the table. "I'll do one last thing for you two girls; I'll run the bath for them."

"Thank-you, Harry." As he moved off, Izzy whispered, "Make sure you sound happy about it all, Jess."

"Of course I will, Izzy. I am happy."

"Then show it, for goodness sake!"

*

An hour later, when the children were all scrubbed and ready for bed, Jess sat on Ben's bed, and asked them to sit with her.

"I want to talk to you, children," she said, as Grace clambered on to her knee.

"What about, ma?" Ben had picked up that his mother had something important to discuss with them.

"It's about Beau," began Jess.

"Where's he gone?" interrupted Edward. "He said he was coming for Easter."

"I know, Edward, and he's just as disappointed as we are, but his friend, Matthew, who runs the medical centre where he works, has been taken ill with the influenza virus."

"Like the one that killed dad?"

"The same one, Edward."

The boys were quiet for some moments.

"Before he went away," began Jess tentatively, "he did something rather special."

"What?"

"He asked me to marry him."

"You're going to marry Beau?" Ben looked puzzled. "But he's our friend."

"I know, Ben. Does that mean he can't marry me?"

Ben shook his head. "No, but what do we call him then?"

"Will he be our dad?" asked Edward bluntly.

"Edward, your dad will always be your dad, so no, you'll still call him Beau."

They were silent as they took in what their mother had said.

"Do you want to marry him, ma?" asked Ben matter-of-factly.

"Yes, Ben, I do."

"Do you love him as much as dad?"

This took Jess by surprise, and she struggled with an answer.

"I loved your dad very much, Ben, but he's no longer here to look after us. Beau wants to look after us, because we are all special to him. He is very special to me, and I do love him, but your dad will always be here in my heart, just as I hope he will always be in your hearts."

Grace, who had been sitting quietly, was now asleep in Jess's arms.

The two boys were silent.

"We won't have to go and live somewhere else, will we, ma?"

"I shouldn't think so, Edward."

Jess had to confess that she hadn't given the matter a thought until now, but it was a very important point; one that had to be talked about before any other arrangements could be made.

Matthew

Beau walked slowly up the stairs towards his office. He was weary. The train trip from Melbourne had been long and tiring. There had been no private compartments available, so he had sat up all night, listening to the clatter of the wheels, and thinking about the overwhelming problems that would surely face him on his arrival in Sydney.

The door to his office was unlocked. He walked in and put down his case. Loosening his tie, he went to the window, and pulled open the drapes. The view was still the same, but today the sea was grey to match his mood.

He heard footsteps along the corridor, and turned as Celia entered the room. Her brown eyes were large and luminous in her pale face, and he sensed the tears that lurked beneath the surface. She smiled wanly at him.

"I'm glad you're back, Beau."

"How is Matthew?"

Beau watched the tear that escaped and traced a course through her heavy make-up. "He's not doing well, I'm afraid."

"Is he out at Serendipity?"

"Yes." Celia cleared her throat. "When you're ready, can we drive out there?"

"Yes, I'm ready whenever you are, Celia."

"I'll fetch my coat, and meet you downstairs. The car is parked on the street."

She turned and walked out of the room. Beau took a deep breath, looked around the office and followed Celia, closing the door behind him. He headed downstairs.

Matthew's motorcar was parked several yards along the street. Beau stood beside it as he waited for Celia. She didn't take long.

Beau opened the door for her. Celia stepped elegantly up on to the running board, and sat in the passenger seat.

Within minutes they were out of the city area, and heading towards the leafy suburbs. Beau, who had been wondering about the lack of traffic on the roads, suddenly realised that it was Easter Sunday.

Celia was uncharacteristically silent as they drove out to Serendipity, and Beau noticed how she tied and untied the edges of her scarf. She was afraid, and he felt sorry for her. What would she do if anything happened to Matthew?

As they pulled into the driveway at Serendipity, Beau noticed Charlie toiling away in the garden. He saw them and waved. Beau smiled and waved back. Here was one lad who had found a purpose, and he felt pleased.

The wheels crunched on the gravel as the car slid to a halt at the front door. Beau climbed out quickly, and opened the door for Celia. She alighted, and gave him a tight smile.

Together they climbed the steps to the front door, and entered the foyer.

"Do we have any other cases here at the Lodge?" asked Beau, as they walked up the stairs to the wards.

"There are four, but only two from here; Matthew and one of the cleaning staff."

Beau looked up quickly. "Not Mrs. Evans?"

"No." Celia's brow creased. "A young lass by the name of Milly."

Beau sucked in his breath. *Matthew, how could you have been so foolish?*

As they neared the roped-off quarantine area, nurse Flanagan bustled out from one of the wards.

"Doctor DuBois, Mrs. Morley, I'll get some masks."

She hurried away, and returned a few moments later with white surgical masks and coats. "Put these on, please."

"How is my husband?" asked Celia.

"He's much the same; no better and no worse than when you saw him yesterday."

"And the other patients, nurse? How are they?" asked Beau, as Nurse Flanagan pulled back the rope barrier.

"I'm sorry to say that one passed away over night. The other two are like Doctor Morley; they're holding their own."

Beau smiled grimly from beneath his mask.

With a rustle of starched uniform, Nurse Flanagan led the way to the room where Matthew lay.

"He's just had morphine a few minutes ago. Doctor Freeman said to administer it every hour."

They stood beside the bed, and Beau looked down on his friend. How different he looked in a matter of days. His face was flushed and puffy, and his chest rattled as he breathed. He looked up at the two standing by his bed, and tried to speak, but the effort was too much for him.

Celia gave a little sob.

"If it's any consolation," said the nurse quietly, "his temperature is not as high as it has been. We're hopeful that the fever will break soon."

Celia walked swiftly from the room.

"Give him some oxygen, nurse. We need to keep him as relaxed as possible until the fever breaks, and change the compress every fifteen minutes, if you can. You're not here alone, are you?"

"No, I have one other nurse with me. There are only three patients here now, so we're coping alright."

"I'll look in on the other two, but you seem to be handling the situation very well."

"We're getting plenty of practise, I can tell you!" Nurse Flanagan laughed softly. "We thought the worst was over, but there's been a wave of new cases."

They walked into the corridor. Celia was leaning against the wall, her face awash with tears. Beau stopped in front of her.

"I want to look in on the other two patients, and then we'll go and find something to eat, and you can tell me how it all happened."

Celia nodded mutely.

Beau followed Nurse Flanagan into the next room where Milly Saunders lay, her face feverish, and her eyes oozing pus.

"How's her temperature?"

"Coming down slowly. I think she'll be lucky. She's young and healthy enough to fight it."

"Good. Keep up the oxygen, and wipe those eyes with some salt water."

"Yes, Doctor."

A nurse was attending to the third patient, so Beau quietly left instructions to bring down the fever as quickly as possible.

He took Celia's arm, and escorted her back along the corridor, where they discarded the coats and masks, throwing them into a basket.

"We need to have a talk, Celia, and as I'm ravenous, we'll find somewhere quiet to have some breakfast. I haven't eaten since I left Melbourne last night."

Celia stared at him, aghast.

They headed downstairs, and out to where the motorcar was parked.

"We'll head back into the city. There's a nice little cafe below my room. We'll have something to eat there, and then I can get changed out of these clothes, which I have been in longer than I care to admit."

"Whatever you say, Beau."

Beau stole a look at her profile. He had to admit that Celia was a beautiful woman, even in repose. It was a pity that her personality sometimes destroyed the image of physical perfection. She was certainly afraid, but was it fear for Matthew's welfare, or her own uncertain future?

Beau brushed the thoughts away, and concentrated on getting them both back to the city safely. Neither spoke for the duration of the journey.

They pulled up in front of Angela's Patisserie, and Beau alighted.

"So this is where you live?" Celia glanced up at the building.

"This is it, I'm afraid. They do have nice cakes and pastries." Beau smiled. "French pastries."

"Oh, I see."

Once inside, Beau motioned Celia to a small table, covered with a red and white check cloth. He knew that it would not be the sort of eatery Celia would choose to dine at, but it was where he was comfortable.

He went to the counter displaying a lavish assortment of cakes and sweet pastries, and turned to Celia.

"Tea or coffee?"

"Black tea, thank-you."

A fresh-faced young woman appeared at the other side of the counter, and smiled widely at Beau.

"Bonjour, Beau!" she exclaimed warmly. "What can I get you?"

"Two black teas, please Angela, and a plate of assorted pastries; your choice."

"Certainement!" There was a twinkle in her brown eyes.

"Merci."

Beau returned to where Celia was seated. Her expression was one of amusement.

"Is she French?" she whispered.

Beau shook his head. "No, but it adds to the ambience of the place."

"Hm." Celia was looking around. To her way of thinking, the décor was tacky, and a little overdone, with artificial flowers in heavy vases, and potted palms in every available nook.

"You don't like it?"

"Let's just say that I wouldn't have chosen it, Beau, but as you are the hungry one, then it's your choice." Celia smiled sweetly.

"We need to talk about Matthew, Celia." Beau was suddenly serious.

"What day did you catch the train to Melbourne, Beau?"

"Wednesday."

"Well, that was the day Matthew fell ill. I wasn't sure what was wrong with him, but he seemed pretty certain, and asked to be admitted into Serendipity. He didn't want to go to the General Hospital." Celia shrugged. "Of course, you know I can't drive the motorcar, so I had to call on daddy. He drove us out there."

"I see." Beau leaned forward. "You will have to monitor your own health for a week, Celia," he said in a low voice. "If you feel sick at all, you must let me know."

Celia stared at him. "You mean I could have caught this thing from Matthew?"

Beau looked around. They were the only customers in the café.

"It's a possibility."

"What's the likelihood of him recovering?" Celia's voice had a slight tremor.

"Fifty-fifty, I'd say. He's strong and healthy, so he stands every chance, and he got on to it very quickly. He did have the vaccine, I presume?"

"Yes, we both had the vaccine."

"It's not a guarantee, but it could help minimise the symptoms." Beau smiled at her stricken face. "We have to stay positive, Celia."

Angela chose that moment to bring the tea tray.

"Here you are then." She glanced from one to the other. "I hope you enjoy the pastries I've chosen."

"We will. Merci, Angela."

"You're welcome." Her brow creased. "Je vous en prie."

"Excellente, Angela."

The young woman giggled as she moved away.

Celia studied her with a hooded stare. "Is all that necessary, Beau?"

Beau shrugged. "Angela enjoys the banter."

"As do you, Beau." She let her gaze linger on him for a moment. "Tell me, how was your short trip to Bendigo?"

Beau looked up from pouring the tea. "Too short, unfortunately."

"And Jess?"

Beau handed Celia a cup of tea. "She's well." He placed the teapot on the table. "As a matter of fact, I've asked her to marry me."

Celia's porcelain features registered no emotion. She was silent for several moments, during which she took a sip of tea and then returned her cup to its saucer. Her movements were slow and controlled, as was her voice when she finally spoke.

"Beau, three years ago you walked away from me, leaving everything behind. You owned nothing. As I can see it, you still own nothing. How can you expect to support a wife, who already has three children? You have nothing to offer her!" Her eyes flickered as she focused them on Beau. "You can't do this, Beau! It makes no sense. It wouldn't be fair on her. Besides, we need you here."

Beau took a moment to compose what he needed to say.

"Celia, don't you think I've thought of all that? Getting a job won't be a problem, and as for me owning nothing, it's not high on my priority list."

"It should be! It would be on my priority list."

"Jess has a house, and I'm sure we can work things out."

"In other words, you haven't discussed it with her?" Celia's tone had a sting to it.

"We hardly had time, did we?"

"What if Matthew doesn't recover?" Her eyes glittered.

"Celia, I'm not going to leave you in the lurch at a time like this. I will wait and we'll see what happens. Matthew's recovery is at the top of my priority list, and I will do my best for him. You will do well to stay away from him, and make sure you haven't contracted the virus yourself. That's all we can do at present."

"If the cleaner at Serendipity is the only other person from here to have this disease, how is it that Matthew has it? He wouldn't have contact with the cleaner!"

"I really don't know, Celia." Beau had a horrible feeling in the pit of his stomach.

"We are all at risk of catching it, because we work in its environment."

Unexpected Surprises

Jess was like a cat on hot bricks, as she waited for news from Beau. She had a path beaten to her in-laws house.

"Jess, love, you can't keep walking around here on the off-chance that Beau will telephone. I'll let you know when he does." Margaret smiled at Jess's anxious face. "He only left here yesterday morning."

"I know, Margaret. I'm sorry."

"Don't be sorry, Jess. It's a terrible thing to have happened, and just when things are starting to go well for you." Margaret touched Jess lightly on the shoulder. "He told us all about it, and we're pleased for you, my dear, really pleased."

"You don't think I'm being too hasty?"

"No, I don't." Margaret sighed as she looked off into the distance. "He's a good man, and we wish you every happiness."

They were sitting on Margaret's front verandah, soaking up the last of the autumn sunshine. Jess smiled suddenly.

"When I told the boys, they seemed a little perplexed by the fact that I wanted to marry their friend, as though this would mean the end of that friendship."

"Children see things differently, Jess. Are they happy about it?"

"Yes, I think so, although they did ask me some very difficult questions."

"I'm sure they did."

The telephone rang shrilly from inside the house.

Jess leapt to her feet. "That could be him, now."

Margaret smiled as she got to her feet. "I'll see, shall I?"

Jess waited, her heart pounding, as Margaret walked slowly along the passage to the telephone. The seconds ticked by.

"It's for you, Jess."

Margaret handed Jess the receiver, and moved quietly away.

"Beau?"

"Yes, my dearest, it's me."

He sounded tired.

"What's the news, Beau? How is Matthew?"

"He's gravely ill, Jess, but I'm hopeful that he'll pull through. I'll do my best, anyway, to see that happen."

"I'm sure you will, but don't neglect your own health, please?"

Jess heard his soft laugh, and suddenly wished she were standing in the circle of his arms. He was speaking again.

"Celia is falling apart, Jess."

Of course she is! "All the more reason for Matthew to recover."

"I told her about us, Jess."

"And?"

"As I expected, she was less than enthusiastic. She reminded me that I have no worldly goods; nothing to offer you, so should not be considering marriage."

Jess swallowed her anger.

"I don't think that will be an issue, Beau."

"But it is something we need to talk about."

"There are a few things we need to discuss, but I'm not going to let them bother me. They will all be sorted out in time. In the meantime, you must take care of yourself." She added wistfully, "When will I see you again?"

"I don't know, Jess. There are quarantine camps being set up along the border now, so when I come down again, I'll probably have to stay for a week before I can continue into Victoria."

"So Swan Hill will have a quarantine camp?"

"Yes."

There was silence for a moment. "Are you extending?"

"No," said Beau quickly. "Take care, my love. We'll talk again soon."

Jess just had time to say, "I love you, Beau," before the line went dead.

She sighed as she put the receiver on its cradle, and when she looked up, she saw Margaret watching her from the kitchen doorway.

They smiled at one another.

"I must get home," said Jess quietly, "Izzy will think I've deserted her."

*

Easter Monday dawned, with the promise of pleasant weather, and the household was keyed up with the anticipation of once again going to the procession. The boys talked of nothing else, and Jess was about to chastise them, when there was a knock at the front door.

"I'll get it!" Yelled Edward, as he charged towards the door.

Jess stood shaking her head. "Ma, its Sally!" she heard him shout.

Jess hurried along the passage, and Edward flung open the wire door. The two women fell into each other's arms. Sally was crying.

"Oh, Jess," she sobbed, "I'm sorry it's taken me so long to come and see you."

"Don't be sorry, Sally." Jess untangled herself from Sally's embrace. "I know you've been busy. Come in, please!"

Izzy had appeared at the kitchen door. "This calls for tea, I suppose?" she said cheerfully. "Hello, Sally. I do like your new hairdo; very chic and modern."

Sally touched her bobbed locks, and smiled. "When in Rome, Izzy."

"Indeed." Izzy turned to the kettle.

"Sit down, Sally," said Jess, making way for Sally to sit at the table. "How is life in Melbourne?"

"Oh, with the influenza virus, we all have to be very careful. The hotels are closing earlier, and a lot of the community buildings are being used as temporary quarantine stations. I've been helping out, as the number of patients is outrunning the number of nurses."

"But you're not a nurse, Sally."

"I know first-aid, Jess. Besides, I don't have a teaching job at the moment. I'm doing some more study, so I need money to pay for my keep. Grandfather left me a tidy sum, but it will run out if I don't work."

"Of course."

"I have a young man I'm walking out with, too, Jess." Sally's cheeks flushed.

"You have? I'm so pleased, Sally." Jess paused briefly. "You knew, of course, that Martin Weatherall has returned to France. He has a young lady there, I believe."

"Oh, yes. Martin did write to me and tell me."

Edward had been sitting beside Sally, listening intently to the adult conversation.

"Ma's going to marry Beau!" he announced.

There was a stunned silence. Sally's features registered a number of expressions as she looked from one to the other.

"You're shocked?" Jess watched her young friend closely.

"Well, yes, you could say that, Jess." A frown creased her brow. "I think I've missed something here. I thought Beau had died."

Jess put a hand to her face. "I'm sorry, Sally. I hadn't told you, had I?"

Sally shook her bobbed head

"It's a very long story, Sally, and I will tell you sometime, but no, he didn't die. He's been in Sydney, and like you, has been caught up in the virus epidemic. He was here for Easter, but he had word that his colleague is very ill with the virus, so he had to leave."

Sally took a few moments to register what had been said, and then she smiled at Jess. "Jess, I'm so happy for you."

Izzy, who had been occupied making the tea, put the cups on the table.

"Where are you staying, Sally?" she asked.

"I still have grandfather's house, and I'm clearing it, ready for sale."

"Good! You'll make time to come to the procession with us, of course?"

"Of course."

*

That evening, as they sat in the lounge, discussing the events of the day, they all agreed that the procession had been much better than the one of the previous year. The Chinese dragon, Loong, was naturally the main topic of conversation, and even Grace and Freya had shown their excitement this year. It was the noise and smell of the firecrackers that had sent them running to their mothers' arms.

"Well," said Izzy finally, when the children were showing signs of sleep, "we'd better start packing our things, Harry. We'll have to catch the morning train whether we want to or not."

Harry sighed heavily. "I didn't realise how much I missed the pub scene, until now. Helping Jean O'Malley has reminded me of all the camaraderie."

Izzy smiled lazily as she rose from the couch, Freya asleep in her arms.

"It's a bit late for that, Harry."

"Oh, I don't know." Harry had a twinkle in his eyes.

"Harry!"

"Yes, my love?"

"Stop stirring, and come and help me get this child to bed."

Harry winked at Jess, who merely shook her head. She had to admit it would be nice to have Izzy and Harry close by, but she dismissed the thought, and turned her attention to getting three tired children to bed.

*

It was three o'clock the following afternoon, and Jess had just walked through her front door, after spending several hours at the Grey Goose. Izzy, Harry and Freya had departed on the morning train, the boys were at school and Grace was with Margaret, so the house was quiet.

She opened up the stove, and pushed the kettle over to boil. Her feet were aching, and she needed to sit down with a quiet cuppa, and let her thoughts unwind. Jean had spent the morning talking about Harry, and wishing that he lived closer.

"He certainly knows how to run a bar, Jess," she had said on several occasions.

Jess kicked off her boots, and pushed her favourite chair in front of the stove. Her head ached from the smoke that permeated the bar, and her clothes had a distinct tobacco smell. Jack had never smoked in the house, and had frowned upon those who did, and she had only ever seen Beau smoking outside. For a moment their faces drifted before her; Jack's with his soft brown eyes and gentle smile, and Beau's with his unfathomable grey eyes and slightly lop-sided grin. They were the two men she loved most in the world; one had gone from her, and the other was trying desperately not to be torn away from her.

Jess sighed and rose from the chair. As she lifted the kettle to pour water into the teapot, she heard voices on the back verandah, and Margaret, Charles and Grace appeared.

"Just in time for a cup of tea." She smiled at them.

"Everything back to normal, Jess?" Margaret began setting the table.

Charles pulled out a chair, and Grace scampered off to her room.

"I suppose it's as normal as it can get at present," sighed Jess, pouring the tea.

Margaret sat opposite Charles, and as Jess handed them both a cup, she looked across at him and nodded her head.

"Sit down, Jess," she said softly. "Charles has something he wants to say to you."

Jess frowned as she sat and looked from one to the other.

"What's this about, Charles?"

Charles cleared his throat, took a sip of tea and replaced the cup on its saucer.

"Margaret and I want to do something for you, Jess. Times are going to be difficult for you with Beau being in Sydney, and we'd like to make things easier, by having a telephone installed for you."

"A telephone?"

"That's right, dear," said Margaret. "You can't keep running around to our place to take his calls. Besides," she glanced covertly at Charles, "what you have to say is between the two of you. You don't need us listening in on your conversations."

"Yes, but…"

"There will be no 'buts', Jess," said Charles in his most commanding voice. "I have already been to see about the installation." He smiled, a rare event for Charles.

Margaret was also smiling at her, but her eyes were swimming with tears.

"How can I thank you?" Jess whispered, her throat tight.

"You don't have to, Jess." Margaret wiped her eyes on a white handkerchief. "We want to see you happy, and this is our way of showing that we care about you, and agree with what you are doing."

Jess reached across the table and took each of them by the hand.

"I am so grateful to both of you, for being here for us, and I'm sure Beau will feel the same. Thank-you."

"Don't get all wishy-washy on me, you two," growled Charles. "You know I can't tolerate weeping women."

Margaret smiled knowingly at Jess.

"No, Charles."

Beau's Dilemma

"Doctor DuBois?"

Beau turned before descending the staircase at Serendipity Lodge, and saw Edwina Evans hurrying towards him. The lower part of her face was covered with a white cotton mask, and her slight frame was enveloped in a large white apron.

She stopped as she reached him.

"How is Doctor Morley?"

"He's showing signs of improvement, I'm pleased to say."

He sensed rather than saw her smile.

"That's good. I can't imagine this place without him."

"No." Beau smiled wearily

"And Milly Saunders? Is she improving?"

Beau took a deep breath and shook his head.

"Not as I would have hoped, but we haven't given up on her." He looked keenly at her. "How are you coping, with the whole workload now on your shoulders?"

She shrugged. "I'm managing. Mind you, some help would be nice. Charlie helps me sometimes, when he's finished his own work."

"I'll see what I can do about getting you some more help." Beau turned to head down the stairs, but stopped when Edwina spoke again.

"I don't know whether I should mention this to you, but as you might be wondering why Doctor Morley and Milly are the only ones infected with this virus, then I feel I should tell you…"

"Tell me what?" Beau knew what was coming.

Edwina hesitated. "It's just that I accidentally came across them…" She stopped as Beau came up the stairs towards her.

"Mrs. Evans –Edwina- you don't strike me as the kind of person to engage in idle chit-chat."

"Oh, I'm not, Doctor DuBois. That's why I'm speaking to you. Their…intimacy surprised me." She spoke quietly.

Beau stared at her for a moment.

"Edwina," he said finally, "I want you to keep this to yourself. I do know about their relationship, and I would prefer that Mrs. Morley didn't find out about it from a member of the staff. She has already expressed concern to me over the coincidence."

"I'm really sorry, Doctor, but Milly has a very loose tongue, and had let the matter slip into conversation, on more than one occasion."

"Conversation with whom?"

"Some of the kitchen staff."

Beau sighed. This was not going to go away, he feared.

"Please, I'm begging you, if you hear anything more, try to quash it. We are doing our level best here, to see that they both survive this virus." Beau smiled thinly.

Edwina nodded. "I understand your predicament, Doctor."

Beau watched as she turned and walked swiftly along the corridor.

Oh, Matthew, we're not going to get out of this one, easily.

*

That evening, Beau sat, as he always did, on the tiny concrete balcony that overlooked the busy Sydney streets, and contemplated the significance of the events unravelling around him. Matthew's indiscretion was surely going to get him into serious trouble, not only with Celia, but also with the Board of Management. He had to circumvent it somehow, but just like the virus, he feared that news was spreading faster than it could be contained. He sighed and reached for his tobacco pouch. As he did, he heard a knock on his door. Frowning, Beau went to open it. It was Celia.

"May I come in, Beau?" Before he had time to answer, she had brushed past him, and entered his small domain. "So this is where you hide when you're not working?" Her eyes skimmed briefly around the small room.

"Come in, Celia," Beau said wearily, as he closed the door.

"I'll come straight to the point, Beau."

Celia looked too elegant for the small, cramped room in which she stood. Her aristocratic head was tilted back slightly, and her brown eyes looked too large for her pale face.

"What's the problem, Celia?"

Her jaw was working. "I need to know what is going on out at Serendipity, Beau?"

"What do you mean, Celia?"

"You know damned well what I mean!" Her fists clenched and unclenched. "What has been going on between my husband and the cleaner?" She spat the last word out.

"What have you heard?"

Celia blinked, and for a moment she looked completely vulnerable.

"What do you think I've heard, Beau? Shenanigans in the store-room, the utility room, anywhere away from prying eyes!" She sniffed loudly. "How do you think that makes me feel?"

Beau exhaled. "Sit down, Celia." He picked up the chair from the balcony, and put it down beside her. Celia sat heavily. "Who told you this?"

"Does it matter?" Celia turned tear-filled eyes towards him. "You knew, didn't you, Beau? You knew, and you didn't tell me."

Beau sat on the edge of the bed. He would have to be careful with his words.

"I guessed something was going on, before I headed down south; just before Matthew and Milly came down with the virus."

"Don't you dare use her name in the same sentence!"

"Be fair, Celia. Blame doesn't only go one way."

"In this case it does! Matthew would never have looked at her, if she hadn't seduced him."

"Don't you think it would be best to wait until Matthew can tell you himself?"

"You sound as though you condone what he has done."

Beau shook his head. "Of course I don't, Celia, but if we're going to be honest here, we both know Matthew's weaknesses."

"We're talking about a cleaning lady, Beau! It is not the same thing!"

"Isn't it?"

Celia stood up, smoothed her black velvet skirt, and looked across at Beau.

"Anyway, the other thing I came to tell you was that daddy wants to see you at the Clinic at eight o'clock tomorrow morning. Don't be late!"

With that, she swept past him, opened the door, and was gone.

Beau slumped.

Who had told her? Celia shouldn't have been out at Serendipity.

*

Beau straightened his tie, pushed a comb through his hair, and surveyed his reflection in the small mirror on the door of the bathroom cabinet. He grimaced.

He was about to be given a grilling by Celia's father, Clarence Bonner-Smythe, and he needed to look reasonably respectable. Under his present circumstances it was difficult, to say the least. If he'd had enough notice, he would have sent his suit to the cleaner to be pressed, but time had not allowed for that. It would have to do.

He looked at his watch, picked up his keys, and opened the door.

It was only a short walk to the Clinic, and it would help him clear his head, before going into the lion's den.

As he climbed the stairs to the Clinic, his steps slowed. The lion was already there;

he could hear his voice clearly. Beau looked at his watch. It wasn't yet eight o'clock. He slipped the watch back in his breast pocket, and continued up the stairs.

The door of his consulting room was ajar, and he heard Celia speaking.

"Daddy, you must make him see reason. We can't afford to lose him, especially now, with Matthew so ill."

"Never fear, my dear, I have it all in hand. He won't be able to resist."

Beau tapped on the door, and entered. Clarence Bonner-Smythe turned from his position at the window, and walked towards Beau, his beefy hand outstretched.

"Beauregarde!" he thundered. "How are you, my boy?"

Beau felt his hand crushed in a vicelike grip, and tried not to wince.

"I am well, sir." He glanced across at Celia, who stood to one side, the light from the window playing on her shimmering silver blouse. She returned his look, and then moved from the window.

Clarence Bonner-Smythe was a powerfully built man, with steely grey hair, and a well-clipped beard. He stood head and shoulders over Beau, and in his immaculate brown wool coat with its fur collar, he was an intimidating sight.

"I won't beat about the bush, Beauregarde," he began, as he drew himself up to his full height. "I have a proposition for you." He stopped, as though waiting for Beau to interject. When he didn't, he continued. "I have put in a recommendation to the Board, to make you a full partner in the Clinic and Serendipity Lodge."

Beau frowned, but remained silent.

"Beau!" Celia's sharp voice penetrated his brain. "Are you listening? Did you hear what daddy said?"

"Yes, I heard, Celia." Beau looked up into Clarence's piercing blue eyes. "May I ask why, sir?"

"You may well ask why, Beauregarde. I feel that you have earned the right to be a full partner, with Matthew and Celia, and in the absence of Matthew, due to his illness and probable confinement, then the timing is perfect, as I see it."

"And if it's not what I want, sir?"

Clarence's high forehead folded into a scowl. "Not what you want? Of course it's what you want! Besides, there will be an apartment to go with this position, and your wages will double." He made a harsh coughing sound. "Celia tells me that your accommodation is ordinary, to say the least."

Beau's head was spinning. He was being offered a full partnership, but as he looked at Celia, he knew exactly who had been behind this sudden move.

"I will have to give it some thought," he said thickly.

Clarence picked up his hat from the desk.

"I'll give you twenty-four hours. I shall expect your answer tomorrow morning."

The door rattled behind him and Beau was left staring at Celia.

"You would be a fool to knock back this opportunity, Beau." She was mocking him. "I can assure you, it won't come again."

As he looked at her, the expression in her eyes was triumphant.

Decisions

Jess looked cautiously at the elegant rosewood telephone, taking pride of place on a small table in the passage, outside her bedroom door. Charles stood beside her.

"It won't bite you, Jess," he said, laughing at her expression.

"No, I dare say it won't, Charles, but it will take some getting used to."

"You'll wonder what you did without it." He touched the slim lines of the receiver. "It's a later model than the one we have, of course, and takes up a lot less room. I think you'll be very happy with it."

Jess could see that he was enormously proud of the moment, and smiled her gratitude.

"I am extremely grateful to you and Margaret, Charles. I'm sure it will be a godsend."

"When the technicians have finished connecting it, I think Margaret would be pleased if you gave her a call. You know our number, of course?"

Jess nodded. "What do I have to do?"

Charles picked up the receiver. "Just pick it up, turn the handle on the base, and someone at the telephone exchange will ask you what number you want. It's as easy as that." He looked at his watch. "You should be connected to the exchange by this afternoon. I must go now, Jess, so enjoy your new telephone and we will look forward to hearing you speak to us."

"Yes, of course, Charles."

The door slammed behind him, and Jess was left alone with the modern contraption. "I suppose I'll get used to you," she muttered, trying to feel convinced.

Later that afternoon, as Jess returned home from the Grey Goose, the sound of the telephone startled her as she opened the front door.

Gingerly she picked up the receiver.

"Mrs. Jess Stanley?"

"Yes."

"This is the Bendigo telephone exchange, Mrs. Stanley. You are now connected to the system, and your number is 687. Let us know if we can be of any assistance to you. Your telephone is now ready for use."

"Thank-you," said Jess, quietly, and received a jolly laugh in reply.

"Don't be afraid of us, Mrs. Stanley. We're here to help."

"Well," said Jess hesitantly, "I would like to speak with Mrs. Charles Stanley." She paused. "Dear me, I've forgotten what their number is."

"That's not a problem, I can assure you. Hold the line, please."

Jess waited, and soon she heard Margaret's voice.

"Hello, Bendigo 176. Margaret Stanley speaking."

"Margaret, it's Jess."

"Jess, dear! How marvellous! You're connected already?"

"Yes. I've just arrived home from work."

"Splendid! You will be surprised at how easy it makes your life. Do you want me to bring Grace home yet?"

"No, she can stay a little longer. It will give me a chance to catch up on my housework before the boys get home. Jean told me today that she will be employing a young man to take over the bar work. I must say I'm relieved."

"That's good, dear. Charles and I have been worried about you. It's too much, when you have children to look after."

"Margaret, when Beau rings again, please let him know that I now have my own telephone, and that my number is 687."

"687. Yes, I'll do that, Jess. He will be surprised." Margaret giggled suddenly. "This is going to be fun, Jess; being able to talk to you, without leaving the house."

"I must go, Margaret, or I won't get my work finished before the boys get home."

"Of course, dear. 'Bye for now."

Jess heard the click as Margaret replaced her receiver. She did the same. The house was silent. For a few moments it had seemed as though Margaret was standing beside her in the passage. Now she was alone.

*

When the boys arrived home half an hour later, they rushed into the passage to examine the new telephone.

"It's not like grandma's!" enthused Edward. "Will we be able to use it, ma?"

"It will only be for special use, Edward."

"Can we tell Mr. Granger at school?" asked Ben.

"Yes." Jess nodded. "Mr. Granger will need to know our number."

"And Mrs. O'Malley?"

"Yes, I'll let her know tomorrow."

"Boy! The kids at school will be jealous, ma."

"There's no need to tell them," said Jess hurriedly, not wanting a repeat of the behaviour that had occurred when Charles had driven the boys to school in his motorcar. "Is that clear?" Both boys shrugged. "Now off you go; there are chores to be done."

*

As Jess was clearing the table later that evening, she heard the telephone ringing.

"I'll get it!" Edward leapt up from the table.

"No!" Jess said sharply. She sensed that it would be Beau. "I'll get it."

She walked into the passage, and slowly picked up the receiver.

"I have a trunk line from Sydney, Mrs. Stanley. Will you be receiving it?"

"Yes," said Jess, and waited.

There was a crackle on the line, and then she heard Beau's voice.

"Jess? Are you there?"

"Yes, Beau, I'm here."

"You have your own telephone now? That is a wonderful surprise."

"Charles thought it would make things easier for us." There was silence. "Beau? Are you still there?"

"Yes, my love."

"Is something wrong? Is it Matthew?"

She heard him sigh. "No, I think Matthew will pull through."

"What is it then?" Her heart began to hammer loudly.

"Something happened today, Jess, that has put me in a quandary. I honestly don't know what to do."

"Tell me."

"Celia's father, who is on the Board of Directors for the Clinic, is recommending me for a full partnership in the practice, and he wants my answer by tomorrow morning."

"Oh." Jess felt her world crumbling around her. "Are you going to accept it, Beau?"

"I don't know, Jess. I feel my arm has been twisted by Celia, but I also know that I'll never have this opportunity again."

Jess leaned against the wall for support, and her voice trembled as she spoke.

"Your work is important, Beau."

"You are important, Jess, and I would die rather than lose you." He paused. "Would you be prepared to move to Sydney?"

"I want to be with you, Beau, more than anything, but Celia wouldn't be happy with that arrangement."

"I can deal with Celia."

"Can you? She doesn't want us to be together, Beau."

"Are you extending?" A voice crackled in their ears.

"Yes," said Beau quickly.

"Beau, you have to do what you think is right." Jess felt the sob rise in her voice. She heard him take a deep breath.

"I haven't been given any time to think about this."

"And if you turn down the offer? What then?"

Jess heard his harsh laugh.

"I wish I could talk to Matthew, but he's not up to that yet."

"What then, Beau?" Jess insisted.

"I'll probably find myself out of work sooner than I had planned."

"I won't stand in your way, Beau." Jess's voice sounded hollow and far away.

"Jess, I won't leave you out of this; I can't, not now."

"Let me know tomorrow what you've decided. I'll stand by your decision."

"I love you, Jess. Don't ever forget that." Jess nodded, unable to speak. "I'll speak to you tomorrow."

The line went dead.

Jess hung up the receiver, and slid to the floor, her back against the wall.

Had it all been too good to be true? Beau would not be allowed to turn down such an offer, and she would not be allowed to be with him. That much she already knew in her heart. Bitter tears slid down her cheeks. She had been too quick to grasp at happiness, and now it was slipping out of her hands.

Beau and Celia

Beau put down the receiver, his hand trembling. He was overwhelmed by feelings of anger, frustration and unbearable sorrow. How could she do this to him? How could she have put him in this position where he had to choose between his job and the woman he loved?

He thumped his hands on Celia's desk. He needed to confront her; ask her why she was doing this now, when Matthew was temporarily out of the equation?

Beau hurried down the stairs. The building was empty, so he locked the big oak doors, and headed along the street. A fretful breeze was swirling leaves and papers along the footpath, and people walked with their heads down, anxious to be off the streets. There was a storm brewing.

Ten minutes later, Beau stood at the door of Celia's apartment. He waited for a moment before he rang the bell. His mood was sour, and he knew that he would have to be in control of his words, once Celia opened that door.

After several minutes, the door opened, and Celia stood there, wrapped in a blue satin gown, her hair in a towel.

"You should have given me prior notice, Beau," she said coolly, "before you came barging up here."

"I'm sorry, Celia, but I do need to talk to you."

She let her gaze move over him slowly.

"Give me ten minutes to get dressed, and then I'll see you."

The door closed in his face, and he knew that she would probably telephone her father. He sighed. He wasn't going to win this battle, if Clarence was firing the bullets.

Beau waited for more than ten minutes, and then the door opened. Celia was now dressed in a cream skirt and blouse, her wet hair hanging on her shoulders.

She stepped aside, and Beau entered the comfortable living room, with its plush green velvet chairs and elegant oak dining setting. Celia beckoned him to sit.

"Thank-you, but I prefer to stand."

"Then you won't mind if I sit?" Celia curled herself on to one of the velvet chairs. She opened a silver cigarette case, and proceeded to light a cigarette. Beau sensed that she was deliberately trying to unnerve him. Her movements were slow and calculated.

"What do you want to say to me, Beau?" she asked finally, as she blew smoke into the air.

Beau stood with his hands behind his back.

"Why are you doing this, Celia?"

"Doing what, Beau?"

"Forcing me to make a choice."

"I'm not *forcing* you to do anything, Beau. I am merely giving you the opportunity to advance your career. What father and I are doing is for your own good, Beau. You belong here."

"And what of Jess?"

"She doesn't belong here, Beau; surely you can see that."

"How dare you presume that Jess doesn't belong here? She belongs with me, and if she's not included in this job opportunity, then..."

"Then what, Beau?" Celia's elegant eyebrows lifted, and her eyes challenged him.

"Then I will have to turn down the offer."

Celia paused, blowing a plume of smoke in his direction.

"You won't do that, Beau." She gave a soft laugh. "I know you too well. I know what's good for you."

Beau closed his eyes momentarily. She was laughing at him; mocking him.

"What right have you got to say what's good for me?"

"I have every right. You are part of this Practice, and Matthew is going to need you more than ever now. You cannot desert us, Beau!"

"I can, if Jess is not welcome here."

Celia laughed scornfully. "She's a country girl, Beau! She doesn't belong in the city. She doesn't belong in your world."

"My world? And what exactly is *my world*, Celia?" She was staring at him now. "I have been a soldier, a vagrant, a barman, I have lived under trees for shelter, killed rabbits for food, walked in shoes with no soles, scrounged from generous people, and you talk about *my world?*"

"You know what I mean, Beau. I mean this world, this life you have made for yourself here."

Beau shook his head.

"I haven't made a *life* for myself, Celia. The only time I am truly content is when I am with Jess."

Celia crushed her cigarette into a silver ashtray, and Beau could see by her sharp movements, that she was becoming angry.

"You walked away from me once before, Beau, and I won't let you do it again!"

He had the answer he had come here looking for.

"So that's it? That's why you are going to all this trouble?"

"Of course it is!" She glared at him.

"And what about Matthew?"

"What about him?"

"Don't you think he deserves better?"

"He doesn't complain." Celia laughed. "Matthew's motto has always been *love the one you're with*. We both know where that has led him."

Beau stared at the woman he had once loved, and saw only bitterness and resentment in her classic features.

"Thank-you, Celia."

"For what? Making you see reason?"

"No; for making my decision easy." Beau turned on his heel and headed for the door. "I'll see myself out."

Celia sat for several moments, staring into the space that Beau had left behind. Then she reached for the telephone.

The Lion's Den

The door to Beau's office was ajar, so he pushed it open and walked into the room. Celia stood at the window, and for a brief moment Beau was reminded of a black widow. She was dressed entirely in black, and her dark hair was pulled back tightly into a bun at the nape of her neck.

"Daddy isn't here yet," she said without turning.

Beau crossed the room to stand beside her at the window. The scene below was full of everyday activity, as people moved about on the busy streets. The tram clanged its way through horse-drawn carriages and motorcars, and nothing was out of place.

Beau swept his gaze beyond the noisy streets, to the quay, where white-capped waves tossed a few gallant yachts about, and the ferry ploughed its regular course across the bay. It was a scene that was etched into his brain, but today it held no fascination, as storm clouds gathered across the horizon.

"What have you decided?" asked Celia, her eyes still focused on the scene below.

Beau was saved from answering her, as the door swung open and Clarence Bonner-Smythe strode into the room. The space seemed suddenly diminished by his size. He pulled off his gloves, threw a manila folder on to the desk, and sat heavily on Beau's chair.

"Good morning, Celia. Beauregarde?"

They both turned.

Celia planted a kiss on the top of her father's head. "Good morning, daddy."

Beau muttered a curt "good morning, sir," and moved to the opposite side of the desk. Clarence looked up.

"Sit down, my boy," he said, as he leafed through the papers before him.

"I prefer to stand, if you don't mind, sir."

"Suit yourself." Clarence sat back and surveyed Beau over horn-rimmed spectacles. "Well, what do I tell my committee?" His thick eyebrows beetled.

Beau was silent for a moment.

"Tell them I appreciate the offer, sir, but I have to turn it down."

Beau heard Celia draw a ragged breath, and Clarence stared at him, his expression frozen in the moment.

"What did you say?"

"I must turn down your offer, sir."

Clarence exhaled. "I thought that's what you said. Good God, man, you must have a very good reason to turn down an offer like this."

"Yes, he has a reason!" Celia whirled on Beau. "Haven't you, Beau?"

Clarence glared at his daughter, and raised a hand.

"Celia, I want to hear what Beauregarde has to say, so kindly hold your tongue."

Celia's lips compressed, but her eyes remained on Beau.

"Well, sir, I am planning on getting married in the near future, and I don't think it would be advisable for my wife to live here, in Sydney." Beau glanced swiftly at Celia. Her eyes narrowed.

Clarence smoothed a hand over his beard as he reflected on an answer.

"I don't see what difference it makes, whether you have a wife or not. The offer can include a wife." He spread his hands. "The apartment I had in mind for you, is large enough for two."

"She has three children!" Celia was still glaring at Beau.

"Three children?" Clarence sat back in the leather chair. "Well, in that case we could look at finding a larger apartment. How would that be?"

"It wouldn't work, sir."

"Why ever not? Unless they're from another planet, I cannot see a problem."

Celia snorted, and Beau clenched his fists as he struggled to control his anger.

Why was it that people like the Bonner-Smythes thought that if they snapped their fingers, everyone would jump to attention? Beau gritted his teeth.

"Look," said Clarence smoothly, "why don't I go through the details of the contract, and we look at it calmly and rationally?" He looked from Celia to Beau.

"I'm sorry, sir, I've made up my mind."

"And what about Matthew?" Celia's voice was high-pitched and almost out of control. "You owe it to him to stay, Beau! You can't walk out on him!"

Beau turned to Celia, his expression stony.

"I will stay until Matthew is well. I promise you that much."

"And if he doesn't get well?"

"He will."

"How can you be so sure?"

"I can only go by the progress he's making. He shows every sign of recovery."

"And how long will that take?"

Beau took a deep breath. "I can't be sure. A week? A month?"

"He will never forgive you, Beau."

"Oh, I'm sure Matthew will forgive me."

"Meaning I won't?"

"I didn't say that, Celia."

"No, but you implied it."

Clarence, who had been listening to the verbal exchange, shook his head impatiently.

"This is getting us nowhere. What do I need to do to make you change your mind, Beauregarde?"

"I'm afraid you can't, sir, and believe me, it pains me to say no."

Clarence drummed his fingers on the desk, and looked up at Beau.

"You are a very valuable member of this team, Beauregarde, and I am loathe to let you go on such a flimsy excuse. Your own war experience has put you on the forefront of ideas to deal with situations we haven't dealt with in this country. I must ask you to reconsider." The chair creaked as he sat back again. "I'm not a man to beg, but I implore you to think about it. I will give you more time to discuss this with your future wife, and then when Matthew is up and about, we can discuss it again, with him." The idea pleased him.

Beau didn't want to procrastinate, and then find he had to answer the same questions at a later date. He could not, would not put Jess through the ordeal of having to deal with Celia. It was unthinkable. It would be like throwing her to the wolves. No, he had made up his mind. He had to walk away, for everybody's sake.

Beau squared his shoulders and looked straight at Clarence.

"No, sir. I have made up my mind."

"That's it?"

"That's it, sir."

Clarence drew a long breath.

"Very well. I can say no more."

"Thank-you, sir." Beau shot a look at Celia, whose expression was one of unbridled anger. "Now, if you will both excuse me, I have something I need to do before surgery."

Beau nodded curtly, and turning on his heel, he exited the room. He felt like a soldier again, having to explain himself to a senior officer. Now he had to telephone Jess and tell her of his decision.

*

"I can't believe how easily you let him off the hook, daddy!" Celia rounded on her father. "What happened to the offer he couldn't refuse?"

Clarence removed his spectacles, folded them, and slid them into the pocket of his immaculate white shirt. He looked up at his daughter.

"His mind was already made up, Celia." He shrugged. "There was nothing I could do."

"His loyalty is to Matthew! He can't leave like that!"

Clarence stared at his daughter for some moments, seeing perhaps for the first time, the struggle she was having with all of this. There was a kind of desperation etched on her features.

"Celia," he said finally, and as gently as he could, "I don't believe it's Beau's loyalty to Matthew that concerns you the most; it's his loyalty to you. Am I right?"

Celia merely blinked and moved towards the window.

"You can believe what you like, daddy! Beau belongs here!"

"Celia, you are Matthew's wife. Your relationship with Beau ended a long time ago. You will never recreate the past, no matter to what lengths you may wish to go. Beau is free to marry who ever he chooses, and in my opinion, he must love this woman very much. Let it go, my dear." Clarence lifted himself out of the chair. "Matthew is the one who needs your attention right now." He picked up the manila folder. "We will find somebody who is willing to accept this offer."

"They won't have Beau's experience." It was just a whisper now.

Clarence moved across to Celia, and placed an arm around her rigid shoulders. "Ah! It's times like these that I wish your dear mother could smooth out the road for you. I've never been the best at that." He patted her shoulder. "Come, my dear. Why don't we go and have some breakfast at Mario's?" He pulled out his watch. "You do have time before the Clinic opens its doors, don't you?" Celia nodded her head.

"Good girl." Clarence was back on relatively safe ground. "Dry your eyes, and we'll be off. We can discuss another strategy while we eat."

*

Beau hurried down the stairs after leaving the surgery. He decided that it was best if he didn't use the telephone in Celia's office, so he headed along the street towards the Post Office. His feelings were mixed, and he was anxious to hear Jess's voice. She would calm the storm within him. The one thing he couldn't tell her about his decision was that it had been made to spare her from Celia's obvious vendetta. No, that wasn't entirely true. He had to admit to himself that Celia's behaviour was irrational, and he needed to distance himself from her, even though he knew that Matthew would be disappointed by his decision.

Beau walked slowly up the Post Office steps to the telephone booth. Stepping in, he pulled the door shut. Stale cigarette smoke lingered in the air.

Within a few minutes he was listening to the telephone ringing at the other end of the line. He waited.

"Hello," he heard above the crackle.

"Jess, darling, it's Beau."

"Oh! Hello Beau." He heard the hesitation in her tone.

"I've turned down the offer, Jess."

There was silence at the other end, before Jess spoke.

"You have? Beau, are you sure that this is what you want to do?"

"I'm sure, Jess."

"I'm really pleased, naturally, but I know how important this work is to you, and…"

"Jess, I am sure. I'll find work down south, of that I am confident. In the meantime, I've said that I will stay until Matthew is well enough to go back to work."

"What was their reaction to your decision?"

Beau paused.

"They weren't happy, but I have to think about us now, Jess, and taking you away from all that's familiar to you is out of the question."

"So you made your decision based on my needs?"

Beau gave a short laugh.

"Not altogether, my dearest. I have to admit that I yearn for the quiet life again."

"Are you extending?"

"Yes."

"Beau, I hope you won't regret this decision down the track, and blame me for it." Jess's tone was warm, and Beau sensed the smile on her lips.

"Would I do that? No, my place is with you, and even if I have to beg Mrs. O'Malley for my old job back, there will be no regrets."

"Oh, Beau, you have made me so happy. I must confess that I haven't slept since we spoke last."

"Well, my darling, you can sleep easy now, and so will I."

"When will we see you?"

"It depends on Matthew's progress, but I can assure you that when we next meet, I will be there to stay."

"I will look forward to that. In the meantime, please, please stay well."

"Good-bye, my dearest."

"Good-bye, Beau. I…"

The line went dead.

Beau didn't hear "I love you."

Part Three

Resolution

Matthew's Recovery

Beau stood looking down on Matthew. His skin was still pallid, his eyes sunken, but his breathing was regular. No longer did he have that ominous death rattle. He had turned the corner, and Beau was confident that he would recover from the virus that had taken hold so quickly.

Matthew opened his eyes and stared up at Beau.

"Hello, old chap," he croaked, as he tried to smile.

"Welcome back, Matthew." Beau patted his friend on the shoulder.

"How long have I been here?" Matthew tried unsuccessfully to sit up.

"A week." Beau shifted Matthew's pillows, so that he could recline.

"My goodness! That long?"

"I'm afraid so, but you're over the worst of it now, thank God, and you can look forward to tackling all those tasks that have been piling up, waiting for you." Beau grinned, and received a weak smile in response.

"You jest of course, Beau. I couldn't tackle anything at the moment."

"Yes, of course I jest. The important thing is to get you well, so that…"

"So that you can break the good news to him, Beau?"

Beau stared at Celia as she entered the ward, her face partly covered by a mask.

"What good news?" Matthew stretched out a hand towards his wife, but she refrained from taking it.

"It can wait, Matthew," said Beau quickly.

"No, it can't! Matthew, I…"

"Not now, Celia!" Beau's tone was sharp.

Matthew was staring from one to the other, across the bed. Their eyes, above the masks that obscured their faces, glared across the space.

"What is going on?" he whispered.

"Beau is leaving us," said Celia quickly, and switched her gaze to Matthew.

"Beau? Is this true?" Matthew's shoulders slumped with the exertion of trying to sit up on the pillows.

"It's true, Matthew, but we don't need to discuss it right now."

"I think we do!" Celia's brown eyes bored into him. "Daddy has recommended Beau for a full partnership in the Practice, and he has turned him down."

"What?" Matthew began to cough, and his forehead beaded with perspiration.

Beau ran to the door.

"Nurse!" he called out. "Bring a compress to Doctor Morley's ward, please!"

Turning back into the room, he glared at Celia. "Now is not the time, Celia!"

"Oh, I think it is, Beau." She turned to Matthew. "I think it's time for a lot of things. There's plenty of dirty linen needs attending to, and no time like the present."

At that moment, a nurse scurried into the room, a compress in her hand. She laid it across Matthew's brow, as Beau grabbed Celia by the arm and propelled her out into the corridor.

"How dare you, Celia! Have you no concern for Matthew's health?"

"Let me go, Beau! You're hurting me!"

Beau released her, and stood back.

"I know what you were going to say, Celia, and I forbid it!"

"You forbid it?" she spat the words out. "You?"

"Matthew is my patient, and I can't allow you to go back into that room, Celia. He may be recovering, but he's still fragile."

"Matthew is my husband, and I'll see him when I like!"

Beau raised his hands, as if in defeat. "Look, Celia, let's not get into a slanging match here. There are things we need to discuss, but not here, not right now."

Celia fixed her gaze on him, as the nurse rushed past them. She shrugged.

"Very well." She paused, staring off into the distance. When she returned her gaze to Beau, he sensed that she was smiling behind her mask. "It's not going to make a great deal of difference really, because when Jess receives my letter, the whole situation should reverse."

"You wrote to Jess?"

"I did."

"Saying what, exactly?"

Celia pulled off her mask. She was smiling. "You'll find out soon enough, Beau."

With that she turned on her heel, and walked away, her slim hips swaying, and her heels clicking on the linoleum.

Beau clenched his teeth as he watched her disappear around the corner of the corridor. What did she have left in her arsenal now? He walked slowly back into the room. Matthew was breathing quickly. He looked at Beau, his eyes troubled.

"She knows about Milly, doesn't she?" he whispered through cracked lips.

"I'm afraid she does." Beau pulled up a chair, and sat heavily. "Milly also has the virus, Matthew."

"Oh, God, no!" he croaked. "How is she?"

"Hopefully she will recover."

Matthew was silent for a moment. "I'm a bloody fool, Beau."

"No more than the rest of us."

"What did Celia mean when she said you'd turned down an opportunity to become a full partner?"

"I suppose I might as well tell you; the cat's out of the bag anyway."

"It certainly is, old chap."

"I've asked Jess to marry me."

For a moment, Matthew's eyes gleamed with pleasure.

"Glad to hear it, Beau, but why turn down Clarence's offer?"

"I couldn't bring Jess and the children up here, Matthew. Let's be honest. Celia would make life a misery for all of us."

Matthew sighed.

"Celia is becoming very irrational, Beau. I sometimes wonder whether she's going to finish up like her mother."

"In an institution? The thought had occurred to me, too, Matthew."

"How long do you think I'll have to recuperate?"

"I don't know. Another week, maybe?"

"So what is your plan, Beau?"

"My plan is to see you back on your feet, and then I'll leave." He patted Matthew on the shoulder. "Of course, we all know plans can change."

And I'm sure they will.

Celia's Letter

Jess felt a sense of relief after talking with Beau. He had reassured her that everything could now go as planned, and that he had no regrets. What he was doing was for her and the children, and nothing would change that.

As another Anzac Day was approaching, the boys announced that Mr. Granger would be holding a special service at the school, even though the viral epidemic had stopped many of the public celebrations.

Jess read the note that Ben handed her, and knew it was something she had to face. There had been no physical recognition of what had happened, until now, and she needed to lay Jack to rest.

She put the note on the sideboard and turned to Ben.

"Are you going to write a poem this year, Ben?"

"I have already, ma."

"Good. I look forward to hearing it. What about you, Edward? Have you written anything special?"

Edward shrugged. "Maybe."

Jess ran her hand through his tousled blonde hair.

"And you're not going to tell me? That's a change for you, Edward."

"It's a secret, ma."

"Well, I'm very glad you're both doing something to honour your father." She felt her voice quivering, so she changed the subject. "Would you two like to walk around to grandma's and bring Gracie home?" They were about to argue. "I'm sure grandma will have something delicious for afternoon tea."

Hearing that, they decided that they would both go and get Grace.

Jess walked to the front door with them, and after watching them cross the road, she lifted the lid of the letterbox. There was a letter. It wasn't from the Base Records Office. Not recognising the neat handwriting, she turned it over. On the back she read: Celia Morley, and a Sydney address.

Her heart did a little plummet. Why was Celia writing to her? Was there something wrong with Beau?

She hurried up the front steps, and sitting on the bench seat, opened the letter. It began:

> *Dear Jess,*
> *I know you would not have been expecting to hear from me, but I felt I had to write and put you in the picture.*
> *Matthew and I are worried that Beau is making the wrong decision by leaving his work here, when he has so much to give.*
> *This practice needs him if it is to make its mark in all the new techniques that are developing because of the war. His experience is vital.*
> *What he doesn't need is a wife and three children to hold him down. I know he doesn't see it that way at present, but he will come around to our way of thinking, and I'm afraid you would find yourself out of the frame. I know Beau. I was married to him for six years, before the war took him away from me. His work was everything to him.*
> *I should like to think that you have his best interest at heart, in which case you need to reconsider his proposal.*
> *I am prepared to do whatever it takes to keep him here. His loyalty has to be to Matthew and me.*
> *I trust you understand, and will do what is necessary.*
> *Celia*

Jess was shaking inside. This was preposterous! She was not going to be a party to it. Pushing the scented paper back into the envelope, she decided that she needed to show it to Jean, but first she had to telephone Margaret.

"Yes, dear, the children can stay a while longer," came Margaret's voice. "There's nothing wrong, is there?"

"No. I just need to see Jean."

"Alright, dear." There was a pause. "Charles says he'll drive them home at five o'clock. Is that enough time for you?"

"Yes, thank-you, Margaret."

Within a few minutes, Jess was hurrying along the street towards the Grey Goose. The side door was open, so she let herself in. Jean was behind the bar with her new young apprentice barman, Norman Reed.

Jess tried to attract Jean's attention, and eventually Norman looked her way, and whispered something to Jean. She shuffled over.

"Jess, love, did you forget something this morning?"

"No, Jean. Could we talk, please?"

"Certainly, Jess." She turned. "I'm going to my sitting room, Norman."

"Yes, Mrs. O'Malley."

"Good." Jean turned back to Jess. "He's a quick learner, like you, Jess. Now come on, I want to know what this is all about."

Jean shuffled along the passage, and into her private sanctuary. She sat in one of the two large lounge chairs, and beckoned Jess to the other.

"Take a weight off, Jess." She sighed.

Jess sat stiffly, and took the letter out of its envelope.

"I want you to read this, Jean, and tell me what you think."

Jean held the letter away from her face.

"The writing's a bit small, isn't it? My old eyes can hardly see it. Who's it from?"

"It's from Celia."

Jean looked up sharply and frowned. "*The* Celia?"

"Yes."

Jean scanned the page, squinting every now and then. When she had finished, she folded it, and handed it back to Jess.

"Well, well!"

"What should I do about it?"

"I would screw it up and throw it in that fire over there, but if that had been your intention, you would have already done it."

"She has a point, of course. His work is important."

Jean leaned forward, her eyes glittering. "Jess, you've heard the old saying 'hell hath no fury like a woman scorned'?"

"I have."

"That is Celia. You must recall how anxious she was to have Beau back, after his suicide attempt? She must have left no stone unturned then to track him down. She has him in her circle now, and she is not about to let him go."

"But she's Matthew's wife. She has no hold over Beau."

"You think not?" Jean leaned back in her chair. "The war took him away from her, remember? I don't think she was prepared for that."

"Do I answer it? Do I tell Beau?"

"Neither, at the moment. Let her stew on it for a few days."

"And Beau? What if he telephones?"

"No, I wouldn't say anything, unless she's told him, of course." Jean frowned.

"What else is troubling you, Jean? Do you think I have been too hasty in all this?"

There was silence for a moment. "You do, don't you?"

"No, my dear. Beau loves you. It's just that…"

"It's just that Celia is determined to destroy what we have? Is that what you're trying to say?"

"Yes, I think so." Jean looked seriously at Jess. "The point is, are you strong enough to withstand what she obviously plans to dish out? Are you both strong enough?"

"I hope so."

"Well then, I've told you what I think. Now I'd better go and help Norman." Jean rose slowly. "By the way, Jess, I did hear on the grapevine that Sid O'Connor is back in town. I thought you might be interested to know."

Jess looked up quickly.

"Sid O'Connor? That's all we need, Jean."

*

Jess was busy washing the dishes after tea, when the telephone rang in the passage. Drying her hands on her apron, she rushed to answer it.

"Trunk call from Sydney, Mrs. Stanley."

"I'll take it," said Jess quickly.

After a few moments she heard Beau's voice. "Jess?"

"I'm here, Beau."

"How are you? How are the children?"

"We're all very well. And you?"

"Oh, I'm alright, I think."

"You think? What's wrong, Beau?"

There was a moment's silence.

"Jess have you received a letter from Celia?"

He knew. "Yes, I did, today."

"What does she say, Jess? I need to know."

"I'll get it, and read it to you. Just a moment."

Jess put the receiver carefully on the small table, and hurried to the kitchen, where she retrieved Celia's letter from the dresser.

Back in the passage, she picked up the receiver.

"Are you still there, Beau?"

She heard him take a deep breath. "Yes."

"I must admit it puzzled me why Celia would be writing to me, but I think she makes herself very clear, Beau."

"Does she. You'd better read it to me."

"Are you extending?" a voice interrupted.

"Yes," said Beau sharply. "Go on, Jess."

Jess read what Celia had written. She heard Beau's sharp intake of breath.

"She had no right, Jess! I'm so sorry that you have to endure this."

Jess heard the bitterness in his voice.

"Beau, we will both endure this. I won't let it stand in the way of our being together, no matter what she says. If you love me, and I know you do, you must not let Celia destroy us." She felt the sob rising in her throat.

"She will try, Jess."

"She can try all she likes; I won't be moved! I won't!"

Jess heard his short laugh. "I'm very tired, Jess, what with all the problems in the medical field at present, and having to deal with Matthew's patients as well. I don't need this, but I'm very pleased to know that you're not going to back down. I only hope you know what you're dealing with."

"Jack had a saying, and I can't remember the exact words, but it means we will never be tested beyond our endurance."

"That's not always the case, Jess."

"I have a saying, too, my dearest. 'Something worth having is worth fighting for.'"

"Yes, it is."

Anzac Day

It was Friday, April 25th, and families were gathered in the school quadrangle, while Mr. Granger organised teachers and pupils for the short commemorative service about to take place.

A temporary podium had been set up, and several children were standing quietly in front, each carrying a wreath of fresh flowers. Edward was among them.

It was nine o'clock in the morning, and a fresh breeze was already chasing the fallen leaves from the Liquid Amber trees. Jess pulled her coat around her, as she stood with Margaret and Charles. Grace jumped excitedly in front of them.

"That's enough, Gracie," said Charles sternly. "Stand still now; it's about to start."

Grace grinned up at her grandfather, and took his proffered hand. Jess and Margaret looked at one another and smiled.

Mr. Granger stepped on to the podium, and the noise in the quadrangle ceased.

"Good morning, ladies and gentlemen and pupils," he began in a loud voice. "As you already know, ANZAC services for our soldiers have been curtailed this year, because of the influenza virus that sweeps across our nation. I thought that, as a mark of respect, we would hold a small gathering, and reflect individually on what it has meant for our community. We will begin with the raising of the flag, and the National Anthem."

He nodded to Miss Tyrrell, who played a loud chord on the piano that had been wheeled out for the occasion. Everybody sang lustily.

Following God Save the King, Mister Granger nodded to a young man standing beside the flagpole. He raised a trumpet to his lips, and men removed their hats as the strains of The Last Post rang out. Silence followed, and then the Reveille.

As Jess wiped her eyes, she heard Mr. Granger's voice reciting The Ode to the Fallen.

"They shall grow not old, as we who are left grow old.
Age shall not weary them, nor the years condemn.
At the going down of the sun, and in the morning
We will remember them."

Margaret placed an arm around Jess, as she stood trembling uncontrollably.

"You're allowed to cry, Jess," she whispered.

"And now," went on Mr. Granger, "I will read out the names of the fallen from our own community, and the children you see before me, will lay a wreath for each one, at the foot of the flagpole."

As he proceeded to read out the names, Jess closed her eyes, and squeezed hard on Margaret's hand. When she heard Jack's name, she opened her eyes to watch Edward walk towards the flagpole. He carried a wreath for his father. It was almost too much for her to bear. She swallowed the lump in her throat, and blinked rapidly. She was laying Jack to rest and her heart was heavy.

When all the children were standing with their classmates, Mr. Granger once again took the podium.

"I'd like to finish this solemn occasion with a poem by one of our pupils. He wrote such a memorable one last year, that I thought it fitting to ask him to write one for this year. I speak of Benjamin Stanley."

Jess watched as Ben made his way to the podium. Mr. Granger said something to him, and he shook his head, before standing erect beside the podium.

"What is your poem called, Ben?" asked Mr. Granger.

"It's called 'I Don't Understand.'"

When the clapping had died down, Ben began:

> *"I don't understand it – war, I mean;*
> *How it takes people far away.*
> *Some come home, but others don't, and it's these we remember today.*
> *Everyone will pay respects,*
> *And I know my ma will cry,*
> *When they raise the flag and say the ode, and the Last Post fills the sky.*
> *I can just remember the day dad left,*
> *And I knew everyone was sad.*
> *He said to me, 'Look after your ma; I'm depending on you, my lad.'*
> *No, I don't understand what war is about*
> *Or why my dad had to go.*
> *I've been told that it was to keep us safe*
> *But I don't think I'll ever really know."*

*

The short ceremony was over. Jess walked across to where the wreaths lay beside the flagpole, and stooping down, she read the notes that had been written on each one. When she got to Jack's, she saw that it had been written in Edward's hand. Jess knelt and turned it over. Edward had written a few lines, which read:

> *"Dad, I was a bit young to remember you on the day you went away,*
> *But I do remember our cricket match, and how we made you play.*
> *You weren't very good at catching, and we laughed when you got hit.*
> *Goodbye dad, we all miss you, and more than just a bit.*
> *Love Edward.*

Jess crumpled to the ground, as she let her tears fall unashamedly. A hand touched her shoulder, and she looked up to see Edward standing beside her, his eyes large and unblinking. Jess gathered him into her arms and wept.

"Your father would be so proud of you, Edward," she whispered into his hair.

"I'm glad you read my poem, ma." His voice was husky. "Mr. Granger was pleased with me. He said I'd give Ben a run for his money."

"Did he say that?" Jess tried to smile. "Maybe you will, Edward. Maybe you will."

Edward pulled away from his mother's grasp. "I'd better go back to class, ma."

"Yes, Edward, off you go."

Jess watched as her son ran across the quadrangle and disappeared into the school building. She got to her feet. Margaret and Charles were standing a little way off, and they came forward, Gracie skipping beside them.

"That was lovely," said Margaret. "Ben did very well again."

"Yes." Jess wiped her eyes. "Edward has something here you should read, too."

They moved across to the wreaths and Jess stood while they read each one. When she had read Jack's, Margaret turned, her eyes filled with tears.

"I think Jack will live on in both those boys," she whispered.

Jess nodded. "He will." She took Gracie by the hand. "Now I must get home."

"We must, too," said Charles, and Jess could see by his expression, that he was moved by what he had read. "Come, Margaret. We'll see you later on, Jess."

Jess watched them walk away, and as she moved off, she heard a voice beside her.

"Jack would be proud of his boys, Jess."

She turned to see Audrey Maitland standing beside her. Jess smiled.

"Yes, Audrey; very proud."

"There's a wreath here for my Frank; written by one of the children. It's all very touching, isn't it? Mr. Granger sets a lot of store by these sorts of things."

"Yes, he does. What is Frank's message?"

Audrey leaned over and picked up a wreath. She read the card.

"It says: Frank Maitland. He died in the line of duty, and lies buried far away, but we will remember what he did, and forever be grateful."

"That's lovely, Audrey."

Audrey sighed. "I'd say the teachers helped out, but it's very nice; very nice."

Jess looked at her care-worn face and smiled.

"How is Billy getting on?"

"Oh, he's alright. His job at the railways keeps him occupied, and I'm very grateful for that. So many of the boys are out of work, and that's a recipe for disaster."

"Come home with me and have a cup of tea, Audrey. I know I'm ready for one."

A brief smile lit her eyes. "That would be lovely, thank-you, Jess."

"I would normally be working for Mrs. O'Malley, but she has a young man behind the bar now, and to tell you the truth, I'm glad."

"Our lads need the jobs, Jess. Has he returned from the war?"

"I believe so."

They walked in companionable silence, until they turned into Oleander Street, and Jess stopped, a frown creasing her brow.

"Is that someone standing outside my gate, Audrey?"

"It looks like it." Audrey shielded her eyes from the glare of the autumn sunshine.

"It looks like Sid O'Connor. Jean said he was back in town."

Jess's mouth went dry, as she recalled her last encounter with Sid O'Connor.

"The last time I saw him," she whispered, "he threatened me, and then stole blankets from my sleep-out. I wonder what he wants?"

"He'll be up to no good, if I know him."

The two women walked on, until they were within a few yards of the pacing figure. Gracie ran on ahead.

"Gracie! Come back here!"

Jess saw Sid turn at the sound of her voice, and dropped the cigarette he'd been smoking. Crushing it beneath his heel, he then lifted his cap.

"'Mornin', Mrs. Stanley." He smiled, and Jess caught a glimpse of yellow teeth.

"Good morning, Sid. What brings you back into the neighbourhood?"

"I'm back f'good." He smiled at Audrey. "'Mornin' Mrs. Maitland."

Audrey ignored him. After all, hadn't he been the cause of Billy's brush with Military law enforcement?

"What are you doing here, Sid?" Jess repeated stiffly.

Sid pulled off his greasy cap, and began twisting it in his hands.

"Firstly, I wanna say I'm sorry f'my behaviour the last time we met." Audrey snorted. "Secondly, I've returned the blankets I stole from y'sleep-out." He nodded towards the front verandah. "I put 'em up there."

"You've got a nerve coming back here!" Audrey sniffed with disapproval.

Sid looked down at his feet. "Tell the truth, it all fell apart with Phyllis an' me, an' she took off with another bloke." He shrugged. "Dunno where she is now."

"What happened to the child?" Audrey asked quickly.

"She'll be twelve months old now." He smiled suddenly. "Her name's Hope."

"Is she with her mother?" This came from Jess.

"Yeah." Sid looked at Audrey. "I dunno whose child she is, Mrs. Maitland. I think Billy's lucky to be out of it. I don't think she's mine, either, but she's a little doll, or she was when I last saw 'er."

Jess looked at Audrey. "So you've come back to look for work?"

"I'd like t'get me old wood run back again."

"Surely you don't expect that people have been sitting around, waiting for you to return?" Audrey was indignant. "It's like your cheek!"

For a fleeting moment, Jess almost felt sorry for him. There was a hangdog look about him now. The cocky Sid O'Connor was certainly not visible.

"Get on with you, Sid O'Connor!" Audrey meant business. "You won't get work in this neighbourhood!"

Sid put his cap on his head, and looked at Jess.

"What about you, Mrs. Stanley? I heard what happened to Jack; I'm real sorry."

"I'll have to think about it, Sid. After all, you did leave under rather a cloud."

Sid nodded glumly. "I'll come back in a day or two, to see if you've changed y'mind." He lifted his cap. "Good day t'both of ya."

As he shuffled off along the street, Audrey turned to Jess, her eyes wide.

"Jess, you're not going to take him back again? He's bad news is Sid O'Connor!"

"I know, Audrey, but he's obviously been dealt a cruel blow from Phyllis."

"That little tart! I'm not really surprised, but that's not our fault. You be very careful, Jess. I wouldn't trust him as far as I could kick him." Audrey laughed. "Come to think of it, I couldn't kick him very far."

"I have to admit," said Jess, as she opened the front gate, "that Sid was the only woodman who stacked the wood for me. The chap I have now, throws it out of the cart, and the boys have to stack it."

Jess smiled as she had a sudden picture of Beau delivering her wood. He stacked it meticulously. Audrey saw the sudden smile.

"What is it, Jess?"

"I thought of someone else who stacked the wood for me."

"Oh?"

"Yes. Come inside and I'll tell you something exciting. Gracie! Leave those blankets alone." Jess looked at Audrey. "I'll have to wash them before I use them, but he did have enough decency to return them."

Matthew

Beau walked into his office. Celia was standing at the window, staring down at the street below. She turned as he entered.

"What are you doing in here, Celia?" Beau hung his coat and hat on the wooden coat stand beside the door.

"I came to see you." She met his gaze.

"Well, here I am. What do you want?" Beau moved to his desk, and leafed through the mail that was there.

Celia sighed. "Do I always have to 'want' something, Beau?"

Beau looked up. "Yes, Celia, you do, so what is it this time?"

Celia perched herself on the edge of the desk. Her perfume pervaded the room.

"Have you talked with Jess?"

"I have."

"And what did she have to say?"

Beau put the letters carefully on the desk. Celia was provoking him, and he knew that two could play at that game.

"She's very happy that I'll be leaving here as soon as Matthew is well, and the matter of staffing has been addressed."

"Is she now?" Celia paused. "Did she say anything about my letter?"

"She did."

"And?" Celia waited. "Honestly, Beau, it's like dragging blood from a stone, trying to get information from you. What did she say, for heaven sake?"

"She's determined that it's not going to make an ounce of difference, Celia."

"I can make it very difficult for both of you, Beau." There was a note of warning in her tone. "Doesn't she see that?"

"Jess would never stoop to your level, Celia." Beau looked up at the clock above the filing cabinet. "Now isn't it time you returned to your office? There'll be patients arriving soon."

Celia slid gracefully off the desk.

"I will get you to see reason, Beau," she said, her hand on the door. "You know that, don't you?" Her red lips curved into a smile. "I know things about you, Beau, that could be an obstruction, if you leave here. Remember that."

She was gone, with a draught of cool air and perfume.

Beau sat on his comfortable leather seat, and drummed his fingers on the desk. Celia was arming herself for battle, and he hoped he would be strong enough to withstand the blows that he knew would come. She was right. His past was probably going to come back and haunt him. Celia only had to whisper the words 'suicide' and 'disciplinary action' and nobody would want him.

Beau reached down and unlocked the bottom drawer of his desk. He drew out the picture of Jess, and laid it carefully in front of him. She had that wistful expression that he found so endearing, and as he looked at her eyes, he could hear her saying: *something worth having is worth fighting for.*

The door opened and Celia appeared, followed by a young man in Service uniform. She placed a file on the desk.

"Your first patient, Doctor; Private Simon Williams." Her eyes rested fleetingly on the picture of Jess. "I think you'll find all his information in the file."

Beau slid the picture back in the drawer, as Celia gave him a tight smile and then left the room, closing the door quietly behind her.

Beau smiled at the young man, and motioned him to sit. Reaching across the desk, he picked up the file. Here was another returned Serviceman with scars left from the war, and no quick fix for any of them.

*

The morning progressed slowly, and Beau was glad to see the last patient leave at midday. He wanted to go and see Matthew, preferably without Celia, so he closed his office and hurried downstairs before she could catch sight of him.

Matthew's motorcar was parked on the street. Beau slid into the driver's seat, and within a few moments, he was making his way out into the traffic. He knew Celia would be livid, but he wanted to speak with Matthew alone and uninterrupted.

Serendipity was shimmering in the autumn sunshine, as he headed along the bumpy driveway. He waved to Charlie, who was hoeing a new garden bed, and received an enthusiastic wave in response. The lad was safe and doing well.

In the hallway, Beau said "good morning" to Shirley, and headed up the stairs.

The linoleum was gleaming, and squeaked beneath his shoes. Edwina Evans was certainly an asset to the daily running of the lodge, and he wondered briefly if she had anyone to assist her, now that Milly was out of circulation.

He reached Matthew's room, but not before nurse Flanagan had him wrapped in a white coat and surgical mask.

"Can't be too careful, Doctor," she chastised, as he tried to protest.

"I suppose you're right, nurse."

Matthew was seated at the window when Beau walked into the ward, and he turned, a smile lighting his pale features.

"Hello, old chap! Nice to see you." He looked beyond Beau. "No reinforcements?"

Beau smiled behind his mask. "No, I managed to escape without them."

"Good." Matthew turned back to gaze out of the window. "I know that's a terrible thing to say, but I can do without Celia's antagonism at present." He sighed. "I have no ammunition to fire back."

Beau sat on the edge of the bed. "We need to have a serious talk, Matthew, but firstly, how are you feeling?"

"Stronger by the day, Beau. I do believe I'm very fortunate that I suspected influenza, and came straight to hospital." He looked directly at Beau. "I've been told that Milly is also recovering?"

"Yes, she'll live, thank God!"

"How did Celia find out?"

"I don't know, Matthew. It's surprising how things get around a place like this."

Matthew nodded. "So when are you leaving us, Beau?"

"I'll wait until you're strong enough, and my position has been filled."

"I'll miss you, old chap." Matthew looked suddenly forlorn.

"I can't stay, Matthew." Beau paused. "Celia has sent Jess a letter."

Matthew's head jerked up. "She did what?"

"I can't subject Jess to this sort of thing, Matthew. I have to make the break, although it pains me to leave my work here."

"I'm sure you'll find work in Melbourne. The hospitals there will be screaming out for men with your experience."

"We'll see."

Matthew screwed up his eyes. "You're not so sure?"

"My past might beat me there."

"What do you mean? You've done nothing to be ashamed of; no scandals, no malpractice." Matthew winced, as if in pain.

"No, but there are other things that could be looked at unfavourably."

"Only if they know about them." Matthew stared at Beau for a long moment. "I'm not going to tell them, if that's what you're worried about."

"Of course not, Matthew."

"But someone else is?"

"That's just it, Matthew; I don't know."

Matthew exhaled. "She's threatened you, hasn't she?"

"Not me, exactly; Jess."

"What can I do, Beau?"

"Nothing, Matthew. I'm hoping that once I've gone, and everything settles down, Celia will realise her mistake and forget all about it."

"Beau, you and I both know that Celia does *not* forget. It is not in her nature."

"Well, whatever the consequences, I have to leave. I'm sorry to lump you with it,

Matthew, but that's the way it has to be."

Matthew turned towards the window. "What's she like, your Jess?"

Beau closed his eyes. He should have brought the picture to show his friend. "You'd like her, Matthew. She's sweet, and kind and…"

"And everything that Celia is not."

"You're the psychiatrist, Matthew. I think Celia needs your professional skills."

"I do love her, old chap, in case you're wondering, but I have to admit that her behaviour baffles *me* sometimes."

Beau patted his friend's arm.

"Then pay more attention to her, Matthew."

*

Celia walked into Beau's office, and frowned as she discovered it empty. His hat and coat were no longer on the stand. He had gone, and she wanted him to take her out to see Matthew. Was that where he had gone, and without her? She pressed her red lips together, and walked purposefully towards his desk.

Slowly she opened the bottom drawer, glancing towards the door as she did so. A woman's face smiled up at her. Celia picked up the picture and stared at it.

"So you're the reason Beau is leaving all this behind?" she whispered.

Celia closed the drawer, and with the picture in her hand, left the room.

Beau's Discovery

It was late in the afternoon when Beau pulled the motorcar over to the kerb, and jumped out. The Clinic was in semi darkness; only the pale light from a streetlamp seeped in to the hidden corners.

The front door was locked. Beau took some keys from his pocket, and within a few moments was making his way up the stairs. His office door was locked.

In the pale light that filtered through open, unoccupied rooms, he managed to find the right key for his door.

Turning on the light he walked across to his desk. He needed to rescue the picture of Jess, and take it with him. The drawer was unlocked. Beau frowned. He thought he'd locked it.

The picture was gone. Annoyance turned to anger as he realised that Celia had seen it on his desk that morning. He rummaged through papers in the drawer and conceded that Celia must have taken it.

Beau locked the drawer and stood for a moment, contemplating his next move. It was too late to confront her now. He didn't want to knock on her door, to find her in her night attire. He would have to leave it until the morning. Why was she doing this to him? It was as if she didn't want to see him happy.

Beau switched off the light, locked the door, and made his slow way downstairs. Out on the street a light breeze was stirring the Elm trees, and leaves swirled around his feet as he walked the short distance to his room.

Angela's Patisserie was buzzing with activity as he reached the building, and feeling the pangs of hunger, he decided that the warmth of an eatery far outweighed the cold loneliness of his room.

Angela looked up as he entered and gave him her winning smile.

"All alone, Doctor? On a balmy night like this?" She laughed gaily.

"I'm afraid so, Angela. Your lights looked very welcoming, so I decided that, seeing as I haven't eaten since breakfast, I am very hungry."

"What can I get you? A sandwich perhaps?"

"A sandwich sounds perfect, and I'd like a cup of tea to go with it."

"Certainement, Doctor DuBois." Her brown eyes twinkled.

"Merci beaucoup, Angela." Beau reached into his coat pocket for his wallet.

Customers listened to their banter, amusement written on their faces.

Beau handed Angela a pound note, and she snorted.

"Is this the smallest you've got, Doctor?"

"I'm afraid so, Angela."

"Lucky you, I say."

"Do you have change?"

"Je fais."

Beau grinned. "Excellente!"

"Find a seat," laughed Angela, "and I'll bring it over."

Beau found an empty seat, and sat at the table with its red and white check tablecloth. He looked around. Couples were enjoying the intimacy of the small tables and hidden alcoves, and the warm sound of laughter encompassed him.

He didn't wait long for Angela to appear, with a plate of freshly made sandwiches, and a steaming cup of tea. She looked around the café. Nobody needed her attention, so she sat opposite Beau.

"You look as though you need cheering up," she said brightly. "Been a long day, has it?"

"You could say that." Beau picked up a sandwich.

"Cheese and pickles; I hope you like them."

"Lovely, thank-you," said Beau, through a mouthful.

"No lady friend tonight?"

Beau frowned, and then remembered that he had sat here with Celia recently. He shook his head.

"No. She's not a 'lady friend', as you so delicately put it, Angela. It's rather a long story; Celia is the wife of a colleague."

Angela nodded knowingly.

"That's good. I thought she was a bit stuck-up for you." Beau smiled. "What's more, she didn't eat any of my pastries."

"And that's as good as an insult?"

"It is indeed!" Angela was thoughtful for a moment. "How's it going with all this influenza that's about at present? I know my customer numbers are down, and it's the same story all around the streets."

"We thought we were on top of it, but there's another outbreak, unfortunately.

The vaccines we have at our disposal are helping, but not eliminating."

"It's a worry, isn't it?"

"Indeed it is. My colleague is actually recovering from it. He's been one of the lucky ones." Beau took a sip of tea. "I'm waiting for him to fully recover, because I'm planning on moving south to Victoria."

"You're leaving us?" Angela's brown eyes registered shock.

"Yes. I'm getting married, and my wife-to-be lives in Victoria."

"Can't she move up here?"

Beau shook his head. "I'm afraid not."

Two customers moved towards the cash register, so Angela got to her feet.

"Well, don't you leave without saying au revoir to me, comprenez?"

Beau grinned. "Je comprenez."

Angela leaned across the table. "She's a lucky girl, that's all I can say," she whispered, before moving away.

Beau finished his sandwiches and tea, and with a wave in Angela's direction, headed out on to the street. Slowly he climbed the narrow staircase that led to his room. He had had a few minutes of emotional release, and now he must gird his loins for the morning's confrontation with Celia.

*

Beau walked into the reception room at eight o'clock the following morning. He knew Celia was already there; he could smell her perfume. She was not at her desk, so he waited.

It wasn't long before he heard the click of her heels on the linoleum, and the door opened. Celia saw Beau standing beside her desk, and halted. The look on his face told her that he was not especially pleased to see her. However, she smiled.

"Good morning, Beau. What can I do for you?"

"I'm getting a little tired of your games, Celia." Beau's tone was stiff.

Celia cocked an eyebrow, as she moved around the desk to her leather chair.

"I don't know what you mean, Beau." She began to sort the files on her desk.

"Yes, you do! You took a picture from my drawer; a picture of Jess."

"You must have mislaid it." Celia continued sorting files.

"I haven't mislaid it, Celia!" Beau thumped his hand on the desk.

Celia looked up, and her eyes were glassy as she stared at Beau.

"How dare you come into my office and accuse me of theft!"

"I know you took it, Celia. What I don't know is 'why'? If it's back in the drawer when I return from Serendipity this afternoon, I'll say no more about it."

As Beau strode towards the door, he heard a strangled sound, which made him glance around. As he did so, patients' files caught him in the chest, sending him staggering against the door.

"Celia!" he shouted. "Enough is enough! You are losing all sense of reason, and I think you need help."

Beau bent to retrieve the files. He placed them calmly on the desk.

"You can't leave us, Beau!" Her voice was tight and her eyes blinked rapidly, in an effort to stop the tears that threatened to overflow. "This Practice will fall apart if you do." She began to rummage in her desk drawer.

"That is nonsense, Celia! The Board will make sure it keeps running smoothly. Your father will see to that."

Celia threw Beau's picture across the desk. There was scribble across Jess's face. Beau picked it up, stared at it aghast for a moment and then looked at Celia.

"Why do this? It makes no sense."

"It does to me, Beau! Everything was going well until she..."

"Celia." Beau tried to stay calm, although his heart was hammering loud enough to be heard. "Jess is everything to me, and I will not change my mind, no matter what you throw at me. Now, stop behaving like a spoilt child! We have a Clinic to run, so I suggest you finish sorting those files, and then see who is waiting on the other side of this door."

"You will not change your mind? Neither will I!"

They glared at each other across the space, before Beau turned away, and strode through the door. People standing awkwardly in the passageway, stared at him as he passed them and made his way to his consulting room.

This couldn't go on! The sooner he got away the better it would be for everyone.

An Unexpected Visitor

Jess hadn't heard from Beau for several days, but she consoled herself with the thought that he would have a lot to sort out before making the final move south. She kept herself busy working a few hours each day for Jean, and endeavouring to plant her winter vegetables before the cold weather set in.

It was during one mild morning, when Jess was pushing cabbage seedlings into the turned soil, that she heard a woman's voice call her name. Turning towards the house, she saw a figure coming towards her, a hand raised in greeting.

"Jess! When you didn't answer the front door, I thought I would try the back."

Jess scrambled to her feet, pushed back the stray hair that had escaped from her scarf, and wiped her soiled hands on her apron. She smiled at her visitor.

"Mary! How nice to see you. You should have told me you were coming."

Jess walked towards Mary Walker, and they embraced.

"It was a last minute decision, I'm afraid. I took advantage of George being home to look after Lachlan, and caught the train." Mary looked beyond Jess to the garden. "Looks like I caught you in the middle of being productive."

"That's alright. Come into the house and we can chat in there. It's time I knocked off, anyway. If Margaret or Charles catch me digging in the garden, they scold me like a naughty child." She laughed.

They had reached the back verandah, where Jess kicked off her boots, and slipped her feet into slippers. They stepped into the warm kitchen.

"Sit down, Mary, and I'll be with you as soon as I clean myself up."

The kettle was singing.

"I'll make the tea, if you like." Mary was already removing her gloves and the pretty pink straw hat that covered her short brown hair.

"Certainly." Jess smiled. "I think you know where everything is."

Mary busied herself at the stove, while Jess retreated to the bathroom to make herself presentable. She removed the soiled apron, washed the dirt from her fingers, and pulled the scarf from her head. Shaking out her hair, she ran her fingers through it, and wondered fleetingly how she would look if it was short.

No, she wouldn't risk it, not yet.

When Jess entered the kitchen some minutes later, Mary was seated at the table, two steaming cups of tea set before her.

"Wonderful!" laughed Jess. "I should hire you, Mary."

"George might have something to say about that, Jess."

"You're right." Jess sat opposite Mary, and for a moment they were silent.

"How are you, Jess?" Mary asked eventually.

"Oh, I'm doing well, and I have some news to tell you, but firstly I want to know about your friend Meg Harper. I believe you received a letter recently."

"I did! It was from a Doctor DuBois in Sydney. He knows you, I believe?"

Jess hid the smile that lurked at the corners of her mouth.

"Yes, I know him very well."

Mary's eyes narrowed as she looked at Jess. "Oh?"

"I'll tell you about that in a moment," Jess said hastily. "Tell me about Meg. She would have known Jack, I presume?"

"Yes, we all knew Jack." Mary reached for her bag. "I have Doctor DuBois's letter here. Read what he has to say."

Jess took the letter from Mary's outstretched hand. Beau's handwriting leapt out at her, and her fingers trembled as she slid the letter from the envelope. Mary was watching her as she opened the paper and began to read.

> *Dear Mrs. Walker,*
> *It is with mixed emotions that I write to you today, concerning a dear friend of yours, Meg Harper. I believe you both nursed on the Western Front. Let me explain. I am a doctor, and I have been working in Sydney with returned Service personnel. I don't need to tell you what trauma that has brought home.*
> *Miss Harper came to our clinic seeking relief for sleeplessness. Unfortunately I was unable to help her with what she wanted, and she undoubtedly sought help elsewhere.*
> *Several days later she was brought to our facility, which had been set up for patients with the influenza virus. Yes, Meg Harper had the dreaded influenza.*
> *In her final moments she begged me to find you, and let you know what had become of her. I can tell you that she died bravely, and she said to tell you*

that the matron was proud of her.
Finding you was incredibly simple. You see, I know Jess Stanley, and I had met her husband, Jack, two Christmases ago, before he left to fight overseas. I contacted Jess (yes, we do correspond) because she had mentioned your name, and I thought it couldn't be a coincidence, and it wasn't.
Jess has told me all about your connection with Jack, so I feel I am writing to a friend. I'm sorry to be the bearer of bad news, but please know that Meg Harper now rests in Sydney's Lane Cove Cemetery. I can get you the details if you would like.
Please accept my sympathy.
I am yours faithfully
Beau DuBois

Jess wiped her eyes as she folded the paper and slipped it back in the envelope. Mary took it without a word, and returned it to her bag.

After a few moments, she looked up at Jess.

"So what's the connection between you and Doctor DuBois, Jess?"

"It's a very long story, Mary, and if you have the time, I'll tell you."

Mary looked up at the clock above the mantel. It was eleven o'clock.

"I'll have to catch the 2.15 to Melbourne, so I'm all ears, Jess."

Jess began the story of her friendship with Beau, and she watched Mary's eyes grow large as all the dramatic details unfolded. When Jess had finished, Mary sat back and exhaled.

"My goodness!" she exclaimed. "And now you are going to marry him?"

"Yes. He's been very good to me, Mary, and I know it may seem sudden to you, but I do love him, and the children are very fond of him."

"It's not for me to criticise, Jess." Mary smiled suddenly. "I shall expect an invitation to the wedding. I'm intrigued, and would love to meet him."

"I'm not sure how soon he'll be able to leave Sydney. His colleague has the influenza virus, and although he's improving, it could be a while."

"I'm happy for you, Jess." Mary paused. "Jack was away a long time, wasn't he?"

"The last time I saw Jack was the eleventh of May, 1917."

"Two years ago."

Jess nodded, and they were both silent.

Finally Mary stood. "I think it's time for another cup of tea, and we can chat about the children. Where is young Gracie, by the way?"

"She's with her grandparents. They see more of her than I do. We can walk around there after lunch, if you like, and you can meet Jack's parents."

"I would love that, Jess." Mary had made herself at home in Jess's kitchen, and was pouring water for another cup of tea. "What do they think about the idea of you marrying again?"

"Oh, they're very supportive. They've even had a telephone installed for me, so that Beau can call me."

"That's wonderful." Mary returned to the table with the cups of tea. "I would think that makes it so much easier for you, having their support."

"It does." Jess smiled brightly. "Now tell me all about Lachlan. He must be growing like a mushroom."

"Oh, he is, Jess." Mary's brown eyes softened. "He is so precious to both of us, that we can't imagine life without him now."

*

The 2.15 train to Melbourne had just left the station, and Jess stood on the platform, watching as it disappeared around the bend. It had been lovely spending time with Mary, and she had promised to come back when Jess had a wedding date.

"Be happy," she had whispered, as Jess hugged her and said good-bye.

Jess was alone once more, and she made her slow way up the steps and across the pedestrian bridge. A cool breeze forced her to wrap her shawl closer around her, and she stepped it out as she headed towards home.

As she reached her gate, she heard a voice behind her. It was Sid O'Connor.

"Excuse me! Mrs. Stanley, can I 'ave a word with ya?"

Jess turned, her hand on the gate.

"What is it, Sid?"

He was twisting his greasy cap in his hands. "I was wonderin' whether you'd 'ad a chance t'think about me deliverin' your wood?"

Jess frowned. "No, I haven't, Sid. After the way you treated me in the past, I don't think I want to trust you."

"It won't 'appen again, Mrs. Stanley, I promise."

"How can I be sure of that, Sid?"

He shrugged his lean shoulders. "Let's just say I've 'ad me guts kicked in, an' I wanna start again. I'm real sorry for me behaviour." He gave a sudden smile. "Mrs. O'Malley has given me what for, an' a tongue-lashin' like ya wouldn't believe!"

"Has she?" Jess paused. "If I say 'yes', Sid, I want a solemn promise from you that you will only enter my yard when I can see that you are sober."

Sid nodded effusively.

"I'm off the booze, Mrs. Stanley, an' you're not the only one who's said that."

"I'm glad, Sid."

"So I can start deliverin' ya wood then?"

"You can start in two weeks time. I have enough to last until then. I want you to come to my front door first, do you understand?"

"Yeah!" Sid's head jerked up and down. "Thanks, Mrs. Stanley."

"Don't let me down."

"I'll see ya in a fortnight, then?"

Jess nodded, and Sid headed off along the street, a bounce in his step.

As she opened the gate, Jess wondered whether she'd been too easy with Sid. He had certainly given her some anxious moments in the past. Had he really changed? One thing was certain; Beau would not be pleased with her decision.

Beau was not pleased with her decision when she told him, on the telephone that afternoon.

"I thought we'd seen the last of him. You're not seriously going to give him another chance, Jess?"

"Everyone deserves a chance, Beau. I seem to remember someone else coming to my gate and asking for a chance." Jess gave a little laugh.

"That was different, Jess."

"No it wasn't. I had no idea who you were, and I admit I was a little anxious." She paused. "Anyway, how is Matthew? Has he recovered?"

"He's on the road to recovery. I should be able to leave here in two weeks, if everything goes to plan. Unfortunately the virus has had a reoccurrence, and at present we have six patients at Serendipity."

"Oh, before I forget, I had a visit from Mary Walker today. She showed me your letter, and of course I told her all about our connection."

"What did she say?"

"She wished us well, and expects an invitation to the wedding."

Beau was silent.

"Beau, are you still there?"

"Yes, my love."

"You're not getting cold feet, are you?"

"Certainly not."

"But something's wrong. What is it?"

"Nothing that we can't overcome, Jess."

"Are you sure?"

"Yes, I'm sure. Now before we're interrupted, I have to tell you that the border is closed, and when I leave here, I will have to stay for a week in a quarantine camp at Albury."

"It doesn't get any easier, does it?"

A droll voice interrupted: "Are you extending?"

"No. Good-bye, Jess. I'll call you in a few days time."

The line went dead.

Jess put the receiver down, and stood for a moment. Something was wrong. Beau sounded very subdued. She hoped that Celia wasn't causing him any more anxiety. Jess had difficulty understanding the relationship between Beau and his ex-wife. Was it that she couldn't accept the idea that he wanted to be with somebody else, or was there more to it than that?

Jess sighed. The sooner he was able to leave, the better it would be for all of them.

As she moved away from the telephone, it rang shrilly. Jess picked it up.

"Hello."

"Jess!" Izzy's voice sounded loud in her ear, and she was obviously distressed.

"What's wrong, Izzy?"

"It's mother, Jess." She gulped. "She's not very well, and I think you should come."

"What do you mean, Izzy? Is it her heart?"

"She's having trouble breathing, and the doctor says she has pneumonia." Izzy stopped to take a deep breath. "Are you able to get away? I'm sorry to land this on you, Jess."

Jess's head was spinning. "I'll catch the train tomorrow morning. I'll have to see if Margaret can have the children, and I'll let Jean know that I'll be away for a couple of days. I've just been talking to Beau, so I'd better let him know what's happening. Oh, Izzy, do you think it's really serious?"

"I don't know, but I think you should be here."

"Alright. I'll hang up now, Izzy, and I'll call Beau. He should still be at the clinic, hopefully. Good-bye, Izzy. I'll see you sometime tomorrow."

Jess hung up the receiver. She had a lot to do if she was to catch the early train to Swan Hill. Firstly she must try to catch Beau. Her fingers fumbled through a notepad that lay on the hall table. His number was there somewhere.

She found it and picked up the receiver. When she heard the operator's voice, she quickly asked for a trunk line to Sydney.

Eventually, after a lot of crackling, she heard ringing on the other end. *Come on, Beau! Please be there!* Jess's heart was thudding.

A female voice answered. "Norlane Street Clinic. How can I help you?"

Jess breathed deeply. It had to be Celia.

"Is Doctor DuBois there, please?"

"No, I'm afraid not. Who's calling?"

"It's Jess Stanley. I'm calling from Victoria."

There was silence for a moment.

"I see. I'm afraid Doctor DuBois has just left. Can I take a message?"

Jess hesitated. "Could you tell him, please, that my mother has been taken ill, and I'll be going to Swan Hill on the morning train."

"And Doctor DuBois needs to know that?" The voice was short and clipped.

"Yes. Yes, he does." Jess felt her own voice rising.

"Very well, but I won't see him until tomorrow."

"That's alright. As long as he gets my message."

There was a short pause. "I'll make sure he gets it."

The line went dead. Celia had hung up.

Jess had no time to ponder on the possible outcome of that telephone conversation. She had to hope and pray that Celia would deliver the message.

Now she had to see if Margaret was available to have the children, and she had to tell Jean that she would be away for a few days.

Thank goodness for the telephone. It meant that she could do all the arranging without leaving the house. Margaret was eager to assist, and Jean told her not to worry about a thing. She needed to be with her mother at a time like this.

It was time to tell the children. Jess called them.

"Ben! Edward! Gracie! Come to the kitchen, please."

The three children appeared from their rooms, and sat at the kitchen table.

"I have to go to Swan Hill tomorrow, children. Your grandmother is very ill, and

Aunt Izzy wants me to be there. You will stay with grandma and granddad while I'm away."

"Is she going to die?" Ben's brown eyes were large.

"I don't know that, Ben, but Aunt Izzy is very worried about her." Jess smiled at his troubled face. "We'll remember her in our prayers tonight."

*

As the train thundered its way towards Swan Hill, Jess sat back on the creaking leather seat and gazed out the window at the scenery rushing by. She pondered on how quickly circumstances could change, and the uncertainty of life.

Beau

Beau opened the door to Matthew's room. It was empty. He frowned, and headed out into the corridor where he saw Nurse Flanagan.

"Nurse! Where is Doctor Morley?"

Nurse Flanagan scowled above her mask.

"He's discharged himself from these wards, Doctor. You'll find him back in his own domain. His wife had him moved, apparently, without our knowledge!"

"Oh! I see. He must be feeling much better."

"Humph! Whether he is or not, he's back among vulnerable people, and I think it was a very bad move."

Beau had to agree, but he said nothing.

"Thank-you, nurse. I'll go and find him." Beau made to move away, but stopped. "Anybody moving into Doctor Morley's room?"

"Yes. Two more patients are coming from the Coast Hospital later this afternoon. I'm told that they are recovering, so will be under observation."

"Good. How many serious cases have we at present?"

"Only two. Doctor Freeman thinks the worst might be over."

"Let's hope so. By the way, nurse, I'm moving to Victoria very soon, so I'd like to say how much I've appreciated your efficiency." Beau smiled at her startled expression. "You've made the job easier for us."

"You're leaving us? We'll miss you, Doctor DuBois." Nurse Flanagan lowered her voice. "I can't say that about everyone here."

Beau laughed. "Thank-you, nurse."

"Good luck then, Doctor." She smiled, nodded, and bustled away.

Beau stripped off his mask and white coat, and headed out of the isolation area. Rounding the corner of the corridor, he headed towards the nurse's station. A young nurse busy writing on a clipboard, looked up as Beau approached.

"Good afternoon, Doctor DuBois!" Her smile was wide.

"Good afternoon, Rachel. I believe Doctor Morley is here."

"Yes, he is, Doctor. He's in room 12."

"Thank-you, Rachel." Beau knew room 12. Charlie had been there for a time. The door was open. Beau knocked.

"Come in." He heard Matthew's voice.

Beau entered. Matthew was fully dressed, and seated at the window which looked out on to the rose garden.

"Good afternoon, Matthew."

"Beau, old chap! Welcome!" Matthew turned. "Pull up a chair, and tell me how things are in the outside world."

Beau seated himself beside Matthew. Looking down on to the rose garden, he saw Charlie busy raking up leaves.

"He's a good worker, Beau," said Matthew, following his gaze. "Fell on his feet."

"I'm glad." Beau turned to look at Matthew. "You're looking well, I must say."

"Never better, old chap. I should be back on my feet in a week's time. How are things with you?"

"I'm waiting for you to get back to the Clinic, and then I can leave."

Matthew was silent for a moment.

"It won't be the same without you, Beau." He sighed. "I wish it were possible for you to bring Jess up here."

"You know that will never work, Matthew. I need to get right away."

"Yes, I know." He shifted his position on the chair. "The Board has been busy interviewing medical students, and have short-listed down to two."

"That's good, Matthew. It will all work out for the best, I feel sure. You have to admit that working relations have been very strained of late, for all of us." Beau paused. "Celia may settle down once I'm gone."

Matthew nodded. "I hope so." He looked straight at Beau. "You know it's all about the Clinic, don't you?"

"Is it?"

"Definitely! It's what makes her tick." Matthew turned back to the window. "Maybe if she'd had children, it would have all been different."

"Maybe." Beau stood up. "Anyway, it's good to see you looking so well. New cases are slowing down again, I gather."

"I believe so. Milly is on the mend."

"Yes. You've both been very fortunate, Matthew."

"Time to start afresh, eh?"

"For all of us. I'll telephone Jess and give her the good news."

"I will expect an invitation to the wedding, old chap."

Beau patted Matthew's shoulder. "Definitely. I wouldn't have it any other way."

"I hope she makes you happy, Beau."

Beau nodded, unable to meet Matthew's gaze.

"I hope I can make her happy, Matthew." One more pat on the shoulder, and Beau hurried from the room.

He reached the motorcar, parked near the front door, and slumped into the driver's seat. He hated leaving Matthew, but he knew he had no choice if they were both to avoid the fallout from Celia's irrational behaviour. Matthew had no knowledge of her destruction of Jess's picture, and he wanted to keep it that way.

Beau drove back through the Sydney streets, as the late afternoon sun dipped behind the buildings. Parking outside the Clinic, he debated whether to use the telephone there or walk around to the Post Office.

There was a light upstairs, which meant that Celia was still there, so he locked the vehicle, turned up his coat collar against the cold wind that had sprung up, and headed for the Post Office.

Jess wasn't answering. He tried again, with the same result. Maybe she was at Margaret's. He put through a call to Margaret's telephone, and eventually he heard her voice.

"Hello."

"Margaret, it's Beau. Is Jess at your place? I've been trying to call her."

"Oh, hello, Beau! No, Jess is not here. She left on this morning's train to Swan Hill. Her mother is very ill. I thought she said she'd left you a message."

"I didn't get it." Beau paused. "Who took the message?"

"Er – Celia, I think she said."

Beau's mouth went dry. "When was this?"

"Yesterday afternoon."

Beau had seen Celia at the Clinic that morning, and she had not mentioned it. Had she forgotten, or was this another of her little games?

"Thank-you, Margaret. What's Izzy's number? I'll try to reach her there."

"Oh, just a minute. I have it here somewhere." There was a pause. "Here it is. It's Swan Hill 137."

"Thanks, Margaret."

Beau was running out of coins. He scooped his remaining silver on to the bench beside the telephone and called the operator.

The moments ticked by, and finally he heard Izzy's melodic voice.

"Hello. Isobel Dalton speaking."

"Izzy, it's Beau. Is Jess there?"

"Beau! How lovely! Yes, I'll put her on." Beau heard her calling out, and then he heard Jess's voice.

"Beau?"

"Yes, my darling girl." The relief was almost too much. "I've just heard about your mother. How is she?"

"She has pneumonia, Beau. The doctor doesn't hold out much hope."

"I'm coming down."

"How?" Jess's voice broke.

"I'll find a way, even if I have to crawl."

"That's not possible, Beau."

"I need to be with you, Jess."

"Yes." It was just a whisper.

Beau put his last coin in the slot. "I'm out of money, so we'll get cut off, but I will see you as soon as I can get there. I promise."

He heard her intake of breath, and the line went dead.

Beau thumped his hand on the bench. Celia had known about this yesterday, and she had said nothing. Anger boiled up inside him as he walked out of the telephone cubicle and down the steps to the street.

Workers were hurrying by, anxious to get home out of the wind. As Beau passed the Clinic, he looked up. There was still a light upstairs. He stopped. Should he confront her now? What was the point? He didn't have time for all this anger. He had to find a way to get to Jess.

Beau climbed on board a crowded tram as it clanged past, and hoped it would take him to George Street and Central Station. It did, eventually, and there he sought the 'information' counter.

A young man looked up as he approached.

"What can I do for you, sir?"

"I need to get to Swan Hill as soon as possible."

The young man frowned.

"Not possible on the train, sir. We can get you to Albury, but you're on your own after that." He shrugged. "Maybe you can beg a lift on a truck going to Mildura."

"Is the border still closed?"

"I think it is, sir, but it's a bit of a hot potato, if you know what I mean. There are plenty of people going straight through to Melbourne."

"Thank-you. So I can get as far as Albury, and see what happens after that?"

"Best we can do, sir, apart from going to Melbourne and then up to Swan Hill."

Beau nodded and moved away.

The earliest train to Albury would be departing at 6.00am the following morning. Beau purchased a ticket and walked back out on to George Street. The evening crowd was thinning out, and he found a seat on the next tram heading north towards Norlane Street.

As they rattled past the Clinic, he glanced up. There was still a light in Celia's office. He pulled on the cord, and the tram slowed enough for him to jump off. It was a risky manoeuvre with his injured hip, but he made it to the footpath safely. Unlocking the front door, he closed it behind him and trudged upstairs.

Light was seeping beneath Celia's office door. Beau knocked and waited.

"Celia, it's me, Beau!" he called out.

The door opened. "What do you want, Beau?"

"Jess left a message for me, yesterday." Her eyes widened. "I didn't get it."

"I'm very busy here, Beau. I can't be expected to remember personal messages."

"This one was important, Celia."

Her hand remained on the door handle. "I'm sorry."

"I'm leaving for Albury at 6.00am tomorrow, and I don't know when I'll be back."

"You can't do that, Beau!" Her tone was sharp. "You can't leave your patients, without any warning."

"I'd have to if I was sick. Reschedule them for next week."

Celia flung the door open wide. "You're making a big mistake, Beau!"

"Not the first one I've made, Celia, and probably not the last."

"You'll be sorry, Beau!" Celia's voice followed him as he turned and walked away.

It was after midday when the train arrived at the Albury station. Beau grabbed his bag and shouldered his way through the crowd milling on the platform. A voice was speaking through a loud hailer, instructing those who were travelling through to Melbourne, to assemble further along the platform. There was a great deal of vocal dissention among passengers who wanted exemption from having to stay in a quarantine camp for a week.

Beau skirted the crowd, and headed for the 'information' desk, to be greeted by a fresh-faced young man in uniform.

"If you're going through to Melbourne, sir, you need to line up with all the others over there." He jerked his head in the general direction of the crowd.

"No," said Beau pleasantly. "I need to get to Swan Hill, today if possible."

"Swan Hill?" The young man laughed. "You won't get to Swan Hill, sir, not today or any day, unless you want to walk."

"I know there's no train, but if you know where I can access road transport, I would be very grateful."

"Oh." His brow creased. "Well, there's Peterson's Haulage up the road a bit. They travel to Mildura regularly. You might be lucky."

"Thankyou. Just up the road a bit?"

"Yeah." The young man jerked his head again. "That way. Best of luck, sir."

Beau moved away. Hunger pangs gnawed at his belly. He hadn't eaten since the previous night, so he went searching for the canteen.

Once satisfied with sandwiches and coffee, Beau set off in the general direction of the haulage company. After tramping for about a quarter of a mile along a much-used dirt road, he came across the trucking yard, surrounded by wire fencing, and a gate securely padlocked.

Beau was wondering what to do next when a truck rattled up beside him. The driver leaned out.

"What d'ya want, mate?" He grinned at Beau through a bushy grey beard.

"I need to get to Swan Hill, and I wondered if you had a truck heading that way."

The driver climbed down from the cab of the Bedford, and walked towards the locked gate. Taking a key from his pocket, he thrust it into the padlock.

"Headin' there meself in half an hour or so. Want a lift, do ya?"

"I would appreciate it."

"I can probably do that. Don't always have company on these long trips." A grin revealed a mouth devoid of teeth, but there was a merry twinkle in his crinkled blue eyes. "Name's

Alf Peterson." He swung open the two iron gates, and then heaved his bulk back into the cabin. "If you wait 'ere, I 'ave to collect somethin' from the depot. You're lucky I 'ad to come back. I'd've been gone, otherwise."

"I'm much obliged," said Beau, relief flooding him. "My name's Beau DuBois."

"A Frenchie, eh?"

Beau smiled. "Not exactly."

"Alright, Beau, be with ya in a tick."

The truck with its canvas canopy jerked forward, its wheels spinning in the gravel. Beau stood back, as dirt scattered around his feet.

He waited for twenty minutes before the truck re-emerged from the depot. Alf swung out of the cabin, locked the gate, and climbed back again.

"Jump in!" he shouted above the noise of the engine. "We're good to go!"

Beau stepped up into the passenger seat, and the truck shuddered as Alf found the gear he wanted. Soon they were bumping along the dirt road, away from the depot, and Alf turned to Beau.

"So, what takes you to Swan Hill?"

"It's rather a long story, I'm afraid."

Alf gave his toothless grin.

"We've got about six hours to fill in, so fire away. I'm listenin'."

Sarah

Jess put the receiver down, and turned to Izzy, who was hovering beside her.

"Beau's coming down from Sydney, Izzy."

Izzy put an arm around Jess's shoulders, giving her a squeeze.

"That's wonderful, Jess. You need him here with you."

"I know, but getting here could be difficult."

"Beau will find a way, my dear. Now, it's your turn to sit with mother while I see about our tea." Izzy laughed softly. "We still have to eat, and Harry will be looking for something shortly."

Jess made her way to the room where she had slept with the three children on their last visit. The room was in semi-darkness, and Sarah lay on the big bed, dwarfed by its size.

Jess sat quietly beside her mother, and held her clammy hand. Looking at the pale face on the pillow, Jess was reminded of a time long ago; a time almost forgotten, when as a small child, she had watched her grandmother fade away. She remembered her mother whispering to her that her grandmamma was on a journey to a much better place, and that she, Jess, must not be too sad.

Jess blinked away the tears that threatened, and thought of all the times she had been too busy to travel the distance to see her mother. Sarah always understood, but Jess knew now that she must have felt some disappointment, even though she always said,

"Your children come first, Jessie."

Sarah suddenly opened her eyes and stared at Jess. The rattling in her chest stopped for a moment, and she smiled. As Jess watched, she thought she heard a faint whisper.

"I won't be long, Jim."

Jess leaned forward, but Sarah's eyes closed once more, and the rattle in her chest resumed. Jess sat back, as Izzy tiptoed into the room and sat on the bed.

"Any change, Jess?" she whispered.

"She said something just now, and it sounded like 'I won't be long, Jim.'"

Izzy's blue eyes rounded.

"Do you think that means…?" She stopped.

"Maybe we need to call the doctor."

"Yes, I'll do that now." Izzy touched Jess's shoulder as she stood. "Oh, sis, this is going to leave a big hole in our lives."

Jess nodded, and squeezed her mother's hand. "Yes, it is."

*

Doctor Barton folded his stethoscope and looked at the two women standing silently beside the bed.

"I doubt your mother will last the night, Mrs. Dalton. I'll inject some more morphine to keep her as comfortable as we can, and nature should take its course. I'm sorry I can't be optimistic about a recovery here."

"We understand, Doctor Barton. Mother has wanted to leave this mortal coil for some time now, so we have to let her go." Izzy squeezed Jess's arm.

Doctor Barton smiled as he closed his medical bag. He was a portly man, in his late sixties, with a kindly face and sympathetic brown eyes behind heavy-framed spectacles.

"I'll say goodnight, and I expect to hear from you when it happens."

He nodded in Jess's direction, and followed Izzy from the room.

*

Through the long night, the sisters kept their silent vigil beside Sarah's bed, and just before the dawn, Jess noticed that her breathing had stopped. Leaning forward, she placed her fingers against her mother's neck. There was nothing.

"She's gone," she whispered, as the tears welled up inside her.

"I'll call Doctor Barton." Izzy moved quietly from the room.

Left alone, Jess bent over the bed and kissed Sarah's forehead.

"Goodnight, mother. Sleep well." Her tears slid down Sarah's cheek and on to the pillow.

"Doctor Barton is on his way." Izzy had returned. She knelt beside Jess, and the sisters held each other tight. "It's what she wanted, Jess. We can't be sad for her."

"We can be sad for ourselves, Izzy."

"Yes, but we mustn't dwell on it, Jess. Mother wouldn't want that."

Harry appeared at the doorway.

"I'm cooking some tomatoes. You girls need something to eat. It's been a long night for you both."

Izzy smiled. Good old Harry. He knew what was important.

"Thankyou, Harry. We'll be there in a moment."

*

Jess and Izzy stood silently as Doctor Barton wrote their mother's time of death on a form. He folded it, placed it in an envelope, and looked up at the two women watching him.

"I'll give this to the Coroner. I've arranged for the undertaker, so he should be here soon. I'm very sorry, Mrs. Dalton. Your mother was a fine woman." He closed his bag. "Is there anything else I can do for you? A sleeping draught, perhaps?"

"I don't think so, Doctor," said Izzy, looking at Jess's pale face. "What about you, Jessie? Do you need something to make you sleep?"

Jess shook her head. "No."

"Very well. You know where I can be reached, if you need me. Good-day, ladies."

When Doctor Barton had gone, Harry poked his head around the door of the bedroom. Jess and Izzy were gazing silently down on Sarah's waxen features. He cleared his throat, and they both turned.

"Nancy has just arrived," he said quietly. "I've left her in charge of the shop while I make you a cup of tea. The doctor has gone, I see."

"Yes." Izzy sighed heavily. "Now we wait for the undertaker." She smiled at Harry. "A cup of tea sounds marvellous, doesn't it, Jess?"

Jess nodded, and together they followed Harry to the kitchen.

"Are you expecting Beau to arrive today?" asked Harry, as he busied himself making a pot of tea.

"I don't know, Harry." Jess sat at the table. "I think he's set himself an impossible task, seeing as there are no trains from Albury."

"Don't you worry about Beau," said Izzy, as she pushed a cup of tea towards Jess. "If there's a way, he will find it, I'm sure." She smiled. "Now can we cheer up a little? Mother wouldn't wish us to walk around with long faces."

Harry picked up a steaming mug, and headed for the kitchen door. "I'll go back to the shop, and I'll send Nancy in to see you."

"Thank-you, Harry." Izzy sat opposite Jess, and picked up her cup. "You look done in, Jessie. I think you need to have a sleep once the undertaker has gone."

"You don't look so wonderful yourself, Izzy." Jess yawned. "It was a long night." She looked up at the kitchen clock. It was nine o'clock.

"I'd better telephone Margaret shortly and give her the news."

"Hello, Jess." Nancy appeared at the kitchen door. "I'm so sorry to hear that Sarah has gone." She gave Jess a gentle hug, and sat beside her. "I'll miss her, too."

"Hello, Nancy." Jess turned to look at the quiet woman who had become an integral part of the working life of the Swan Hill family. "You look well."

"Working in the shop has been a godsend for me."

"Nancy, do you want me to tell Jess about the ideas we've been thrashing out over the past couple of months?" Izzy slid a cup of tea in front of Nancy.

"Yes, if you like."

Jess looked from one to the other, as Izzy continued.

"Nancy has decided to sell the farm. Martin's not interested in taking it on, so we all had a thought that maybe, when the farm is sold, Nancy can move in here, and we'll move into mother's house. It makes perfect sense."

"I had already told you to move in to the family home, Izzy," Jess chastised gently. "Of course it makes sense." She turned to Nancy. "That sounds like a wonderful idea." Her brow creased. "Is Martin going to stay in France?"

Nancy's pale blue eyes lit up. "Yes, but he's coming home for Christmas, and bringing his French lass, Fleur, with him. They want to get married here."

"Nancy! How wonderful!" Jess was genuinely pleased.

Nancy put her cup on the table, and smiled at Jess. "A little bird has told me that you're getting married, too."

Jess coloured and looked swiftly at Izzy. "That's right, Nancy, but not yet."

"I'm so happy for you, Jess. Beau is a lovely man."

"Yes, he is."

"We can have a double wedding," said Izzy gleefully, "when Martin comes home!"

"Izzy! Today is not the day for discussing weddings."

"Why not?" Izzy met her sister's startled gaze. "Mother won't mind, and it is a thought, you must admit."

"Stop it, Izzy! Have you no sensitivity?"

Harry's appearance at the door saved them both from further verbal conflict.

"The Undertaker's here, Isobel."

"Oh!" Izzy's body slumped, and she smiled thinly at Jess. "Come on, Jessie. I'm not doing this on my own." Jess had risen from her chair, and Izzy took her arm. "I'm so sorry, Jess," she whispered contritely. "I wasn't thinking."

"That's your trouble, Izzy; you speak first and think later." Jess tried hard to sound displeased, but inside she knew that Izzy would never change.

"I know."

Nancy made a hasty retreat back to the shop, followed by Harry.

"What was all that about?" he asked as he closed the door.

"I think I started it," said Nancy, "by mentioning weddings."

"I see." Harry shook his head. "I think we are in for a long few days, Nancy. Isobel's emotions will be seesawing backwards and forwards, and she'll say things completely out of place." He sighed. "It's not what Jess needs at present. She's had enough to deal with."

"They'll get through it, Harry. After all, they're sisters, and their love for each other will outweigh any differences."

Harry cocked an eyebrow. "Don't be too sure about that, Nancy."

"Oh, but I am."

*

Jess and Izzy watched silently as the Undertaker and his assistant gently attended to their mother's body before removing her from the bed. They carried her on a litter, out through the kitchen, and to the waiting hearse.

The Undertaker returned alone, to where Izzy and Jess were folding the bed linen.

"We'll leave you now, Mrs. Dalton." He was a soft-spoken man in his later years, with a full head of steel grey hair and a beard of equal proportions. He stood in the doorway, his black hat in his hands.

Izzy turned at the sound of his voice.

"Thank-you, Mr. Hobson. We'll come and see you tomorrow to make final arrangements for the funeral service."

"Very good, Mrs. Dalton. Please accept my condolences."

Izzy nodded, and Mr. Hobson took his leave.

Izzy and Jess stood and listened to the sound of the hearse, as it was turned in the back yard, and driven down the bumpy driveway to the street. Silence followed.

Izzy looked at Jess.

"We'd better get this bed made up, Jess. You'll have to sleep here, I'm afraid."

Jess's eyes widened. "I can't sleep in here, Izzy! I'll sleep on the couch."

For once, Izzy didn't argue. "Very well. I'll get you some blankets."

Beau's Arrival

It was a long day, as the constant stream of friends and neighbours came by to offer their condolences to the family. Sarah had been a loved and respected member of the community, and the word of her passing had spread like wildfire.

Jess and Izzy had no chance to catch up on well-needed sleep. Freya constantly demanded her mother's attention, and they were kept busy making pots of tea.

Finally, at about five o'clock, everyone had gone, and the sisters collapsed into each other's arms, completely exhausted.

"If I have to drink another cup of tea, I swear I'll burst!" Izzy exclaimed, just as Harry emerged from his exclusion zone; the shop.

"Well, you can make me one." He winked at Jess. This was Harry's idea of a joke.

Izzy threw a pot mitt in his direction. "Make it yourself! I'm done!"

Harry shrugged. "What's for tea, or do I have to get that as well?"

Izzy looked at Jess. "What a good idea. Come on, sis, we can retire to the lounge while Harry gets the tea." She ushered Jess towards the door.

"Take your daughter with you!" called Harry to their retreating backs. "I'm not looking after her as well!"

"Why not?" Izzy grabbed Freya by the hand. "She's perfectly happy playing here with her dolls."

"Out!" said Harry, playing along with his wife's lighter mood. In an hour or so it might be a different story.

Jess was sitting back on the couch, her eyes closed, when Izzy entered the lounge.

"We're in charge of Freya while Harry cooks us some tea, Jess."

"Hm." Jess's eyes remained closed.

Izzy collapsed into an armchair opposite her sister, while Freya found another collection of toys in the corner of the room.

"Do you know that Freya will be two next week?"

Jess opened her eyes. Yes, she knew, because Freya had been born just after Jack had sailed for the Western Front. "I know," she said quietly.

Izzy was silent for a few moments.

"It doesn't seem like two years. I sometimes wonder what we did without her." She yawned. "Did you get on to Margaret?"

"Yes, I did."

"What did she say?"

"What could she say, Izzy? She's very sorry."

"Will they come up for the funeral, do you think?"

"They have the children, Izzy; I've told them not to."

"Hm." Izzy closed her eyes. "When do you think Beau will get here?"

"That's a very good question. Providing he can travel through to Melbourne, I don't see him getting here for at least a couple of days."

"Quarantine still happening in Albury?"

"I imagine so."

"So he may not be able to travel through to Melbourne?"

"No."

"I'm surprised he hasn't telephoned to say where he is."

"Let's wait and see, shall we?" Jess closed her eyes again. Suddenly her head felt disconnected from her body, and the scene inside her eyelids was spinning around and around. "I'll dispense with tea, Izzy, if you don't mind," she muttered. "I need to give in to sleep right now."

Izzy heaved herself out of the lounge chair, and threw a blanket across Jess's knees. "Alright, Jessie. We'll leave your tea on the hob. Come on, Freya, let's see what daddy is cooking up for tea."

Jess heard the door close behind them, and she felt herself sinking into that blessed darkness brought on by total exhaustion. Sleep claimed her in a matter of moments.

*

Jess was awakened by a voice at her ear. "Jess!"

She struggled to emerge from the fog that surrounded her.

"Jess!" There it was again. She felt something brushing gently across her forehead.

Blinking rapidly, she tried to sit up. A face swam before her, and her focus slowly returned. It was Beau. Her fingers clutched at his jacket, and her breath came in gasps, as his arms surrounded her. With her face pressed against his neck, Jess had no control over the tears that welled up inside her.

"It's alright, darling girl," Beau murmured against her ear. "I'm here now."

When her tears finally subsided, Jess looked up into his eyes.

"What time is it?" She wiped her fingers across her wet cheeks. "How long have I been asleep?"

"It's ten o'clock, and you've been asleep for at least two hours."

"Two hours?" The fog hadn't quite lifted. "How long have you been here?"

"I arrived about eight o'clock." Beau grinned suddenly. "Izzy said I wasn't to wake you, or I'd have her to deal with. They've gone to bed, and I couldn't wait any longer." He brushed his fingers through Jess's tangled hair.

"I must look an absolute fright."

"Not to me," he whispered tenderly, as Jess slid her feet on to the floor, and nestled her head against his shoulder.

"How did you get here so soon?"

She felt him laugh. "I had a bone-shaking ride in a truck, with a man who wanted to know everything about us."

"Us?" Jess turned to look at him, seeing for the first time the stubble on his chin, and the dark shadows around his eyes. She touched his cheek.

As their eyes locked, Beau took her hand and gently kissed each of her fingers.

"I have missed you so much, Jess." His hands cupped her face and his mouth closed on hers, igniting a flame inside her.

They clung together, aware only of each other as the moments ticked by.

It was Beau who finally broke the spell, lifting his head and sighing deeply.

"I'm sorry I wasn't here when your mother passed," he whispered against her hair. "Izzy told me all about it." He laughed softly. "Apparently I'm to sleep in the spare room."

Jess lifted her head quickly, her eyes wide. "That's where mother died."

Beau nodded. "I know. Izzy told me."

"Did she also tell you that I refuse to sleep in there?"

"She did."

Jess felt her cheeks burning, as she realised the implications of what she had just said. Her hands flew to her face. Beau smiled at her discomfort.

"Don't worry," he whispered. "I've been given the house rules, and I have sworn solemnly to obey them." He kissed the tip of her nose. "At this moment I'm very tempted to disobey them."

"And have Izzy on your back?" Jess reached for another kiss. "That would take a very brave man. You're already bending the rules."

"I can't be punished for bending the rules, surely?"

"What Izzy doesn't know, won't hurt her." Jess traced her fingers down his scarred cheek. "I am so happy to see you, Beau. The whole thing has been awful."

"Darling girl, I'd have walked on hot coals to get to you if I'd had to."

"Yes, I believe you would."

"Don't make me leave you just yet."

"You're willing to risk Izzy's wrath?" Jess smiled at his downcast expression.

"For a few more minutes with you, my darling, I'd risk the wrath of God."

Jess gasped. "Beau! You mustn't say things like that!"

"It's true. Now let's not waste our precious minutes."

He drew her to him on the narrow couch, and felt their hearts beating together.

*

An hour later, Izzy, deciding to check on Freya, tiptoed silently along the passage. Noticing a light beneath the lounge-room door, she quietly opened it. Jess and Beau were sound asleep, curled up together on the couch.

Izzy smiled softly, and turning down the light, retreated from the room, closing the door quietly behind her.

"You make sure you take good care of her, Beau," she whispered to herself, as she padded towards Freya's room, "or you *will* answer to me."

"So how did you sleep, Beau?" Izzy, clad in a pink dressing gown, was at the stove, stirring the porridge.

Jess glanced quickly at Beau, sitting across the table from her. He met her glance and smiled.

"I slept very well, thank-you, Izzy."

"The bed wasn't too soft?"

Izzy's question hung in the air, while Jess waited with bated breath for what would surely come.

"As a matter of fact," said Beau, his eyes remaining on Jess's face, "I didn't make it to the bed. The couch was comfortable enough."

Jess was horrified.

Izzy turned, the porridge pot in her hand.

"Was it indeed?" She ladled porridge into bowls.

"Izzy, it wasn't like that," began Jess, her cheeks flushed.

"Wasn't like what?" Izzy looked across at Beau. "Did you break a promise, Beau?"

"No, Izzy, I didn't."

Izzy smiled suddenly. "Well that's alright then. You both looked very cosy when I peeped in at about eleven." She shrugged. "You'd left the light on."

"Good morning, everyone." Harry appeared at the kitchen door, sleep tousled and clad in pyjamas and dressing gown. "Sleep well?"

Izzy smiled benignly. "Oh, yes, Harry. We all slept very well."

"Good." He sniffed the air. "Porridge? Is that the best you can do, Isobel?"

"Would you like to wear it, Harry?" Izzy's expression was completely bland.

"No." Harry sat beside Beau. "I'll eat it."

Jess tried to suppress a giggle, but it escaped, and within a few moments, they were all laughing helplessly.

"Well!" exclaimed Izzy, as she set the porridge pot back on the side of the stove. "That cleared the air, didn't it?"

Jess wiped her eyes. "You two are as funny as a circus."

"It's called 'being married', Jess," laughed Harry. "No, that's not quite true. It's called 'being married to Isobel'." He ducked as a pot mitt sailed over his head. "I'm sorry, Beau. We're not always like this. You must be wondering what sort of family you're marrying into?"

"Oh, I'm not concerned." Beau grinned at Jess. "I'm only marrying Jess."

"Don't be too sure about that." Between mouthfuls of porridge, Izzy managed to organise the day. "That's enough hilarity! We need to get down to the serious business at hand. Harry?"

"What is it, my love?"

"Is Nancy coming in today?"

"Yes." Harry looked up at the clock on the mantel. It was eight twenty. "As a matter of fact she'll be here in ten minutes."

"Good. I'd like her to look after Freya, while Jess and I go to see the Funeral Director."

"Oh! Alright."

"Beau, what would you like to do today?"

Beau looked at Jess, who pulled a face as she lifted a spoonful of porridge.

"I hadn't thought about it, Izzy. What do you suggest?"

Izzy put down her spoon. "I suggest that you spend the morning checking out our wonderful town, and then after lunch, Jess can take you to the family home." She pushed back her chair. "Right! That's all settled. Now I need to get Freya up, while *someone* does the dishes."

"That *someone* won't be me," said Harry, also pushing back his chair. "I must get dressed before Nancy arrives." He left the kitchen.

Izzy looked at Jess and Beau. "It looks like you're left with the dishes." She smiled sweetly. "There aren't many. You're lucky that Harry didn't cook up a storm."

When they were alone, Jess stacked the porridge bowls.

"We have been told." She smiled at Beau's bemused expression.

"I really want to spend my time with you."

"Izzy and I do have to organise the funeral, Beau, and then we can spend time together. How long do you think you'll stay?"

"Alf is returning from Mildura on Friday, and he'll take me to Albury, if I'm ready to go. When do you think the funeral might be?"

"What's today? I'm losing track of time."

"Today is Tuesday."

"Then we'll have to arrange the funeral for Thursday."

Beau nodded slowly. "I must be with you for that, Jess. I didn't meet your mother, but from what Izzy told me about her last night, you must be like her."

"Yes." Jess felt tears prickling behind her eyes. "I wish I had made the effort to see her more often."

Beau clasped her hands across the table. "No self-recrimination, Jess. You did the best you could." He squeezed her fingers. "My mother died when I was a child, so I don't even remember her."

"And your father?"

"He died around the time I went into Medical College."

"I know so little about you, Beau."

He smiled. "I'll tell you one day."

Matthew and Celia

Celia stalked into Matthew's room, her red lips set in a straight line. Matthew, who was standing at the window, turned, his smile quickly becoming a frown.

"What seems to be the problem, Celia?"

"Problem? What makes you think there's a problem, Matthew?"

Celia flung her handbag on the neatly made bed and stood beside her husband, her hands on her hips.

"Whatever it is, you'd better tell me." Matthew looked sideways at her profile.

Celia swung around to face him. "It's Beau! He's gone!"

"Gone where?" Matthew's eyebrows arched.

"Where do you think? To her, of course!"

Celia reached for her handbag, and pulled out a packet of cigarettes. Her fingers trembled as she attempted to light one. Matthew waited until she had exhaled before he spoke.

"You'd better tell me about it."

"She rang to say her mother was ill, so he caught the morning train to Albury." Celia released another cloud of smoke. Matthew turned away, as the fumes caught in his throat. He coughed harshly.

"Her name's Jess, Celia. Why can't you call her by name?"

"Because I'm too angry." Her foot tapped rapidly on the linoleum. "I've had to reschedule all the patients at the Clinic."

"When did he say he'd be back?"

"A week. He'd better be back by then!"

"It must have been serious, Celia. He wouldn't have gone otherwise."

Celia looked around for something in which to flick her ash. There was a cup and saucer on the window ledge. She removed the cup and flicked her cigarette ash into the saucer. Matthew began to cough again.

"Please don't do that, Celia!" he rasped.

"My smoking has never bothered you before, Matthew."

Matthew turned his head away, breathing hard.

"How did you get here?" he asked finally.

"Yes, well that's another thing!" Celia stubbed her cigarette into the saucer. "I had to catch the tram." She rolled her eyes. "People weren't wearing protective masks, and I had an old woman coughing on me. Thank goodness my face was covered."

"So people should still be covering up?"

"Out on the street? Yes, of course. The newspaper reports that influenza cases are on the rise again. The hospitals are struggling to keep up with them."

"How many do we have here?"

"We have six."

"Serious cases?"

"Three recovering, and three not out of the woods yet."

"What about deaths?"

"We had two deaths here while you were so sick, but nothing since."

Matthew sat on the edge of the bed. "I have to get back to work."

Celia turned to stare at him. "You're not fit for work yet, Matthew."

"Yes, I am! I need to catch up with what's going on out there. Find me a nurse, please, Celia?"

"No, Matthew!"

"Very well." Matthew stood up and walked to the door. "I'll find one."

"Nurse!" he called as he looked along the passage. "Nurse!"

Hurrying footsteps were heard, and the nurse, Susan, appeared.

"Yes, Doctor Morley?"

"I wish to be discharged, nurse. Can you make the arrangements for me?"

Susan glanced at Celia, and hesitated.

"Is that wise, Doctor Morley?" she asked cautiously.

"No, it isn't!" snapped Celia. "You're going back to bed, Matthew."

"The 'discharge' papers, nurse! My Practice is suffering because of my absence. I need to get back to it."

"Matthew! Don't be absurd!" Celia followed him, as he hastily began to change out of his pyjamas, into trousers and shirt. "You're still not well."

Susan hovered uncertainly in the doorway, while Celia tried to stop him by grabbing his shoes from beneath the bed.

"How are you going to get home, Matthew? The car isn't here."

"I'll get home, Celia! Don't you worry about that! Now give me my shoes!"

There was a scuffle as Matthew prised his shoes from Celia's grasp.

"Matthew!" She panted. "Please be reasonable. You are not ready to go home yet. Nurse, could you fetch an orderly, please?"

Susan darted away.

Matthew glared at Celia, and it was then that she noticed the two red spots that had appeared on his cheeks. His breathing suddenly became laboured and he slumped against the bed, coughing fitfully.

Celia tried to prevent him from falling to the floor, but she was not strong enough.

"Matthew!" She dragged at his arms.

A sturdy young orderly appeared in the doorway, followed closely by the nurse.

"He collapsed!" sobbed Celia, as the orderly lifted Matthew effortlessly, and laid him on the bed.

Susan placed a thermometer beneath his tongue, before loosening his clothing.

"He seems to have had a relapse," she said, as she removed the thermometer. "It's what I was afraid of; his temperature is 101." She slipped the thermometer in her apron pocket. "We need to cool him down." She ran from the room.

Celia stood helplessly to one side, as Susan returned with a bowl of cold water and compresses. She applied one to Matthew's forehead, and another across the back of his neck.

"He needs to be back in the other wards," she said, looking in Celia's direction, "but I don't think there are any spare beds."

Celia's eyes were large and genuinely fearful.

"So he could be contagious again?" she whispered.

"I don't know, but we'll need to wear masks while we're attending to him." She looked at the orderly, standing quietly by the door. "Could you get us some masks, please, Steven?"

When he had gone, Susan turned to Celia.

"I'm sorry to do this to you, Mrs. Morley, but could you change the compresses every ten minutes? It's vital that his temperature comes down."

Celia nodded mutely.

Susan smiled encouragingly. "I'll go and see if Doctor Freeman is still here."

Sarah's Funeral

It was Thursday, the day of Sarah's funeral. The rain was falling, and a chill wind wrapped itself around the crowd of mourners gathered at the graveside to say their farewells. People battled with black umbrellas, as the wind tried to wrench them from gloved hands.

The Minister, his long black robes flapping against his legs, spoke quickly about Sarah's long-time loyalty to the town she and her husband, James, had called home. Rain droplets fogged his spectacles, and the pages of his Bible were tearing away from his fingers. Harry held an umbrella above his head, but it flapped violently, threatening at any moment to be blown inside out.

> *"Forasmuch as it hath pleased Almighty God of His great mercy to take unto Himself the soul of our dear sister here departed, we therefore commit her body to the ground; earth to earth, ashes to ashes, dust to dust; in sure and certain hope of the Resurrection to eternal life, through our Lord Jesus Christ. Amen."*

A final gust of wind blew the umbrella inside out, as Harry wrestled with it. The Minister whispered something to him, and Harry beckoned several men in the crowd to come forward. They left the shelter of umbrellas, and moved towards the casket. Standing three to each side, they carried it to where the earth had been prepared. Carefully they set it on the ropes and eased it into the ground.

Jess and Izzy stood close together by the grave as their mother was lowered slowly to her final resting place. Tears mingled with the rain on their faces as they clung together. When the casket was down, they showered rose petals on to the lid; roses picked from Sarah's garden.

The Minister, anxious to get everyone out of the rain, raised his hands.

"Please, can you all move to the Sunday School Hall? I think you'll find it will be much more comfortable, and the ladies are serving up a lovely afternoon tea."

He began to usher people forward, like a shepherd trying to move his flock. Beau made his way to Jess's side and placed an arm protectively around her, while Harry took Izzy's hand. Together they picked their way across the sodden grass to the hall. Jess shivered with the cold. She had not brought her thick coat with her, and so had to make do with a light jacket and her favourite shawl; the one Izzy had given her so long ago.

The hall was warm as they stepped inside, but the smell of wet clothing lingered in the air. Cups of tea were being handed around, and plates of fresh scones were quickly being consumed. Beau ushered Jess to a seat.

"I'll get you a cup of tea, Jess." He rubbed her cold fingers. "And a scone if there are any left." He smiled and left her there.

Izzy sat beside her. "It's a pity about the rain, Jess, but I suppose there are a lot of farmers out there, and in here, who are extremely happy about it."

"Judging by the chatter, I would say you are right, Izzy." Jess pushed back her wet hair, as she looked around the crowd of strangers. "I don't know any of these people. Should I, Izzy?"

"Well, there are one or two faces you should remember, Jess. There's Mrs. Teesdale over there, talking to Mr. Robertson." Izzy nodded towards a man and woman, deep in animated discussion. "The Teesdales own Riverview Farm, and Mr. Robertson has been the dentist here forever."

Jess smiled. "Oh, yes, I do remember Mr. Robertson. Mother had to lead me, kicking and screaming, to see him." She shuddered.

"Who was kicking and screaming?" Beau had arrived, juggling two cups of tea and a plate of scones.

"Jess was," said Izzy quickly, "when she had to see Mr. Robertson, the dentist."

"He's over there." Jess took a cup, and placed the plate of scones on her knee.

"I see." Beau glanced briefly in the direction of the grey-haired gentleman with the ample paunch, who was laughing uproariously. "Oh, Izzy, Harry is getting you a cup of tea."

Izzy stood up. "Sit here, Beau. I'll go and look for Harry." She smiled and moved away through the crowd.

Beau sat beside Jess. "You look weary, my love." He took a scone.

"I am." She smiled at his concern. "I've been away for so long, Beau, that I'm the stranger here. These people were mother's friends, and I don't remember them." Jess took a sip of tea. The cup was warm in her cold hands.

"Don't feel bad about it, Jess. That's what life does, I'm afraid."

Doctor Barton took that moment to approach Jess, and he lifted his hat politely.

"Mrs. Stanley, forgive me, but I was unaware that you are Mrs. Dalton's sister until now. You must think me very rude not to have acknowledged you the night your mother died. Please accept my apologies."

"That's perfectly alright, Doctor Barton." Jess looked at Beau. "Doctor Barton, let me introduce you to Doctor DuBois, who works in Sydney."

"Ah!" Doctor Barton's eyes lit up. "You're not at the General Hospital, by any chance? I hear the influenza has forced the set up of field hospitals like they had during the war."

"No, I'm not at the General. I'm actually involved with a Clinic set up to deal with returned soldiers and all the psychological and emotional problems that they've brought home with them. With the influenza now plaguing our city, we have all opened our doors to extra patients."

"How interesting. I would like to talk more fully about this, if you can spare me a few minutes." Doctor Barton looked apologetically at Jess.

"Go ahead, Beau. I don't mind."

"Are you sure?"

Jess nodded. "Here, take these scones with you."

Jess watched as the two men walked to a quiet corner of the hall.

"Beau has found Doctor Barton, I see." Izzy sat beside Jess, and gently eased her feet out of her shoes. "These are killing me," she complained.

"Izzy, I've told you before that your shoes are not suitable, especially on a day like today; teetering about on the slippery grass."

"I know." Izzy yawned. "I just want to go home and put my feet up by the fire. It's been such a long day."

"We can't very well sneak out, while everyone is having a jolly time, reminiscing."

"Is that what they're doing? I think they're enjoying your scones, little sister."

"It was one way to fill the morning."

"I can't make scones to save my life. You must have got that talent from mother. Her scones were always as light as a feather." Izzy's eyes wandered across towards Beau and Doctor Barton. "The good doctors seem to be enjoying themselves. They have a lot to discuss, I expect."

"Hm."

"So Beau's leaving tomorrow?"

"Yes. The driver who dropped him off here on Monday, is coming back this way tomorrow, and is happy to have the company back to Albury."

"I'm sure he is." Izzy patted Jess's hand. "We're all going to miss him, Jess. He fits in comfortably with our eccentric family." She paused for a moment. "When are you going to put him out of his misery, Jess?"

Jess turned startled eyes on her sister. "What do you mean?"

"I mean 'when are you going to marry him'?"

"We haven't had time to talk about it, Izzy."

"I suppose not." Izzy paused. "Can I tell you something, little sister; something that I've never disclosed before?"

"And what is that?"

"Harry and I didn't wait until we'd tied the knot." Izzy looked her sister straight in the eye.

"You didn't?" Jess looked across at Beau, who at that moment, glanced in her direction. He smiled.

"No, we didn't."

"Why are you telling me this, Izzy?"

"No reason. I thought you might like to know." Izzy smiled at Jess's pained expression. "When two people are meant for each other, it's a natural progression. Now be a good girl, and don't let that wonderful man wait too long."

Jess looked across at Beau. "Do you remember what you said to me the first time you met Beau?"

Izzy groaned. "No, but I imagine it was something out of place, or you wouldn't be reminding me of it now."

"You said 'now there's a face only a mother could love'."

Izzy shuddered. "Did I really say that, Jess? How horrible!"

"He's still the same man, Izzy. See how your concept of him has changed?"

"I'm so sorry, Jess." Izzy looked contrite. "You could always see beneath the scars.

It has taken me a little longer."

Harry was heading towards them. "You two look as though you need to go home." He seated himself beside Izzy.

"We do." Izzy linked her arm in his. "Do you think you can spirit us away, Harry?"

"I can try." He smiled indulgently at his wife, and Jess had a sudden image of them sneaking away to some secret rendezvous. She turned away to hide the smile.

*

"Aaaah! That's better." Izzy stretched her bare feet towards the flames that crackled up the lounge room chimney. "What a long day!"

She was seated beside Jess on the couch that had been Jess's bed for the past few nights. Harry was at the big oak sideboard, pouring red wine into glasses.

He handed the sisters a glass each, and then settled himself in the big old lounge chair with its crocheted rugs and plump cushions.

"It's good to relax, I must admit." He sipped his wine and sighed contentedly. "The poor Reverend had a nasty time of it, what with the rain and wind." He grinned. "And then, the umbrella had to blow itself inside out. I nearly went up with it."

Izzy laughed into her wine glass. "Come on, Harry, it would take more than an umbrella to lift you off the ground."

Harry looked at Jess, his eyes twinkling. "This woman has no respect for her husband. Have you noticed that, Jess?"

Jess shook her head. "You knew what Izzy was like when you married her."

"I say! Are you both going to gang up on me? I need Nancy here to defend me."

"She only defends you because she works for you." Izzy wriggled her toes. "It was very good of her to look after Freya today. I don't think I'd have coped with a child around my feet all day."

"Well you didn't have to, and my children are safe at their grandparents' house, so we're both very fortunate." Jess looked into her glass. "The boys are going to want to know all about it. Jack…" She stopped.

"What about Jack, Jessie?" Izzy put her arm around Jess's shoulders.

"Nothing. It doesn't matter." Jess stood and put her glass on the sideboard. "I'm going to find Beau."

"He was on the back verandah, having a smoke, when I last saw him," Harry said over his shoulder.

Jess made her way through the darkening kitchen and opened the wire door. She could see the glow of a cigarette, further along the verandah.

Beau turned as she stood beside him. He took a last puff and dropped the butt on to the verandah, where he crushed it with his shoe.

"Harry said I'd find you out here." Jess slid her arms around him and he held her close, his chin resting on the top of her head.

"I have to go back to Sydney tomorrow, Jess." There was remorse in his tone.

"I know, but it won't be for long, hopefully."

Jess felt him take a deep breath. "Once Matthew is completely well, I'll leave." His hands slid down her body, pressing her against him. "I'll come to you with nothing,

Jess, just as I arrived at your gate nearly three years ago."

Jess looked into his eyes, shadowed in the last of the evening light. "Your love is enough, Beau. Everything else will sort itself out."

"Do you mean that, Jess?" His face was close to hers.

"Don't doubt me, Beau. Don't ever doubt me."

"I love you so much, Jess; I always have, although I tried to deny it."

"It's strange the way life is mapped out for us. We have no say in it really."

"It's a good job we don't."

"Do you know what Izzy said to me today?"

Beau gave a short laugh. "Tell me."

"She asked me when I was going to put you out of your misery and marry you."

"My misery?"

"That's what she said."

"Darling girl, find me a preacher and I'll marry you right now."

"So we can plan on it being soon then?"

"As soon as you want it, my love. I'll leave the planning in your hands." He leaned back and studied her face. "It's not going to be a big affair, is it?"

"No, not if I have any say in it."

He kissed her then, and as their bodies melted together, each knew that the night was going to be agonisingly long, knowing that they were only a room away from each other.

"I can't wait much longer, Jess," Beau whispered into her hair. "In the meantime, I'd better let you go to your lonely bed, and I'll go to mine." His fingers slowly traced the contours of her face. "Tomorrow is going to be another very long day."

*

Friday dawned with a watery hint of sunshine after the bleak chill of the previous day. The family had gathered at the table, but this morning there was no sign of the usual banter that accompanied breakfast.

Porridge was eaten in silence; there was no comment from Harry. He finished eating and excused himself. Izzy pushed her chair away from the table, and after placing her bowl in the sink, also excused herself.

"I'd better go and see to Freya." She smiled thinly at the two still seated.

When Izzy had gone, Beau reached across the table and took Jess's hands. Her eyes were moist as she looked at him, and she clutched at his fingers.

"What time are you expecting your ride?" she asked, her voice husky.

"Mid-day. Alf hopes to be here by then. He'll have lunch at a pub, and then pick me up on the roadside." There was silence. "When are you going home?"

Jess cleared her throat. "Probably tomorrow. Margaret and Charles have had the children long enough. I need to go home."

Beau rubbed her fingers. "I hope I can get away soon, Jess. Matthew must be ready to go back to work by now." He released her hands and sat back with a sigh. "I'll have some explaining to do when I get there. I had no time to talk with Matthew, so goodness knows what Celia has said to him."

"What could she say to him?"

"She could say anything, and feel completely justified." Beau pushed his chair back from the table. "I'd better go and pack my bag."

Jess watched him move from the kitchen. Once again she wanted to halt time so that she didn't have to say goodbye. It seemed that her life was filled with goodbyes, and only snatches of good times in between.

Jess rose slowly from her chair and carried their plates to the sink. She stared at the dirty dishes for a time, before consciously rousing herself to wash them.

After drying her hands, she wandered into the passage and found herself outside Beau's room. Slowly she opened the door. Beau was standing at the bed, his bag open in front of him. He turned as Jess entered, and opened his arms. She walked into his embrace, and they stood close together in silence. In another two hours, he would be gone.

"I have something for you," he whispered into her hair.

Jess lifted her head. "Something for me?"

"When Izzy sent me out to explore her lovely town on Tuesday, I came across a jeweller, and I bought you something."

"Oh?"

Beau released her and put his hand into his trouser pocket. "I know you love your mother's ruby pendant, so I bought you something to match."

"Beau! You didn't!"

In his hand he held a small red velvet box. Jess's eyes widened as he opened the lid to reveal a ring with a ruby red stone surrounded by tiny diamonds. Jess looked up at him in amazement.

"It's not a ruby, Jess; it's a garnet, and the diamonds are quartz, but it was the nearest I could get to the real thing. Do you like it?"

"It's beautiful, but you shouldn't have."

"I needed something tangible to join us together." He took her left hand and slipped the ring on her third finger. "Now I can say you belong to me."

Jess held her hand up, and the precious stones winked in the sunlight that glanced through the window. She looked at him, her eyes shining.

"You've had this with you since Tuesday, and you waited until now to give it to me?" Jess chastised gently.

"I didn't think it appropriate to give it to you before now."

"No, I suppose not." Jess slid her arms around him once more, and lifted her face for a lingering kiss.

"Oh!" Izzy's voice brought them apart. "I'm sorry. I didn't mean to interrupt."

Jess turned and held out her hand towards Izzy, who gave a squeal of delight.

"What's this then? Is this the official word?"

"You could say that." Beau was smiling as Izzy stretched out her arms.

"Then how about a hug for your future sister-in-law!" She pulled him into an enthusiastic embrace. "Does this mean we can plan a wedding now, Jess?"

Jess looked at Beau as he untangled himself from Izzy's arms. "We're not having a big wedding, Izzy; just something quiet with the families."

"What family do you have, Beau? You've never mentioned any."

"My parents are both dead, but I have a sister somewhere. I haven't seen her since I was a child. She's ten years older than me." His brow creased. "Her name's Charlotte, and sadly, I know nothing about her."

"You have a sister?" Jess was staring incredulously at Beau.

He shrugged. "I don't know her, Jess," he said apologetically.

"Yes, but…"

"Well that shouldn't be too difficult then." Izzy laughed a little too loudly. "Come and show Harry and Nancy. We all need some cheering up this morning." She turned to Beau. "How long have you been keeping this quiet, may I ask?"

"Since you sent me out to explore the town on Tuesday."

"Since then? Shame on you, Beau! Now come on!"

Harry and Nancy were duly impressed, and asked the same question of Beau. Harry slapped him on the back. "While there's nobody about, I think this calls for a little celebration. I'll get us all a drink. Wait here."

He disappeared into the house.

"So you won't be waiting until Martin gets home at Christmas?" Nancy asked quietly.

"I don't think so, Nancy." Jess looked at Beau, who shook his head.

Harry returned with glasses and a bottle of wine.

"Your daughter's awake, Isobel," he said as he poured the wine.

"She'll have to wait until we've drunk a toast." Izzy raised her glass.

"To Jessie and Beau. I hope life is kind to you; you both deserve it."

Harry and Nancy raised their glasses.

"Now," said Izzy, putting down her glass, "I must go. A child awaits."

*

Two hours later, Jess and Beau stood by the roadside, waiting for Alf Peterson's truck to arrive. It wasn't long before Beau saw it approaching, canvas flapping.

"Here he comes, Jess."

They watched as the truck slid to a halt on the wet gravel. Alf leaned out of the cabin, his whiskered face wreathed in a smile.

"So is this the lucky lady, eh Beau?" Alf was smiling at Jess.

"Yes, Alf, this is Jess, and I think we are now officially engaged."

"Jolly good. Pleased to meet you, Jess." He turned his grin to Beau. "We have about six hours for you to tell me all about it."

"Six hours!" Beau was smiling. "If I remember correctly, Alf, it took seven hours to get here."

"Yeah, but that was only because the bloody engine kept overheatin'. Anyway, there won't be a train to Sydney tonight, so what's ya hurry?"

"No hurry, I suppose."

"Alright then, if y've said y'goodbyes, we'll be away!"

Beau turned to Jess, and gathered her into his arms for a final kiss.

"No more goodbyes, Beau," he heard her murmur.

"No more goodbyes, I promise."

Then he was gone, and Jess watched until the truck was out of sight. She walked slowly back to where Izzy stood outside the shop. Silently they embraced.

"Well, Jessie," Izzy whispered, "I thought you might have responded to my confession yesterday, but I gather it went right over your head."

Jess stared at her sister. "Meaning?"

"Meaning I gave you permission to break the house rules, and you didn't take it."

Jess's eyes widened, and colour suffused her cheeks.

"Oh, Izzy, I don't believe you said that."

"It must have crossed your mind, surely?"

"That's not the point. This is your home, and I...we had to respect that."

Izzy shook her head slowly. "Don't say I didn't try."

Jess was silent, suddenly feeling very vulnerable and yearning for her children and the security of her own home.

"I'm leaving tomorrow, Izzy."

Izzy nodded as she gave Jess's shoulder a gentle squeeze.

"You always had more conscience than I did, Jess."

"No, Izzy; that's not true."

"Well, anyway, you have our blessings, and I hope it all happens soon."

Storm Clouds

Beau knocked on the door of Celia and Matthew's terrace apartment. It was four in the afternoon, and he had just stepped off the train from Albury. He was travel weary and dishevelled, and should have stopped by his own room to tidy himself up, but he needed to see whether Matthew was home.

Nobody answered. It was Saturday afternoon, so they wouldn't be at the Clinic. Beau knocked again, a little louder. This time he heard movement behind the door, and it opened. Celia stood there, her face devoid of make-up, and her eyes puffy and red-rimmed. Beau stared at her.

"What's the matter?" he asked finally.

"Matthew's in the hospital." Celia hiccoughed.

"What?"

"He's been taken to Sydney General." She pushed a hand through her untidy hair.

"Is that Beauregarde, Celia?" Clarence's voice could be clearly heard.

"Yes."

"Then you'd better let him in."

Celia opened the door, and Beau stepped into the warmth of the living room.

Clarence was seated on the couch, a glass of red wine in his hand. Beau stood inside the door, as Celia closed it and went to sit beside her father.

"Perhaps you'd better tell me what's going on," ventured Beau, glancing from one to the other.

"Come and sit down." Clarence indicated the lounge chair opposite him. "Would you care for a wine?"

"No, thank-you, sir." Beau sat on the edge of the plush velvet chair and waited.

Celia blew her nose, and then stared across at Beau, while Clarence placed his glass carefully on a small polished table beside the couch.

"Matthew collapsed," began Clarence, "and Doctor Freeman had him transferred to the Sydney hospital for tests."

"And?"

"He has tuberculosis."

"Tuberculosis?" Beau shook his head. "How could this have happened?"

"It seems that Matthew had pneumonia as a boy, which left him with a weakness which the influenza virus quickly attacked. That has now been overtaken by the tuberculosis bacteria, and well, we all know what that does to the lungs."

Beau shut his eyes for a moment.

"So what happens now?"

"He'll have to convalesce for several months." Celia was watching Beau closely. "Time and complete rest are the two things that will get him through this."

"I see." Beau took a deep breath.

"So you see, my boy," said Clarence, his eyes also on Beau, "I'm afraid we cannot release you for some time." He shrugged his shoulders. "I'm sorry. I know this is not what you wanted to hear, but that's the way the dice has been thrown."

It was like a hammer blow to Beau's chest. He looked at Celia. Her eyes told him nothing; they were hollow and expressionless.

Beau found his voice. "I presume he will be transferred to a sanatorium? "

Celia nodded. "Yes." It was barely audible.

"We've chosen a private facility, up in the mountains," said Clarence, "where the air is clean, and he will stand the best chance of recovery."

Beau looked down at his dusty shoes, so out of place in this elegant room, and tried to tuck them beneath him.

"This means we have to discuss the future of the Clinic."

"We do." Clarence picked up his glass. "Are you sure you don't want a drink?"

"No, thank-you."

"The Board has interviewed several applicants, and we are down to two young men who have completed their training; one in psychiatry and one in general practise. They are both very keen to gain experience, and I think if they work with you over the coming months, while Matthew is away, then we should have an excellent team." He sipped his wine. "We only need this blasted influenza to disappear. It keeps rearing its ugly head and putting everything behind."

Beau's head was whirling. He had not seen this coming, and now he was powerless to do anything other than stay put. This could take until the end of the year, if they were lucky; twelve months worst case scenario.

"Can I go and see him?"

"Not a good idea, Beauregarde," said Clarence. "We have to stay away, too."

Celia moved to the sideboard and poured herself a glass of wine.

"The place he is going to is called Willowbank Sanatorium. It's very picturesque, and hidden away in the hills. I'll go and stay there once he's established."

"Damn rotten luck really!" Clarence drained his glass.

Celia was speaking again. "We haven't asked about you, Beau. How was your visit to Swan Hill?"

Beau shook away the thoughts that had crowded his brain. "Jess's mother died before I got there, so I stayed for the funeral."

"I'm sorry."

Beau studied Celia's face. Never had he seen her contrite, but in this instance, he thought he caught a glimpse of contrition.

"How did you get to and from Swan Hill, may I ask?" Clarence joined the conversation. "There aren't any trains."

"I got a ride with a truck driver going from Albury to Mildura." Beau looked down on his dishevelled appearance. "Hence the state of my clothes."

"So you've come straight from the train?"

"Yes, I have."

"Have you eaten?"

'Not since breakfast."

"Well then," said Clarence cheerfully, "you must allow us to take you to dinner." He smiled at Celia. "How about Mario's, Celia?"

Celia cocked an eyebrow at Beau, and her moment of contrition vanished. "Only if you go home and change, Beau."

"Celia!" Clarence flapped a hand at his daughter. "You need to do something about your own appearance, if I might be so bold as to mention it."

"Yes, daddy, seeing as you mentioned it!"

"Thank-you, sir," said Beau stiffly. "That's very kind of you."

"It's about time you called me Clarence." He looked at his pocket watch. "Shall we say six o'clock? We'll pick you up in the motorcar."

Beau nodded as he stood and followed Celia to the door.

"Don't keep us waiting, Beau." Celia gave him a tight smile.

Beau stepped out on to the street. His legs felt like jelly, and his head hurt. What did he do now? It was clear where his duty lay, but his heart cried out against it. He needed to talk to Jess, but what was he going to say to her? That they had to wait perhaps for another twelve months? Twelve months? That seemed like a lifetime. His steps faltered as he made his way along the deserted streets, and he thought of Matthew, struck down now with tuberculosis, with the prospect of being locked away in a sanatorium for possibly twelve months.

Now he had to dress and be presentable to dine with Clarence and Celia, where discussion would surely turn to the Clinic and what would happen next.

What *would* happen next? He could no longer make a prediction.

He thought about Jess. Would she be home from Swan Hill yet? He would have to leave it until the following morning to telephone her. He desperately needed to talk to her, but how much more bad news could she be expected to endure?

Beau unlocked the door to his humble room. The air was cold and stale. He shut the door behind him, and for a brief second wanted to run from the world that kept throwing him against the rocks. Sweat beaded his forehead, and a cry tore at his throat. He couldn't do this; it was too hard.

He clenched his fists until his nails bit into the flesh.

"Jess!" he cried into the empty room. "Help me!"

Part Four

Reconciled

The Package

Jess unlocked the front door and stepped into the passage. It felt good to be home. Closing the door behind her, she walked into her bedroom, put her case on the bed, and removed her hat. She shook out her hair, dropped her shawl on the bed, and slipped her feet out of her shoes. Putting on her slippers, she headed for the kitchen. It was warm, and the kettle was singing on the side of the stove.

Jess smiled to herself. Margaret had been and set the fire, so that she didn't have to come home to a cold house. Looking around, Jess could see that Margaret had left other small touches of comfort for her. There was a small vase of violets on the table, and a plate of biscuits. A letter lay on the table, and beside it, a package.

Jess picked up the letter. Her heart beat quickly as she read the sender address. It was from the Base Records office, and she knew that the package would contain Jack's few possessions.

Slowly she removed the brown paper and stared at the small cardboard box for a few moments, before lifting the lid. Blinking back the tears, she saw Jack's well-worn Bible, a collection of notebooks, the pictures that the boys had drawn for their father, his beloved pipe, and the scarf that his mother had knitted for him. On the bottom of the box lay her photograph, with the letters she had written.

Jess had to sit as she spread the collection in front of her. Picking up Jack's Bible, she laid it against her cheek, breathing in the smell. It was musty, and signs of mildew encrusted the cover, but it was so familiar that Jess put her head on the table and wept. This small package of his treasures was all that was left of her beloved Jack.

Jess wiped her eyes, and opened the letter. It was from the Base Records office, and merely gave an inventory of the articles contained in the box. Jess read it, and placed it back in the envelope. There was nothing of a personal nature written there, and no other explanation. She sighed as she gathered the items and placed them back in the box. The children would like to see that their father had kept their drawings.

Jess saw a movement on the back verandah, and heard her children's voices. She waited as Margaret opened the back door, and they all filed into the kitchen. Three faces lit up at once when they saw their mother sitting at the table, and they rushed into her arms. Margaret followed, closing the door behind her.

"Hello, Jess," she said, above the noise of their chatter. "I think we're all pleased to see you home."

"It's good to be home." Jess clung to her children.

"Have you had a cup of tea, yet?"

"No. I haven't been here long."

"We heard the train, and they all wanted to come and see you." Margaret moved to the stove, where she pushed the kettle across to boil.

"Thank-you Margaret, it was lovely coming home to a warm kitchen."

"I thought you'd appreciate it."

Ben, who had spotted the open box on the table, pulled it towards him.

"What's this, ma?"

"That's your father's belongings, Ben, or what's left of them." Jess looked up at Margaret, whose eyes glistened.

The boys began delving through the papers, discovering their own handiwork.

"Dad kept our pictures?" Edward's eyes were shining.

"Yes, Edward, he did, and now they are yours again."

"Children," said Margaret quietly, "I'd like to speak with your mother, so could you go to your rooms for a little while?" She smiled softly.

Ben nodded, and grabbing Edward by the sleeve, hauled him away from the table.

"Here," said Margaret, "take a biscuit with you."

Grace was not so easily moved, and clung like a limpet to her mother.

"She's alright, Margaret. That's the longest we've ever been apart."

Margaret handed Grace a biscuit.

"How was it, Jess? I'm sorry we didn't get there. Charles wanted to go, but I told him what you had said, and I think he saw the sense in it."

"It was rather harrowing, Margaret," said Jess, over Grace's head, "but we all got through it. The day of the funeral was bitterly cold and wet."

"Yes, it was here, too." Margaret placed a cup of tea in front of Jess. "Oh! What a lovely ring! Is that one of your mother's?"

"No." Jess shook her head. "Beau gave it to me."

"Beau was there, Jess?"

"Yes, he managed to get away from Sydney. It was rather tricky, but he got a ride with a truck driver from Albury, who was kind enough to pick him up on the return journey yesterday."

"I'm glad he was there, Jess." Margaret had Jack's pipe in her hand, and she ran her fingers along the well-worn stem. "Jack didn't go far without this."

"No. I'm pleased to have it back."

Margaret put the pipe carefully back in the box. "Keep it for the boys."

The two women were silent for a time, while they sipped on their tea, and thought of Jack. Grace remained attached to her mother.

"Anything happened here while I was away?" asked Jess finally.

"Nothing significant." Margaret's brow puckered. "Oh, I did have a visit from Sid O'Connor while I was here getting the house ready for you."

"Oh?"

"He said that you were willing to 'give him another chance', (his words) and he wanted to know when he could drop a load of wood here." Margaret paused. "I told him he'd have to wait until you came home. What did he mean, Jess?"

Jess sighed. "The last time Sid O'Connor came here, before both he and Phyllis Powell disappeared, he was extremely aggressive, and stole blankets from the sleep-out."

"What!" Margaret's eyes widened. "And you're going to give him another chance?"

"Only with certain rules attached."

"Jess, I'm sorry, but isn't that being rather foolish?"

Jess picked up Jack's Bible. "Jack would have given him a second chance."

Margaret shook her head. "Well, I hope you know what you are doing."

Jess placed the Bible back in the box. "How's Jean?"

"She's alright." Margaret sat back. "She seems happy with her new barman."

"Good."

There was another short silence.

"When does Beau hope to leave Sydney?"

"As soon as his colleague is well enough."

"Soon then?"

Jess nodded. "I hope so." She touched the precious stone on her finger. "He gave me this ring, as something tangible to hold us together."

Margaret reached out and took Jess's hand. "It will. I know it will."

*

The following morning, Jess was enjoying a sleep-in, while the children played quietly in their rooms. Her eyes were closed, and she could hear the boys laughing. It was a soothing sound, and she was tempted to go back to sleep. Suddenly the telephone rang in the passage.

As Jess swung her legs out of bed and reached for her dressing gown, she heard running footsteps.

"I'll get it, ma!" she heard Ben shout.

The telephone clicked as he picked up the receiver, and she heard him answer. There was silence, and then he spoke again.

"Beau! I'll get ma! Wait a minute."

Jess tied her dressing gown around her, and as she hurried from the room, Ben handed her the receiver.

"Its Beau, ma!"

"Thank-you, Ben." Jess took a deep breath. "Beau?"

"You got home alright, Jess?"

"Yes, and you? Where are you?"

"I'm at the Clinic. There's nobody else here."

He was silent.

"Beau? Are you alright?"

"It's Matthew. He…" Jess heard the quaver in Beau's voice, and she waited for him to continue. "He has tuberculosis."

"Tuberculosis?"

"Yes. He'll be taken to a sanatorium, where he'll stay for some months."

Jess felt the wall coming towards her. She put out a hand to stop from falling.

"What are you saying, Beau?" Her voice was coming from far away.

"I can't leave here, Jess." She heard the anguish in his voice. "I have to stay."

"Are you extending?" a droll voice cut in.

"Yes!" Beau answered harshly. "Jess, I am so sorry. I don't know what to say. God knows when I'll be able to see you again." Jess was unable to speak. "Jess, are you still there? I need to know that you're still there. You are my world, darling girl, and I would do anything to be with you right now, but I'm at a loss." He stopped to compose himself. "I can't lose you, Jess. Say something, please? Help me, Jess?"

"How?"

"By reassuring me."

"Something worth having is worth fighting for, Beau. Remember?"

"Yes, I remember, and I have a feeling it will be a fight."

"I'll be here. I'll wait for you, Beau, I promise." Jess gave a shaky laugh. "We may have a Christmas wedding, after all."

"I love you, Jess. Whatever happens, know that I love you."

"I know." Jess looked down to see Ben staring anxiously at her. "And I love you." The line went dead.

Jess slowly replaced the receiver.

"Are you alright, ma?" Ben's brown eyes were full of concern.

"I have to be, Ben." Jess brushed a hand through his tousled hair. "Come on, let's go and have some breakfast."

Celia

Beau put down the receiver, and walked across to the window. He gazed out on to his favourite view, but today the sea was grey and turbulent. Boats were being tossed about like corks, and as he watched, the ferry disappeared behind a wave. It re-emerged some seconds later, only to be swamped again and again.

Elm trees growing along the street beneath him, bent with the wind, like ghostly skeletons. The sky was dark, just like his mood, and he wondered if he would ever feel secure about the future. He felt like the ferry out there, being swamped time and again, with no chance to find an even keel.

Jess had reassured him, but was he being fair to her? If he let go now, she would have a chance to find a life for herself. She deserved happiness, not uncertainty.

Beau leaned his head against the cold windowpane, and felt the vibration as the wind tore at it. Did he have the courage to let her go? Is that what it was all going to come to? He looked down at his hands resting on the windowsill. Turning them over, he saw the red marks where his fingernails had dug into his palms.

What had Clarence reiterated last night during dinner at Mario's?

"The offer is still on the table, Beauregarde. In fact, it seems more likely now that Matthew will return in an advisory capacity only. That means you will be running the show, my boy."

Sitting back in his chair, he had smiled indulgently at Beau, and then at Celia, whose eyes had never left Beau's face.

He heard her footsteps now on the linoleum outside the door. They stopped, and the door opened. Beau lifted his head from the window.

"Oh, I didn't expect to find you here, Beau." Her tone was cool.

"I had to use the telephone." Beau turned to face her. "Public telephones have been closed because of the influenza."

"Who were you calling?" Celia moved towards the desk, a pile of manila folders in her arms.

"I was calling Jess."

Celia looked up sharply. "Does she know about Matthew?"

"She does now."

"And?" Celia tapped her foot impatiently.

"And she's prepared to wait for me."

Beau heard Celia's sharp intake of breath.

"Does she know how long that may take?"

"Yes."

Celia began sorting the folders into small piles on the desk, her movements carefully controlled.

"You heard what daddy said last night, Beau. You can be in control of all of this, if you want to be."

"I know."

"So why is it so difficult for you to say 'yes'?" Her movements stopped.

"You know why, Celia."

"No, I don't! Spell it out for me, Beau."

"It doesn't include Jess."

Celia was silent as she straightened each pile of folders. She looked up at Beau.

"Make the break now, Beau. It will be a lot less painful for everybody."

Beau clenched his jaw. He couldn't tell Celia that he'd just had similar thoughts. It wasn't the path he wanted to go down. He had never before considered himself to be a coward, so how could he possibly even consider it? He stared at Celia.

"I won't do it, Celia. I love her too much to put her through that."

"But you're prepared to put her through months of anxiety, not knowing when you'll be together, if ever?"

Beau frowned. "What do you mean, 'if ever'?"

"Beau, Matthew's recovery from all of this is not guaranteed." Celia was being brutal now. "What is your plan if he doesn't recover?" Beau was silent. "You don't have one, do you?"

"I prefer to think that he will recover."

"You're being unrealistic, Beau!" Her voice was rising dangerously. "It's a very real possibility; one we need to be prepared for. Promise me you'll think very carefully about it?" Celia clamped a hand across her mouth, and Beau saw her tears.

"I can't promise anything, Celia."

Celia now clenched her fists. "Do the right thing, Beau! For everybody's sake!"

Beau sat at a secluded table in Angela's Patisserie, concealed by a potted palm. His fingers were pressed to his eyes, and for the second time in two days, he wanted the earth to swallow him. He had been offered the chance of a lifetime, and he was afraid to take it. The consequences were too overwhelming. 'Do the right thing, Beau'! He could still hear Celia's voice as he had stormed out of the office.

"What can I get you, Beau?" Angela's voice brought him back to the present. "Are you alright? You look a little pale."

Beau gazed into her frank, open face. "I'm alright, Angela."

The brown eyes regarded him solemnly. "No, you're not." She turned. "Sandra! Mind the counter for fifteen minutes, please. Oh, and bring us two cups of black tea and a plate of those fresh custard pastries."

"Righto!"

Angela pulled out a chair and sat opposite Beau. "Come on now, let's have it! I think I know you well enough now, Doctor DuBois, to see that something is troubling you."

Beau gave a crooked smile. "That will take more than fifteen minutes, Angela."

"Well, however long it takes, I'm listening."

Beau folded his hands in front of him. He knew he had to talk to somebody, or his head would burst. Angela's eyes bored into him, as though she could already read his mind.

So Beau talked and Angela listened, her eyes never leaving his face. It all came out; the hostility, the jealousy, the concern for Matthew's welfare, the fleeting moments with Jess, and the offer that was designed to tear them apart.

Two cups of tea sat before them getting cold, as Beau told Angela as much of his story as he dared. When he sat back, the cup of tea still untouched, she shook her head slowly.

"That's some story, Beau." She paused. "What is it *you* want?"

"What do I want? That's not the point, Angela."

"Isn't it? I think it's very much the point. What is your heart telling you?"

"My heart tells me to run to Jess." He sighed. "That's when I'm afraid."

"Do you know what I think?"

"What do you think, Angela?"

"I think you should get Jess up here, and introduce her to Celia."

"You can't be serious! It would be like throwing her to the wolves. Besides, she wouldn't come."

"Have you asked her?"

"No, not exactly."

"Then don't assume what Jess would do, Beau." Angela sat back and picked up her teacup. "I think you underestimate your Jess. She's stronger than you think." She shuddered. "Urgh! This tea is cold."

"I know she's strong, Angela, but I don't think meeting Celia will solve anything."

"Do you have a better idea?"

"No, sadly."

"Put it to her and see what she says." Angela picked up a custard pastry. "I think she needs to see firsthand what her man is going through up here."

Beau smiled suddenly. "Maybe you should be working at the Clinic, Angela."

She gave a tinkling laugh.

"Doing what, may I ask? Serving tea?"

"No, I think you have far more talent than that."

Angela picked up the teacups.

"I'll get you a hot cup of tea." She laughed as she moved away from the table. "Any more comments like that, and I might take you up on it."

Jess's Decision

Jess resumed her daily routine, and life began to flow in an orderly fashion. She spent the mornings helping Jean with the everyday running of the hotel, and the afternoons were taken up with tending her winter vegetables, or catching up with those sewing jobs that seemed never ending. The boys were hard on their clothes, and invariably came home from school with holes in the backsides of their pants.

"I don't know what you do to wear out the seat of your pants," she complained one night, to which the boys had looked at one another and giggled.

"We slide down a hill behind the school," said Edward, his hand over his mouth.

"All the boys do it, ma," offered Ben as an explanation.

"I don't care what the other boys do, Ben!" Jess was angry. "You are not to do it again, do you hear? I can't afford to keep replacing your clothes!"

"No, ma." They were both contrite, and Jess's mood softened.

"I'm sorry, boys, but I don't have spare money to throw around."

"Sorry, ma." Ben looked as though he wanted to say something else.

"Yes, Ben, what is it?"

"Edward, go away! I want to talk to ma in private."

"Go and see what Grace is doing, Edward. She's been very quiet, and that's a bad sign." Jess smiled at him. "Off you go!"

Edward headed reluctantly from the kitchen, and Jess turned to Ben.

"Now, Ben, what is it you want to say?"

"Um, it's Edward's birthday next week, and I wondered if I could use some of that money that Beau gave me, to buy him a present."

Jess hadn't heard from Beau for several days, and was starting to worry.

"That's very sweet of you, Ben, but I'd rather you hang on to that money for now. We'll do something special for Edward on his birthday."

Ben nodded slowly. "He needs another cricket bat, ma."

Jess frowned. "Why? What's wrong with the one he's got?"

"It's splitting, ma."

"Is it? Let me worry about that, Ben." Jess smiled at his downcast expression. "Off you go now. It will soon be time to get ready for bed."

Ben moved off, and Jess was left to muse on the coming birthday. Edward would be eight, and her mind immediately went back to his sixth birthday; the day he had fallen out of the apricot tree and dislocated his shoulder. All the associated memories came tumbling into focus, and her eyes misted. That was the first time she had seen Beau laugh, when Ben had estimated that he would turn sixty the following day. So Beau would turn forty-two the day after Edward turned eight.

It was also the day she had seen something in his eyes when he had looked at her, that had made her tremble.

How was he, she wondered? Their last conversation had not been encouraging; everything seemed to be working against them.

Jess looked down at the ring on her left hand. It was a symbol of Beau's love for her, but right now it represented all the things that stood between them. What was it about a ring that stood for love? Was it the completeness of the circle, unbroken, that meant so much to the giver and the receiver? It had to be.

The telephone rang shrilly in the passage. Jess went to answer it.

"Henry Granger here, Mrs. Stanley. Sorry to trouble you at this hour, but I have a request, and I didn't want to spend the night brooding over it."

"What is it, Mr. Granger?" Jess was instantly relieved that her boys were not the reason for the call.

"I need someone to assist with the new third grade reading program, and I wondered how you would be placed to fill that role?"

Jess was being offered a job.

"Oh!" Jess had heard about the program, because Edward was in grade three.

"Yes. It's designed to help those pupils who may be struggling with their reading, for whatever reason. Sometimes it's because their parents are unable to help them; it may be that they just need that extra tuition, or maybe they're just lazy. As I said, it's to help them gain a better understanding of the written word. I thought that with your boys being so interested in the English language, you might be interested in helping out. You would receive a small remuneration, and it would be for three mornings a week." He stopped.

Jess's head was whirling. It was something she would like to do.

"Mr. Granger, I am flattered that you have asked me, and yes, I would be very interested, but there are a few people I need to speak with first."

The relief was evident in his voice. "Are you saying that you will take it?"

"Not exactly, but if you can give me a few days, I will have an answer for you."

"That's heartening, I must say. I will speak to you again in a few days time."

The telephone went dead. He was gone.

Jess replaced the receiver, and turned to see two pairs of wide eyes.

"What did Mr. Granger want, ma?" asked Ben anxiously.

"We're not in trouble, are we, ma?" cut in Edward.

"No, Edward, you're not in trouble. Should you be?"

Edward shook his head vehemently.

"Mr. Granger wants me to work at the school, helping with a new reading program for grade three."

"There's a lot of dummies in my grade," said Edward matter-of-factly.

"Edward! That's not nice."

"Well, it's true!"

"Edward, a lot of children don't get help from their parents, and they struggle to keep up with the rest of the grade. Mr. Granger wants them to have a little extra help, because, as you know, reading is very important."

"Are you going to, ma?"

"I'll talk to Beau, and Mrs. O'Malley, and grandma of course, before I make a decision. Now," she added, "I think it's time that three children started getting ready for bed. It's a school day tomorrow."

*

Jess desperately needed to talk to Beau, but she was reluctant to ring the Clinic in case Celia answered the telephone. He had been silent for three days now, and she wondered what could possibly be happening all those miles away.

Jean had been in favour of Jess taking the position at the school.

"Wonderful news, Jessie, love! I can find another washerwoman. You say 'yes' to Mr. Granger." Jean had flapped her thick arms at Jess. "When will you start?"

"I don't know, Jean; possibly next term. I won't leave you without help."

"You've got me through the rough times, Jess. I'm managing now. I'll ask Audrey Maitland if she'd like to earn a few shillings a week."

"I'm sure she would."

Margaret was delighted with the news. It meant that she could look after her granddaughter for the couple of hours Jess was at the school.

"It's what you need, Jess. It will stop you moping about, wondering how all this business with Beau is going to be resolved."

"If it ever is resolved."

"Now, that's no way to talk, Jess," chided Margaret gently. "I'm sure Beau is doing all he can to sort it out, although I must say it couldn't have happened at a worse time."

*

Jess waited anxiously to hear from Beau. He would be thrilled for her, she felt sure, but she had to speak to him before Mr. Granger needed an answer.

It wasn't to be that way. Mr. Granger telephoned later that week, and Jess had to make a decision.

"I'd be very happy to help out, Mr. Granger. When do I start?"

"That's wonderful news!" He almost came through the telephone. "You can start next week, but if you wouldn't mind coming to see me tomorrow, I can go over the program with you. Shall we say ten tomorrow?"

"Yes, alright."

"Good." Then he was gone.

Jess replaced the receiver. Should she telephone Beau? Maybe she would leave it for another day. *Perhaps he'll call tonight.*

Beau did call that night, after Jess had sent the children to bed. He sounded desperately tired, and Jess wished that she could put her arms around him and make it all go away. She asked after Matthew.

"He's gone to a sanatorium, and we can't see him just yet. Celia will go and stay close by, once he's stable."

"Do you think he's going to come through this?"

"Right now I couldn't say."

"What about the Clinic? Are you managing all that on your own?"

"We've closed the doors until further notice."

"How are *you*, Beau? I'm very anxious about you, and I wish there was something I could do to help you."

"You couldn't come up here for a few days, I suppose?" It was said very softly.

"What?" Jess wondered if she had heard right. "You want me to go to Sydney?"

"I'm sorry, Jess. It was just a thought. Forget I said it."

"But you would like me to, wouldn't you?"

"I would, but it doesn't matter."

"Yes, it does." Should she tell him about the job at the school? Maybe not right now. "I'll see what I can do, Beau…"

"Are you extending?"

They both said "yes!"

"If Margaret is prepared to have the children again, I'll come." She stopped. "I've never been that far on my own before."

"You're not afraid of meeting Celia?"

"At the moment, Beau, I feel very sorry for her. No, I'm not afraid of meeting her. Actually, it could be a good thing for both of us."

"Darling girl, you don't know what a relief it is to hear you say that."

"I'll talk to Margaret in the morning, and if you call me tomorrow evening, I should be able to give you an answer." She paused. "I do want to come. I need to see what it is you are sacrificing for me."

Beau was silent for a moment. "I'll call you tomorrow night."

There was a faint sound and the line went dead.

Jess leaned against the wall to steady herself. Beau wasn't coping, and she needed to be there. It would take all her courage, but she had no choice.

Preparations

It was almost 10am. Jess sat in the cold corridor of the school, waiting for Mr. Granger. Her mind was racing over all the things she needed to do, if she was to head up to Sydney. Was it even possible to get to Sydney with the border closure? She needed to find out.

There was also the problem of Sid O'Connor, who would be arriving at her door any day soon, with a load of wood. She was duty bound to give him the chance she had promised him.

Finally, what was she going to say to Mr. Granger? Would he be receptive to her delaying the starting time for the reading program? She was about to find out.

"Mrs. Stanley, come on in." Mr. Granger's voice broke through her reverie.

Jess was ushered into the cluttered office, and sat stiffly on the straight-backed chair in front of the massive desk. Mr. Granger moved around to his chair, and surveyed her over the rims of his horn-rimmed spectacles. He always reminded Jess of a wise old owl.

"Now, Mrs. Stanley," he began, "I am very pleased that you have agreed to help out with our reading program. So many of our children are falling behind in their literacy skills, and I am hoping that this will give some of them the boost they need to take them into grade four." He stopped.

Jess used the pause to launch into her apology.

"Mr. Granger, something of a personal nature has come up, which means I have to go away for a few days, possibly a week."

"So you're asking if you can start at a later date?"

"Yes, I'm afraid I am."

"I don't see a problem with that. This is an initiative I have proposed for our own school, so it doesn't really matter when you start." He smiled benignly. "You do what you have to do, Mrs. Stanley, and we'll be ready for you when you return."

Jess was relieved. "Thank-you, Mr. Granger. You've taken a load off my mind."

"While you're here, I'll outline the program, and we'll see how it develops from here." He pulled a sheet of paper from a precarious pile on the desk, and reached across towards Jess. "This is my plan…"

Twenty minutes later, Jess left the school, her head spinning. This was going to be a little more than simply listening to children read.

Jess hurried to her in-laws' house, where she tapped the shining brass knocker. Within moments, she heard running footsteps.

Margaret and Gracie appeared at the door.

"Jess! Come on in. You're just in time for morning-tea."

"Lovely." Jess stepped into the warmth of her in-laws' home.

Gracie rushed ahead of them to the kitchen, but was pulled up short by her grandfather, who had stepped out from the front lounge-room.

"Gracie! No running in the house!" boomed Charles, to which Gracie silently scrambled up on to her chair, her face creased into a scowl.

Margaret busied herself making the tea, and Charles sat heavily at the head of the table, picking up the newspaper as he did so.

"Sit down, Jess," breezed Margaret. "How was your interview with Mr. Granger?"

Jess didn't know where to start.

"I've had to put him off for a week or so."

"Oh? Why?" Margaret's hand stopped midway over the teacup.

Jess glanced towards Charles and the open newspaper.

"I need to go to Sydney."

There was silence. Margaret's jaw dropped, and Charles appeared from behind the newspaper.

"Is Beau alright?" Margaret glanced quickly at Charles.

"Well that's just it, I don't really know. I don't think so."

"Is he sick?" Charles was staring intently at Jess.

"No, but his colleague now has tuberculosis, and will spend some months in a sanatorium." It was like a bombshell.

Margaret eased herself on to the chair opposite Jess, and put the teapot carefully on the table. "Oh, my goodness!"

"So Beau is running whatever it is they do up there?" muttered Charles.

"Yes. The Clinic is closed, but there's still the institution for returned servicemen and women. They have some influenza cases as well."

"So you want to go into all that mayhem in Sydney?"

"Yes, Charles, I do."

Charles pursed his lips. "What is your plan for getting there?"

Jess swallowed hard. "It all depends on whether you can have the children again so soon."

"Of course we can," cut in Margaret, before Charles could open his mouth.

He glared at her, but she was looking at Jess.

"Is this wise, Jess? After all, the sickness is still very prevalent up north."

"I know, Charles, and at this point I'm not even sure if the train runs straight through. I'll go to the station and find out."

"If you *can* go, when will it be?"

"It's Edward's birthday on Thursday, so I thought I could leave on Friday, providing it's alright with you."

"Of course, my dear." Margaret reached across the table and clasped Jess's hands.

"If you do go, Jess," said Charles emphatically, "I am going to insist that you have a private compartment." He folded his newspaper. "I don't want you travelling with all the riffraff. A woman on her own is a prime target for ne'er-do-wells."

"Why don't you go to the station with her, Charles, and check out what needs to be done. After all, you have made that same trip yourself on several occasions."

"Yes, I'm well aware of what needs to be done, Margaret." He sounded a little condescending, to Jess's way of thinking, but then, that was Charles.

"I'm very grateful to you both for helping me through all this. It can't be easy for either of you, and yet you are here to support me and the children."

"You're the only family we have now, Jess." Margaret's eyes were brimming, and she dabbed at them with a handkerchief. "Come on, let's drink our tea, or it will be cold, and Charles doesn't like cold tea, do you, dear?"

"Certainly not."

Grace, who had been silent throughout the preceding conversation, now made her presence felt.

"Can I have a biscuit, please, grandma?"

Margaret smiled. "Of course, sweetheart." She handed Grace a biscuit, and turned to Jess. "Don't worry about Edward's birthday, Jess. I'll make him a cake, and you can all come here for tea on Thursday."

That was settled.

When the morning-tea ritual was finished, Charles insisted on walking with Jess to the railway station.

"I need the exercise," he declared, as Jess tried to put him off. "Doctor Simmons told me I should walk for at least half an hour every day, for my heart."

They set off at a brisk pace, and within ten minutes were standing at the window of the ticket office. Nobody was in attendance, so Charles hit the bell that stood on the window ledge. A young man sauntered into view.

"Can I help you, sir?" he queried.

"You certainly can, young man." Charles had an air of authority about him that was very seldom ignored. "We need to know whether trains are going through to Sydney at present."

"I believe they are, sir."

"And the border quarantine?"

The young man shrugged. "It hasn't altogether been a success, sir. It was early in the piece, but people got a bit lax, if you ask me."

"Right! In that case, I would like to make a booking from here to Melbourne on Friday." Charles looked at Jess. "Probably best to go down on the 10.15, and catch the Sydney train that leaves at 4.00. That way you're not hanging about the station for hours." He turned back to the young man. "Can I book a private compartment on the Sydney train, from here?"

"You can, sir, but I will have to put through a call to Spencer Street Station."

"Very well."

The young man moved away from the window, and Charles turned to Jess, who had been standing quietly by, a little bemused by the take-over.

"When do you anticipate coming home, Jess?"

"I'm not sure, Charles. I can't stay away too long."

"Well, what if we book a return ticket for next Tuesday? That gives you three full days. Is that long enough?"

"I suppose so." Jess hadn't had time to think about a return journey.

The young man was speaking, his hand over the telephone receiver. "Was that a return ticket from Melbourne to Sydney, sir?"

"Yes, returning from Sydney on Tuesday."

"Will that be the 6.00 a.m. train, sir?"

Charles looked at Jess, who nodded vaguely.

"Does it get into Melbourne in time to catch the last Bendigo train?"

"Yes, sir."

"Very well."

"You realise, sir, that you have to change trains at Albury?"

"Yes, yes! I am aware of that."

The young man went back to his conversation on the telephone, and Charles reached into his pocket for his wallet. Jess was quick to re-act.

"No, Charles, I'll pay for my tickets."

"Nonsense!"

Jess knew that it was no good arguing with Charles.

"I'm sure Beau will reimburse you the money spent, Charles."

"Very well."

The young man returned to the window.

"Who's actually going to Sydney?" he asked casually.

"I am," replied Jess, before Charles could answer.

"You'll have to pick up your Sydney ticket, when you get to Spencer Street, ma'am." He smiled in Jess's direction. She nodded.

When the transaction had been made, Charles pocketed his wallet with a grunt of satisfaction. "That's done!" He looked at Jess. "I hope you know what you are doing, Jess. You make sure you keep your face covered when you're in public places. We don't want you contracting this wretched influenza."

Jess smiled. "I'll be very careful, Charles."

"See that you are."

*

The telephone rang shrilly that evening, just as Jess was getting Grace to bed.

"I'll get it, ma!" shouted Ben, taking off along the passage at full speed.

Jess bent to give Grace a kiss, and then walked slowly to where Ben was talking rapidly into the telephone, and nodding his head vigorously.

"Its Beau, ma!" He handed Jess the receiver.

"Thank-you, Ben." Jess put the receiver to her ear. "Hello, Beau."

"Ben is getting used to answering the telephone, Jess. He sounds very confident."

Jess laughed. "It's usually a race to see who can reach it first. Edward was handicapped tonight; he's in the bath."

"Oh, I see."

"I have my tickets, Beau. I'm leaving here on Friday, catching the night train to Sydney, so I'll be there on Saturday morning." There was silence at the other end of the line. "Beau? Did you hear what I said?"

"Yes, I heard, Jess. Are you sure about this?"

"Yes, I'm sure. Are you having second thoughts?"

"No, of course not, but I don't want you to feel obligated."

"Beau!" Jess felt a twinge of annoyance. "I'm coming, and that's all there is to it! Charles has paid for my tickets, and insisted that I have a private compartment."

"Good!" There was relief in his tone. "I'll repay Charles, of course."

"It's your birthday on Friday." Jess softened her tone. "I remember, because it's Edward's birthday on Thursday."

Jess heard him laugh. "That's right. I remember, too."

"We can celebrate when I get there."

"Are you extending?"

"Yes. Celebrate? Jess, I'll be forty-two! What's there to celebrate?"

"Everything, Beau. We'll be together. That's enough to celebrate, surely?"

"Yes, darling girl, you're right, and I'll look forward to that."

"Beau, I have something to tell you."

"What is it? Not bad news, I hope."

"No. I've been offered a position at the boys' school; helping children with their reading and writing skills."

"That's wonderful, Jess. I'm sure you can cope with that."

"I'll be paid a small fee, and it will be for three mornings a week."

"Good!"

"It will help fill the days until you are able to be here."

"I don't know when that will be, Jess. There's been no more news about Matthew; we're all waiting to see what the next move will be. Celia is like a cat on hot bricks, and I'm hoping she is called soon to the Sanatorium. It will be a relief to both myself and her father when that happens."

"Will you tell her I'm coming?"

"I don't know."

"You must tell her, Beau."

"And give her time to select her arsenal?"

"That's hardly fair, Beau."

"Jess, you don't know her. Celia is capable of a lot of things."

"She must be a very unhappy woman, Beau."

"She shouldn't be! She's indulged by both Matthew and her father."

"I don't think that's what it's about."

"Well, you can judge for yourself when you meet her, Jess. All I'm asking is that you don't accept her at face value. I know you, Jess. You believe there's a best in everybody."

"There is, Beau. Sometimes it takes longer to find."

"Maybe. We'll be cut off shortly, Jess, so before that happens, I want to say how much I love you, and Saturday can't come soon enough."

"Just be at the station to meet me, Beau…"

He was gone.

Jess slowly replaced the receiver. It seemed that they were continually raising each other up from depths of despair and isolation. Was that how their love would always be, or could they look forward to good times ahead, when all of this was over? She certainly hoped so.

*

The next few days flew by, as Jess prepared for her brief trip to Sydney. She was nervous and excited at the same time. Spending three days with Beau was precious. The hardest part was going to be the journey. Jess had never undertaken anything quite so adventurous before; she had always had the protection of family around her. It was not a good time to be travelling, with the influenza still causing problems in the cities, and Beau on the front line, but she knew how to protect herself, and if she didn't do it now, then she feared for their future together.

Jess selected her wardrobe carefully as she packed what she thought she would need. The red dress was placed neatly at the bottom of the case. They might dine out, and she didn't want to embarrass Beau by having nothing suitable to wear. For travelling she chose a plain green skirt and cream blouse, with pintucking across the front. She would need a coat, and the only decent one she owned was the light brown one that she had wrapped around Beau, that fateful day in the bush. Izzy's fringed shawl went very well with it, so she would wear that.

As she packed her white cotton nightdress, she wondered fleetingly where she would sleep, and her fingers trembled as she laid it in the case. She hadn't actually given that a thought until now. They would be alone, with no family telling them what to do, and no prying eyes watching them. Jess remembered Izzy's comment, and a brief smile touched her lips. Shaking away the thought that followed, she took the ruby pendant from its black velvet pouch, and turned it so that the sunlight could dance on its many facets.

Memories of that Christmas two years ago flooded her mind, and the breath caught in her throat. Jack had been home on leave, and neither could have known that it would be their last night together.

"Oh, Jack," whispered Jess to the silence of the bedroom, "I will always remember what we had, and now I need you to be happy for me in this next important decision that I have made…"

A loud banging on the front door brought Jess back to reality. Tucking the pendant back into its pouch, she placed it carefully in the case, wiped a hand across her wet cheeks, and hurried to the door.

Sid O'Connor stood on the other side.

"Mornin', Mrs. Stanley!" He swiped the greasy cap from his head, and grinned.

"Good morning, Sid."

"Got a load o'wood out the back for ya!" He laughed. "An' I'm as sober as a judge, in a manner of speakin'."

"Are you?" Jess suppressed her own smile. "Alright, I'll unlock the back gate for you. How much are you charging, Sid?"

"Nine bob; same as it used to be."

"Very well."

Jess watched as Sid bounded down the front steps, out the gate, and disappeared along the street. Closing the door, she headed for the kitchen. There was enough money in her tin on the mantel to pay Sid, so she took out nine shillings, slipped the coins in her apron pocket, and went to open the back gate.

Sid was there with his horse and cart. He clucked his tongue, and the black beast picked its way past her and down to the dwindling woodheap. Leaping down from the cart, Sid tethered the horse to a post near the chook pen, and stripped off his jacket. Jess handed him the money from her pocket.

"Thanks, Mrs. Stanley." He jiggled the coins before slipping them into his trousers pocket. "I'll stack the wood, t'save the young'uns havin' t'do it."

"I'd appreciate that, Sid."

Jess walked back to the house, musing on his change of heart. Life had certainly not been kind to Sid O'Connor, and contrary to public opinion, she hadn't the heart to kick him while he was down. It wasn't in her nature. If she was wrong about him, well then, she would just have to admit it, but until then, she would give him the benefit of the doubt.

*

It was Thursday, Edward's birthday. Jess had managed to buy a second-hand cricket bat from the thrift store. It looked to be in relatively good order, and the shop manager assured her that it would suit an eight-year-old.

So when the morning dawned and Jess heard pounding feet along the passage, she was prepared. The bat was wrapped and ready for its new owner.

Edward leapt on to the bed, making it creak ominously.

"Happy Birthday, Edward."

He spied the present and pounced on it with glee.

"Another cricket bat! Thanks, ma!" The paper was ripped off in an instant.

"Give me a hug." Jess opened her arms, and Edward fell against her, almost toppling her from the bed. "Steady on! I said 'a hug', not a tackle!"

They were both laughing, and Jess felt good. There had been very little laughter in the house over recent months, and that needed to be addressed.

"Are we going to grandma's tonight?"

"Yes, Edward. Grandma is going to give you a party."

"It'll be good when Beau can come to our parties again, won't it, ma?"

"Yes, Edward, it will be very good indeed."

*

As the birthday candles were lit, and the light was turned down, Jess looked around at her family. The children's faces glowed with pleasure, and they all sang lustily. Her glance caught Margaret's, across the table, and Jess saw concern in her brown eyes; concern for her step into the unknown. Jess felt a tremor run through her body, and she prayed that she was making the right decision.

Jess's Journey

Jess stood on the platform, her coat securely fastened against the keen wind that tried to go straight through her. A last minute addition to her wardrobe, a green felt beret, was pulled firmly down over her ears, muffling the sound of the train as it thundered into the station.

Jess picked up her case and climbed aboard. Entering a carriage occupied by a young couple and their two children, she smiled apologetically at the young woman, and received a shy smile in response.

"I'm sorry for the intrusion, but the train is full today."

"That's alright," replied the young woman quietly. "We're only going as far as Kyneton."

The young man looked up from behind his newspaper, and glanced briefly at Jess as she sat opposite him.

"I hope you don't mind children," he said, as the small boy scrambled on to his knee. "Careful, Christopher!" he chided.

"No, I don't mind children. I have three of my own."

The train jerked into motion, sending the small boy tumbling to the floor. He began to cry, and his mother gathered him up into her arms, trying unsuccessfully to console him. Jess estimated him to be about two years old. His sister stood staring at Jess as the train gathered speed, and risked losing her balance as well. Jess smiled at her. She was a plump child with a head of red curls, and a sprinkle of freckles across her nose. She was possibly as old as Edward.

"What's your name?" she asked abruptly, and received a nudge from her father.

"Alice! Don't be rude!"

"It's alright," said Jess smoothly, turning to the child. "My name is Jess."

"Where are you going?" The brown eyes studied Jess.

"I'm going to Melbourne, and then I have to catch another train to Sydney."

"That's a long journey," said the young man, putting down his paper.

"It is, and to tell the truth, I'm a bit nervous about the whole idea."

"You've left your children at home?" The question came from the young mother.

"Yes. They're with their grandparents."

The young woman nodded. "We're taking our children to my parents in Kyneton, and then we have to go to Melbourne, where David's father is very ill with the influenza virus." She looked at her husband.

"I'm sorry." Jess felt a twinge of sympathy for the family. "I know what that's like."

"You do?"

"My husband died of the influenza virus last November, just after the war ended. He's buried over in England."

"That must have been terrible for you," said the young man.

"It was." Jess smiled wistfully. "With three children to raise, I had to stop feeling sorry for myself and get on with life." Needing to change the conversation, she said, "Are you from Swan Hill?"

"Yes," said the young man.

"I have a sister in Swan Hill. Her name is Isobel Dalton."

The young woman's plain features suddenly glowed.

"I know Isobel," she said enthusiastically. "Her Freya and my Christopher are the same age. We see each other regularly."

So the conversation continued, and the young woman became quite animated as she talked about Isobel and what a wonderful person she was. Jess listened, sometimes with amusement, as her sister's virtues were praised, and she wondered briefly, whether they were talking about the same person.

When the Kyneton station was announced, the young man got up quickly and dragged their large suitcases from the luggage rack.

"We have to go, Sandra," he said, as he slid the compartment door open.

"I have enjoyed talking to you." The young woman lifted the sleeping child as she stood up, and smiling at Jess, followed her husband and daughter into the corridor.

"Likewise," said Jess, as the compartment door was shut, and the family disappeared from view.

Jess sat back in her seat and closed her eyes. She didn't want any more conversation, and fortunately nobody interrupted her solitude.

She thought about the instructions that Charles had given her as she left.

"When you get to Spencer Street, go straight to the ticket office, get your tickets, and fill in your time at the cafeteria. Don't go wandering about, Jess. Make sure your purse is not on view, and trust nobody."

Margaret had simply hugged her, and whispered, "Take care, Jess."

The motion of the train lulled her to sleep, and it seemed like no time before the whistle startled her awake, and the train began to slow as it approached its final destination. Jess pulled her case from the rack and waited for the final hiss of steam as the train stopped. Opening the compartment door, she stepped into the corridor, and joined the jostling crowd making its way on to the platform.

As she stood looking around her, she heard a voice at her elbow.

"Can I help you, ma'am?" A man in blue railways uniform smiled down on her from behind a white facemask.

"I need the ticket office," said Jess, returning his smile.

"Follow me." He walked quickly across the parquetry floor to where a sign indicated the purchase of tickets. "Here you are, ma'am, and if I can be of any more assistance, don't hesitate to ask."

"Thank-you. Where is the cafeteria?"

"Straight along to your left." He indicated with his hand. "Take my advice and cover your face, ma'am. Part of this building is being used as a hospital at present, for the influenza patients, so I beg you to be careful."

"Oh! Nobody told me that before I left Bendigo."

"No, they wouldn't." He laughed. "Where are you headed, may I ask?"

"I need to catch the Sydney train at 4.00 o'clock."

"Well, come and find me when you're ready, and I will personally escort you to the train. My office is just along to the right, and in case you're wondering, I am employed to look after the welfare of travellers, especially those travelling long distance."

"Thank-you."

"If I may be frank, ma'am, you are a perfect target for ne'er-do-wells who gather in places like this."

"You mean I look completely out of place?"

"You do, and the fact that you are alone…." he shrugged, "makes you even more of a target."

"I'm grateful to you."

"Name's Andy." He smiled. "I expect to see you later."

He sauntered off, while Jess asked for her tickets. When she had them securely in the pocket of her coat, she picked up her case and headed in the direction of the cafeteria.

Many people were scurrying through the station, their faces masked by scarves or coloured cloth, so Jess pulled her shawl across her nose and walked quickly.

Once in the cafeteria, she bought a cup of tea and a scone, and went to sit in an isolated corner, away from other people. She felt alienated and a little fearful. Nobody spoke or smiled, and she wished she could see a familiar face, or hear a familiar voice.

The time passed slowly as Jess sat in that secluded corner, but eventually the station clock read 3.30. It was time to go and find Andy. His had been the only friendly face in a moving sea of humanity.

Jess wrapped her shawl around her face, picked up her suitcase and made her way back towards the ticket office. As she walked slowly past, she saw Andy's tall frame heading in her direction. Two other people were staying close to him, and Jess guessed that they too were waiting for the Sydney train.

"There you are!" His cheerful voice instantly relaxed Jess's jangling nerves, and she smiled from behind her shawl. "Good! I have two other country travellers going to Albury."

Beside him stood an elderly couple, their faces almost obscured by coloured cloth. Their eyes smiled at Jess, and she responded with a nod of her head.

"Follow me!" Andy headed off with his long-legged stride, and they all hurried to keep up with him.

Breathless, they eventually arrived at the platform where the Sydney train was quietly belching steam. Andy took his leave then, with a quiet reminder to Jess to be very careful when she got to the Sydney station.

"Is anyone meeting you in Sydney?" he asked.

"Yes."

"I'm very glad to hear that. You take care now." Then he was gone, moving through the crowd with ease.

Jess turned to see the elderly couple trying to board the train with their suitcases.

"Can I help you?" Jess moved forward to assist.

After some manoeuvring, cases and travellers were safely on board.

"Thank-you," said the woman.

"Glad to help." Jess turned to head in the opposite direction. "I have a private compartment, so I need to go this way."

Her case was light in comparison, and she wondered fleetingly what they could possibly be carrying that was so heavy. Her steps led her along a narrow corridor, and she looked for compartment No. 8.

Sliding the door open, she stepped inside. A leather seat ran along one side of the small space, and opposite was the bed, still folded up against the wall. In front of the window was a small folding table, on which lay a couple of magazines.

The light was dim, and outside the window the evening was fast approaching. She placed her case on the leather seat, and sat beside it. Sighing, she slipped her feet out of her shoes, and wriggled her toes. It had been a long day, and she was very tired.

As she sat contemplating what lay ahead, Jess heard a light tap on her door. She got up to open it. A man in a white coat stood there.

"Hello, Mrs. Stanley," he said pleasantly, "I'm Harold, and I'm your steward for this journey. When would you like me to return and pull your bed down?"

"Oh!" Jess shrugged. "Maybe in an hour or so. Is there a buffet car, where I can get a meal?"

"There certainly is. It's the next carriage to your right, or if you prefer, I could bring something to you. It's not a good time to be mixing with other people."

He reminded Jess of Jean's Rodney, fleshy with a ruddy complexion. His thick brown hair was slicked down with oil and he smelled strongly of aftershave.

That would be most welcome," said Jess. "What do they have on the menu?"

His brown eyes twinkled, "I suggest the steak and kidney pie with mashed potatoes and peas."

Jess suddenly realized that she was hungry. "That sounds lovely. I'd like a cup of tea with that, please."

"Very well." He scribbled in a notepad, smiled, and hurried away, sliding the door shut behind him.

Jess relaxed against the seat, and looked forward to a substantial meal.

As she sat there, gazing at her reflection through the window, she thought of Beau, and wondered what he would be doing. She hadn't had time to call him again before she left, so she had to trust that he knew what time the train would be arriving in Sydney.

The lights outside the window started to move as the train jerked into motion. They were on the way. Jess pulled her coat around her and pushed her hands into the pockets. They encountered her tickets, and that was all. Her purse was not there. Jess felt a moment of panic. It must be in her case. Quickly she opened the catches, and her hands felt amongst the clothes. No, it wasn't there.

She stood up, and pushed her hands back into her pockets. Her purse was gone.

How could that have happened? She had been so careful. At no time had she been close enough for anybody to steal her purse. She sat heavily.

What should she do? Report it to the steward, Harold? She would have to. Jess's mind went back over her movements since arriving at the station, and there was no way she could have been robbed. She felt sick inside. Andy had warned her to be vigilant, and somewhere along the line she had let her guard down. She would have to wait for Harold to return. There was nothing else she could do. How was she going to pay for her meal?

Jess felt a tear trickle from the corner of her eye. She brushed it away impatiently. This was no time to get teary. Consequences had to be met head-on.

There was a light tap on the door, and Harold appeared.

"I have your meal for you," he said cheerfully, as he set a tray on the small table.

"I'm sorry, but I can't pay for it." Jess's voice shook. "My purse has been stolen."

He frowned as he looked at her. "Are you sure?"

"Yes, I'm positive."

"Hm. You are not the only one who has reported such an incident." His lips puckered. "Leave it with me, and in the meantime, enjoy your meal."

As the door slid closed quietly behind him, Jess pondered on the situation. The only time she had been in close contact with anybody was when she had helped the elderly couple with their luggage. It couldn't be them, could it? No, surely not.

It was a puzzle. She would mention them to Harold when he returned. In the meantime, the smell of the steak and kidney pie was very enticing, and she was extremely hungry.

The evening wore on, and weariness overcame Jess as she waited for Harold to return. Closing her eyes, she let the motion of the train lull her into a light sleep.

Finally she heard the door open, and Harold appeared.

"I'm sorry for barging in, Mrs. Stanley. I did knock."

Jess rubbed her eyes. "That's alright. How did you get on?"

He was smiling. "Describe your purse to me, Mrs. Stanley."

"Oh, it's small, red and has a gold clasp. I had three pounds in it."

"Voila!" He drew his hands from behind his back. "Is this it?"

"Yes! Where did you find it?"

"I'm afraid we do have thieves in our midst."

"An elderly couple?"

"What makes you say that?"

"I've been wracking my brain, and the only people I've been close to were an elderly couple. I helped them on to the train with their luggage."

"They're not elderly, I can tell you, and they have been at this game for some time now, apparently. The conductors have had their eye on them, but have been unable to catch them with the goods. You'll be pleased to know that they are now under guard, and will be handed over to the police in Albury."

"Their cases were very heavy, and I did wonder what was in them."

"They've been very busy in Melbourne. Wearing face covering made it easy for them, you see."

"So how did you eventually catch them?"

"A gentleman who'd had his wallet stolen, recognised it when they tried to pay for food in the buffet car."

"I am so relieved."

"So was he, I can tell you. Now, I will prepare your bed for you, so that you can have a few hours sleep." Harold deftly pulled down the bed, and straightened the linen with experienced hands. "You do know that we have to change trains at Albury?"

"Yes, I am aware of that."

"It does tend to disturb passengers' sleep, but there's nothing we can do about it." He smiled. "I'll leave you now, and I'm very pleased to have been able to retrieve your purse."

"I won't have to speak to the police in Albury?"

"No. The police will have enough on this couple to stop them in their tracks." He picked up the plate and cup from the table. "Make sure you fasten the door."

Beau

After the change at Albury, Jess slept fitfully, dreaming of strangers and masked thieves, and running to catch trains that disappeared from her sight.

Finally, before daybreak there was a tap on her door. Jess struggled out of bed, pulled on her dressing gown and turned on the light.

It was Harold with a cup of tea in his hand.

"My apologies, but it's five o'clock, and we have to stir passengers."

"That's alright." Jess yawned, and ran her fingers through her hair.

"Cup of tea?"

"Yes, thank-you." She took the proffered cup.

"I hope you slept well, after all the drama last night."

"Reasonably."

"Is someone meeting you at the station?"

"Yes, my…friend is meeting me."

"Good. It's not a safe place for a woman on her own."

"Thank-you for your concern, Harold, but I'm sure I'll be safe."

He smiled. "We can't be too careful in this strange time we're living in." He turned. "Make sure you keep your face covered."

When he had gone, Jess closed the door, and sat to drink her tea. It was hot and sweetened with condensed milk. As she drank, she looked out the window. All she could see was her own reflection, and shimmering lights as they moved through the darkness. It would soon be daylight, and Beau would be waiting for her.

Jess took care getting dressed. She wanted to look her best. After brushing her hair, she decided to leave it loose, and sit the beret on top. Her face was pale, so she patted some powder across her nose, and pinched her cheeks to give them some colour. With fingers that trembled slightly, she applied a small amount of lipstick, and was pleased with the reflection that looked back at her from her small compact mirror. She was like a young girl, about to go on a first date.

The sky had lightened by the time Jess was ready to leave, and she sat silently watching the buildings moving past. The train began to slow down, and the whistle blew at every level crossing.

Finally they stopped, and slamming doors could be heard, as people merged into the corridor. Jess waited until they had stopped passing her door, and taking one last look around the compartment, she stepped out into the corridor. Her nerves were jangling with anticipation as she stepped on to the platform. People hurried by her, their faces covered with scarves or cloth. Jess wrapped her shawl firmly across her nose, and her eyes searched the crowd for Beau's familiar figure.

Stepping back out of the way, she decided that it was probably safer if she stayed where she was, rather than go wandering in search of him. So she waited while the rest of the passengers drifted by, and eventually the platform was empty.

A tiny panic button was triggered inside her, as she stood on the now deserted platform. Where was Beau? Something must have happened; he wouldn't just abandon her. If he didn't come, what would she do?

"Your friend hasn't arrived?"

Jess spun around to see Harold standing beside her. He was now dressed in a heavy black overcoat, and had a grey woollen scarf wound around his face.

"Something must have delayed him."

"Where is he coming from? Maybe I can take you there."

"I don't know." Jess was close to tears. "He has a medical clinic in the city, but I'm not sure where it is."

"Well, I don't think it's a good idea to stand here all alone. Come over near the ticket office." He looked at his watch. "I have an errand to run, which should take about fifteen minutes. When I get back, if you're still here, we'll work something out." He smiled behind the folds of his scarf, and taking her arm, led Jess to a seat beside the ticket office.

"Thank-you, Harold. You have been so kind."

"We need to look after our passengers. If you've gone when I get back, I'll presume that all is well."

Jess nodded mutely, and Harold left her there. Confusion overwhelmed her, and she groped in her pocket for a handkerchief. Had she been stupid to undertake this journey, only to be left in the lurch? No, Beau wasn't like that! He loved her, she was certain. Was he ill? After all, he was working with patients who had the dreaded influenza. All she could do was sit and wait.

Then she saw him; she recognised his lopsided gait, as he ran along the platform. Jess stood up. "Beau!" she cried. "I'm here!"

He headed in her direction, and they collided in the middle of the platform.

"Oh, Jess! I am so sorry!" He buried his face against her shawl, and Jess felt his body trembling against hers. "There was no tram, and I had to walk."

"You had to run, you mean."

They held each other tight, until Beau's heartbeat had slowed enough for him to raise his head. He looked at Jess, her eyes swimming with tears, and choked back his own emotion.

"If anything had happened to you, my darling girl, I would never have forgiven myself. Here, take that wretched covering off your face and let me kiss you."

"Only if you're not infectious." She tried to sound flippant.

"Infectious! Jess, I've been exposed to this wretched thing for four months. I think if I was going to get it, I would have by now."

"That's alright then."

Jess pulled the shawl from across her nose, and felt the pressure of Beau's lips on hers. His arms tightened around her, until she could hardly breathe.

Finally she broke away, laughing shakily.

"I'm here now, none the worse for my journey, and I have quite a story to tell."

"What sort of story?"

"One with a happy ending, fortunately."

"Good." Beau picked up her case. "Come on, tell me your story while we walk."

"Walk?"

"The trams aren't running, Jess." Beau tucked her arm through his, and smiled. "I am so pleased to see you, my darling. I wasn't sure that you would be able to come, what with all the confusion at the border."

"There's no confusion at the moment."

They stepped it out, leaving the station behind, and headed along George Street. Jess told Beau what had transpired the night before, and her timely rescue by the observant Harold. Beau groaned.

"Oh, Jess! I had no right to expose you to all this."

"Hush! It's not your fault, and I survived the ordeal. Now, where are you taking me? For some breakfast, hopefully."

"You didn't have breakfast on the train?"

"No. Harold brought me a cup of tea, that's all."

Beau pulled her close against his side. "I should be jealous of this Harold. Was he young and handsome?"

Jess laughed. "No, silly! He actually reminded me of Jean's son, Rodney; rather plump, but with a more cheerful disposition."

"That's alright then." Beau grinned suddenly. "I can't have you let loose amongst eligible bachelors, now can I?"

Jess smiled at him. He suddenly looked boyish, and she caught a glimpse of Beau as he might have looked when he was younger. There was an eagerness about him that stripped away the lines of tiredness and stress. Their eyes locked as they walked, and everything around them fell away; it was as if they were alone on the streets of Sydney. Passers-by stepped around them, and some even smiled as they perhaps recalled their own heady days of romance.

When they reached Norlane Street, Beau pointed out the Clinic, saying that they would return there later. They walked on until Angela's Patisserie came into view.

"That's where we'll have breakfast," said Beau, " but firstly we need to go upstairs to drop your case off, and I'll show you the place that I call home."

"Upstairs?"

"Yes." He looked up, and Jess followed his gaze. "I live up there where you see the balcony. I'm the lucky tenant; I have a room with a view."

"Oh."

Beau took her hand, and they climbed the brick stairway that led up from the alleyway. When they reached a wooden landing, he dug in his pocket for a key, and opened the first door to their right.

"Welcome, Jess."

She stepped into the small space and looked around her. The room contained a bed, covered roughly with a blue chenille cover, a small table and chair, a wardrobe and a cabinet on which stood a gas ring with a kettle. A door across the room was open to reveal what Jess presumed was a bathroom. French windows, dressed with light organza curtains, looked out on to the street.

Daylight was beginning to creep across a pink sky, and the noise of traffic carried through the open window.

"My balcony." Beau put down Jess's case, and stepped out through the window. "Come and look at my view."

Jess moved out on to the small balcony with its wrought-iron balustrade, and stood beside Beau. Together they gazed down on to the already bustling street, and across the opposite building to a gap in the masonry, where they caught a glimpse of white-capped waves.

"I sit out here and think of you." Beau slipped an arm around Jess's waist.

"It's beautiful." Jess was awestruck.

"It's especially beautiful this morning."

Jess turned to look at him, and her heartbeat quickened as she read the expression in his eyes. She turned away, pretending to gaze down on the street.

"Where am I going to stay, Beau?" She hardly dared ask the question that had been on her mind for some time.

He took a while to answer. "I'd like you to stay here with me, Jess." At her hesitation, he added quickly, "I have a friend downstairs who would be very glad to have you stay with her, if that's what you'd rather do."

Jess shook her head. "No. I'll stay with you. Do you remember when I asked you that same question, Beau?"

"How could I not remember?"

"And you wouldn't."

"I couldn't, Jess. I would have dishonoured you, and discredited myself. I wasn't prepared to let you live with that."

"Everything's different now, Beau." She turned to face him. "I want to spend every moment with you, and if that is frowned upon by others, then I don't care."

"Do you mean that, Jess?"

She ran her finger gently down his scarred cheek. "Yes, I mean it."

He took her hand and led her back through the French windows, closing them behind him. Jess released her hand, and walked across the room. Her heart was thudding against her ribs. Removing her shawl, she placed it carefully over the back of the chair. Then slipping her arms out of her coat, she folded it across the back of the chair. Lastly, she pulled off her beret, and shook out her hair.

Beau was behind her; she could feel his breath as he lifted her hair and kissed the nape of her neck. The fluttering of long-suppressed desire filled her, and she leaned back against him. His arms slid gently around her, and as his hands caressed every curve and hollow of her body, Jess felt herself slowly relaxing into him. All the nervous tension was gone, and she knew that this was where she belonged. She was loved and cherished.

"Are you sure this is what you want, Jess?" Beau whispered in her ear, and he slowly turned her to face him.

She nodded. He lifted her effortlessly and carried her to the bed.

There in that tiny room, above the noise and bustle of early morning on the busy city street, they consummated their love, slowly, deeply and with infinite tenderness.

When they finally lay quiet, Jess brushed the damp hair from her face and looked up at Beau. His eyes were closed, and his face was in repose. Jess thought back to the day she met the quiet stranger whose life had been turned upside-down because of the war. She had felt sorry that he had to endure the taunts of people as he walked the country, existing on handouts and his own ingenuity. Now here they were, totally immersed in each other, and she loved him unconditionally.

Beau opened his eyes, and saw her studying him.

"What are you thinking?" he asked drowsily.

"I was thinking about the day we met."

Beau laughed softly. "I was a sorry mess, wasn't I?"

"Yes, you were."

He leaned over and kissed her. "Just look at us now. Who would have believed that we would come to this? I certainly didn't."

"Nor I. Izzy believes that there has always been a strong link between us."

"And what would Izzy say about this?"

"She would approve."

They lay quietly for a few moments, until Jess suddenly remembered something.

"Happy birthday, Beau," she murmured.

She felt the chuckle that ran through his chest. "What a birthday present you've given me, Jess. Thank-you, my darling girl." He kissed her, and then lying back on the damp sheet, he sighed. "We could stay like this all day, but I think we need to get you some breakfast before you fade away."

Propping himself on one elbow, he looked down on the woman who had long ago stolen his heart. He brushed a hand across her flat stomach, marvelling at the pale smoothness of her skin.

"You are so beautiful," he breathed.

Jess pushed his hand away. "If you're going to talk like that," she chided softly, "I'm not going to get any breakfast."

Beau smiled. "How many days have we got?"

"Until Tuesday, but let's not think about that."

"No. Let's think about breakfast." He sat up reluctantly. "There's someone I want you to meet. Her name's Angela and she has the patisserie (a bakery in common terms), where we will dine while you are here."

"Oh? Angela?" Jess said teasingly. "Is she young and beautiful?"

Beau turned to face her, and his grey eyes became serious.

"Not as beautiful as you, darling girl."

A Day in the Sun

Half an hour later, they were clattering down the staircase that led to the street. Beau took Jess's hand, and guided her to the building alongside. He opened a wire door and ushered her inside. The air was fragrant with the aroma of bread, and Jess suddenly felt very hungry.

There was nobody behind the counter. Beau led Jess to a table hidden behind green foliage, and pulled out a chair for her.

"Sit here, Jess," he whispered, "and I'll find Angela."

He headed towards the counter, and pressed his hand on a bell. It rang sharply.

Jess, peeping from behind the foliage, saw a woman appear from the rear of the shop. Her brown hair was fastened up in a floral scarf, and her round face was flushed. She saw Beau at the counter and smiled broadly.

"Bonjour, Beau!" she exclaimed. "You're late this morning."

"Bonjour, Angela," Jess heard Beau reply. "Yes, I am, rather."

"What can I get you? The usual?"

"Yes, but make that two."

"Two?" Her brown eyes scanned the patisserie. She spied Jess behind the foliage, and smiled knowingly. "Oh, I see. That would be Jess, I presume?"

Beau nodded.

"You go and sit down, and I'll be with you shortly."

"You could add a couple of your famous custard tarts to that order, please Angela, for us to eat later."

"Oui!"

"Merci."

Beau headed back to Jess and sat opposite her. He reached across and took her hands in his. She smiled softly.

"You speak French, Beau?"

"No, not really, but Angela and I have this little game going. It amuses the customers." He looked around. "Sadly, the customers are light on this morning."

They were silent as Beau gently massaged Jess's fingers. He touched the ring that shone on her left hand, and looked deep into her eyes.

"We should get married, Jess."

"Now, you mean?"

"Yes, and then I wouldn't feel so guilty about all this."

"I don't want you to feel guilty, Beau." Jess released her hand and touched his scarred cheek. "I made this choice, and I have no regrets."

"Are you sure?"

"Yes. Besides, what would Izzy say if she could hear you talking like this?"

Beau smiled. "She would probably say 'deprive me of a wedding, would you?'"

"Exactly."

Angela appeared beside the table, and they moved apart.

"Here we are then! Breakfast for two."

"Merci, Angela." Beau helped move the cups and plates from the tray, while he introduced the two women. They smiled at one another, and Jess was immediately drawn to the dark-haired woman who reminded her of Mary Walker.

"I'm very pleased to meet you, Angela," she said, as Beau moved a cup towards her, "although I don't speak French."

"Oh, neither do I!" Angela looked at Beau. "We just have a bit of fun, really." She turned to Jess. "Did this man tell you that I suggested you come up here?"

Jess raised her eyebrows at Beau. "No, he didn't." It was her turn to embarrass him. "Did he tell you that it was his birthday yesterday?"

Angela placed her hands on her ample hips and her smile was mischievous.

"No, he didn't. Secretive, isn't he?" She paused. "I'll tell you what I'll do to mark this special occasion; I'll prepare a sumptuous meal for you both tonight. How does that sound?"

Beau's face flushed slightly. "That sounds wonderful, Angela, but only on condition that you join us."

"Alright then. Shall we say six o'clock?"

Beau looked at Jess. "Is that alright with you, my love?"

"Yes. It sounds marvellous."

"Good, then I'll leave you to your breakfast." Angela bustled away.

"So it was Angela's idea?" Jess bit into a slice of toast.

"Yes, actually."

"She's very nice."

"And very practical. I bend her ear on many occasions."

"I can see why."

They finished eating in silence.

Beau sat back, wiping his mouth on a serviette.

"I hope you feel better for that, Jess." He leaned forward. "What will we do with the rest of the day?"

"Well, I need to make a telephone call to Margaret, to let her know that I've arrived safely."

"We can do that from the Clinic. I'll take you down there now, and show you where I spend half my time. I don't have to be at Serendipity until tomorrow, so we have the rest of this day free." He paused. "How would you like to go across the Bay on the ferry?"

Jess's eyes widened. "I've never been on the ocean," she admitted.

Beau laughed. "It's quite safe, and we can spend some time on the beach at Manly. It might put some colour in your cheeks."

"Oh!" Jess touched her cheeks. "I didn't think I looked that bad."

"You don't, my dearest, but some good salt air will do you good."

*

A ten minutes walk brought them to Norlane Street, and Beau unlocked the big wooden doors of the Clinic. They entered, and he ushered Jess up the stairs to the offices on the second floor.

"We'll go to reception and use the telephone before I show you my office," said Beau, as he led the way.

The door to reception was open. Beau frowned. Celia must have forgotten to lock it the previous night.

They entered, and Jess was immediately drawn to the large window that overlooked the city and beyond to the harbour.

"What a wonderful view!" she exclaimed, as she stood gazing out upon the panorama.

Beau came up behind her, and instinctively wrapped his arms around her.

"Isn't it marvellous?" His chin brushed against her hair.

They stood for several minutes, absorbed in the activity outside the window, and they didn't hear the footsteps echoing along the passage behind them.

"Well!" said a familiar voice. "What a pretty picture you make, Beau!"

Beau turned quickly. Jess was slower to re-act.

"Celia! I didn't expect to see you here today."

"Obviously not." Her eyes were on Jess, as she turned from the window. She recognised her from the drawing that she had defaced. "Jess, am I right?"

Jess nodded, and tried to smile. "I'm pleased to meet you, Celia."

Celia snorted, and her dark eyes shifted to Beau. "What are you doing here?"

"I'm showing Jess the Clinic, Celia. You don't have any objections, do you?"

She shrugged her shoulders. "No, not particularly." Celia walked to the desk, opened a drawer and took out a file. "By the way, I have permission to stay with Matthew, as of next Friday." She glanced at Jess before fixing her eyes once more on Beau. "Daddy and I would appreciate it if you could have the two new staff members installed here before then. We need to open these doors again."

"Everything's in hand, Celia. The only thing missing will be someone to take your place at reception, while you are away."

"That's covered. You don't have to concern yourself with that, Beau."

"Good."

Celia headed for the door, and turned to fix her gaze once more on Jess.

"I'm sorry, Jess, if I'd known you were coming, I would have welcomed you properly. Good day to you both." Then she was gone.

Jess turned to Beau. "You didn't tell her?"

He shrugged. "I told you, I didn't want her preparing her arsenal."

"Beau!" Jess sighed. "I've told you before; I can take care of myself."

"I just wanted to protect you, that's all."

"I'd like the chance to really speak to her, Beau."

"You'll get that chance, I'm sure. Now," he steered her towards the telephone, "you have a more pressing conversation with Margaret."

Jess looked at the telephone. It was a different design to hers. Beau saw her hesitation, and picked up the receiver. He turned the handle and waited.

After a few moments a voice asked him for the number.

"I'd like to put through a trunk call to the Bendigo exchange, please."

He waited, and then Jess heard him say, "Bendigo 176, please."

Finally he handed the receiver to Jess.

"Hello? Margaret? It's Jess." Her voice trembled slightly, and she felt Beau's arm around her waist.

She heard Margaret's voice, loud and clear. "Jess, dear, you have arrived?"

"Yes, Beau met me at the station." She didn't want to go into details.

"That's wonderful, dear. We've been wondering where you were. The children are all here, waiting to say 'hello'. Here's Ben."

Jess heard Ben's voice. "Hello, ma! Granddad is going to take us to the park!"

"That sounds wonderful, Ben! Beau is taking me on the ferry, across the water."

"Ooh, ma! You be careful."

"I'll be safe, Ben, don't you fret!"

Edward's voice came across the line. "Where are you going, ma?"

"I'm going on a ferry, across the water."

"Don't fall in, ma!" Jess heard him giggle. "You can't swim."

"I won't, Edward. You enjoy your day at the park."

"I'm taking my new cricket bat, ma."

Jess heard Grace's voice, high-pitched and anxious.

"Where are you, ma? I can't see you!"

Jess felt her eyes mist, and she had to force her voice to be controlled.

"I'm a long way away, Gracie, and I want you to be a good girl for grandma. I'll see you in a few days, alright?"

"Yes." Jess heard the tears, and then Margaret came on the line.

"Gracie's going to help me make biscuits while the boys are at the park this afternoon. How is Beau?"

Jess looked at Beau. "He's alright. We're at the Clinic at the moment."

"Are you extending?" a voice interrupted.

"No," said Jess slowly. "Goodbye, Margaret, goodbye, children. I'll call again when I have more news."

The line went dead. Jess replaced the receiver and wiped a hand across her eyes. She felt Beau's arms around her, and she buried her face in his chest.

"I really don't like leaving them," she sobbed into his jacket.

"I know, sweetheart." He held her tight. "I know."

*

Some time later they were seated at the quayside, sharing fish and chips with the seagulls, and waiting for the arrival of the ferry. The day was unexpectedly warm, and a light breeze stirred the water into tiny silvery caps. Jess was transfixed. She had never been to the coast, let alone set foot on a vessel, and the prospect made her excited and a little anxious.

"Are you sure it's safe, Beau?" she asked tentatively, as she shooed a pesky seagull from the last of her chips.

Beau laughed. "People travel on the ferry every day, Jess. It's perfectly safe, and today is so gloriously calm, we will simply glide across the bay." He brushed a hand across her cheek. "I won't let anything happen to you, I promise."

Jess turned away from the intense look in his eyes. All her strength seemed to vanish when he looked at her, and her body responded with flutters of desire. She folded up the empty fish and chip paper, and walked across to a rubbish bin.

When she returned, she was back in control of her emotions. Beau was sitting with his eyes closed, and as she sat beside him, she heard him whisper,

"Wouldn't it be nice if the whole world would just go away?"

"Yes, it would, but it's not going to happen." Jess leaned across and spontaneously kissed him lightly on the cheek. Beau opened his eyes and stared at her.

Then, with people strolling by, he pulled her down into his arms, and kissed her so fiercely that Jess was taken by surprise.

"Beau!" Her face was flushed as he released her. "People are watching!"

"Darling girl, I want everyone to know that I am the luckiest man alive."

"Beau, hush!" Jess felt the colour rise in her cheeks.

"Well, it's true." A young couple passing by smiled coyly at each other. "Don't be afraid to tell her you love her!" Beau called out.

The young man turned. "We're getting married next Saturday."

"Congratulations!" responded Beau.

Jess pulled her shawl across her face to hide her embarrassment. "Stop it, Beau!"

He was laughing, and suddenly Jess knew that he needed this little diversion to remind him that life still held precious moments. She began to laugh with him.

Soon the laughter spread like an infection, and people began to chuckle as they walked by. Beau wiped his eyes and uttered a contented sigh.

"Suddenly it feels good to be alive." He turned to look at Jess. "Let's savour this moment, Jess, as one of our truly happy moments. We can tell our children how we infected everyone around us with laughter."

"Our children, Beau?"

"Yes, my dearest, *our* children. I want lots of them."

The sound of a foghorn saved Jess from further embarrassment. Beau jumped to his feet, and grabbing her hand, hurried her to where the ferry was spilling out passengers on to the jetty. They joined another queue of eager people waiting to step on to the gangway.

"You'll enjoy this, Jess!" shouted Beau above the noise of the pulsing engine.

"I hope so."

Beau squeezed her hand. "Let's sit outside. That way we can taste the salt spray, and feel the wind in our hair." He laughed at Jess's startled expression. "Trust me, darling, that's exactly how it will be."

They moved towards the bow of the ferry, and Beau chose a seat directly in front of the cabin. Sitting close together, he reached into a rucksack that was slung over his shoulder, and retrieved a rug to tuck around Jess's knees.

People moved about, finding their ideal seat, and conversation hummed around them, but on this special day, they could well have been on their own.

The engine made a grinding sound, and the vessel began to turn, slowly, until it was facing out on to the bay.

"It's so beautiful," breathed Jess. "My boys would love this."

Beau smiled, his eyes never leaving her face. "They would."

As the ferry churned through the water, Beau pointed out significant landmarks that made the harbour unique, like Pinchgut Island, or Fort Dennison as it was currently known. The island had been a convict prison in the early days, and Jess shivered as he told her about the prisoners who had perished while trying to escape. It looked harmless enough now, with the water lapping around the rocks.

It didn't take long for the ferry to complete its journey, and soon they were pulling up alongside the jetty at Manly.

Beau folded the rug, returned it to his rucksack, and grabbing Jess by the hand, headed eagerly for the gangway. He was like a schoolboy today, and Jess smiled secretly as she let him lead her on to the jetty.

They passed through a building where their tickets were checked, and then they were free to explore the glittering sands of Manly Beach.

"This is what we've come for!" cried Beau, as they stepped on to the white sands that seemed to stretch forever. "What do you think? Isn't it glorious?"

Jess stood in amazement, staring at the glittering sea as it made its rhythmic journey to the shore. People were gathered in groups, some simply taking in the crystal clear view, while others paddled up to their ankles in the moving tide. There were squeals of delight from children as they frolicked at the water's edge, and women with parasols kept an eagle eye on them, in case they ventured too far. The sun shone on the white sand, causing Jess to blink and shade her eyes.

"It's beautiful!" she exclaimed.

"Come on, we'll find a place to sit and watch."

Jess struggled on the soft sand as Beau pulled her forward, and her boots seemed to fill with every step.

Finally they stopped, and Beau reached once more into his rucksack for the rug.

"Here will do." He spread the rug on the soft sand, and gestured for Jess to sit. He fell down beside her, and stripped off his jacket. "It's unseasonably warm."

Lying back, he placed his hands under his head, and gave a sigh of satisfaction.

Jess looked down at him, and marvelled at the change in his features. His eyes had a sparkle she'd not seen before, and his brow was smooth. He'd left all his worries behind him for the time being. Any thoughts of influenza had been pushed to the back of his mind.

He caught her studying him, and reaching up a hand, pulled her head down so that he could kiss her.

"Beau!" She sat up and looked around to make sure nobody was watching. "This is unseemly."

"Unseemly?" Beau reclined on one elbow. "Jess, people here don't care about that sort of thing. They're free with their affections, and nobody takes any notice. Now lie back here with me and let's enjoy this freedom together."

Jess lowered herself on to the sand and stared up at the blue sky. It reminded her of a time long ago.

"Izzy and I used to lie down in the paddock and watch the clouds," she reminisced softly. "We could see all sorts of things in the clouds." She chuckled. "One day we were so engrossed in our study of the sky, we forgot that we hadn't shut the gate, and all the cows were wandering down the road."

Beau was watching her closely. "What did you do?"

"We had to go and round the cows up, and received a harsh word from our father." She turned to look at Beau. "My father wasn't a harsh man, but he loved his cows, and to see them all heading towards the milking shed before their udders were full, was too much for him. We weren't allowed to have our cup of fresh milk that night." Jess giggled. "We were a mischievous pair."

"Yes, I'm sure you were."

Jess was quiet for a moment, as she stared into the grey eyes so close above her. "Beau?"

"What is it, my love?"

"Do you ever think about your sister?"

Suddenly the sparkle left his eyes, and he frowned. "Why do you ask?"

"Because I find it unthinkable that you don't know anything about her. Somewhere out there you have a sister, Beau. Her name is Charlotte, and that's all you know about her." He moved away, and Jess realised that she had touched a very raw spot. "You told me that you'd tell me about yourself one day."

"And I will, but not today, Jess. This day is ours, and I don't want anything to spoil it." His eyes were once more intense as he looked at her.

She smiled slowly. "Alright, but if I'm going to marry you, I want to know everything about you." Beau didn't answer, but sat up and began unlacing his boots. "What are you doing?"

"Take off your boots, Jess. I want you to walk in the sand with me, and feel the water lapping around your toes."

"What?"

Beau knelt at her feet and began undoing the buttons of her boots. Jess felt a wave of embarrassment, but his smile told her that she had no choice in the matter.

Once her boots and stockings were off, he held out his hands and lifted her to her feet. Jess felt the warm sand beneath her toes and suddenly she had the urge to run and frolic, as many children were doing along that glittering stretch of water.

"Come on!" Beau pulled her gently, and together they ran across the sand to where the waves were lapping. Jess stopped on the wet sand, feeling the coolness now underneath her feet, and Beau bent to roll up his trousers.

"You have to feel the waves, Jess. Tuck your skirts up, like those women over there, and let the water wash over your feet."

Jess looked across to where two young women were frolicking in the shallows, their skirts pulled up to reveal bare limbs.

Jess shook her head. "No, I can't."

"Yes, you can, Jess. Nobody is watching you."

Reluctantly she hitched her skirt, and held it in one hand as she stepped gingerly towards the water's edge.

The first shock made her gasp as the water and the sand covered her feet and then pulled away again. Another wave came, this time not so cold, and so they continued on their never-ending journey towards the dry sand.

Beau was laughing at her expression, as he stood calf deep in the water.

"Isn't that a wonderful feeling, Jess?"

"It's a bit of a shock. I didn't expect it to be so cold."

"Exhilarating is the word, Jess! Exhilarating!" He bent, and scooping up a handful of salt water, tossed it in Jess's direction.

She caught her breath as cold droplets landed on her face. Laughing, she scooped up a handful of water and tossed it back at Beau.

Soon they were both saturated, but they didn't care. They were carefree for this brief period of time and it felt good.

Finally, panting with the exertion, Jess called for a halt.

"That's enough, Beau! I need to sit down." She made her way back to the rug and flopped down, breathing hard.

Beau landed beside her, and after brushing back his dripping hair, reached for the rucksack. He produced two paper bags and handed one to Jess.

"Angela's custard tarts," he said, as he opened his bag. "I hope they're not too squashed."

They weren't, and so they completed their afternoon by tucking into the delicious softness. Beau licked his fingers and sighed with satisfaction.

"We'd better start heading back soon, Jess. The last ferry leaves at four, and we'd do well not to miss it."

Jess wiped a hand across her mouth and stared out across the beach.

"It's been a wonderful day, Beau," she whispered. "Thank-you for everything."

"We will have more days like this, Jess, when the world comes back to normal."

She smiled softly. "I hope so."

*

That evening they recalled their adventure to Angela, who watched them both closely as they tucked into a meal of pork pies and vegetables. She had not seen Beau so animated, and concluded that the woman in the red dress, seated beside him, was the reason for this change. Their eyes only left each other when she, Angela, was speaking, and she sensed that they were desperate to be alone.

There was one thing left to do, however, and so as their plates were emptied, Angela brought out a birthday cake, complete with candles.

"I don't know how old you are, Beau," she said as she placed the cake on the table, "so I guessed at forty. You have four candles; one for every ten years."

Jess and Beau looked at one another and smiled, as they both recalled Edward's birthday two years ago, when Ben had estimated Beau to be sixty, because there were six candles.

"Forty-two, actually," said Beau, and Jess related to Angela the tale of Ben's mistake, and his embarrassment when Beau finally had to correct him.

"Well," said Angela, as she collected the dirty plates, "I'm sure it's been a long day for both of you, so I won't keep you from your slumbers. The rest of the cake is yours to have when you want it."

"Thank-you, Angela." Jess smiled into the friendly brown eyes. "We are deeply grateful to you for doing this." She looked at Beau. "I must admit I am weary."

"I'll see you both tomorrow." Angela turned to Beau as she added, "You make sure you take good care of this girl, Doctor DuBois. She is a treasure."

"Don't worry, Angela, I already know that."

"Good! So I'll wish you both a good night." She winked mischievously at them. "Off you go then!"

*

As they walked slowly up the stairs to the landing, Jess leaned against Beau.

"I think Angela approves of me," she whispered.

Beau looked down at her. "Of course she does; who wouldn't?"

He unlocked the door to his room, and they stepped inside. Switching on the light, Beau walked across to the window and drew the heavy grey drapes across, muffling the sounds from the street below. They stood awkwardly for a moment, one each side of the room, before Beau opened his arms and Jess walked into his embrace.

"Our first night together," he whispered into her hair.

"Not quite, Beau. Have you forgotten Swan Hill?"

"It wasn't quite the same, Jess."

He held her away from him then, and his grey eyes were serious.

"This is a big step for you, Jess, and I want you to be certain."

"I am, Beau. We're both old enough to know what we're doing, and if we truly love one another, then waiting seems…"

"Unnecessary?"

Beau removed the shawl from her shoulders, and began to unfasten the hooks down the back of the red dress. Jess shivered with anticipation as the red dress slowly slipped to the floor. Stepping out of it, she lifted her arms and curled them around Beau's neck. His hands caressed her back, pushing up her camisole until they found bare flesh. Jess lifted her face for the long kiss that followed.

Jess and Celia

Beau rose early the following morning, and after dressing quickly in the cool morning air, he turned on the kerosene heater so that Jess would wake to a warm room. She was still sleeping soundly, and reluctantly he leaned over the bed and brushed the hair from her face.

"Jess," he whispered, "I must go over to Serendipity." She stirred, and blinked in the morning light. "Stay there as long as you like, and I'll come back for you later in the morning."

"What time is it?" Jess yawned.

"It's eight-thirty. I'll leave the key for you, and when you're ready, go down to Angela's and have some breakfast."

Jess nodded. "Don't be gone too long."

"I promise." He kissed her lightly on the cheek, and she heard the door close behind him.

Left alone, Jess pulled the blankets over her bare shoulders, and tried to go back to sleep, but a nagging pain in the back of her head, forced her to rise. Slipping into her dressing gown, she went into the bathroom. There she opened a small cabinet above the basin, and amongst the masculine paraphernalia, she found a box of headache powders. She read the label and decided that they would do her no harm, even if they did no good.

Back in the bedroom, she opened a wooden cupboard, found a glass and filled it with water. She emptied one of the powders into it, shook it, and drank it. The sediment remained in her mouth, making her shudder.

Moving to the window, Jess pulled the drapes back, revealing a bright, sunny day. She pulled back the organza curtains and stepped out on to the balcony. It was a Sunday morning, but already the street was bustling with motorcars and horse-drawn carriages. A tram clanged its way through the centre of the activity and people, their faces covered, ran to catch it.

Jess sighed. All of this was a world away from where she lived, and her longing for home welled up inside her. She blinked. This was Beau's world, not hers.

Suddenly she was wracked with grief and guilt, as a picture of Jack flitted before her mind's eye, startling her. Jack's loving was uncomplicated, warm and predictable. Her union with Beau was different; he was sensual, exciting, and she found their desire for one another overwhelming. Jess shivered, but not from cold. It was all moving too fast.

Her head still ached. The past two days had caught up with her, and although she loved Beau with every fibre of her being, she knew that she would have to slow down. She stepped back into the room and closed the door.

Taking her time, she dressed in front of the kerosene heater, and then bathed her face with cool water. As she brushed the tangles out of her hair, she studied her reflection in the mirror above the bathroom basin. Her eyes were too large, and she noticed dark circles above her pale cheeks. She would have to put some colour back before Beau saw her, or he would think something was wrong.

When she was finally happy with her reflection, Jess picked up the scattered clothing from the night before, and straightened the bed.

Turning off the kerosene heater, she picked up Beau's keys, let herself out of the room, and headed down to Angela's. She opened the screen door, to be greeted by Angela, who held a tray of steaming pastries. Her face was flushed from the ovens, and she smiled warmly at Jess.

"Good morning, Jess. I trust you slept well?"

That brought the colour to Jess's cheeks. "Yes, thank-you, Angela."

"Good! Now I'll just pop these little beauties in the cabinet, and if you'd like to find a table, I'll be with you in a moment."

Jess escaped to a table at the back of the patisserie, and waited for Angela. Customers came and went, buying their fresh bread and pastries, and the constant banging of the screen door, jarred on Jess's thumping head.

Finally Angela was free to attend to her, and she approached Jess's table with a wide smile.

"What can I get you, Jess?"

"Just some toast and tea, thank-you, Angela."

Angela peered at her. "Are you alright? You look a bit peaky."

Jess smiled at her concern. "I have a bit of a headache, but I've taken some powders, so hopefully it goes away soon."

"Hm, I hope so. If it doesn't, you'd better check with that man of yours."

"I don't want to bother him, Angela. I'm sure it's because the past two days have been extremely hectic. If I'm quiet today, I should be alright."

"Beau is so excited to have you here, Jess. He just needs a gentle reminder that you are a long way from home, and therefore a little anxious. Make sure you tell him."

"Of course."

"Yes, well I'll bring you some breakfast. How about an egg with that toast?"

"No, I couldn't eat an egg, Angela. Just some jam will do."

"Very well."

When she had gone, Jess sat back, closed her eyes and tried to relax. She needed to feel better by the time Beau returned. She couldn't tell him what was on her mind, and yet he needed to understand that she was way out of her depth. These feelings she was experiencing were all new to her, and perhaps they both needed to step back.

Angela brought her breakfast, and Jess enjoyed the fresh toast and sweet black tea. Her headache was easing, and as she finished the last crust with a dollop of strawberry jam, she decided that a short walk in the fresh air might fill in the morning, and steady her erratic thoughts.

Wrapping her shawl around her shoulders, Jess approached the counter.

"All finished, Jess?" Angela looked up and smiled.

"Yes, thank-you, Angela. Do I pay you, or…"

"No, no! Beau has an account here. He'll fix it up at the end of the week."

"Oh!" Jess added, "I might go for a walk now, Angela. If Beau comes looking for me, I'll be down on the quayside. We were there yesterday, and I think I can find my way back there."

"You take care, Jess," warned Angela. "This is Sydney, and there are a lot of ne'er-do-wells out there. Cover your face, too."

Jess nodded, swept her shawl across her face, and opened the screen door. Angela watched her go, a frown creasing her brow.

Jess hurried in the direction they had taken the previous day. Before long she found herself away from the tram route and the noisy main streets.

The quayside was bustling with families, all waiting to catch the ferry on this perfect Sunday morning. Jess sat on the seat that she and Beau had occupied, and watched the passing parade. Seagulls circled overhead, waiting to snatch food from unsuspecting visitors, and children cried when they had hot chips taken from their hands. Jess smiled. Her children would love this.

The morning passed quickly as she watched the activity, and saw the ferry leaving in a flurry of white foam. Her headache had passed, and she felt that there was colour back in her cheeks. She closed her eyes, and breathed deeply, tasting the salt air through the folds of her shawl.

A sudden movement on the seat made Jess look around. Beau was there beside her. The smile died on her face as she saw the expression in his grey eyes.

"Jess, what on earth do you think you're doing?" His voice was sharp.

Jess blinked, unsure how to re-act. "I'm enjoying the sunshine, Beau!" she retorted. "I had a headache, and I needed some fresh air. Why?"

"This is not Bendigo, Jess. I don't want you wandering about on your own!"

"I'm perfectly safe, Beau!" Indignation was rising in her chest. "There are plenty of people about. I don't know why you're going on so!"

His shoulders slumped. "I don't want anything to happen to you, Jess. You're my responsibility while you're here."

"But I don't need a gaoler, Beau; I can look after myself."

"You've already proved that you're too trusting, Jess. Believe me, there are people out there just waiting for the opportunity to pounce on people like you."

Jess turned away. "Alright! I'm sorry, I won't do it again!"

"Jess, please let's not be angry with one another." Beau took her hands. "When Angela said you'd come down here, I'm afraid I panicked." They stared at one another for a long moment. "Can we both be reasonable now?"

Jess considered this statement. "Yes, but don't treat me like a child, Beau."

"I'm sorry." He squeezed her fingers. "Shall we go? I have Matthew's motorcar, and I want to take you out to Serendipity."

Jess tried to smile behind her shawl. "I'm sorry too, Beau. I didn't mean to make you angry."

"Not angry, my darling girl; terrified for your safety."

Jess pulled down her shawl, and reached over to kiss him. "I'm safe now, so come on, let's go."

They hurried along the promenade, and up a grassy embankment towards the road where Beau had parked Matthew's motorcar. He helped her in to the passenger's seat, and climbed in beside her. Turning the vehicle into the traffic, they left the quayside and headed for the quieter suburban streets. Neither spoke as they passed through leafy streets, with the sun dappling on the shiny paintwork of Matthew's motorcar.

Finally they turned into the long driveway of Serendipity, and Jess gazed around her at the colourful gardens and shady gum trees.

"It's beautiful!" she exclaimed.

"Wait 'til you see the Lodge. It was a private home before Matthew turned it into a respite centre for returning soldiers."

They rounded a bend, and Jess saw the impressive two-storey stone residence, with its green painted window frames, and massive stone dogs guarding the door.

"My goodness! Who could afford to live in a house like this?"

"Only the very wealthy, I'm afraid."

Beau pulled up at the front door and handed Jess down on to the gravel path. Together they entered into the impressive foyer with its black and white linoleum, and Beau crossed to the receptionist's window.

"Shirley!" he called.

Shirley appeared. She smiled at Jess as she said, "Back again, Doctor?"

"Yes, I've brought my fiancé, Jess, to have a look at the place."

"Very well, but I wouldn't let her go beyond the restricted area, Doctor."

"No, she certainly won't be going there."

"Alright." Shirley smiled at Jess.

They moved on, and as they climbed the wide staircase, which reeked of phenyl, Jess tugged on Beau's hand.

"Your fiance, Beau?"

"Of course. That's what you are, Jess."

Jess smiled. "Yes, I suppose I am."

At the top of the stairs they encountered Edwina Evans, mopping the linoleum along the corridor. She stopped as she saw Beau.

"Hello, Doctor DuBois!"

Jess saw an attractive woman, probably in her mid-forties, her brown hair swept back from her face, and a large pinafore tied around her slight frame. Her face was flushed from the exertion, and her smile was wide.

"Hello, Edwina. I'd like you to meet my fiancé, Jess." Beau turned to Jess. "Edwina's son, Charlie, is one of my success stories. I think I told you about him. Charlie now works in the gardens here, and has proved that not every story has a bad ending. If you go and have a wander in the garden, you'll probably meet Charlie."

Jess was tempted to make a remark about 'wandering about alone', but changed her mind. "I'm very pleased to meet you, Edwina."

"Likewise, Jess. This man performed a miracle with my Charlie, and I'll forever be in his debt." She smiled at Beau, who flushed with embarrassment.

"That's not really true, Edwina," he protested.

They continued along the corridor towards the nurse's station. Beau pointed out the different rooms, and they entered an empty one, where Jess saw for herself the sparse use of furniture. She commented on this.

"We can't have anything in here that a patient might be able to use to end his life." Beau looked seriously at Jess, and she shuddered as she thought of his attempt to end his own emotional trauma.

"I see." She turned her face away as tears threatened to spill.

Beau noticed and touched her arm. "I'm sorry, Jess. Trauma is very real in a place like this, and we have to read the signs very quickly."

"I understand."

They headed back into the corridor, and as they approached the nurse's station, they saw a figure coming towards them, her hips swinging in the tight black skirt that reached just above her ankles.

Celia acknowledged Jess with a brief smile, before turning her attention to Beau.

"I'm glad you're back, Beau. You are required in quarantine. Doctor Freeman hasn't arrived, and we have two new patients requiring attention. Nurse Flanagan is at her wits end." She rolled her eyes dramatically.

Beau smiled apologetically at Jess.

"It looks like I have to go, Jess. Have a stroll in the garden while you're waiting."

He took off at a run along the corridor, and the two women watched him disappear around the corner. Celia sighed.

"This is what happens all the time, Jess. The job comes first."

"I imagine it has to." She paused for a moment. "It was the same with my husband, Jack, and I knew I couldn't stop him from going to fight overseas."

Celia looked at her closely. "Beau is very dedicated to his work and he is very good." She picked up a clipboard from the counter of the nurse's station, and began to peruse it. "In fact, it's what he thrives on; always has."

"And Matthew? Is he the same?"

Celia pursed her red lips. "Those two are like chalk and cheese, but one can't do without the other. They've been friends for a long, long time, Jess. I always think of them as Matthew being the brawn and Beau being the brains." She laughed. "So you must understand why this partnership is essential." Her eyes suddenly misted. "Even more so, once Matthew recovers." She turned her attention back to the clipboard, and hastily scribbled something in the margin of the attached list.

"Rachel!"

A nurse appeared from the ward opposite. "Yes, Mrs. Morley?"

"I've checked the supplies list. See to the purchases as soon as possible, please."

"Yes, Mrs. Morley."

Rachel scurried away with the clipboard.

"How is Matthew?" ventured Jess warily.

"Beau has told you what happened?"

"Yes."

"I don't know. I haven't seen him since he was taken to a sanatorium some miles away, in the foothills of the Blue Mountains." Her haughty face was suddenly downcast. "I'm leaving here on Friday to be with him for the foreseeable future." She looked at Jess, and her voice trembled slightly. "He must recover, or all this will have been for nothing, and that is not acceptable." Her eyes blinked rapidly. "Now, if you will excuse me, I have work to do."

Jess watched as Celia moved quickly towards the stairs. At the head she turned.

"Please tell Beau that I want a ride home when he's finished. I'm not going on that blasted tram again!"

Jess listened to the sound of her heels as she descended the stairs, and suddenly she had a clearer picture of Celia, and what had driven her to behave as she had.

*

Jess spent the following hour wandering through the garden and sitting beneath an arbour of rose bushes. She watched a young man deftly wielding a shovel, and she presumed this was Charlie. He didn't see her as she sat hidden by foliage, but she heard him humming as he worked. Beau had 'performed a miracle', according to his mother, and Jess could see by simply observing, that Charlie was doing well.

Jess turned as she heard footsteps crunching on the gravel path, and looking up, she saw Beau approaching. She smiled as he sat beside her.

"It's all very peaceful here," she said.

Beau was looking in Charlie's direction. "Yes, it is. Have you spoken to Charlie?"

"No, he seems very absorbed in his work."

"Come and meet him, Jess."

Jess put a restraining hand on his arm. "Not yet, Beau. You might be interested to know that I had a conversation with Celia."

"Was she her usual caustic self?"

"No, she wasn't."

Beau turned to look at Jess. "Go on then, surprise me!"

"She told me that she has always considered your relationship with Matthew as, and I quote, 'Matthew being the brawn and Beau being the brains'."

"What!" Beau laughed. "Celia said that?"

"Yes, and I believe that all of this conflict is about Matthew. She wanted him to succeed, and knew that he couldn't do it without you." Jess looked away. "Matthew's sickness now means that it is even more important that you stay and get him through this."

"Jess, I'm sorry, but everything has always been about Celia; everything!"

"Maybe you don't know her as well as you think you do, Beau."

"I lived with her, Jess. I know her intimately." He grimaced. "I'm sorry, my love. That was an unfortunate turn of phrase."

Jess smiled at him. "I believe this is all about Matthew."

Beau shook his head. "You always believe the best in people, Jess." He sighed. "I don't suppose I'll ever change that."

"No." Jess took his hand. "Now, come and introduce me to your success story, and before I forget, Celia wants a ride back in to the city, when you're ready."

"Does she now?" Beau leaned across and kissed her cheek. "Have I told you today that I love you, Jess Stanley?"

"I believe you're telling me now."

The Last Day

Jess awoke the following morning to the sunlight streaming through the window. She was alone, and the other side of the bed was cold. Stretching, she wondered if Beau had left for work already. No, she could hear him moving about in the bathroom. She smiled to herself as she heard him whistling quietly. He was happy. How would he be when she left him the following morning?

Jess pushed back her hair, and lay back on the pillow. The nagging pain had returned to her head and she needed to take some more of Beau's headache powders, preferably without his knowledge.

While she was contemplating her next move, the bathroom door opened and Beau appeared. He was dressed in a dark grey suit, with a white shirt and grey tie. His hair was wet, and Jess noticed that he had shaved. A red woollen scarf was draped around his neck. Sitting on the edge of the bed, he smiled at her.

"Good morning, my darling! How did you sleep?"

"Like a top." Jess propped herself up on one elbow. "You're heading off to work?"

"I'm meeting our prospective medical personnel at the Clinic, and showing them around, before the Chairman of the Board of Directors, (Celia's father) gives them the final once-over. Hopefully we can then re-open the doors later this week."

"That will be a good thing."

"It certainly will." He frowned. "There must be a lot of desperate people wandering around out there, waiting for some attention." He touched her face. "Now, I suggest that you take your time getting up. I have a tub of hot water waiting for you in the bathroom, if you would like to have a soak."

"That sounds lovely." Jess lay back again. It would certainly help her head.

"When I've finished at the Clinic, we'll have breakfast together, and then I'm afraid I must return to Serendipity."

"I'd like to telephone Margaret some time today, if that's possible."

"We can do that from Serendipity." Beau smiled at her. "I'll leave you now, Jess. I might be a couple of hours, so take your time." He bent to kiss her cheek. "Every moment away from you is agony," he whispered into her ear.

Beau left her then and as he closed the door behind him, Jess had a sudden feeling of helplessness. She would be leaving him come the following morning, and there were no guarantees that they would see each other in the foreseeable future. Her eyes misted. Now that their union was complete, they would both find the separation unbearable.

Throwing back the blankets, Jess reached for her dressing gown, and slipped it over her shoulders. The thought of a soak in a hot tub was extremely inviting, so she retrieved her under garments from the chair where she had left them the night before, and made her way into the bathroom. It was still warm, and smelled strongly of Pears soap.

Jess opened the cabinet and found the headache powders. A twinge of guilt went through her, as she thought that perhaps she should have told Beau how she was feeling, but he had been so loving, she had put the thoughts to the back of her mind. The pressure at the back of her head had to be as a result of all of this.

When she had poured herself a glass of water and dropped one of the powders into it, she stood at the open window while she stirred the contents to a milky paste. She shuddered as the mixture went down her throat.

Suddenly there was a loud knock on the door. Jess jumped.

"Doctor DuBois! Are you there?" she heard a woman's voice shouting.

Jess moved uncertainly towards the door.

"Doctor DuBois! It's me, Mrs. Patterson! I have your washing." There was silence, and then Jess heard, "Doctor DuBois?"

Slowly she unlocked the door. On the other side stood a large woman, her head swathed in a floral scarf, and her bulky form encased in a matching apron. In her arms she carried a wicker basket filled with freshly laundered clothing. She stared open-mouthed at Jess.

"Blimey!" she said finally. "Who are you?"

"I'm Doctor DuBois's fiancé," stuttered Jess. "Who are you?"

The woman thrust the basket towards Jess. "I'm Mrs. Patterson. I do the doctor's washin', and I'd be obliged if you would take it, and give me what needs doin' this week." Her small, close-set eyes were peering at Jess.

Taking the basket, Jess placed it on the floor.

"What does he usually give you to wash?" she asked.

"Well, everythin', I suppose. You'd better give me the sheets and towels, an' whatever clothes he's been wearin'. Oh, and you'll have t'empty the basket. It's the only one I've got."

Jess quickly took the fresh clothes from the basket, and placed them on the small table. Then, under the watchful eyes of Mrs. Patterson, she stripped the sheets and pillowslips from the bed. In the bathroom, she picked up Beau's wet towel, and a pile of clothes that he'd left there. Her fingers searched the pockets before she threw them all into the basket and returned it to the woman at the door.

"I hope this is all you want," she said, as Mrs. Patterson took the basket.

"I want me five bob." Her eyes never left Jess's face.

"Oh!" Jess couldn't remember seeing any money lying around. "Just a minute."

Finding five shillings in her own purse, Jess handed it to the woman, who took it and pocketed it in her apron.

"Thanks." With one last look in Jess's direction, she made her heavy way down the stairs. "Fiance, my eye!" Jess heard her mutter under her breath.

Closing the door, Jess leaned on it. She could imagine what stories the woman might relay to her friends.

The water in the tub was still hot when Jess lowered herself into it. She sighed as she pulled her knees up and rested her head against the rounded edge. Beau had left a cake of Pears soap on a stool beside the tub, so she lathered herself with it, and then closing her eyes, relaxed in the fragrant suds. The thumping in her head slowly began to subside.

Feeling refreshed after a long soak in the fragrant water, Jess finally stepped out of the tub. Towelling herself dry, she dressed in a clean grey skirt, soft pale green blouse and a lightweight grey wool vest. She twisted her hair on top of her head, and after studying her pale features in the foggy mirror, patted some powder on her cheeks. The water in the tub would have to stay there until Beau came home, as Jess could see nowhere to empty it.

After hanging up fresh towels in the bathroom, she remade the bed with clean linen, and put Beau's clothes away in the wardrobe. Then she stepped out on to the balcony to wait for him. Leaning over the balustrade, she watched people hurrying by, and wondered where they were all going.

The door opened and Beau entered the room. He threw a briefcase on to the bed, and headed out on to the balcony.

"How did it go?"

"Excellent." Beau gathered her into his arms. "We should be able to open the doors by next Monday." He buried his face in her hair. "You smell good enough to eat," he murmured.

"I had a visitor while you were gone."

Beau lifted his head. "A visitor? Who?"

"A Mrs. Patterson."

"Oh, Jess, I'm sorry! I completely forgot that she would be here this morning."

"She asked for your washing, so I gave her what I could find."

"Did she ask for her money?"

"I paid her five shillings."

"She must have been shocked when you opened the door."

Jess laughed. "I don't think she believed me when I said that I was your fiancé."

"She probably thought that I had a fancy woman."

"You may have some explaining to do when she returns."

"She can think what she likes, now come on, we both need to eat before heading out to Serendipity." He took her hand. "How does a tram ride sound?"

"Don't you have Matthew's motorcar?"

"No, not today. Celia and Clarence have gone shopping for her expedition to the mountains to be with Matthew."

Jess picked up her shawl, and together they headed down the stairs and into Angela's Patisserie.

Angela laughed when Jess related her encounter with Mrs. Patterson.

"My goodness!" she exclaimed, as she brought their tea and toast. "Doctor DuBois, you have certainly had your reputation ruined this morning, and no mistake."

Beau merely smiled as he looked at Jess. "I don't mind in the least," he retorted.

"It will be all around the washing circle by now," Angela reminded him.

"Let them talk. I don't care."

Angela was still chuckling as she left them to their breakfast.

When they had finished, they said goodbye to Angela, and headed out on to the busy street. Beau took Jess by the hand as they negotiated the traffic, and they made it safely on to a tram. They squeezed on to a vacant seat as the tram rattled its way out of the city. It was crowded with passengers, so Beau carefully took the ends of Jess's shawl and wrapped it around her face, covering her nose.

He did the same with the red woollen scarf that he was wearing.

"Can't be too careful when you're travelling, Jess," he whispered. "We don't know where these people have been, or who they've been in contact with."

Jess smiled at him above the folds of her covering, and taking his hand, she squeezed it tightly.

The ride was slow, and they sat close together, their hands entwined, while laughter and conversation buzzed around them. This was their last day together.

Finally Beau stood up. "We'll have to walk from here, Jess."

He pulled on a cord and the tram screeched to a halt. Jumping off, he turned to lift Jess down, just as the tram jerked into motion. She lost her footing and collapsed into his arms.

"Damn drivers!" Beau shouted angrily. "They don't look to make sure everyone is off safely. Are you alright, Jess?"

"Yes." They were still standing in the roadway. "Do you remember the day you caught me when the horse unbalanced me?"

"I'll never forget it, Jess. You took my breath away then, and I still haven't got it back." Beau smiled into her eyes. "Now we'd better get off the road before we're both run down. Come on."

They headed for the footpath, and made their way along a street lined with Elms, and overlooked by grand buildings. There was a slight uphill gradient, and Beau walked quickly. Jess suddenly found the pace too fast. She grabbed his arm.

"Please slow down, Beau. I can't keep up."

She was breathing hard, and Beau frowned as he looked at her.

"Are you alright, Jess?"

"I'm out of breath, that's all."

Beau slowed his pace, and tucked her arm in his. "I'd better give you a check-up while we're at Serendipity. You shouldn't be breathless. It's not much of a hill."

Jess was still reluctant to tell him that she had been struggling with headaches over the past two days. If she could manage to get through this day, tomorrow she would be gone, and the headaches would probably be gone too.

As they crunched along the gravel drive to Serendipity, they heard a voice calling out to them, and looking around, saw Charlie waving enthusiastically. They waved back.

"When I first met Charlie," said Beau, "he was in a permanent foetal position, rocking backwards and forwards, and unable to speak."

"Look at him now."

"I'm so glad I could help him, Jess."

Jess looked into his grey eyes. "Yes, I'm sure you are, Beau. It's wonderful work that you are doing here, and you should be so proud."

Nothing more was said as they entered the building. They climbed the staircase at Jess's pace, and Beau frowned as he watched her.

"I'm going to check you over before I do anything today. You should not be so breathless, my darling girl."

"It's just that I'm not used to city life, Beau. People move a lot quicker here."

"Hm, we'll see."

He took her to an empty room, where she sank gratefully on to a bed.

"Wait here." Then he was gone.

Jess waited, and he returned with stethoscope and thermometer. After sliding the thermometer underneath her tongue, he removed her shawl.

"Unbutton your vest, Jess, and I'll check your lungs."

Beau was now her doctor, not her lover, and he worked with skilled hands while Jess sat silently.

"Well," he said finally, "your temperature is slightly elevated, and your lungs are a little wheezy, so I suggest you spend the rest of the day sitting out in the sunshine." He smiled at her worried face.

"I have had a headache on and off over the past two days," Jess confessed, "so I took some powders that I found in your bathroom cabinet."

Beau shook his head. "Why didn't you tell me, Jess?"

"I didn't want to worry you. It was a combination of several things."

"And it's my guess," he said quietly, "that you're near the end of your menstrual cycle. Am I right?"

"I-" Jess felt her face flushing. She nodded mutely.

"Jess, think of me now as your doctor. I do know about these things."

"I know."

Beau whispered against her ear. "Don't keep things from me, Jess."

She gazed into his eyes as she struggled to remain calm. "I'm sorry, Beau."

"Well, now I think it's time for you to get some sunshine while I do my rounds, and I'll see if I can find you a tonic in this place. You need boosting up."

Jess pulled her vest on, and buttoned it. Suddenly she felt like a naughty schoolgirl, caught out for being secretive, and chastised by the headmaster.

Beau was watching her as she wrapped her shawl about her shoulders and stood up. She would have to get used to him being two different people in her life; the man she loved and the man who would see to her medical needs.

Returning his smile, she walked to the door.

"I'll come and find you in an hour or so," said Beau, as she walked out into the corridor.

Jess nodded and continued towards the stairs.

Once outside, she found a seat hidden away in an arbour of rose bushes, and she sank on to it. What a strange ending it was going to be to their idyllic few days?

Jess closed her eyes and let the late autumn sunshine play on her face, while her thoughts drifted from her desire for Beau, to her family waiting at home, and finally to Jack, and the times they had together. Jack would never have talked about the personal issues of a woman's life, and Jess smiled as she remembered his embarrassment when Ben was about to be born.

"It's nice out here in the sun, isn't it?" A voice interrupted her reverie.

Opening her eyes, Jess saw Charlie sitting beside her. He was wiping his perspiring brow on a handkerchief.

"Yes, it is, Charlie."

"So you and Doctor DuBois are going to get married?"

Jess sighed. "That is the plan, Charlie, but it won't be for some time yet."

"Is that because of Doctor Morley?"

"Partly, Charlie."

"Mum an' me will always be grateful for what he did for me."

Jess looked at his fresh youthful face, and wondered how one so young could have experienced such atrocities during the war.

"He pulled me out of a very dark place, too, Charlie."

"Oh?"

"My husband died of this dreadful influenza at the end of the war, and didn't make it home. Beau – Doctor DuBois – made me see that I couldn't give up on life."

"He's had plenty of dark times in his life. He told me some of it."

"Yes, he has, Charlie; very dark indeed."

They were silent for a while.

Charlie was talking again. "Where are you from, Jess? You don't mind if I call you Jess, do you?"

"Not at all, Charlie. I'm from a town called Bendigo, down in Victoria."

"That's a long way away."

"Yes, it is," said Jess wistfully.

"I had a mate over in the training camp, had a friend who came from Bendigo."

"A lot of men went from Bendigo, Charlie."

"His name was Jack, I think." Charlie's brow was puckered.

"Jack?" Jess's throat was dry.

"Yeah. I don't know his other name."

"My husband's name was Jack, Charlie."

Charlie's brown eyes narrowed as they met Jess's, and he tried to remember his encounter with the soldier from Bendigo.

"Do you reckon it could a been him?"

"It's very possible, Charlie."

"Small world, eh?"

"Yes, it is."

*

Later that evening, Jess and Beau sat quietly on the balcony, enjoying the spectacular sunset, and munching on Angela's special salad sandwiches. They both had a lot to think about as the precious hours ticked away.

Jess had not been able to contact Margaret, and could only hope now that Charles would be at the station to meet her the following evening. She would have liked the opportunity to speak once more to Celia, but that was not possible. Charlie had unsettled her as he talked about the 'bloke from Bendigo', and she wanted to think that it was her Jack.

She looked over at Beau. He was staring out into the darkening sky.

"Are you going to be alright?" she asked tentatively.

He turned to face her, and in the gathering darkness, she couldn't read his expression.

"I'll have to be, won't I?" was all he said.

Jess placed her hands against his cheeks, and her vision suddenly blurred.

"Talk to Angela if you need somebody. Don't do this on your own."

He smiled and took her hands from his face. "I'm going to miss you more than I could possibly say," he whispered.

"I don't want to leave you, but I know I must. We will get through this, Beau. We have to be optimistic." She smiled tremulously. "Now, let's not waste the hours we have left."

"Are you sure you're feeling alright?"

Jess laughed. "That foul-tasting tonic you gave me, has perked me up no end!"

As they melted into each other's arms, Jess knew that she was in denial. Sharp pains had begun again, at the base of her skull, and as her body trembled with desire, she pushed everything else out of her mind.

The darkness closed around them as they stood locked together on the tiny balcony, and only the faint breeze shared their sighs.

Deadly Consequences

The sky was still dark the following morning when Beau stirred, and he moved to see the clock. It was four-thirty. He had another half hour to hold Jess before he needed to wake her. Curling up against her back, he slid an arm beneath her head. Something was wrong. The pillow was wet. He jerked himself awake and touched her shoulder. Her cotton nightdress was also wet. His hand trembled as he felt for her forehead. It was burning beneath his touch.

"Oh, God, no!" he whispered to himself. "Jess! Jess! Wake up!"

There was no response. Beau leapt out of bed, switched on a light and hurriedly pulled on his clothes. Rushing into the bathroom, he plunged a face cloth beneath cold running water, wrung it out, and placed it across Jess's forehead. He placed another one beneath her head as the sobs rose within him.

"Jess! Please wake up!"

He had to get her to Serendipity. His mind was racing. Perhaps Angela would sit with Jess while he went to get Matthew's motorcar.

Beau hurried from the room, and down the stairs. Angela lived behind the shop, and her door was in the alleyway. He found it in the darkness, and banged loudly.

"Angela!" he called. "It's Beau! I need your help!"

He saw a light go on inside, and in a few moments, Angela appeared, sleep-tousled and tying her dressing gown around her.

"Beau! What the dickens is going on? Do you know what time it is?"

"Yes!" he panted. "Angela, it's Jess! She has a fever, and I must get her to the hospital. Could you sit with her while I go and get Matthew's motorcar?"

Angela was suddenly alert. She slammed her door, and followed Beau.

"Yes, of course. Off you go. I'll take care of her."

"Try to keep her cool, Angela."

"Yes, yes! Go!"

Beau turned at the corner of the alleyway, as Angela made her way up the stairs.

He ran as fast as his hip would allow, along the dark deserted streets until he came to Celia's terrace house. Normally a ten minutes walk, it took five minutes this morning, and he gasped as he leaned momentarily on the wrought-iron fence.

On legs that trembled, he climbed the steps to the front door. His pounding must have disturbed Celia's neighbours, for lights appeared in windows.

Celia took her time coming to the door. He pounded again.

"Celia! It's Beau! Open up, please!"

The door finally opened, and Celia stood there, wrapped in a pink dressing gown, her dark hair falling untidily around her face.

"What is the meaning of this, Beau? Do you want to wake the dead?"

"It's Jess!" he gasped. "I need to get her to Serendipity. She has a fever. Can I have Matthew's car, please?"

Celia's black eyes, devoid of make-up, studied Beau for a moment.

"Wait five minutes and I'll come with you."

"I can't wait, Celia! This is serious!"

"Five minutes!" Her voice was sharp.

She disappeared from the doorway and Beau was left standing, helpless and agitated. He had no choice but to wait.

True to her word, Celia appeared a short time later, dressed in a heavy black coat, a cream wool scarf wrapped around her face. Her hair was tucked beneath a cream beret, and her face was devoid of the usual colour.

"Come on!" she said, as she closed the heavy front door. "We have no time to lose."

Beau followed her, slightly dazed, to where the car was parked on a driveway between the terrace houses. They climbed in, and Beau backed on to the street.

"The neighbours will be talking about this, Beau." Celia was smiling.

Beau drove recklessly along the still deserted streets, until he came to his own place. Jumping out, he left the motor idling while he took the stairs two at a time. Celia climbed out slowly, and stood by the open door. There was no point in her following.

Beau burst in to his lodgings to see Angela slipping a clean nightdress over Jess's head. He touched her forehead. It was still burning.

"I've been doing as you said, Beau."

"Thank-you, Angela." Beau proceeded to wrap Jess in a blanket, before lifting her into his arms. "I'll let you know if there's any change."

"Yes, yes! Just get her to the hospital. I'll tidy up here and lock the door."

Beau nodded. "Keys are on the bedside cabinet."

He carried Jess down the stairs to where Celia was waiting beside the parked car.

"I'll sit in the back seat with her," she said matter-of-factly, as she climbed in.

Beau laid Jess carefully across Celia's knee.

"Make sure that compress stays on her forehead."

"Yes, Beau! You drive; I'll take care of Jess."

Beau was too bemused to realise that this was a changing game for Celia. He climbed in to the driver's seat, and the car jerked into motion.

Traffic was beginning to emerge on to the streets with the approach of daylight, and horns blasted as Beau pushed his way through slow-moving vehicles, both horse-drawn and motorized.

Once out of the city maze, he cranked the car up a notch, and the road bumped beneath them.

"Careful, Beau!" shouted Celia, above the engine noise. "You'll kill us all the way you're going!"

Beau ignored her. He had to get to Serendipity. Every second was crucial. Soon the building loomed ahead of him, and he raced through the big gates and along the driveway, pulling up with a jerk at the main door. Turning off the motor, he jumped out, and flung open the door to the back seat. Celia lifted Jess's shoulders, and Beau was able to slide her towards him, where he lifted her carefully.

"I'll get one of the staff to help you," said Celia, as she climbed out of the car.

"No, I'm alright."

Beau climbed the steps, and Celia ran ahead to open the door.

Their footsteps echoed across the quiet foyer as they headed up the stairs to the second floor. Beau made straight for the quarantine area and Celia followed.

Nurse Flanagan met them at the roped-off entrance, and her eyes narrowed above her mask.

"Doctor DuBois! So we have another patient?"

"Yes." His voice was ragged. "My fiancé, Jess."

"Oh!" She called out, "James! Come quickly!"

James appeared from one of the rooms, and quickly assessed the situation in the corridor. He was swathed in white from top to toe. Taking Jess from Beau's arms, he hurried along the corridor and disappeared into a ward.

Beau staggered back against the wall, suddenly spent.

"Are you alright, Doctor?" Nurse Flanagan asked, and she looked at Celia. "Mrs. Morley, I think you should take Doctor DuBois to the canteen, while we make the patient comfortable." She turned to Beau. "Is it the influenza, Doctor?"

Beau nodded. "I haven't taken her temperature, but I suspect it's over 100."

"Alright." She smiled behind the mask. "I'll see to her, doctor, while you go and calm yourself."

Nurse Flanagan hurried off, and Celia took Beau by the arm.

"Come on, Beau, we've been given our instructions, so we'd better obey."

Together they stepped over the rope barrier, and headed back along the corridor towards the stairs.

"I don't want to go to the canteen, Celia. Let's go into Matthew's office. I can't face people right now."

Celia noticed that he was staggering slightly as they made their way to Matthew's office, so she gripped his arm tightly.

Once in the office, Beau sank on to one of the straight-backed chairs, while Celia moved across to the window to open the curtains.

"I can't lose her, Celia." His voice was just a whisper.

Celia turned from the window. "You won't lose her, Beau." She crossed the floor, and wrapping her arms around his stooped shoulders, she held him tight.

Beau felt his eyes fill as Celia held him, and suddenly he wondered where all this had gone wrong. Celia was speaking again, her voice muffled by her scarf and the emotion that at that moment overwhelmed her.

"Why is it, Beau, that the two people we love most in the world, have to suffer, while we get off scot free?"

"Not scot free, Celia. Our suffering will come if anything happens to them."

"This is all my fault, Beau." Celia raised her head. "I'm responsible for what has happened to Matthew and Jess." Celia stood up and walked to the window. "What I did was childish, Beau; I can see that now. Can you ever forgive me?"

Beau wiped his eyes. "Celia, what's happened is not as a result of your behaviour. We've both said and done things that are regrettable, but they didn't cause the sickness. What we have to do now is try to bury the hatchet. Two people are depending on us, and they need our undivided attention."

Celia turned, but Beau couldn't read her expression, as the light from the window obscured her features.

"I only spoke to Jess very briefly, but she seems very nice."

"She means everything to me, Celia." He pressed his fingers into his eyes. "Now I have to make a call to her family, and tell them what's happened. Jess was supposed to catch the train this morning."

"Do that from here, Beau, while I go and see if I can get us a cup of tea." Celia unwound her scarf, and smiled. "You're going to need your strength, Beau."

She walked from the room, closing the door quietly behind her.

*

Beau made the necessary telephone call to Margaret, who was understandably distraught, and he promised to keep them posted on Jess's progress.

As he put the receiver down, Celia returned with cups of tea and sandwiches.

"I must get back upstairs," he protested, but Celia laid a hand on his arm.

"Beau, Nurse Flanagan is very capable of dealing with the situation. Now I want you to eat something."

"I need to be with Jess."

"After you've eaten." Celia was insistent.

Beau gulped down the tea and sandwiches, and then headed for the door.

"I must go, Celia." He stopped, his hand on the brass knob. "I appreciate your being here this morning, but you need to remember that Matthew is your primary concern. You must ensure your own health, if you're going to him on Friday."

"I know, and I will." Celia smiled briefly. "I'll telephone daddy to send a car for me. You keep Matthew's car as long as you need it, Beau."

"Thank-you."

"Take care, Beau. We both have something precious that we must protect."

Beau looked at Celia, and suddenly her mask of indifference seemed to be stripped away, leaving her face bare and vulnerable.

"You take care, too, Celia, and say 'hello' to Matthew for me."

"I will."

Beau hurried away, afraid of his feelings right now. He took the stairs two at a time, ran the length of the corridor, and around the corner to the quarantine section. At the rope barrier, he donned a white gown and mask, and strode along the corridor to the room where he'd seen James take Jess. The door was open.

Beau stepped inside. Nurse Flanagan was tucking a sheet around Jess. She turned as he entered.

"Her temperature is 101, Doctor. I've just replaced the compresses, and she's breathing regularly at the moment."

"Thanyou, Nurse. I'd like to sit with her."

"Certainly, Doctor. If I need you elsewhere, I'll come and get you, but I did hear Doctor Freeman arrive about ten minutes ago, so you possibly won't need to be disturbed. I'll come back in ten minutes with fresh compresses. Call for James if you need anything else."

Beau pulled a chair up alongside the bed. Nurse Flanagan bustled out of the room as he sat heavily.

Taking Jess's hand in his, he studied her face as she slept. Her skin was flushed and glistening with perspiration. He turned the compress, feeling the warmth of it already.

"Darling girl," he whispered, "I am so sorry for what has happened. If I hadn't needed you so much, you could still be with your family, and free from this dreadful disease. I should have listened to my head when you said you'd taken my painkillers. Instead I listened to my heart, and now I have to sit and watch you suffer." He stifled a sob. "Don't leave me, my darling. I cannot even imagine life without you."

A coughing spasm wracked Jess's body, and Beau turned her so that she could retch into a small basin that nurse Flanagan had left beside the bed. Thick yellow mucus dripped from her mouth, and Beau could hear the rattle in her chest as she struggled to breathe.

When the spasm had subsided, he wiped her mouth, and laid her back on the pillow. A crackling groan escaped her lips, and her breathing was laboured. Beau rushed to the door.

"James!" he shouted into the empty corridor. "Oxygen, now!"

James appeared a minute later, and together they connected Jess to the oxygen cylinder. His heart broken, Beau could only stand by and watch as his beloved Jess fought for her life. Never had he felt so helpless.

Part Five

Reunion

Beau's Anguish

The following days melted into a blur as Beau attended to Jess's needs. Concerned duty nurses tried to encourage him to take a rest, but he stubbornly refused.

"Jess is my responsibility," he would say resolutely.

The only times he left her side were to telephone Margaret and Angela.

Nurse Flanagan shook her head at him on several occasions.

"You're going to collapse if you don't rest, Doctor, and then you'll be no good to Jess at all."

"I am not leaving her, and if it is within my power, I will see her through this."

Hour after hour he sat holding her hand and talking quietly to her. He attended to her bodily needs, and held her as she tried to cough up the thick mucus that clogged her chest. He sponged her down with cool cloths, and changed her compresses every ten minutes. He mixed honey with ginger and lemon juice, and fed her through a syringe. Sometimes she was able to swallow it, and other times she spewed it back out on to the bed sheet.

On several occasions Beau tried massaging her back and chest with camphorated oil, to help her breathing. If she was aware of his hands on her body, she gave no sign. Her temperature remained high, in spite of the constant changing of compresses.

During those moments when her energy was spent, and her breathing, although shallow, was regular, Beau would hold her hand and tell her over and over again how much he loved her.

On one occasion, as he sat holding her hand, he talked about his childhood.

"I know I promised you that one day I would talk about my sister, and my childhood, so I suppose now is as good a time as any. I don't remember much about my mother, Jess; she was a shadowy figure, regularly confined to her bed, and on those occasions, my father wouldn't allow us anywhere near her.

My sister, Charlotte, was ten years older than me, so I didn't have much to do with her either. I was a lonely child, Jess, and spent most of my time with a tutor."

He smiled to himself.

"The one I remember most was a Mr. Pratt. He disliked me intensely, and I must say the feeling was mutual. He used to tell my father that I was a morose little boy, who stubbornly refused to do what he asked of me."

He rubbed Jess's hand.

"I had many a caning from my father for disobeying my tutor.

My father spent a lot of time away from home I remember, and mother used to say that his work was important. He worked at the hospital, and that was about as much as I knew about my father.

Mother died when I was eight, and I remember being carried, absolutely distraught, out of her sick room. I didn't see her again. Father, in his grief, forgot that we needed him, and locked himself away in his study for days on end.

It wasn't long after that I remember, that Charlotte left home. Father refused to talk about her, and promptly sent me off to boarding school. I was miserable, Jess; completely isolated and constantly bullied during those years. Then I met Matthew, who became my protector. You see, he was always bigger than me, and in exchange for some personal coaching in those subjects that he wasn't good at, he agreed to act as my bodyguard. Nobody came near me, I can tell you."

Beau laughed then.

"I remember during one of my visits home, my grandmother was there. This was my father's mother, and she was about as comforting as an echidna on a winter's evening. She hated children. I wonder that she ever had my father. I don't remember my grandfather. He was French, as I may have told you. Maybe he went back to France. Who could blame him if he did?

Grandmamma, as I had to call her, would find fault with me, no matter what I did. As I said, Charlotte was not mentioned in our household, until one night when I did overhear father and grandmamma talking about her. They didn't mention her name, but I knew it was Charlotte they were talking furtively about.

From their conversation I got the impression, (and I was only about ten at the time) that Charlotte had disgraced the family, and had been sent to a convent to repent of her sinful nature. What that meant I wasn't entirely sure, but looking back now, I would say that Charlotte might have had a child, or possibly been pregnant, when she was sent away.

So you see, Jess, I didn't have a loving family like yours, and that's why it's important to me to have the family I never had. I can only do that with you, darling girl, so please, please don't leave me."

At that point, Beau put his head on the bed and cried, for all the wrongs that had occurred in his life, and the fragile hope he now had of seeing what life should be like. His last few days with Jess had filled him with some hope, and the thought that it could all be snatched away at any moment, pressed heavily on his already fatigued brain.

He slept then, the tears soaking into his white mask.

*

It was Friday morning, and Beau was returning to Jess's bedside after talking to Margaret. He had prepared her for the worst. Jess was strong, but her strength was waning, and with a heavy heart he had to concede that she couldn't struggle for much longer.

He walked slowly up the stairs, preparing himself for what must surely come. Two patients brought in at the same time as Jess had already succumbed, and they were both young men, strong and seemingly healthy.

Beau's footsteps faltered, and he grabbed the wooden banister for support. He wanted to cry out at the injustice, but he knew that every case was an injustice. Looking up he saw Celia and Clarence standing at the head of the stairs. They watched his slow progress until he was standing beside them.

"We wanted to know how things are, Beauregarde," said Clarence gruffly, "before we head for the mountains."

"How is Jess?" Celia's dark eyes were large and stricken.

Beau shrugged. "She's still with us, but…" his voice shook, "it's been three days, and I have to say I'm beginning to lose hope."

Celia stifled a sob. "Please don't lose hope, Beau! She mustn't die!"

"I've done all I can; it's up to her now."

"The motorcar is still at your disposal, if you need it." Clarence's voice was flat. "I have borrowed another one to take us to Matthew."

"How is Matthew?" Beau pulled himself momentarily out of his despair.

"He's doing well, apparently," said Celia, as she wiped her eyes.

"Good." Beau smiled wanly. "That's something. Now I must get back to Jess."

"Certainly." Clarence took Celia by the arm. "I'll call in on my way back, which will probably be tomorrow. We'll be thinking of you, lad."

Beau watched as they made their way down the stairs, and then pulling up his mask, he walked resolutely towards the quarantine section.

Jess was quiet when he entered her room, and he checked her pulse. His heart beat erratically, when for a moment he could find nothing.

Then he felt it; faint but regular. Beau lowered Jess's hand on to the sheet and stepped back. Looking down on her now, she reminded him of one of Gracie's dolls. Beau turned his face to the wall, and let the tears fall.

He didn't hear Nurse Flanagan enter the room, and he didn't hear the faint whisper that came from Jess's lips. "Beau."

Nurse Flanagan did, however.

She placed a hand across Jess's brow, and slipped a thermometer beneath her tongue.

"Doctor DuBois?" Beau turned slowly. "I think her fever has broken."

Beau knelt beside the bed, and placed a hand on Jess's brow. He looked up at Nurse Flanagan, whose eyes were shining as she pulled the thermometer from Jess's mouth.

"Ninety-eight!" she announced tremulously.

Beau took the thermometer from her hand. He had to make sure. Jess's eyelids began to flicker.

"She's going to be alright, Doctor." Nurse Flanagan patted his arm, and tucking the thermometer back in her apron pocket, walked quickly from the room.

"Beau!" It was just a whisper.

"Yes, my darling girl, I'm here." Beau stroked her face, pushing the tangle of hair from her brow.

Jess's green eyes, large now above hollow cheekbones, sought his, and her hand fluttered on the sheet. Beau held it tightly. His heart was bursting, but the anguish was gone. Jess had been restored to him, and he would be forever grateful to whatever power had made it possible.

"What happened?" Her eyes burned into his.

"You've been on a journey, Jess, but now you've come back to us."

"You took care of me?"

"Yes, my darling, I did."

Her eyes closed, and for a brief moment a flicker of a smile touched her lips.

"I knew it was you."

"How did you know?"

Her fingers moved in his. "Your hands," was all she said.

Beau smiled. So she had been aware of his presence.

"Rest now, Jess, while I go and telephone Margaret to give her the good news."

"My children," she whispered.

"Yes, your children need to know that you are going to be alright." For a moment her fingers clutched his, and he saw a tear slide down her cheek. "You *are* going to be alright, Jess."

Recovery

Beau knew that, although Jess had come through the first stage of the influenza, she still had a long way to go. Her recovery would be long, and he had to prepare himself for possible setbacks. Margaret was relieved when he told her, somewhat tearfully, that Jess had turned the first corner, so they could be cautiously optimistic. They had both cried together.

When Beau returned to the ward, a nurse was busy changing the bed sheets. Jess looked up at him as he entered, and smiled wanly. He returned her smile across the top of his mask, and waited for the nurse to complete her task.

As she quietly left the ward, Beau knelt beside the bed and clasped Jess's hand.

"I've spoken to Margaret, and we both had a good cry," he said softly.

"The children?"

"Margaret will tell them. She hasn't said too much to them, but she senses that Ben, in particular, is aware of what's happening."

Jess nodded. "He would be." She stared up at him. "You need to rest, Beau."

"I need to go home and change my clothes, and thank goodness for these masks. I haven't shaved for four days."

A slight smile played around her lips. She released her hand from his, and reached up to touch his face.

"You go. I'll be alright."

"I'll have to, I'm afraid." He bent to kiss her forehead, and tasted the cloth of his mask. "Not so easy, is it?"

Jess kissed her fingers and laid them across his mask. Their eyes met and held.

"I'll be back before you know I've gone," he whispered, returning the kiss to her lips. "I love you, darling girl."

Jess smiled, and shooed him with her hands. "Go!" she murmured weakly, before closing her eyes.

Beau left her then, and went in search of the duty nurse, to tell her that he was leaving for a while. He didn't find the duty nurse, but he found James in the utilities room, rinsing out bedpans.

"I'm going home for a while, James. Jess seems able to breathe on her own now."

"Great news, Doctor. We all thought she'd be lucky to pull through, but she's defied the odds, and we couldn't be happier."

"I'll be back as soon as I can. In the meantime, if you could make sure she has a little sustenance; some broth, perhaps?"

"I'll see to it, Doctor."

"Thank-you, James."

Beau stripped off his mask and gown, and headed for the stairs. Stepping out into the fresh air, he took a deep breath. When did he last taste fresh air?

Matthew's motorcar responded immediately, and he turned on the gravel driveway and headed for the gates. As he did, he saw a figure running towards him. It was Charlie. He put his foot on the brake.

Charlie came to a halt beside him, and sweeping off his cap, peered in through the glass. Beau wound down the window.

"We heard about Jess, Doctor," he panted. "Is she alright?"

"She is now, Charlie."

"That's good." He was nodding enthusiastically. "She's a nice lady, Doctor."

"The best, Charlie, the best."

"Well, I won't keep you; I just wanted to know how she was."

"I trust she'll keep improving, Charlie."

"She will." Charlie stepped back. "She's got you t'look after her."

Beau smiled at that remark. "Thank-you, Charlie."

The motorcar slid into motion, and Beau headed towards the gates. He couldn't tell Charlie that he was inadvertently responsible for Jess's condition. It was his failure to recognise the early symptoms… He shook the thoughts from his head. He couldn't change what had happened earlier. What he had to do now was make sure that his professionalism was not overrun by emotions.

*

Angela looked up sharply as Beau burst through her screen door. Her hands stopped in mid-air, as she served a customer.

"Beau!"

"It's alright, Angela. Jess has turned the corner. Her fever has broken, so now we can be cautiously optimistic."

"Thank God for that!" Angela completed her transaction, and the customer left the shop. "You look ghastly, I must say."

"That's why I'm here. I need to change my clothes and have a shave, and then I might feel more human." Beau rubbed the stubble on his chin.

"I'll get your keys." Angela disappeared through a door at the rear of the shop, re-appearing a few seconds later. "Here you are. I think you'll find everything tidy up there. I've changed the bed sheets, and washed a few of Jess's things."

"Thank-you, Angela. I'm indebted to you. I don't know what I would have done if you hadn't been here."

Angela flapped her hands. "Glad to help, Beau." She smiled warmly. "I'm so glad that Jess is going to recover. Now you go and clean yourself up! Oh, and you'd better pop in when you've finished, and I'll have a parcel of food for you. You look as though you could do with a good feed."

"Bless you, Angela." Beau grinned suddenly. "You really are an angel."

Angela laughed. "Oh, go away with you!"

Beau hurried up the stairs to his room. Opening the door, he could see that Angela had been busy. He dropped the keys on the bedside table, and began to strip off the clothes he'd been in since Tuesday morning. A soak in the tub would have been very welcome, but he didn't want to be away from Jess for too long.

After shaving the stubble from his face, Beau looked long and hard at his reflection in the bathroom mirror. It had been a handsome face until German shrapnel had ripped apart his cheek. Now it was also beginning to show the ravages of time. Lifting the hair from his forehead, Beau ran a finger across the scar that Jess had stitched, over two years ago. He smiled as he remembered her panic at being asked to do such a thing. It was barely visible now.

Jess loved him, in spite of his physical scars. In fact she seemed to enjoy running her fingers down his damaged cheek. Beau found a bottle of cologne in the cupboard, and splashed a little on his face. It felt cool and refreshing.

It was time to return to Serendipity. Opening Jess's case, he could see that Angela had folded her clothes neatly. Jess would probably have need of some of these things, he thought, as he shut the lid. Locking the room, Beau shoved the keys in his pocket, and hurried down the stairs. Angela met him at the door of the Patisserie, and handed him a brown paper bag.

"Some treats," she said brightly. "There are a couple of custard tarts in there, so don't squash them. I thought Jess might be up to having a little custard."

"Thank-you again, Angela. I'm sure Jess will appreciate it."

"Oh, by the way, you have scrubbed up well. You even smell nice."

Beau rolled his eyes at her, and headed for the motorcar. "I'll be seeing you, Angela. I'll come home to sleep once Jess is quite stable."

Angela nodded. "Righto!"

They waved, and Beau rolled the motorcar into the traffic.

When he arrived at Serendipity, he grabbed Jess's case, and strode into the building. Shirley's voice interrupted his stride as he passed the receptionist's window.

"Wonderful news about your Jess, Doctor."

"Early days yet, Shirley, but she's heading in the right direction."

Shirley nodded vigorously, and he continued up the stairs. Donning gown and mask, Beau stepped over the rope barrier and headed for Jess's room.

At the door he stopped, and his heart did a plummet. The bed was empty; Jess was not there. Turning on his heel, he strode back along the corridor.

"Nurse!" he shouted to the empty corridor.

Nurse Flanagan appeared from the end ward, and hurried towards him.

"Where's Jess? She's not in her room!" There was panic in his tone.

"It's alright, Doctor." Nurse Flanagan raised her hands as if to calm him. "Doctor Freeman has sent her to the hospital for a chest x-ray."

"Without consulting me?"

"You weren't here, Doctor." Her voice remained calm.

"Was he aware that her fever has only just broken?"

"Yes. Her temperature is stable, Doctor."

"How long ago did she leave?"

"Half an hour." She smiled behind her mask.

"Where is Doctor Freeman now?"

"He's attending to the patient in room 1, and I must get back there. He's not doing as well as your Jess."

Beau frowned, and nurse Flanagan leaned a little towards him.

"Doctor Freeman is surprised by Jess's recovery," she said in hushed tones. "I didn't tell him, but I suspect it's the tender loving care she received."

Beau stared at her. "What do you mean?"

"I'm sorry, Doctor DuBois, but your constant vigil didn't go unnoticed." She shrugged her plump shoulders. "It was your will that kept her alive. We can't give the patients that kind of attention."

"And you believe that?"

"I do. Now I must go back and do what I can for Mr. Harding, poor man. He doesn't have a wife to urge him on." She smiled sadly, before bustling away.

Beau stood for a moment, a frown etched on his brow. It was an interesting theory, he had to admit, but sadly not supported by any scientific evidence. Jess had been aware of his presence, but had she actually heard his desperate pleas for her to come back to him? He would have to find out.

Realising that he still carried the suitcase and Angela's bag of pastries, he returned to Jess's room. Placing the suitcase beside the bed, he then opened the bag. The hunger pangs that had been gnawing at him for the past three days could no longer be ignored. On a number of occasions, caring nurses had quietly brought him sandwiches, which he had eaten without thought or interest.

He stood at the window and munched on one of Angela's sausage rolls, while he watched the scene below him. This was the room he had stood in with Matthew, when the influenza had first broken out, and they had discussed how to utilize the space to accommodate infectious patients. It was also the room where he had walked in on Matthew with Milly Saunders. He wondered briefly what had become of her; he had seen neither sight nor sign of her since she had been discharged.

His eye caught sight of an ambulance, bumping its way across the grass. It stopped below him, and two sturdy orderlies jumped out. He watched as they opened the rear door of the vehicle, and began removing a gurney. It carried Jess. Beau quickly placed the bag on the bedside table, and ran from the room. He had to negotiate the back stairs of the building, which had originally been used by the servants. The stairwell was dark, and a damp odour hung there. The door at the bottom was heavy, and resisted his pushing, until finally it creaked open, and the daylight streamed in.

"Well timed," said one of the orderlies. "You must have seen us coming."

"I did." Beau looked at Jess, and she smiled at him.

"Leave the door open please, mate," said the orderly, looking in Beau's direction. "It's as dark as a cow's stomach up there."

Beau grinned as he followed them up the stairs. Once they reached the second floor, he ran ahead of them, to turn back the bed covers, but discovered that a nurse was already there, quietly waiting to see to her patient. Beau stood back.

Jess was lifted from the gurney and carried effortlessly to the bed, where the nurse busied herself with smoothing the covers, and plumping the pillows. Then with a quick look in Beau's direction, she scurried out of the room.

The two orderlies picked up the gurney, and with a nod in Beau's direction, also left the room. Beau carried a chair across the room, and sat beside the bed. Jess reached for his hand, and her eyes searched his. He smiled behind his mask, and squeezed her fingers gently.

"So you've had an x-ray?"

Jess nodded. "Doctor Freeman insisted." Her voice was weak. "I wanted to wait for you, but he said it had to be done straight away."

"That's alright. I should have been here, but it's done now." Beau reached for the bag of pastries. "Angela sent some custard tarts for you. She said the custard would do you good. Would you like some now?"

At that moment the nurse appeared, and placed a thermometer beneath Jess's tongue. There was silence while she placed cool fingers on Jess's wrist, and checked with her watch.

"All good," she said, as she removed the thermometer and wrote on a clipboard. "Temperature stable at 98." She smiled at them and left the room with a rustle of starched apron.

"I'm going to be alright, aren't I, Beau?" It was more a statement than a question.

"Never underestimate the power of love, my darling girl." Beau touched her face. "Yes, you're going to be alright."

*

The following day, Clarence arrived, and met with Beau in Matthew's office on the ground floor. He was heartened by the news of Jess's recovery, and had news of Matthew's progress.

"He's doing well, I'm pleased to say, and seeing Celia, boosted him no end."

Beau smiled to himself. *Is it the power of love at work again?* "Excellent."

"We had a long discussion on the future of the Clinic and of course, this place, and in the process, decided to put it to the Board to have you freed from your current contract, Beauregarde, if that is what you wish. It is up to you, but I'm pleased to say that my daughter has now realised that things don't always go according to her plan, and she has apologised to Matthew for all the friction she has caused." Clarence gave an embarrassed little cough. "She also owned up to several things she has done to you and Jess in recent times, and I humbly apologise on her behalf."

"We need to put it all behind us. We all have altered circumstances, and we must look after those we love."

"I agree, Beauregarde." Clarence held out his hand, and Beau took it. "Of course, we'll be pleased to have you here until such times as Jess has recovered and is fit to return home."

"Thank-you, Clarence. Naturally I won't leave until everything is in place here, but I will be travelling with Jess, when she is ready." A frown creased his brow. "When Matthew has turned the corner, so to speak, I'll make it my business to come and see him. That is a promise."

"Celia's apology won't make you change your mind about staying?"

"No, Clarence. The decision has been made."

"I do understand." Clarence turned to leave. "Oh, one more thing. I'd like to take you and Jess to dinner at Mario's before you leave here."

"That will be a little while yet, Clarence, but thank-you, we accept with pleasure."

"I am so sorry about all this." Clarence gave a slight nod, before leaving.

Left alone, Beau leaned on Matthew's table. It had taken a dramatic turn of events to finally smooth the road for everyone, and now they could all concentrate on those things that mattered.

His steps were light as he headed upstairs to tell Jess the good news.

Wedding Plans

As the days slipped by, Jess became stronger, and was eventually moved from the quarantine ward, to a room amongst the returned servicemen and women. At first she was a little worried by the strange noises that issued from some of the rooms, but Beau assured her that she was safe. He locked her door before leaving her each night, and travelled home to his own room to sleep.

On the days when the winter sun was shining, he would carry her down the stairs and sit her in the garden, where she watched the gardeners turning the soil, pruning the roses, and planting bulbs. She enjoyed those moments, because they gave her time to think about what had happened during those three days when she had lost consciousness. Small stirrings of memory fluttered at the back of her mind, and she recalled a much-loved voice. Beau had talked to her through those days of darkness; told her things that she could vaguely remember.

Jess talked with her children on a number of occasions, reassuring them that she was getting better, and she would see them soon. After each conversation, she would rest her head on Beau's chest and cry until she was exhausted. He would stroke her hair, and hold her tight, in an attempt to transfer some of her anxiety to his own body. It reminded him of the time he had held her after Jack's death, in an attempt to relieve her of her grief.

Angela sent regular packages with Beau. There were pastries to tempt her appetite, and which she sat and enjoyed with him in the sunshine.

It was during one of these moments, when they were both seated in the garden, their knees covered by a colourful crocheted rug, that Beau brushed the crumbs from his lap and turned to Jess.

"We need to get married," he said quietly, wiping crumbs from his mouth.

"We are, Beau." Jess turned puzzled eyes in his direction.

"Yes, but we need to get married now."

"Now?"

"Before we leave Sydney."

"Why?"

He took her hands, his eyes serious. "Because, when we get you back to your family, I don't want to spend my nights at Margaret's or Jean's, as society would expect. I want to be with you."

Jess stared at him for a long moment. "So how do we do that?"

"We have a Chaplain here at Serendipity, and all we need is a witness."

"Go on."

"I'm sure Angela would be very happy to be the witness."

"You have it all figured out, don't you?" Jess laughed softly at his serious expression. "And what do we tell Izzy?"

"Izzy will understand. Besides, we can still have a large family gathering later on, if you really want one."

"I see." Jess stared out across the garden. "Family means your family, too, Beau."

He groaned. "Jess, please don't do this. I've told you my sister left home a long time ago; too long ago. I wouldn't even know her now, even if I could find her."

"I don't know how you can know that you have a sister, possibly here in Sydney, and not make any attempt to find her. What if she has children? You think she has at least one child." Jess was still staring out across the garden.

"What? Who told you that?"

Jess turned to face him. "You did."

"When?" He already knew the answer, but he wanted her to say it.

"I don't know." Her brow creased. "I remember you telling me that your sister may have had a child; that's why she was sent away."

"I told you all that when you were unconscious, Jess."

"You did?" She turned to look at him.

"Yes, amongst other things."

"That's extraordinary."

"Nurse Flanagan was right," he murmured, almost to himself.

"Nurse Flanagan?"

"She told me that it was my will that kept you going through those three days."

"The power of love, Beau?"

"Yes. Now, back to my original question. What is your answer?"

Jess touched his face. "My answer has to be 'yes'."

*

The week that followed was one of frenzied excitement. As word spread around the staff at Serendipity, notes of congratulations appeared on Jess's walls, and coloured bunting appeared, all around the entrance foyer. Jess felt bemused and excited, but she also needed to escape the confines of Serendipity. She felt well enough now to be discharged, but under Beau's watchful eye, she knew it wouldn't happen in a hurry.

"You need to be 100 percent before I let you loose on the town," he said to her on more than one occasion, when she had begged him to take her back to his place. "I'm not taking any more chances. Your x-rays have been fine, and we don't see any lasting damage, but it's still early days. Have patience, my love."

"Have patience? What about our wedding? I do need to do some planning."

"Like what?"

"Like what I'm going to wear, for instance?"

Beau smiled. "I wouldn't be too concerned about that, Jess."

"Of course you wouldn't! You're a man!" Beau laughed at that remark, and tried to draw her into his arms, as they sat on the garden seat, but she held him back. "And where are we going to have this ceremony? Have you thought about that?"

"Calm down Jess. Yes, I have, and I'm thinking it might be nice here in the gardens at Serendipity. The Chaplain is ready whenever we are."

"Is he?" Jess knew she was snapping at him, but her frustration was beginning to show. "Let me in on the plans, Beau, please!"

"I'm sorry, my love, but there is still so much for me to do here before we go, that everything else has temporarily slipped my mind."

"Obviously."

Beau winced. This was their second argument, and he had not intended for this to happen. He took her hands, and held them as she tried to pull away.

"Jess, please don't be angry. This is too important for anger."

"Then tell me what's happening."

"The Chaplain, Pastor Allenby, is happy to officiate, and I suggested here, because I thought it might be something for the Staff to look forward to; a wedding in their own grounds. Are you happy with that?"

Jess decided at that moment that she wasn't going to let him off the hook that easily. She studied his face as she searched for an answer. She saw remorse there.

"What if it rains?"

Beau shrugged. "Well –er- we could move into the foyer, I suppose."

Jess thought about this; it was a logical move. "Yes, alright, we could do that. And Angela? Have you spoken to her about this?"

"No, Jess, I haven't."

"Did you have a day in mind?"

Beau pushed his fingers into his eyes. "Please, Jess, I don't need interrogation right now." His vision was blurred as he looked at her, so he didn't see the smile that played around her lips. "What day do you suggest?"

Suddenly her resolve weakened, and she took his face in her hands.

"What if we discuss that now?" she said softly.

Beau relaxed. "Yes, alright. Believe me, Jess, none of this was intentional."

"I know, and I'm sorry." She sat back on the seat. "Shall we start again?"

"That's a very good idea. Tell me what you think of this as a plan. If I can get train tickets for Friday evening, how do you feel about having the ceremony here, on Friday morning?"

"Train tickets?" Jess turned to face him.

"How would you like to go home on Friday night?"

"Home?"

"That's what I said."

"You think I'll be ready to travel by then? What's today? I have no idea!"

"Today is Tuesday, and yes, you should be strong enough to travel by Friday."

"I can go home?"

"No, Jess, *we* can go home."

Jess nodded vigorously. "That's what I meant. *We* can go home." Her eyes were shining as she reached across and slipped her arms around his neck. "Oh, Beau, I do love you, and I'll marry you on Friday, if that is the plan."

"Good." Beau gave her a gentle squeeze. "In the meantime, if you want to pack up your things, you can go back to my place tonight."

"You mean that?"

"Of course."

"I feel as though I've been here forever."

"Well, I'm discharging you as of today."

Angela

Jess spent the rest of the day sorting out her belongings, and finally being able to strip off her nightdress and dressing gown. She dressed in her grey skirt, pale green blouse with ruffles around the neck, and a jacket, as it was cool in the building. Finally she was able to brush out her hair, and apply a little make-up to her pale face. That done, she filled in time walking the corridors, and checking out the garden, with a view as to where the marriage ceremony might take place. She chose a grassed area, overshadowed by a magnificent ghost gum, its smooth trunk gleaming in the sunlight. Beau should have no objection to her choice.

It was within view of the building, so patients would be able to watch through the windows. Yes, it would be perfect.

Beau spent the rest of the day showing the new Medical staff around the premises, and Jess caught the odd glimpse of them, as she moved freely around the grounds. It really was a magnificent place, and her heart constricted as she thought of Beau giving all this up for her. She chastised herself for being mean to him earlier, and promised herself she must never do it again. He was a special man; a good man, and he loved her. She would do well to remember that.

The afternoon dragged as she waited for Beau to finish, and eventually he appeared at the door of her room.

"Ready?"

"Yes, I'm ready."

"Then let's get you out of here."

As Beau took her arm, and picked up her suitcase, his mind went back to their arrival at Serendipity, when he wasn't sure whether she was going to live or die. He looked at her now, and although she was pale, her eyes had a shine, and her step was light.

As they passed the reception desk, Shirley called out to them.

"Good luck, Jess! All the best for your marriage!"

"Thank-you, Shirley." Jess smiled at Shirley, and then her glance fell on Beau. "It will be a good marriage," she whispered so that only he could hear it.

He squeezed her arm.

*

They stepped out into the sunshine, and Jess stopped, pulling Beau to a halt beside her. She pointed to the ghost gum, standing tall amid the varieties of shrubs, native bottlebrush and roses.

"That's where we need to have the ceremony, Beau!" she declared.

Beau followed the line of her arm. "Do we indeed?"

"Yes. I think it will be the perfect spot, and the patients can watch as well."

"Hm." His eyes were turned away from her. "I'll think about it."

"Beau!" Jess gave him a gentle shove. "Now who's being mean?"

Beau turned to face her, his eyes shining. "It will be perfect, Jess." He opened the car door, tossed the suitcase in the back seat, and handed Jess into the passenger seat. "Absolutely perfect, and I can't wait."

"You'll have to," said Jess primly. "There are still things to do."

"I know." He climbed into the driver's seat. "I've got two days to finish working with the two new doctors at the Clinic, before I can even think about anything else." He looked sidelong at Jess, as the car slid forward. "You can do your feminine planning with Angela. I'm sure she'll be up to the task."

"Beau?" Jess suddenly became thoughtful.

"Yes, my love?"

"Do we tell the family, or wait until we get home, and surprise them?"

"I think we should tell them beforehand. We don't want to give Charles another heart attack."

"Yes, you're right. I'll call them tomorrow."

They were both silent as Beau concentrated on the road, and Jess thought about the reaction their news was going to have. Feelings would undoubtedly be mixed.

The car slid to a halt outside Angela's, and Beau jumped out. He opened the door for Jess, and she stepped on to the footpath.

"Come on, let's go and see Angela."

Jess stood for a moment. "Actually, Beau, I'm feeling rather weary. Do you mind if we go upstairs? I think I need to rest."

Beau took her arm. "Of course, my love."

Together they climbed the stairs to the landing, and Beau delved in his pocket for the key. He pushed the door open, and Jess stepped inside.

"It must be two weeks since I was here, Beau." Jess sighed as she threw her shawl on the neatly made bed. "I see a woman's touch here, am I right?"

Beau put the case on the bed. "Yes. Angela has been in, cleaning up after me."

"We have a lot to thank Angela for."

"Yes, we have." Beau opened his arms, and Jess stepped into his embrace. "Oh, Jess," he murmured into her hair, "I thought I was going to lose you, and it would have all been my fault."

"No, Beau!" Jess tilted her head back to look at him. "Let's not talk about blame. It happened, and we've come through. Let's be grateful for that."

His eyes looked deep into hers. "I know, but if I…"

Jess stopped him, by placing her fingers over his mouth. "Hush! I won't hear another word. Now, I need to lie down before I fall down."

Beau pulled back the covers, and helped her on to the bed, where he unlaced her boots, and eased her feet out of them.

Jess sighed, suddenly aware that two weeks in hospital had sapped her of strength. She smiled apologetically at Beau, as he plumped her pillows.

"I'm sorry to be a nuisance."

Beau pulled the blue quilt over her. "Nonsense." He kissed the top of her head. "You rest now, and I'll go downstairs and have a chat with Angela. She probably saw us arrive, and is wondering why we didn't pop in."

"Yes, you do that. Apologise for me, will you, and tell her I'll see her tomorrow?"

"I can do that. I won't be gone long."

*

By the time Beau returned, night was drawing her mantle over the southern continent, and a chill had crept in to the air. Jess had managed to change into her nightdress, and was sleeping soundly. Beau closed the drapes over the window, and turned on one of the lamps. He lit the kerosene heater, and reaching for his briefcase, decided that he would attempt to do some work in preparation for his meeting with Clarence and the new medical team the following morning.

For two hours he worked in the dim lamplight, until his eyes burned, and his stomach began to protest. Then moving quietly, so as not to disturb Jess, he boiled the kettle on the single gas burner, made a pot of tea, and consumed two sausage rolls that Angela had sent home with him.

It was only nine o'clock, but he decided that he would go to bed. Jess had not stirred, so quietly he undressed, and then after turning off the kerosene heater, and the lamp, he eased himself on to the narrow bed. Jess lay with her back to him, so he gently wrapped his arms around her, cradling her against him.

"Goodnight, my darling," he breathed into her hair.

Jess gave a little sigh, and moved herself just enough to fit snugly against his body.

"Mm," he heard her murmur softly.

*

The following morning, Jess woke to the sounds of the city coming to life. She needed to use the bathroom, but Beau still slept beside her, his arm flung across her shoulder. As she tried to slip from beneath his arm, he stirred, and she felt herself drawn back against him.

"And where do you think you're going?" His voice was thick with sleep.

"I need to use the bathroom," whispered Jess, as his arms circled her.

"Oh!" She was released. "Don't be too long."

Jess twisted away from him. "I won't."

By the time she returned, Jess noticed that Beau had turned on the kerosene heater, and was lying with his hands behind his head.

"Come back here and talk to me," he said, as he threw back the covers.

Jess slipped in beside him, and teeth chattering, pulled the blankets over them.

"What do you want to talk about?" She turned, wrapping an arm around him.

"Well, you were out for the count when I got back last night." Beau tucked an arm beneath her. "I pottered around, and did some work for a couple of hours, and then had some supper, (because we missed out on having tea,) and still you slept."

"I was very tired."

"You must have been." He kissed the top of her head. "I had a lovely chat with Angela, and she's very excited about being part of our ceremony."

"I'm so glad."

"She has one stipulation."

"And what is that?"

"That you spend tonight and tomorrow night at her place."

"Why?"

"Protocol, she called it. The groom should not see the bride prior to the wedding."

"She's right, Beau."

He sighed. "Yes, I know, and I'll have to relinquish you for two nights."

"Don't make it sound like a lifetime." Jess twisted away from him, and swung her legs out of the bed. "As a matter of fact, we can start now."

As Beau made a grab for her, she moved out of his reach. He lay back, shaking his head. "You are so cruel."

"Friday's not that far away. Now come on, I'm very hungry, you have work to get to, and I have a telephone call to make." She picked up her clothes from the chair. "I'm first in the bathroom."

Jess heard him groan as she shut the bathroom door.

*

After a breakfast of toast and jam, and chatter from Angela, it was time to head to the Clinic. Jess needed to talk to Margaret before Beau's busy day started.

Promising to return and talk to Angela, Jess followed Beau from the patisserie. Covering their faces they headed down the now crowded street. Jess tucked her arm in Beau's, and had to run to keep pace with him.

"Slow down, Beau!" she wailed. "You walk too fast!"

"I'm sorry, my love. It's a habit. Nobody strolls in the city. You get run down if you do." He smiled at her. "I'll try to keep to your pace."

Fortunately the way was downhill, so eventually they compromised on their stride, and made it to the Clinic within ten minutes.

Beau unlocked the door, picked up a pile of mail from the foyer floor, and together they made their way up the staircase. Their footsteps echoed in the empty building, and Jess could smell beeswax and polish. The cleaners had been busy.

Beau unlocked the door to reception, and dropped the mail on Celia's desk.

Jess walked across to the telephone, and nervously turned the handle. Her heart was beating a little erratically, as she went over in her head what she would say to Margaret. Beau smiled encouragingly at her as he leafed through the mail.

Finally she heard Margaret's voice, faint and a little weary.

"Hello."

"Margaret, it's Jess. How are you? How are the children?"

"Oh, Jessie dear." Her voice rose slightly. "We're all well. How about you?"

"I'm recovering. Beau is taking good care of me."

"That's good, dear." There was a pause. "Any idea when you'll be home?"

"Hopefully on Saturday. We're planning on catching the night train from Sydney on Friday. Beau is coming with me. He's finally able to leave his position here."

"That's wonderful, dear. The children are getting very anxious, particularly Gracie. I'm running out of things to keep her occupied." She gave a soft laugh. "Charles has taken her to the park, and of course the boys are at school."

"Yes, of course. Have you told Mr. Granger what's been happening?"

"Oh, yes, dear. He said the job's still yours when you return."

Jess took a deep breath. "Margaret, I have something to tell you. Beau and I have decided to get married before we leave Sydney. In fact we are having a ceremony on Friday morning, out at the Institution where Beau has been working."

There was silence on the other end of the line. Jess looked at Beau, and her brow furrowed.

"That's probably a good idea, Jess," Margaret said finally. "Will it be a proper marriage service? I mean, it won't just be a registrar, will it?"

"No. We have the Chaplain from Serendipity Lodge."

"From where?"

"Serendipity Lodge. That's the name of the Institution."

"I see." There was another pause. "So you'll be Mrs. DuBois when we see you."

Jess hadn't thought of that. "Yes, I expect I will."

"You have our blessings, Jessie."

"Thank-you, Margaret. That means a lot."

"Are you extending?" a droll voice interrupted.

"No," said Jess hurriedly. "We'll see you all on Saturday, Margaret. Give our love to everyone..."

The line went dead.

Jess replaced the receiver, and looked across at Beau.

"We have their blessings, Beau," she whispered.

He was beside her in one stride, and gathered her into his arms.

"That's what you needed to hear, Jess."

"Margaret sounds very tired." Jess wiped a hand across her eyes. "They will have had the children for three weeks by the time I get home. That's too long."

"The situation was out of your hands, Jess. You didn't plan on being away all this time. Now come on, I'll walk you back to Angela's before everyone starts to arrive here." Beau took her hand.

"There's no need to walk me back, Beau. I know the way."

Beau lowered his eyebrows. "Can I trust you to go straight there? No detouring to the quayside?"

"I'd love to sit by the quayside and watch the boats, but no, I promise I'll go straight to Angela's."

"Very well. I'll see you there when I've finished, and if it's not too late, we can both go to the quayside and watch the boats."

Jess smiled eagerly. "That would be lovely."

"We might even grab some fish and chips, and behave like tourists." Beau slipped his arms around her, and leaned in for a kiss. "Would you like that?"

"Hm." Jess tweaked his nose. "Then you can walk me home to my new lodgings."

"Don't tease me, Jess."

"I'm sorry." Jess reached for another kiss. "Now I must go." Untangling herself from his embrace, she moved to the door. "Au revoir, as the French say."

"Au revoir, ma Cherie."

She was gone, and Beau stood for a moment before moving to the window. He stared down on to the street, and in a few minutes, saw Jess walking away from the building. She looked up and saw him, and spontaneously blew him a kiss.

Beau responded, and he wanted to capture that moment forever. The light was shining on her hair, as it moved in the breeze, giving her a golden halo. Her face was upturned, and the smile was radiant; the smile was for him.

"I love you, Jess." He mouthed the words, saw her puzzled frown, and then the smile re-appeared and she mouthed the words, "I love you, Beau."

He turned away from the window as the door opened behind him, and Clarence walked in.

*

Jess's steps were light as she made her own way back to Angela's. She had a good feeling about the future. Her children would soon be in her arms, a good man was prepared to share her life, and the bad times were behind them. What more could she ask for? Life with Beau was going to be full of surprises, of that she was certain. There would be large doses of love, and her cheeks flushed as she thought of what that could bring. Maybe children? Beau had already indicated that he wanted lots of children. She would let time take care of that.

Her immediate thoughts were on the wedding ceremony. There had been no time to plan a service, let alone decide what she should wear. She would talk to Angela. Maybe she would have some ideas?

Jess had reached the patisserie, and opened the screen door. Angela looked up from behind the big glass-topped counter, and smiled warmly.

"Jess! You're back!"

"Yes. My telephone call to Margaret went well. We have their blessing."

"Good! Now, what is your plan for the day?"

Jess shrugged. "I've had to promise that I won't go wandering around the city by myself, so I suppose I'll have to stay here until Beau comes back. Then he has promised to take me down to the quayside and have fish and chips."

"How romantic!" Angela sighed. Then she looked across the counter at Jess, and a wicked twinkle appeared in her eyes. "Beau told me last night that you are concerned about what you should wear on Friday. I think I can help you there."

"You can?"

"Yes." She turned and called out behind her. "Sandra! Mind the counter, will you? I'm going out the back to my rooms."

Sandra's head appeared from the kitchen door, flushed from the warmth of the ovens. "Righto!"

Angela moved from behind the counter, and taking Jess by the arm, led her through the back of the shop to where she lived.

As they stepped into the dining room, Jess felt as though she had been transported back in time. The room was small, dwarfed by the heavy oak furniture that filled it. An elaborately carved sideboard took up one wall, and was covered with silverware of every description, from a tea service down to miniature photo frames, displaying people from another age.

An enormous oak table took up most of the room, along with six matching straight-backed chairs with maroon velvet seats. In the centre of the table stood a silver candelabrum, and at either side were silver tureens with matching servers.

Jess knew that her eyes had widened, as Angela pulled back the heavy maroon drapes covering the window. She smiled at Jess's expression.

"My grandmother's," she explained. "I didn't have the heart to get rid of it."

"My goodness!" was all Jess could say.

"Anyway, this isn't what I brought you in to see. Follow me." Angela led the way along a short dark passage, and into a bedroom. Once again she swept back the heavy curtains, allowing some light from the alley to penetrate. "This is what I wanted to show you."

Angela opened a wardrobe door, and pulled a garment from the interior. Spreading it on the wrought-iron bed, she stood back to see Jess's reaction.

"It's a wedding dress!" exclaimed Jess, as she touched the cream silk fabric spread out across the bed. "Whose is it?" She glanced at Angela, whose eyes were glistening with tears. "Is it yours?"

Angela nodded. "I was supposed to be married in February, 1915, but Teddy enlisted to go overseas, and I was left wondering what sort of future we might have. He didn't even make it to the beach at Gallipoli."

"I am so sorry, Angela." Jess felt the tears well in her own eyes. "So we've both experienced loss."

"Yes." Angela wiped her eyes. "Would you like to wear this dress on Friday? I would be very honoured."

"It's beautiful." Jess fingered the soft fabric.

"I know what you're probably thinking," said Angela with a laugh. "You're thinking that it will be too big for you." She patted her ample hips. "Four years ago I didn't have these. I was as thin as a reed, just like you, Jess. I'm afraid I've indulged in too many pastries."

Jess smiled. "I wasn't thinking that at all, Angela. I would be very honoured to wear it."

"I don't have a veil." Angela rummaged in the bottom of the wardrobe, and produced a box. "But I do have these." She pulled out a coronet of gardenias. "They will be perfect in your hair, Jess." Jess didn't know what to say as she stood staring at the silk gardenias. "I'll go back to the shop and see what Sandra is doing, and if you like, you can try it on. I'll come back in about twenty minutes."

Jess nodded. "Alright," she said slowly.

Angela bustled out of the room, and Jess stood awkwardly for a moment, as the realisation penetrated her brain. She had a wedding dress, and a beautiful one at that, thanks to the generosity of a woman she had met only a few weeks ago.

Slowly she began to undress. The gown slipped easily over her head, and cream satin ribbons tied around her waist. Jess noticed that there were tiny pink rosebuds embroidered around the neckline, and on the outside of the close-fitting sleeves. She studied her reflection in a cheval mirror that stood beside the bed. The gown certainly looked as though it had been made for her, and it felt soft and comfortable. She looked down at her black boots and wondered wryly if Angela had a more appropriate pair of shoes. Shaking out her hair, Jess placed the coronet of gardenias on her head, and stared at the woman looking back at her.

It was a moment of realisation, and it brought tears to her eyes.

Angela walked back into the room, in time to see Jess wiping away the tears.

"It's perfect," she breathed. "You look like a bride from one of those magazines. Beau will be stunned when he sees you."

Jess turned to Angela. "Do you think so?"

"Certainly!" She took Jess's hand and turned her around. "It was made for you, Jess." Her eyes were shining. "Beau must not know anything about this, Jess! In fact, he must not see you in the gown until you walk towards him at the ceremony."

"How are we going to arrange that?" Jess laughed shakily.

"Leave it with me." Angela was getting excited. "I know how we can do it."

"There's only one thing, Angela." Jess lifted the gown to reveal her black button-up boots. "I don't have any footwear."

Angela rummaged at the bottom of the wardrobe, and came up triumphantly with a shoebox. She lifted the lid to reveal a pair of cream satin shoes with a tiny heel.

"Never been worn!" she declared. "I'd say we're about the same size."

Jess slipped her feet into the shoes, and smoothed down the front of the gown.

"Angela, you are a wizard. Thank-you so much."

"I am pleased to be able to help, Jess. Beau is a truly wonderful man, and I know you'll both be happy. The love you have for each other simply shines out of you."

Angela held out her arms, and Jess found herself enveloped in a warm, floury hug.

"Now, we'll get all this hung up and ready for Friday. By the way, this is the room you will be sleeping in, I hope you don't mind?"

"No, I think tradition is a wonderful thing, even if Beau is slightly miffed."

They both laughed.

*

By the time Beau returned in the middle of the afternoon, Jess was swathed in a white pinafore, and up to her elbows in flour.

"What's going on here?"

Jess wiped a floured hand across her brow. "I'm making scones for Angela."

"Well, when you've finished there, I need to spirit you away for a while."

Angela appeared at the kitchen door.

"Are they nearly ready for the oven, Jess? They're selling as fast as you turn them out." She turned to Beau. "If you're not careful, I'll keep Jess here to cook for me."

"No chance of that, Angela." He laughed.

Jess placed a tray of scones in the large oven, and removed the pinafore. Her face was flushed in the warmth of the kitchen, but she had enjoyed her time there, and her eyes shone.

"They'll be ready in ten minutes, Angela."

"Good! Now shoo, you two, and do what you have to do."

"You heard the lady, Jess. You have been given permission to leave." Beau took Jess by the hand, and together they made their way through the patisserie, which was jammed with customers, and out on to the street.

"Where are we going?" asked Jess, as they stepped off the footpath, into the traffic.

"To the quayside," answered Beau, as he steered her carefully between the horse-drawn, and motorised vehicles.

Jess ran to keep up with him, and as they reached the opposite footpath, she pulled on his hand.

"Slow down, Beau, please!" she panted.

"I'm sorry, my love, but there's something I want to show you." Beau slowed his pace, but Jess sensed his impatience.

They crossed the grassy slope that led down to the quayside, and found an unoccupied seat along the promenade.

"Now, what's all the hurry, Beau?" Jess was breathing deeply.

"This," said Beau, as he removed a small velvet box from his pocket. He opened the lid, and Jess saw the gold band resting on blue velvet. "Your wedding ring, Jess." His eyes held hers, before he removed the ring, and took her hand.

Beau slipped the ring on Jess's left hand, and she stared at it, gleaming in the winter sunshine.

"It fits," she said finally.

Lifting her arms, Jess wrapped them around his neck, and they clung together on that wrought-iron seat, with passers-by casting curious sidelong glances.

"You'll soon be mine," whispered Beau into her hair, before taking her face between his hands and kissing her thoroughly and unashamedly.

When they broke apart, he delved into his pocket once more, producing tickets.

"I have our train tickets, Jess. We'll be on the sleeper tomorrow night, and we don't have to quarantine at Albury."

"We'll be home on Saturday?"

"Yes, my darling, we will." Beau smiled at Jess's eagerness. "One more thing; Clarence wants to take us out for dinner tomorrow night, at Mario's, which is a very fancy seafood restaurant just along the harbour front. I've said we'll be pleased to accept." Jess nodded. "I have a feeling he wants to provide me with a reference for finding work in Victoria."

"That's the proper thing to do, surely?"

"Yes, it is. Oh, there is another thing, Jess." Beau took her left hand, and sliding the ring from her finger, he placed it carefully back in the box. "I've asked Charlie to be in charge of the ring on Friday. He's very excited about that."

"We've nearly got everything covered then," said Jess carefully.

Beau frowned. "Nearly? What else is there?"

"Nothing else." Jess smiled secretly. "What I want now is some fish with lots of chips, as I say goodbye to this beautiful harbour on this glorious evening."

"Your wish is my command."

Dinner at Mario's

Thursday was filled with frantic activity, as the wedding day loomed. Jess packed and re-packed her case, tried on the gown several times, and tried to concentrate on making scones for Angela, who was like a bee in a bottle, secretly organising a number of surprises for the bride and groom. When Jess questioned her, she merely tapped the side of her nose, and shook her head.

"You'll have to wait, Jess," was all she would say.

Beau was absent the whole day, and didn't appear until well after five in the afternoon. Jess was upstairs, having changed into the red dress at Angela's suggestion. She was in the bathroom, trying to twist her hair up into the tortoiseshell combs, when she heard the door open.

"What time is dinner, Beau?" Jess called out.

"Six o'clock. Clarence will pick us up at five forty-five."

She heard him rummaging in the wardrobe, and opened the bathroom door.

"You haven't got long to get ready then," she said. "I think I've finished with the bathroom. You can have it."

Beau turned from his searching, and looked at her.

"I'd better wear my best suit, if I have to meet your standard." He smiled, and his eyes travelled over her. "Are you wearing that dress tomorrow?"

"No," said Jess coyly. "You'll have to wait until tomorrow for that."

"I see." He grabbed her around the waist, and pulled her close. "You're going to surprise me, are you?"

"I might." Jess wriggled free. "Go and get ready, Beau! We' don't want to be late."

Beau kissed the tip of her nose, before retreating to the bathroom.

Jess wandered out on to the balcony, for a final glimpse of the city, magical under the lights. Traffic moved slowly along the road, and pedestrians wandered the footpaths as the daylight slowly disappeared. Voices carried on the night air, and she could hear laughter coming from a tram, as it clanged its way along the centre of the street. Perhaps they were all heading to a party? Maybe it was a wedding party? Whatever the scenario, they all sounded happy, and Jess felt happy with them. She smiled and waved from the balcony, receiving waves in return.

"Who are you waving at?" Beau had come up behind her, and sliding his arms around her, rested his chin on her shoulder.

"The people on that tram sound so happy, they must be celebrating a wedding."

"Hm, perhaps they are."

They stood for a moment as the tram disappeared from their view.

"I wonder if they are as happy as we are," whispered Jess, as she turned to face Beau. "They couldn't be, could they?" She cupped his face in her hands.

"I don't think so."

Time seemed to stand still then, as they looked into each other's eyes. Jess stopped breathing. Looking into Beau's eyes was like drowning in a deep grey ocean, and never wanting to come up for air.

"Clarence has arrived, Jess. We'd better go down." Beau's voice came to her out of the mist, and she sucked in a deep breath. "Where were you just then?"

"Oh, somewhere." Jess tucked her arm in his. "Let's not keep Clarence waiting."

*

Mario's Restaurant was shimmering in reflected light from the water that surrounded it. Tables were set with crisp white cloths, gleaming silver, and an array of crystal glasses. Waiters in white shirts and black waistcoats moved with ease between the tables, and the soft murmur of conversations blended with the clink of glasses.

Jess found herself clutching Beau's hand as a tall young man led them to a table which looked out on to the shimmering harbour. Having met Clarence, she was immediately tongue-tied, and overwhelmed by his physical presence.

"Relax, Jess," whispered Beau.

"I've never been in a place like this before," Jess whispered back. "Don't let me make a fool of myself, Beau."

"You won't. Just be yourself, and everything will be alright."

The young waiter moved a chair out for Jess, and as she sat, he spread a white napkin across her lap. She smiled nervously up at him, before looking across the table to where Beau was watching her. He smiled encouragingly at her, as the waiter stood poised with a bottle of wine in his hand. Beau nodded at him, and he poured a glass for Jess, before moving around the table.

Jess looked down at the array of cutlery, and knew that she would have to follow Beau's lead, as to what she should use for each course. Having never dined in such elegance before, she felt very uneasy. Clarence, on the other hand, looked completely at ease as he chatted to the waiter, and Jess heard him ordering a bottle of the best champagne that Mario had in stock.

"My young friends are getting married tomorrow," she heard him say, as he looked in their direction, "and I want to drink a toast to their future."

The waiter smiled at her then, before moving away. Beau picked up a menu, scanned it, and then turned to Jess.

"What if I choose our dishes tonight, Jess," he said quietly.

"That sounds like an excellent idea," breathed Jess.

Another young waiter appeared at their table, and the meals were ordered. Clarence sat back with a sigh, as he sipped his wine.

"Isn't this a beautiful place?" he asked nobody in particular.

"It's very nice." Jess had to agree, although it made her feel uncomfortable.

Clarence put down his glass, and removed an envelope from the pocket of his jacket. Jess quaked under the direct scrutiny from his piercing gaze.

"I have something for you, Jess," he began, and he slid the envelope towards her. "It's from Celia, and I'd like you to read it."

Jess glanced at Beau, who nodded.

Picking up the envelope, Jess saw that it wasn't sealed. She drew out the sheet of paper, and unfolded it. Celia's spidery handwriting leapt out at her.

"You want me to read it now?"

"Yes, please," said Clarence, as he folded his hands on the table before him.

Jess took a deep breath and began to read.

> *"Dear Jess,*
> *I hope you can find it in your heart to forgive me for the anxiety I have caused both you and Beau. Please try to understand that the Clinic, and the work that has been going on there, is extremely important to me, and for a time I lost sight of the fact that ultimately it's not up to me to tell you what you should do. Matthew's illness and your own brush with death, showed me what is more important, and I saw how much you mean to Beau. I have no right to jeopardise that, and I'm sorry for the cruel things I did to try to achieve what I wanted. I had no right*

to read Beau's personal mail, and I should never have written you that letter. I'm sorry for that. I should have given Beau the message that your mother was ill. That was despicable. I should not have defaced your picture." Jess looked at Beau and frowned, before continuing. *"That was spiteful. I couldn't bear it that you had such a hold over Beau, and I couldn't understand why, until I met you. Now I see what I couldn't see before. You are gracious and kind, and you will make Beau happy, where I could not. I must concentrate now on Matthew, and try to make amends. There have been wrongs on both sides, and I want to believe that we will find contentment. The Clinic will survive. I can see that now, so I must trust those in charge.*
I wish you both well, and once again I am deeply sorry.

Celia

Jess looked across at Clarence, whose eyes were fixed on the chandelier above their heads.

"What can I say?" said Jess slowly, as she placed the letter back in the envelope.

Clarence moved his gaze to her face, and Jess could see that his eyes were moist.

"Before you say anything, Jess," he began, "there are some things you need to know about Celia." He shifted on his chair, and his wide brow furrowed. "Celia is very much like her mother; they are both highly-strung, and have always lived their lives as though balancing on a highwire. I'm afraid I have given in to both of them over the years, probably to their detriment." He paused. "Celia's mother now resides in an asylum, where she has twenty-four hour care." He stopped, as the waiter served tiny bowls of prawns in a cream sauce.

"I'm sorry," said Jess.

"I'm afraid that Celia will finish up like her mother if she keeps up this constant obsession over things she can't change." He picked up the tiny fork at the end of the array of cutlery, so Jess did the same. "In some respects, Matthew's illness has given us all a reprieve. Celia will stay in the mountains now, for as long as it takes for him to get over this, and in the meantime, you two can get on with your lives, and the Board can get on with the job of running the Clinic and Serendipity." He tasted the prawns. "Excellent!" he beamed at the waiter, before turning once more to Jess. "So it's an ill wind that blows nobody any good, and if it means we can get back to the job in hand, then it's not all bad.

Celia is not one to apologise for anything, and for her to have written that letter, must have taken a great deal of effort and courage. Your forgiveness is paramount, Jess, not just for Celia, but for me."

Jess looked across at Beau. He also had tears in his eyes.

"Of course I can forgive her." Jess felt her voice tremble. "Please tell her that I fully understand why she wanted everything to remain as it was, but I know that it doesn't, and there are changes that we must resign ourselves to. Maybe when Matthew is fully recovered, they might think about paying us a visit." Jess smiled at the two serious faces opposite her. "It's not all that bad down in Victoria."

Clarence was the first to recover his composure.

"Thank-you, Jess, from the bottom of my heart." He pulled another envelope from the breast pocket of his jacket, and handed it to Beau. "Here is a little something, Beauregarde, from the Board of Directors, to show our gratitude for what you have done both at the Clinic, and out at Serendipity."

"Thank-you, sir."

"For goodness sake, how many times have I told you to call me Clarence?"

Beau smiled. "If you can call me Beau, then I'll consider calling you Clarence."

"Very well, Beau." Clarence held out his hand.

The two men shook hands, and Jess smiled as she thought that more than one bridge had been crossed this night.

"Now, Clarence," said Beau, "can we please eat this wonderful food?"

"What a good idea. When the champagne arrives, we will all drink to the future."

The evening continued with a main course of lobster. Jess looked at the creature with dismay, uncertain about the way to tackle it. Beau saw her dilemma, and while Clarence was busy talking with the drinks waiter, demonstrated how to crack the shell and pull out the flesh. Jess handled it with as much dignity as she could, and was grateful for the napkin that covered her dress.

Finally, after a dessert of orange flummery, followed by coffee, Clarence announced that he needed to get home.

"I'm expecting a call from Celia tonight, and I must be there to take it," he announced, as he wiped his mouth on a napkin. "She'll be anxious to hear how you received her letter, Jess."

"We need an early night, too," said Beau "It's going to be a big day tomorrow."

"It certainly is." Clarence pushed back his chair and stood up. "This is on me, Beau. Call it a wedding present."

"Thank-you, Clarence. We have enjoyed it immensely, haven't we, Jess?"

Jess, who was feeling a little light-headed, nodded in agreement. "Yes, certainly."

Clarence pulled out his pocket watch. "I'll take you two home, and then head on to Celia's. I'll call for you in the morning, Beau. Is ten o'clock early enough?"

"Yes." Beau looked at Jess. "What's your arrangement for the morning, my love?"

Jess shook her fuddled head. "Angela has it all under control. I just have to be ready by half-past ten." As she stood, Jess gripped the table for support. "Hold my hand, Beau," she whispered. "I have a feeling I'm going to fall."

"Are you unwell?" He sounded anxious.

"No, but I have had too much wine."

Beau smiled then, and took her hand. "Lean on me, and cover your mouth when you get out in to the fresh air. I don't want you falling into the harbour."

Clarence, unaware of their dilemma, went to pay the account, before leading the way across the short gangway and on to the dock.

"That was a successful evening all around," he announced loudly as he opened the door of Matthew's motorcar.

Jess had the dreadful feeling that she was going to be sick, and she looked panic-stricken at Beau. He read the signs.

"Clarence, if you don't mind, Jess and I would like to walk. It's not far."

"Are you sure?"

"Yes. Thank-you for a lovely evening, and I'll see you in the morning."

"Very well." Clarence climbed into the vehicle. "Goodnight."

As he disappeared from view, Jess turned to the rail, leaned over it, and brought up her meal into the murky depths of the harbour below them. Beau rubbed her back until the onslaught was over.

"I'm sorry, Beau," she said as he handed her his handkerchief. "What a waste of a beautiful meal."

"We won't tell Clarence." He drew her against him.

"I've never eaten food like that before, and I've never had champagne." She laughed shakily. "Do you think I'm drunk?"

"No." Beau laughed. "A little tipsy, maybe."

"I won't tell Angela. She'll say we should have dined at her place."

"And she'd probably be right." Beau released her, and took her hand. "Are you alright to walk?"

"I think so, if you hold me."

"I'll always hold you, Jess." He squeezed her hand.

As they walked slowly up the hill, and away from the harbour, Jess had a question that had been bothering her, since reading Celia's letter.

"What did Celia mean when she said that she was sorry she defaced my picture?"

"My drawing of you at the Easter fair; she scribbled over it."

"Oh!" She paused. "She must have been desperately unhappy." Her brow creased. "Do you think Celia is genuinely remorseful?"

"I don't know, Jess, but I sincerely hope so."

"Maybe she can make something of her life now, with Matthew."

"He was always more understanding of her than I was."

"Perhaps she should have married him in the first place."

"Then, my darling girl, I wouldn't have met you."

"It seems that all things happen for a reason."

"I'm beginning to realise that."

"So Clarence is taking you out to Serendipity tomorrow? That's a bit unusual, isn't it? Your ex-father-in-law?"

Beau shrugged. "After all that's happened, he wanted to do that for me… for us."

They had reached the alleyway, and saw a light over Angela's door.

"I'm going to miss Angela," said Jess softly. "She has become a very good friend."

Beau stopped beneath the hazy glow of a street lamp, and drew Jess into his arms.

"Tomorrow is the start of a new chapter for us, Jess," he murmured into her hair.

"I wonder what we'll see when we turn the page." Jess touched his face.

"Don't anticipate, my love. It will be what it will be."

Jess laughed softly. "That's very prophetic, Beau."

"But it's true, Jess. One thing I do know is that there will be a lot of love."

"Oh, I'm very aware of that." Jess lifted her face for a long goodnight kiss.

"Sweet dreams, Jess."

"I probably won't sleep a wink."

Beau laughed softly. "Oh, I think you will."

The Wedding

Jess awoke to the swish of the curtains being pulled back, revealing daylight. She groaned, and put her hands over her eyes.

"Rise and shine!" came Angela's cheery voice.

"Oh, my head feels like cottonwool." Jess turned her face into the pillow.

"Jess!" exclaimed Angela. "Don't tell me you have a hangover?"

"I don't know what I've got, but I feel terrible."

"Right!" Angela pulled the covers off the bed. "I'm going to run a bath for you, and you're going to have a long, hot soak." She stood at the foot of the bed, hands on hips. "But first, you are going to have a substantial breakfast."

"No!"

"Oh, yes! Boiled eggs and toast."

"I couldn't!"

"Yes, you can, and you will, my girl! I can't have you getting married with a hangover. You should have dined here, where I could keep an eye on you."

"Now you're sounding like my sister."

Angela laughed. "I'd like to meet her. What's her name?"

"Isobel, or Izzy to most of us."

"Well, would Izzy say 'come on, get out of that bed?'"

"Yes, probably."

Angela headed for the door. "Come down to the kitchen when you have your land legs, and I'll fix breakfast." With that she disappeared.

Jess slowly swung her legs over the side of the bed. She had never felt like this before, and she swayed as she stood. After pulling on her dressing gown and slipping her feet into her slippers, she walked slowly to the door.

Her first call was the bathroom, and then she headed slowly along the narrow passage towards the kitchen. Angela was busy raking the coals in the big black stove that occupied one wall.

"It must have been some night!" she exclaimed, as Jess sat heavily at the pine table. "You'd better tell me all about it."

While Angela busied herself preparing breakfast, Jess went through all that had happened the previous night.

"My goodness! And you have forgiven her? Jess, you are too generous."

"Maybe, but I really think she has been suffering, too."

"Still, I don't think I'd have been so accommodating."

"I think you would, Angela." Jess smiled across the table at her newfound friend.

"Well anyway, we have to get you in tiptop condition, so I'm going to give you something to take, to clear your head of the cobwebs."

"What is it?"

"Nothing drastic, I assure you." Angela laughed. "Just some powders." She looked up at the clock above the stove. "It's now eight thirty, and you must be out of here by ten thirty. We should be able to do it."

"Who's looking after the shop?"

"Sandra's in charge today, with the help of two bakers. I'm going to enjoy my day of freedom. Now, I'm going to run that bath."

*

A short time later, after having taken Angela's 'powders', Jess lay in the warm water and contemplated the day ahead. This was a big step she was taking, and a tiny flutter of apprehension niggled at her. She loved Beau; she loved him dearly, but the future still held uncertainties. Her children needed to accept him as a father figure, rather than just a friend. The boys were old enough to remember their father, but Gracie probably didn't have any memory of him, so the transition would be easier for her.

Jess was sorry that her family couldn't be part of what was about to happen today, and she knew that she would have to make it up to them somehow.

"Time to get out, Jess!" Angela's face appeared at the bathroom door. "I need to use the bathroom."

"Give me five minutes." Jess squeezed out the sponge, filled with lavender scented soap, and reached for a towel.

An hour later, Jess stood in front of the cheval mirror and surveyed the image looking back at her. She had to admit that Angela's dress was right for her, and the coronet of gardenias suited her gold hair. She turned to view herself from all angles. What would Beau think? Would he approve of the lengths Angela had gone to, to make her look like a bride?

"You look wonderful, Jess." Angela's reflection appeared beside hers.

"Do you think so?"

"I know so!" Angela, dressed in a suit of pale blue, and with her hair brushed until it shone, held up her hand. "I have these for you to wear," she said smugly.

In her hand she held a pair of silk stockings, and two blue satin garters.

Jess's eyes widened. "I can't wear those!"

"Yes you can. Something old, something new, something borrowed and something blue, remember?"

Jess sighed. Angela was nearly as bossy as Izzy. She took the stockings and sitting on the bed, pulled them over her feet. She had never worn anything so fine, and they felt gloriously soft and smooth against her skin.

"Now the garters," instructed Angela, who stood watching the process. Jess obediently slipped the garters on, and pulled them up to her thighs. Smoothing down her dress, she stood up.

"The stockings feel wonderful, Angela. Do I have you to thank for those?"

"Ah, well, I was under instruction." Angela flapped her hands in the air.

"Beau asked you to get them?"

"Yes, now are you ready?"

"I think so." Jess placed a hand across her stomach. "I do have butterflies, though."

"Only natural." Angela paused as she looked at Jess, thinking about the wedding day that did not eventuate for her. "Jess, I want you to keep the dress, and all the trimmings, to show your family." She smiled at Jess's shocked expression. "Maybe have another wedding, just for your children?"

Jess shook her head. "I can't keep your wedding dress, Angela."

"Of course you can." Angela slapped her plump hips, and laughed. "I'm never going to fit into it."

Jess held out her arms, and the two women hugged each other.

"I'm going to miss you, Angela," said Jess, her eyes moist. "You might be like my sister, but I'll miss you just the same. We must keep in contact."

"Yes, of course." Angela wiped her eyes. "We're not going to get all soppy, are we?"

"It's too late for that," said Jess, dabbing at her own eyes.

"Well, I think it's time to go. Come on."

Together they stepped out into the alley, and Angela led the way to the main street, where Jess saw a magnificent black horse, with a white plume on its head. It was pulling a shiny phaeton with a black hood. She gasped.

"Angela! You didn't?"

"Did you think you were going to walk?"

"No, but…"

Angela laughed gaily. "The horse actually belongs to a friend of mine, who is an undertaker. (I insisted on the white plume.) The phaeton I acquired from another source, you will be pleased to know."

Jess laughed. "An undertaker's horse?"

"Isn't he a beauty?" Angela took Jess's arm, and propelled her forward.

"Your carriage awaits."

The young man seated at the front of the phaeton, jumped down to assist the two women, before climbing back to take up the reins. He was dressed in a black suit and top hat, and Jess wondered wryly whether he was the undertaker.

"This is Andy," said Angela, settling herself on to the padded seat. "And in case you're wondering, he is the undertaker's son."

"Oh. I'm so pleased we're not travelling in a hearse."

Angela laughed. "Would I do that to you, Jess?"

"Maybe."

Andy flicked the reins and the black beast moved into the traffic. Men raised their hats, and women waved, as the spectacle passed them, and Jess felt her cheeks flush as Angela waved gaily back.

When they were out of the congestion of vehicles, Angela took Jess's hand.

"How are the nerves now?"

"I'm a little fluttery."

"Relax and enjoy the ride. You know who'll be waiting at the other end, and I feel sure he's going to be awestruck when he sees you."

"Are you going to give me away, Angela?" Jess was frowning.

"Good gracious, no! I'm just along to witness your signatures. Do you need someone to give you away?"

"No." Jess shook her head. "It will seem strange, that's all."

The gates of Serendipity loomed up ahead, and Jess strained to see across the garden to the ghost gum standing tall among the rose beds. There were a few people gathered, and she could make out Clarence and Charlie. Edwina was there, and she could see Nurse Flanagan and Shirley from reception. Her eyes searched for Beau. There he was, immaculate in a grey suit and pale blue tie. He turned as the phaeton was drawn to a halt, some ten feet from those gathered there. Jess took a deep, shaky breath, and reached for Andy's hand, as he helped her alight. She stepped on to the ground, and smoothed down the front of her dress.

"He's waiting," whispered Angela. "Off you go."

Jess took a hesitant step forward. She sensed that Angela was right behind her.

Beau was watching her, and his eyes never left her face as she stepped up beside him. He took her hand, and she smiled into his grey eyes.

"You look so beautiful," he breathed.

The Pastor, a rotund young man, with a ruddy complexion and twinkling blue eyes, gave them a few seconds to compose themselves, before starting the modified service.

"Ladies and gentlemen, (and I'm pleased to see a few of you here) it is my great pleasure to be able to officiate at the marriage of these two whom you see before you. These are trying times we are living in, and I am pleased to see that those here are keeping an acceptable distance from each other, with exception of the bride and groom, of course. Before I begin, I would like to say what an honour it has been to work alongside Doctor DuBois, in the tending of those wretched souls struck down by the influenza. He is a man of integrity and great compassion, and will be sadly missed here." His blue eyes turned to Jess, and he smiled. "Jess, I saw you several times during your battle with the influenza, but we haven't actually met until now. I wish you both well." He opened his Bible. "Let us begin…"

Jess was acutely aware of Beau standing close beside her, and did her best to concentrate on the words being spoken, but it all seemed surreal.

"Jessie Alice Stanley, do you take Beauregarde Richard DuBois to be your lawful wedded husband, for richer or poorer, in sickness and in health, to have and to hold from this day forward, until death do you part?"

"I do."

He turned to Beau. "Beauregarde Richard DuBois, do you take Jessie Alice Stanley to be your lawful wedded wife, for richer or poorer, in sickness and in health, to have and to hold from this day forward, until death do you part?"

"I do."

"Who has the ring?"

Charlie stepped forward, grinning from ear to ear, and handed Beau the ring.

He slipped it on her finger as he followed the Pastor's lead.

"Jess, I give you this ring as a symbol of my love, and with all that I am, and all that I have, I honour you, in the name of the Father and of the Son and of the Holy Spirit."

"For those whom God hath joined together, let no man tear asunder." The Pastor's voice rang out above the warble of magpies, and the occasional screech of a cockatoo.

Hands clasped, and eyes only for each other, they listened as the Pastor continued with words from scripture, concerning the sanctity of marriage and its important place in society. He finished with the words from first Corinthians:

"Love is patient, love is kind, never jealous or envious, never boastful or proud… there are three things that remain - faith, hope, and love, and the greatest of these is love." The Pastor closed his Bible, and smiled at the two before him. "It is now my pleasure to pronounce you husband and wife."

A cheer erupted from the direction of the building, and all eyes turned to see windows open and arms waving, as patients and staff added their voices to the ceremony. The Pastor was forced to shout over the noise.

"You may kiss your bride."

Beau drew Jess to him, and amid the cheering and wolf whistles, kissed her.

As they parted, the Pastor raised his hand, and from somewhere they could hear a brass instrument playing a shaky rendition of Mendelssohn's Wedding March.

"Food is being served in the foyer," announced the Pastor, as the final note died away. He turned to the bride and groom. "I need signatures before you depart."

"I suppose that includes me." Angela had stepped forward to envelop Jess and Beau in a moist hug. "Congratulations both of you. That was so beautiful."

Clarence had also stepped forward, and was shaking Beau by the hand.

"Congratulations, my boy."

Charlie was dancing from one foot to the other, as he waited to kiss the bride and congratulate the groom. Edwina stood back, waiting her turn, and smiling at her son's exuberance. How different he was now.

Finally they all moved towards the Lodge. The shouting continued from the windows, and Beau smiled as he waved to the men and women who had occupied his working life for the past six months. They were happy for him. He looked at Jess, walking beside him, and his heart was full.

In the foyer, members of the kitchen staff were serving sandwiches and teacakes, and there was even a wedding cake. Jess's eyes popped open when she saw it, and she immediately looked in Angela's direction.

"Did you do this, Angela?"

Angela was beaming. "I thought I'd surprise you."

Jess shook her head. The woman was unstoppable. "Thank-you," she murmured.

"You can't have a wedding without cake," was all she said.

As Beau went to get them both a cup of tea, Jess stood quietly to one side, allowing herself a moment to take in all that had happened. She was now Beau's wife, and the prospect was both exciting and daunting. Watching the animation around her, she was reminded of her wedding to Jack, all those years ago, and her heart gave a little flutter when she realised that she was no longer Mrs. Stanley.

Jack would always be in her heart, but it would now be Beau holding her hand, and walking with her through the rest of their lives.

Beau was walking towards her now, cups in his hands.

"What's the matter, my love? You were frowning just then."

Jess took the proffered cup and smiled at his concern. "Nothing's the matter."

"Good. Can I say that you look wonderful? Where did you get the gown?"

"It was Angela's."

"Angela's? I didn't know she was married."

"She wasn't. Her intended died at Gallipoli."

"Oh, so she never got to wear it?"

"No."

"What a pity. She'd make some man a good wife."

"I don't think she has the time to think about that."

"Well, she's over there now, talking with Clarence, and they look very animated."

"Beau! Shame on you!" Jess was horrified at the implication. "He's old enough to be her father."

"I wasn't suggesting anything, my love, but you must admit they do seem to be enjoying each other's company."

"Clarence has a wife."

"She's in an asylum, Jess."

"Yes, well I don't think it's a good idea for you to be matchmaking!"

Beau laughed. "I don't think I need to. Come on, let's cut this cake and enjoy the food that's been prepared for us."

*

An hour later, when all the food had been consumed, and Beau had been to say goodbye to everyone at Serendipity, they made their way out to the waiting vehicles. Beau and Jess climbed into the phaeton, and Angela was invited to ride with Clarence. This made Beau smile, and Jess shake her head.

As the horse turned towards the gates, Beau looked across at the sandstone building for a last time. Jess saw the look of sadness that passed across his features, so reaching over, she clasped his hand tightly. His gaze moved to her face, and the moment of sadness was gone.

"We'll have a good life, Jess," he whispered.

Jess ran a finger slowly down his scar. "Yes, I'm sure we will."

Epilogue

The Homecoming

A keen wind blew along the Bendigo railway station, moving leaves and sneaking around the legs of those who stood waiting for the Melbourne train.

Margaret, Charles and the three children huddled together, their coats gathered around them, and hats pulled down on their heads.

"When's the train coming?" Grace was jumping up and down in anticipation.

"It won't be long," said Margaret smoothly, her hand firmly clasping that of her granddaughter.

"Hush, Gracie!" Charles laid a hand on her shoulder. "Stand still, for goodness sake! You'll see your mother soon."

"Will she be with Beau?" Ben looked up at his grandmother.

"Yes, Ben, she will."

"And are they married now?"

"Yes, they got married yesterday."

"Does that mean Beau will be living in our house?" Edward's brow was furrowed.

"Yes, Edward, he will."

"Oh!"

"You'll have to do as *he* says now, Edward," said Charles dryly, "with no arguing."

"Yes, Edward!" Ben gave his brother a shove, knocking him into Margaret.

"Enough, Ben!" Charles growled. "Apologise to your grandmother."

Ben looked sullen. "Sorry, grandma."

Margaret smiled thinly. Three weeks with the children had tested them all, and she was looking forward to a quiet house and no confrontations.

"Beau's always been our friend." Edward was pensive. "Does this mean that he'll be the boss of us now?"

Charles and Margaret looked at each other.

"It means," said Charles, "that he'll still be your friend, but you will need to show him some respect. It may be difficult for a time, but for your mother's sake, both of you must try to fit in."

"Hm." Edward's brow was furrowed.

"Here comes the train! Here comes the train!" Gracie resumed her jumping, golden curls bouncing beneath her blue beret.

*

Inside their carriage, Jess and Beau sat gazing out the window at the familiar landscape. They were nearly home. It had been a long twenty-four hours, and they were both tired. Jess bit on her lip as the train slowed, bringing the hills into focus. She clutched Beau's hand.

"Are you alright, Jess?" He noticed her consternation.

"I'm nervous."

"What are you nervous about?"

Jess turned to look at him. "I'm nervous about the reactions we might get."

Beau's brow furrowed. "They're your children, Jess. Don't you think they'll be excited to see you?"

"I know you're right, Beau, but I've been away from them for three weeks, and so much has happened to me in those three weeks."

Beau brought her hand up to his mouth, and kissed her fingers. "Trust them, Jess."

The whistle sounded as the railway workshops came into view. In a few moments they would stop, and they would step out on to the platform.

Jess released her hand from Beau's, and stood as the train thundered into the station. With a loud hiss, steam covered the crowd gathered there, and the train ground to a halt.

Beau opened the compartment door, and together they made their way to the platform. Beau was the first to step down, before reaching for Jess's hand. She took it, and he squeezed it for reassurance.

"It will be alright, Jess," he whispered. Jess nodded, as her eyes searched the crowd. There they were; she could see Charles and Margaret. She moved forward.

"Ma! Ma!" She heard Gracie's squeal, and with a quick intake of breath, opened her arms to receive her daughter. They clung together for several moments, and Jess let the tears fall as she buried her face in Gracie's golden hair.

When she lifted her tear-stained face, five pairs of eyes were watching her. Without letting go of Gracie, who hung on like a limpet, she spread one arm, and the two boys walked into the family embrace.

"Oh, my darlings, it's so good to see you."

They clung together, while Margaret, Charles and Beau looked on in silence.

Finally, shoulders aching from holding Gracie, Jess let her slide to the ground, and stood erect. Margaret walked towards her, and encompassed her in a warm hug.

"Welcome home, Jess. We've all been anxious to see how you look." Margaret held Jess at arms length, and ran a critical eye over her. "You look better than I thought you might."

"I had the best of care." Jess looked at Beau as she spoke.

"Thank-you for bringing her back to us again, Beau."

"I had no intention of losing her, Margaret."

Charles cleared his throat. "You do have luggage, I presume?"

"Oh, yes, in the luggage van."

"I brought the motorcar, so perhaps you and I can get the luggage, Beau?"

"Certainly, Charles."

"Good to have you here," Jess heard Charles say to Beau, as the two men walked away. "Welcome to the family."

Jess turned to Margaret. "It's going to be alright, isn't it, Margaret?"

"Of course it is, dear."

"You're not angry that we married in Sydney?"

"No, dear." Margaret smiled. "It was the best thing to do under the circumstances. Besides, we can have a celebration when everything settles down."

Jess looked down at her children, who were regarding her seriously.

"Did you nearly die, ma?" Edward's blue eyes were questioning.

"I was very sick, Edward, but Beau wasn't going to let me die." Jess took her two boys by the hand, while Margaret took a firm hold of Gracie. "Now, what's been happening here while I've been away?"

"Oh, Jess," said Margaret, "we have so much to tell you, don't we, children?"

The boys nodded enthusiastically.

"Really? Well, how about you tell me while we head for the motorcar. I need to get home" Jess looked up to see Beau coming down the steps of the pedestrian bridge. She smiled softly. "*We* need to get home. We have so much to tell you, too."

Margaret watched, as the distance decreased between them. Gracie let go her hand and ran to meet Beau. He swung her up in his arms, and she smiled down at him. Margaret breathed a soft sigh of relief. There was plenty of time to tell Jess what had really been happening during her absence.

"Come on, grandma!"

Margaret smiled as she walked slowly up the steps.

The first book of the trilogy:

Forget Me Not

An extract from a review:

"The book flowed like a movie for me, from scene to scene, with back stories and timelines running parallel across the oceans. It was a trip into the past, and you walked me through the very landscapes that my grandfather, great uncles and nana lived and endured."

Thank you.
Sue Kidd

The second book of the trilogy:

Forget Me Not – The Journey Continues

"In 'The Journey Continues' we follow Jess Stanley and her family, as they come to terms with the loss of their beloved husband and father.

World War 1 is over, but the world is hit with 'The Spanish Flu' and now, even in Australia, the pandemic is having an impact.

For those who have enjoyed the first novel, 'Forget me not' – this is a must-read.

How does Jess cope with her grief and loss, and look ahead to a life without her Jack? Family life will never be the same.

Valerie Broad OAM

Love your story. Jess's new life begins now, and the challenges continue. Clever ending/beginning.

Francis Wright

Acknowledgements

2020, the year of the global Covid Pandemic, has been challenging for everybody, and a time during which I found solace with my characters. They too, were a part of a global pandemic, one hundred years ago, and so I can identify with their anxiety and uncertainty. Their battles have now become our battles, and the parallel between the two pandemics is extraordinary.

They have become a part of me, and I am thrilled that so many of my readers have become attached to them, too.

Thank-you to all those who have read or are still reading 'Forget me not'. I value your comments and your encouragement, and I have done my level best to deliver a continuing story that is both realistic, and yet human in its content.

Thank-you Joanne Livingstone, for once again designing a cover that depicts the story so beautifully. This whole project would have floundered badly, had it not been for your expertise, and guiding hand through the publishing process.

Thank-you Valerie and Fran, for taking the time to make this journey with me, encouraging me along the way.

I hope you enjoy Jess's journey of discovery, and I look forward to bringing you 'Journey's End' at a future date.

Valmai Harris

Valmai Harris

Growing up in country Victoria, Valmai spent much of her time writing stories, purely for her own amusement. This was curtailed when music became her priority, and piano practise took up much of her time.

Later, when her own family emerged, writing became a thing of the past. It wasn't until later years, when the children were off her hands, that Valmai began writing music. She found this to be both therapeutic and rewarding.

Thoughts of retiring with nothing to do are far from Valmai's mind, as she plans to continue writing stories.

Lightning Source UK Ltd.
Milton Keynes UK
UKHW010645140521
383717UK00001B/127